MISTRUNNER

BOOK 3

MISTRUNNER

BOOK 3

NICHOLAS SEARCY

Podium

Cover design by Pius Bak

ISBN: 978-1-0394-5437-8

Published in 2024 by Podium Publishing
www.podiumaudio.com
Podium

MISTRUNNER

BOOK 3

CHAPTER ONE

THREE YEARS LATER

Mira was lost after what happened in Nova City. For the longest time, I had no idea how to help her. I tried everything. Eventually, I decided that the best thing I could do for her was to give her the space to grieve. Maybe it was necessary, but walking away was the hardest thing I've ever had to do.

—Patrick Ward

I leaned back, enjoying the slight sway of the hammock as I felt the warm sun playing over my mostly bare skin. Reaching down, I grabbed a glass bottle and brought it to my lips. I didn't open my eyes as I took a sip, then let out a sigh of appreciation. "This is much better than the last batch," I said. "Though that's not really a high bar, is it?"

I could practically feel the shake of Patrick's head as he answered, "That's kind of harsh. I'm still trying to figure this brewing thing out."

"Like you were trying to figure out cooking?" I asked, recalling the six-month period where he'd insisted on cooking and eating the meat from mutated wildlife. He'd claimed to have been following some recipe book he'd gotten from an ancient traveling merchant we'd saved from a nest of monstrous mosquitoes, but the results suggested that he'd gone off script. Thankfully, he'd lost that obsession and focused on brewing various alcoholic beverages. The alcohol content didn't really do anything for me, but the taste of the latest batch was still pleasant enough.

"That's not fair," he said. "I was just following Glenda's recipes. I can't help it she had a weird preference for insect meat."

I tilted my head to the side and opened my eyes before pushing my sunglasses to the top of my head. Raising an eyebrow, I asked, "Aren't you the one who saw those ingredients and thought it was a great idea to give it a try?"

"Bugs aren't that different from seafood, and you love that," he pointed out.

"Totally different."

"How? I mean, biologically, there really is a lot of common ground, and—"

"Insects are gross, and seafood is delicious," I stated, leaving no room for argument as I closed my eyes and replaced my sunglasses. "That's the difference, Pick."

Once upon a time, he'd tried to move past that name. But that felt like an eternity in the past; so much had happened since then, and we'd both changed in a thousand different ways. Besides, I was the only one allowed to call him by the nickname, and that was only on occasion. Everyone else knew him as Patrick.

"But think about it," he said. "The first people who decided to eat, say, a shrimp—they probably looked at that thing and thought the same thing we think about . . . I don't know . . . crickets or something."

"Some cultures eat crickets all the time," I said. "Remember that village we found in the African Dead Zone? They raised herds of giant crickets for food."

"And you vomited when you realized what you were eating," he said. "But I'm not debating the viability of crickets as food. They're actually really nutritious. I talked to one guy who used to work in Manhattan—you know, where they do all sorts of research—and he said that insects, pound for pound, are one of the most nutritious foods you can eat."

"Still gross." I leaned back and once again closed my eyes.

"Anyway—my point is that shrimp look just as gross as bugs," he went on. "Like, maybe more so."

"Take that back," I growled theatrically. "Shrimp look and taste delicious. Period."

"That's only because you're used to eating them," Patrick stated. I heard him sit up from his own hammock, and it wasn't hard to imagine him leaning forward, an excited expression painted on his face. "But let's say that you'd never eaten or seen a shrimp before. Then, you find one. What kind of person looks at that and says, 'I think this is going to become my favorite food,' huh?"

"A hungry one."

He sighed, and via Observation, I heard his feet scraping against the ground. "You're really not going to admit I'm right, are you?" he asked.

"Nope. I'm stubborn like that," I said, once again opening my eyes and favoring him with a broad smile. "That's why you love me."

It had taken me a while to get to the point where I could utter any variation of those words, even in jest. But after being with Patrick for almost two years, they felt as comfortable as a cool breeze. And what's more, the sentiment was true. I did love him, and I was certain that he loved me, as well. That surety hadn't always been there, but with everything we'd been through together, I didn't think there was anything that could tear us apart.

"Accepting your flaws isn't the same as endorsing them," he said with a faux-haughty tone. "Besides, I love you for . . . other reasons."

I glanced at him out of the corner of my eye, and I was happy to see his eyes roaming over my body. And rightly so—I was worldly enough to know that I looked good, especially wearing nothing but a bikini. A result of my constant training as well as the effect of my inflated Constitution attribute, I reasoned. Or perhaps it was just good genetics. Either way, he certainly appreciated what he saw.

But the same could be said for me. While Patrick wasn't a frontline combatant, and he preferred to spend his time either at the helm of *The Leviathan* or fiddling in his workshop, he'd never slacked in regard to his own training. So, his stocky body was extremely well muscled.

"The way you're looking at me, I'd think you had something naughty on your mind," I said with mock innocence.

He pushed himself to his feet and fixed me with a blue-eyed stare before saying, "Maybe I do. You don't—"

A familiar sound tickled my ears, and I sat bolt upright. Springing from the hammock with unnatural grace, I summoned my trusty, well-worn assault rifle and whirled around, searching for the sound's source. Seeing that, Patrick did the same, bringing his black-and-gold Tergan Tactical pistol out of his own storage space.

"What is it?" he asked, all flirtation gone from his tone.

"Company," I said, cocking my head to the side to get a better handle on the sound's origin. I never really let Observation drop, but I almost never used the ability at full blast. Not only did doing so result in a distractingly huge volume of sensory input, but it was also unnecessary. Usually, the passive enhancement to my senses was enough. However, that didn't mean I didn't use it when necessary, so I flared the ability, and once I'd categorized the approaching sound, I said, "Three trucks. Heavy ones."

"Troop transport?"

I shook my head, saying, "No clue. Not enough information. Did we piss anybody off lately?"

"There was that thing in the desert," he said.

"That was two thousand miles from here," I countered. "Felicia wouldn't track us down out here. And even if she wanted to, nobody knows where we are."

Patrick was curiously silent at that, and I asked, "Right?"

"Uh . . . I might've gotten drunk a few weeks ago and let some things slip," he said in a small voice. Then he shook his head. "But those were just locals. They wouldn't have—"

I shook my head as the convoy drew closer. It was still a couple of miles out, but I knew that wouldn't last, given their rate of approach. "Jesus, Patrick," I mumbled. "I've told you to watch what you say . . ."

"Nobody's after us, Mira," he said. "We haven't done anything to offend anyone around here. There was no reason to hide."

I just shook my head again and faced in the appropriate direction. Then, I cut my eyes at *The Leviathan* itself. The ship was almost two hundred feet long and half as wide, and she was built like the flying tank she was. She wasn't the fastest thing in the world, but what she lacked in speed, she made up for in durability, versatility, and comfort. Originally, the fuselage was matte black with gold trim, but in the three years since Patrick had bought her, we'd changed the color scheme a few times. Now, it sported a light-blue paint job with bright-red highlights.

"Do we run? You want me in the cockpit?" Patrick asked.

"Yeah," I said. "But don't start anything up. Just be ready to bring the thunder if whoever it is steps out of line."

"Ten-four," he said, racing toward the open bay in the back. In seconds, the ramp had retracted, and the door had begun to close. Patrick was far more valuable at the helm than he'd ever be with his pistol.

I considered hurrying into something more appropriate for meeting strangers, but I decided against it. The convoy was getting closer by the second, and the last thing I wanted was to be caught with only one leg in my infiltration suit. Besides, I felt confident in my abilities—especially backed up by Patrick and *The Leviathan*. If they had issues with seeing me in a swimsuit, then that was their problem.

Of course, I could tell myself that a thousand times over, but there was still a big part of me that was that shy little girl who'd had to use Mimic to hide her blushes when she'd first visited Bourbon Street. I suspected that I'd never quite move past that old version of me, and I had to admit that I was kind of happy about that.

However, just because I wasn't going to get dressed didn't mean I wouldn't prepare. To that end, I summoned my gun belt—and the hand cannon holstered to it—from one of the storage slots in my arsenal implant. With practiced ease, I fastened it around my waist, then moved on to my nano-bladed sword, which I strapped to my back. In only a few seconds, I was fully armed and as ready for battle as I was going to get.

Still flaring Observation, I tracked the convoy as, over the next thirty seconds, they raced across the terrain as they closed in on our position. With the ocean at my back and sand at my feet, I waited, but not for long. Soon after I'd armed myself, the first truck came into view. Then the second. And finally, a third.

The black trucks themselves were typical troop transports, with huge knobby tires and manned cannons jutting from the roofs. But I couldn't make out any identifying characteristics or markings, which told me at least part of the story.

Unaffiliated or under the radar. Either way, that would make them more dangerous. I relayed the information to Patrick, who said, "Give me the word and I'll take out the lead truck."

"Wait."

"I don't like this, Mira," his voice came over my interface.

"I don't, either. These people definitely aren't local," I said.

And that much was obvious. The closest settlement was a town with a population numbering in the four digits, and other than that, there was nothing of note for four hundred miles. Even then, as far as I knew, that city—which was called Danton—was ill-equipped to attack us. More than that, they wouldn't have much reason to. The fact that none of our enemies had a presence in the region was one of the reasons we'd chosen the beach in the first place.

Finally, as the trucks came within my range, I hefted my R-14 and took aim. Outside of one purchase, I hadn't updated my arsenal in a while, but that didn't mean the assault rifle was any less powerful. In my hands, it was more than enough to deal with most threats. And for the ones for which it was insufficient, I had heavier weapons.

The truck pulled to a stop a hundred yards away, and for a long few moments, it felt like we were in a standoff. Then, a voice, magnified by some sort of public-address system, crackled to life. "We don't want any trouble," said a man with a curious accent I couldn't place. The presence of an accent meant that he was speaking English instead of using the language favored by the locals.

"Yeah. Sure," said Patrick, using *The Leviathan*'s own speaker system. "We've heard that one before. Pardon me if I don't shut down my cannons."

Of course, I knew there was only one cannon on the ship, but our visitors couldn't know as much. The more dangerous they thought we were, the better off we would be.

"How do we do this?" the newcomer asked over his intercom.

Patrick and I had protocols for this kind of thing, and he quickly instructed them as to our terms. One person could approach, but the rest would remain with their convoy. One wrong move, and Patrick would engage *The Leviathan*'s weapon systems and blow them away. If they didn't like our terms, then they could turn around and go back to where they'd originated.

Given that they'd tracked us down in the middle of nowhere, I suspected they wouldn't take that final option. They wanted something from us, and they wouldn't leave until they tried to get it.

After a few moments, a figure stepped out of the lead truck and dropped the three feet onto the ground. Then he moved toward me, climbing a sand dune past a few tufts of spiky grass, then awkwardly descending the slope until he hit the beach. After that, his way was clear, and he adopted an exaggerated swagger.

"This guy," I muttered.

"What?" asked Patrick through my interface.

"He looks . . . I don't know . . . I don't like him," I said.

"Don't shoot him yet," Patrick chided.

"But he's wearing, like, ten gold chains," I said. "And do you see the size of that belt buckle? And his pants are so tight I can see his—"

Patrick coughed. "Yeah. Go ahead and shoot him," he said.

Even though I knew he couldn't see me, I rolled my eyes at his statement. By that point, the newcomer had closed to within fifteen yards, and his eyes never left me. Or, more accurately, my scantily clad body. The bikini wasn't exactly immodest, but it still didn't cover much. Under his ogling gaze, I wanted to shoot him even more.

Or blow him up. A quick toss of a grenade, and he'd be torn into hundreds of little pieces. But then again, if I did that, we'd have to pick up and move. And I liked that beach, not least because there were no major predators around, which allowed us to relax. Of course, we'd had to put out a Mist net as a barrier to keep the bigger sea creatures from approaching, but that wasn't that big of a deal.

As I'd already noted, the man was dressed absolutely ridiculously in an obnoxiously bright and sleeveless red shirt, revealing arms covered in snaking tattoos. Around his neck were a half dozen gold chains, each studded with glittering jewels. His lower half was clad in pants tight enough that pretty much everything he had to offer was on display. Finally, a pair of leather boots, the toes capped with shiny steel, completed the look.

"How do you think he gets his hair to stay like that?" asked Patrick over my interface. "Like, it looks like actual plastic. Maybe it's a cybernetic implant or something."

I snorted a poorly timed giggle, and I could practically see Patrick's grin in my mind's eye. The visitor clearly didn't like the idea that I might've been laughing at him, and as he approached, I could see his hands twitching to draw the pistol holstered on his hip. It was a gaudy nickel-plated thing with a pearl handle.

As he drew closer, Patrick muttered, "And he has a soul patch. Bold choice on the facial-hair front. Have to respect the commitment."

"Shut up," I grunted, schooling my face to placidity. As ridiculous as the man looked, he'd obviously hunted us down with a purpose in mind. Still, it was difficult to take him seriously, given his clownish appearance.

"Something funny?" the man asked when he got close enough. He was ten feet away, but even then, I didn't need Observation to get a good whiff of his overpowering cologne.

"No, no—not at all," I said.

"I need to speak to your captain," he said.

"You can speak to me," I stated.

"Offer isn't for you, sweetie," he said. The last word was originally in another language, but my Universal Language ability had translated it. I didn't like his tone, though.

"And if I tell you I'm the captain?" I asked.

"Then I might have two offers for you" was his immediate reply. "Now run along and get your boss. It's time for the men to talk."

I shot him in the leg.

Just a graze, but it sent him tumbling to the ground with a howl. Immediately, the cannons on top of the trucks swiveled in my direction, and *The Leviathan*, under Patrick's control, responded in kind.

I didn't pay attention to any of them. Instead, I stepped forward and kicked the man in the face, sending him sprawling onto his back. Then, I aimed my R-14 at him and said, "Now, this practice ammunition isn't as powerful as the good stuff, but judging by the fact that it still punched a hole in you, you really, really don't want to pick a fight with me. So, I'm going to ask you one time: What do you want? If you answer right, I might treat your wound. If not . . . Well, let's not go down that road, okay?"

"A little heavy-handed, Mira," Patrick said via our Secure Connection.

"I don't know. It felt just about right to me," I responded.

The man groaned, "W-what . . ."

"Wasn't talking to you," I stated. "Now, what do you want? Make it good."

"I . . . We . . . We wanted to hire your ship," he said. "For a job, okay? We have a job, and we're willing to make it worth your while. Please . . . Please don't kill me . . ."

Another voice came over the truck's public-address system, saying, "Please excuse my idiot brother. He doesn't know when to keep his mouth shut."

I shouted, "Then you shouldn't send him to represent you!" Then, I added, "Come on out. We're not negotiating with Captain Tight Pants here."

The intercom crackled, but no voice came out. For a moment, I thought I was going to have to start shooting, but then the door of the middle truck opened, and another man stepped out. He bore some resemblance to the writhing man on the ground, but his style was very different. For one, he didn't wear a single piece of jewelry, and his clothing was almost drab by comparison. Still, he held himself with a similar swagger, though his seemed far more genuine.

As he approached, Patrick said, "Careful. He looks dangerous."

"So are we," I said, mostly under my breath.

THE OFFER

After Nova, Mira was broken. I tried so hard to be there for her, to help her heal, but she needed something I couldn't give her. In the end, that's why she needed to go off on her own. Me sticking around was only going to make things worse.

—Patrick Ward

Oh, grow up. It's just a flesh wound," I said to the ridiculous man writhing on the ground. My shot had barely even clipped him, and though its passage had taken quite a bit of flesh with it, it wasn't anything to get worked up about. Of course, I had a bit of a skewed perspective when it came to injury. I blamed my propensity for getting into dangerous situations where my body was put through a blender, but it probably had just as much to do with my mindset and the effects of my skills.

"You shot me!" he hissed. "You fucking shot me!"

"And I'll shoot you again if you don't shut up," I reminded him.

That definitely closed his mouth, but as the other man approached, I could still hear Captain Tight Pants's whimpers. They were almost soothing, after a fashion.

Finally, the newcomer arrived. He said, "I suppose you're the muscle of the operation, huh? Interesting."

"Something like that. What do you want?" I asked, tiring of the charade. I nodded at the man on the ground and asked, "Want me to take care of him?"

"As annoying as he is, no. I don't—"

"Wait—no. Wrong idea. I didn't mean take care of him. I meant take care of him, you know?" I said. When he clearly didn't understand the difference, I shook my head and elaborated, "I wasn't asking if you wanted me to kill him.

I'm not that big of an asshole. I meant to ask if you wanted me to treat the wound. I have a skill."

"Medic and muscle, huh?"

"Something like that," I said. My Triage ability wasn't all that impactful, but it did enhance my ability to treat injuries by no small amount. I also had a couple of flashier abilities, but I didn't want to reveal the extent of my power. These people were strangers, after all, and giving away too much information was a good way to get killed. Still, I had no intention of letting a man bleed to death just because he was annoying.

"Sure. We have a medic back at our camp, but . . ."

"But they're all the way back there. I get it," I said, stepping forward. I trusted Patrick to have my back, so I wasted no time in kneeling beside my victim. Or patient. He was both, I supposed. In any case, I retrieved a foam bandage, a bottle of water, and a med-hypo from my arsenal implant and went to work. In only a few moments, I'd done enough that I felt sure he would make a full recovery, which was probably more than he deserved. After, I stood as I knocked imaginary dust from my hands, saying, "All fixed up. Maybe next time keep your mouth shut."

He didn't answer. Instead, the man just glared at me. I took it in stride. If I got all worked up over every man—or woman, come to that—who looked at me threateningly, I would've long since gone crazy. It was easier to just ignore people like him.

Or shoot them. Maybe blow them up. There were lots of ways to deal with those sorts, I guess.

"So," I said, looking at the brother. I noticed that his eyes never drifted below my chin, which struck me as stupid. I wasn't certain if he meant it as an ill-considered attempt at chivalry—after all, I was still half-naked—or if he intended it to show he didn't fear me enough to keep track of my weapons. Either way, it wasn't the smartest course of action. "What's your name, anyway?"

"No witty name for me?" he asked, smirking slightly.

"No. You're too normal," I said.

"My name is Isaac. My brother is Huascar," the man said. "And your name?"

"You don't know?" I asked. "You did come to us, you know. Figured you'd at least know who you were coming to see."

"We know the other one," Isaac stated. "Patrick Ward. The pilot. You . . . are . . . a mystery."

"That's me. Miss Mysterious. Or maybe Miss Sterious," I said. "No—that sounds like a bad clothing line. Either way, my name's Mira."

"Mira," Isaac said. "Nice to meet you."

"Oh, yeah—fucking great to meet you!" growled Huascar, who was still sitting on the ground in a puddle of his own blood. "Just amazing."

"Quit whining," I said, my tone dismissive. "You'll be fine."

"You fucking shot me!"

"Call it an aggressive hello," I advised. Then, I said to Isaac, "So, as much as I've enjoyed this—God knows I love shooting arrogant assholes as much as the next girl—I'm going to have to ask you once again why you came here."

"It's simple. You have that," he said, nodding to *The Leviathan.*

"You need a ship. I gathered that much. What for?" I asked.

"A job."

"What kind of job?"

"A confidential one," he answered with another slight smile. "And it will remain so until we come to an agreement."

"And if we can't find common ground?"

"Then I'll collect my brother, and we'll be on our way," he said. "No muss, no fuss. Just a missed connection. But I promise you, you're not going to want to miss this opportunity."

"Yeah? Why is that?" I asked.

"Because we have access to what you need," he said. I expected him to keep going with an explanation, but he didn't.

I rolled my eyes and sighed. "Seriously? Am I going to have to drag it out of you? Just tell me what you want, what you're offering, and give me a risk assessment. Otherwise, we're done here."

"Fine. Risk is moderate."

"Be more specific," I said. I'd taken plenty of jobs before, so I knew precisely which questions to ask in order to determine whether or not I wanted to hear more.

"Aliens. They're actually called Dengyts. They have peak weaponry, good armor, and almost impenetrable defenses," he said. "Most of the time. But we have a way to mitigate the risk, so we'll just have to kill twenty or so to get what we want."

Aliens. It had been more than seven years since my Awakening, and I knew there were only a couple more to go before the Integration began. When it did, the system-enforced quarantine would lift, and the aliens would descend upon us like locusts. Many were already on Earth, having used various smuggling skills, abilities, and classes to circumvent the system's quarantine. And ever since I'd been on my own, I'd made it a point to kill as many of them as I could. So, he was definitely speaking my language.

However, my hatred of the invaders did not overwhelm my good sense, and I knew there were alien enclaves and strongholds I could not assault. More than once, I'd been forced to retreat from such enemies.

Still, he had my attention.

"I'm not familiar with Dengyts," I said. "What do they look like?"

"Short. Maybe three feet tall but with normal proportions. Otherwise, they look almost human, except for having pointed ears and slightly exaggerated features."

"They're gnomes!" exclaimed Patrick, who'd been listening in via our Secure Connection. I winced at the volume of his excited voice. One thing I'd learned since we'd gotten back together was that Patrick had a thing for fantasy stories, and any time we ran into alien races, he would try to categorize them according to Earth's mythology. I would've objected, but calling something an orc was far easier than trying to remember its proper name. Which was Eahimajeaakavith, by the way. The word *orc* was much easier to swallow.

"They're extremely advanced from a technological standpoint, but they lack physical abilities. As far as I know, it's a racial point of pride that they don't go down that road of development," Isaac explained, completely unaware of Patrick's outburst.

"And I'm assuming they have something you need," I said.

At the same time, Isaac said, "Information. I won't say more than that until we've agreed to terms."

Information. I wasn't certain what form something like that might take. Perhaps the gnomes—damn Patrick for putting that in my head—had a data chip that contained said information. Or maybe the would-be thieves intended to kidnap someone knowledgeable. I had no idea, but the basic notion seemed plain enough.

"And what are you offering?" I asked.

"The Dingyts have a store of high-capacity Mist circuits intended for mechanized armor suits," he stated.

Obviously, he thought that meant something to me, but it might as well have been gibberish for all I understood why I should care about such a thing. Sure, it was interesting, but I wasn't exactly a mechanic or an engineer. And—

"Tell him we'll do it!" screamed Patrick, eliciting a wince on my part.

"What's wrong?" asked Isaac.

I held up a finger, adjusting my perspective so I could project a question toward Patrick without having to give it voice. I asked, "What? Just like that? Why?"

"This . . . It's something I was working on for the year we were . . . you know . . . split up," he said. "I'll explain everything once these guys are gone, but . . . I need those circuits. Like, it'll change everything."

I frowned. I hated being reminded of the time we'd spent apart. It had lasted a little over a year, and in that time, I'd engaged in quite a lot of self-destructive behavior. More than that, I'd had to go through it alone. Sure, there were other men. Even a woman or two, just because I saw no reason not to explore. But none of them were Patrick.

I'd always assumed he'd gone down a similar path, but we shared an unspoken agreement that we didn't talk about any of it. It was in the past—just like Nova—and it didn't need to affect our current relationship.

But it seemed that wouldn't always be true.

Shifting back to verbal communication, I said, "And do we get a cut of whatever it is you want to steal?"

"It's not monetary. As I said, we're after information. But whatever else is there, you and . . . Mr. Ward will get your share," he said. "And before you ask, just know that the Dengyts are extremely wealthy."

I shook my head. "Maybe it seems like that to you, but none of the aliens on the surface are well-off," I stated. My every experience with the invaders told me that the smugglers who'd taken the chance of subverting the quarantine were usually desperate, ill-equipped, and weak. Sure, they seemed advanced and powerful to most people on Earth—the ones who even knew they were around, at least—but that was because we were a newly Initiated planet, and people hadn't had the chance to grow into their power. "But I can tell you from firsthand experience that's not the case."

I'd spent quite a bit of my time since the fall of Nova robbing aliens. At first, I'd tried running the Rifts myself, but it didn't take me long to realize just how dangerous that kind of thing was. A few near-death experiences, and I decided it was much easier just to rob the alien mining operations than to risk my life in the Rifts.

Of course, that had the side effect of slowing down my leveling speed, but slow and steady was better than quick and dead.

"I think you underestimate them," he said. "They are not the aliens you've seen before. They sent an entire battalion down here. A research division, as well. And they have almost zero interaction with humans."

"Why go through so much trouble for a few Rift Shards?" I asked. The little crystals were extremely valuable, but I'd found that mining them was far more complicated than my first two Rifts would suggest. Certainly, I'd nearly died both times, but looking back, those two experiences were nothing like what I'd seen since. As such, mining Rifts was a risky—usually deadly, in fact—venture that often proved more trouble than it was worth.

For me and the aliens.

"They're not here for Rift Shards."

"That . . . They're all here for Rift Shards," I said. Indeed, I'd come to believe that the Earth held no other resources the aliens might find valuable.

"Not true. Rift Shards are a valuable commodity, and there's always a market for them," he said. "But for a well-prepared and well-equipped venture, there are some resources that, to the right people, are even more valuable. The Dengyts are one such group. As I said, they sent an entire battalion down here, all to protect their operation."

"What resources are they here for?" I asked, getting annoyed at having to drag every little piece of information out of the man.

"We're not sure what it's called, but it's a mineral of some sort. Perhaps a metal that's useful in their technology. I don't know more than that."

"Unobtanium," provided Patrick.

"What?" I asked silently.

"That's what Remy used to call it," Patrick answered. "It's a made-up name. Like, it's meant to refer to valuable, hard-to-get resources."

"That's a stupid name," I said.

"It's better than the mineral to be named later," he pointed out.

I rolled my eyes, which Isaac clearly thought was a bit odd. One of the perils of carrying on two conversations at once, I supposed. If my Mind attribute had been any lower, I might not have managed it.

"Did I say something amusing?"

"Not you," I said, choosing not to elaborate further. "So, let me get this straight. You want Patrick and our ship. In exchange we get these circuits and whatever we can steal from these gnomes."

"Gnomes?" he asked, narrowing his eyes. Almost instantly, his face softened, and he gave a soft chuckle. "Ah. I see. An apt label."

"Right. So, did I miss anything?" I asked.

He shook his head. "Not really," he said. "But I should point out that, while we didn't come here specifically for you, we will not refuse your help."

I wasn't certain how I felt about being a tagalong. Usually, I was the driving force behind whatever Patrick and I chose to do. He wasn't passive—not exactly—but he was a reasonably easygoing guy. And he only objected to our chosen course if I'd made some grave miscalculation in my decision-making process. Which happened more often than I liked, but in my defense, he was a lot more conservative than I was.

"Alright, then—you're going to need to give me a few minutes," I said. "If you or your people do anything, you'll see the business end of *The Leviathan*'s cannons. And let me tell you—when Patrick shoots, he doesn't take it easy like I do."

"Understood. We shall await your answer," he said. Then, he dragged his brother to his feet before helping him back to their convoy. I didn't move until they were firmly ensconced in one of the trucks. Then, I retreated to one of *The Leviathan*'s hatches, which opened as soon as I got close. After that, it only took me a few seconds to reach the cockpit, where I found a grinning Patrick.

"I like this look," he said, leaning back in the pilot's chair and gesturing to my ensemble. "Very sexy."

"I didn't have time to get dressed before they reached us."

"That's not even close to true," he said. "But whatever you need to tell your-self. You won't hear me complaining, either way."

I rolled my eyes and sat in the navigator's chair. The cockpit was big enough to accommodate three more people, but we'd never really invited anyone else onto *The Leviathan*. Patrick and I were more than capable of flying the ship by ourselves.

"So? What do you think?"

"We're obviously doing it," he said. "Money and killing aliens—what's not to like?"

"The part where the aliens have unknown power?"

"We'll scout it out."

"You mean I'll scout it," I corrected him.

"Yeah. That. C'mon. You're not going to let that trip us up, right?" Patrick asked, an eager expression on his face.

"What's with the circuits? What are they? Why do you want them?"

He sighed, then ran his hand through his hair. "Okay, so when we were . . . on a break," he said. "You know I stayed with Cy for a while, right?"

"I'm aware," I said, knowing that Cy was short for Cirilla Montague, his onetime cybernetic engineering instructor. Or boss. Maybe friend. I didn't really know the nature of their relationship, and I was well past the point where I wanted to find out.

"Right. Sure," he said, sensing my suddenly icy demeanor. Just because I didn't want to investigate what those two had been up to didn't mean I was happy about it. I didn't know when they'd progressed past a mentor-mentee relationship, but it was hard to believe that it hadn't started in Nova City. "Any-way—so, while I was staying with her, we started working on a project together. It was her idea, actually. When she found out that I had a Pilot ability under my belt, she—"

"Just spit it out, Pick," I said.

"Mech suits," he answered. "We were going to build mech suits, okay? But we ran into an issue. Because it would function as an external cybernetic—kind of like your Cutter—it would necessitate very different inner workings. But no matter what we tried, nothing really worked, and eventually, we just gave up. It wasn't until about six months ago when you and I were visiting that town in the mountains that I found out that there was a way around that kind of thing."

"And I'm guessing the Mist circuits are the answer."

"Good guess," he said. "They're only made on one specific planet in the whole galaxy, and they're protected by antitampering mechanisms that—"

"So, you need these circuits to make your . . . mech suits work, right?"

"That's right," he said. "It's . . . I mean, this would be a game changer for us, Mira. I could finally keep up with you, which would mean we could hit Rifts more reliably, and . . . I don't know. It's also . . . I mean, it's incredibly cool, right? A suit of armor that functions like a cybernetic but can hit like a tank? Come on. Tell me you wouldn't want that kind of weapon on your side."

It was a good argument, and one that brushed up against the touchiest subject in our relationship. Patrick never really mentioned the disparity in power between us, but I knew it was on his mind. How could it not be, after the last time we'd tried running a Rift together? As it turned out, the first experience, where the Rift had manifested as a derelict space station infested with mind spiders, was an aberration. The only other time I'd dragged him inside of a Rift, we'd both nearly died. I'd come close to losing a leg, and he was in a coma for weeks. To say it was an eye-opener was an absolute understatement.

So, it was no wonder that he'd sought out a way to augment his own lacking power.

"If we do this, you know they're going to try to betray us, right?" I asked.

He shrugged. "It's not a trap if we see it coming" was Patrick's reply.

"And if we don't?"

"You always see the traps, Mira," he said with perfect confidence. Did he really have so much faith in me?

"Okay. I guess we're doing this, then."

He couldn't hide the wide grin spreading across his face in response to my declaration.

CHAPTER THREE

TRUST

I'm not an insecure person. Or at least, I never thought I was. But that first Rift with Mira, it opened my eyes to how far ahead of me she was. At first, I didn't let it affect me, but after the . . . incident, I couldn't lie to myself anymore. I was slowing her down, and unless I did something drastic to figure out my place in all of this, I would never be more than a deadweight.

—Patrick Ward

After Patrick and I agreed to meet Isaac and his crew the next morning, they turned their convoy around and retreated to their own camp. Isaac was eager to get started, but I insisted that we had some things to button up before we would be comfortable joining them. To that end, I found myself sitting on the sand and looking out over the restless ocean. Night had already fallen, and Patrick was busy grilling nearby—probably something with a disgusting origin, knowing his adventurous cooking habits. The moon cast the world in a silvery glow, which was augmented by the twinkling light of stars above.

I leaned back on my palms, digging my fingers into the sand as I looked up at the purple awning we'd attached to the fuselage. The area beneath was lit by strings of lights—actual electric lights, so they didn't have the blue tint of a Mist lamp. A great bonfire danced merrily just beyond the awning's boundary, and the air was filled with the sound of the surf.

I sat there for a while, just staring out at nothing, until Patrick's voice broke my reverie. "Storm's coming soon," he said, sitting next to me. He handed me a plate of steaming meat; it smelled alright, which boded well. So, I didn't ask after the origin of the meat.

"Yeah. Probably a big one, too," I agreed, taking the plate. I summoned a bottle of water from my arsenal implant.

"We don't have to do this," Patrick said. "You know that, don't you?"

"Of course I do," I said. We didn't do anything unless we both agreed on it. Anything else was a recipe for disaster. "But you need those circuits, right?"

"I . . . I thought so," he said. He took a bite from a haunch of grilled meat. "I used to, at least. I mean, you weren't the only one with issues back then."

Back then.

"You mean when I was an absolute mess from what happened in Nova?" I asked.

"I wasn't much better off," Patrick said.

I knew that much because we'd discussed it more times than I wanted to count. That was the key to working through our issues. For the longest time, I'd thought his problems were secondary to mine. Not because he was inherently less important but, rather, because his issues were.

After all, I'd killed a city.

He just felt bad because his girlfriend was stronger than him.

The two didn't seem comparable at all. But over time, I'd realized that my thinking was incredibly reductive. It wasn't just that I was more powerful than him. He'd known that from the very beginning. Rather, he was afraid of being left behind because he couldn't keep up. He'd seen me taking on giant spiders and aliens—and coming out on top—while he'd struggled to merely survive. Those issues had been laid bare and exacerbated by the mind spiders' soul spike.

As the silence stretched, I chanced a bite of my dinner, and the moment it hit my tongue, I let out of cough of surprise. When I'd recovered a moment later, I croaked, "Spicy . . ."

He grinned. "You like it?"

I gave him a weak thumbs-up.

"Anyway, my point is that I'm over it," he said. "I don't need it anymore. Not like I used to."

"But you still want it," I reasoned.

Shrugging, he said, "I guess. I mean, it could help us both, really. If we were both in real armor, we could—"

"I'm happy with what I have," I said.

"Come on, Mira—you haven't really updated your equipment in almost two years," he complained.

"I added those stabilizers to the Pulsar," I pointed out. "And the extended drum for the BMAP, too."

Indeed, the Mist stabilizers had cut the charge time for Empowered Shot in half, and the BMAP now held almost twice as many shots as it had in its original form. I'd intended to switch out my scattergun for something more lethal, and for a variety of reasons—mostly that there just wasn't much out there that met my parameters, but also because our credit flow was only barely able to keep up with *The Leviathan*'s maintenance needs. It wouldn't have been such a problem if I was willing to delve a few Rifts, but I'd shied away from those for a while.

He sighed and rolled his eyes before shaking his head and taking a bite of that disgustingly spicy meat. As he chewed, he gestured with his fork and said, "Fine. But this would enhance my combat capability to the point where I could probably give you a run for your money. In certain situations, I mean."

"It would be that strong?"

I regretted it the moment I asked the question because it made the gap between us that much more prevalent. But it was an undeniable fact that any armor system that gave Patrick the ability to match me in combat was indeed powerful. We both knew just how far ahead of him I was.

"I didn't mean it like that," I said.

"No, it's fine. You're right."

"It's not fine. You know how much I need you, right? You remember what I did without you, don't you? How lost I was? Literally and psychologically. I can't function without you. None of this works without—"

"I know," he said, cutting me off. "I get it."

And I was certain that he did. After all, we'd worked through the issues over the course of hundreds of conversations. But he'd also seen what I became when he wasn't around. More, he was well aware that I was hopeless as a pilot and navigator, and I couldn't even begin to bring the most out of *The Leviathan*. He filled a role, both as my partner and as our pilot, but the last thing I wanted to tell him was to stay in his lane. He wanted to be able to take care of himself, and I couldn't really argue for anything else. Not without getting his hackles up.

"I don't know why we're even talking about this," I said. "We already agreed to do the job."

"As if we couldn't pick up and be on the other side of the world in a couple of days," he said.

"But there's no reason to do that," I argued. "I'm on board. You want it, too. Let's just focus on doing what we need to do so we're ready when they inevitably betray us."

"You really think they will?"

"Captain Tight Pants will definitely take a chance the moment my back's turned," I said.

"Well, you did shoot him."

"Only a little," I said. "And he deserved it."

"You can't solve every problem with shooting, Mira. We talked about this," he pointed out.

Rolling my eyes, I said, "Sure. Yeah. I know that. That's what explosions are for. When shooting fails, blow stuff up."

He laughed, and so did I—but in the back of my mind, I couldn't help but recognize that I'd only been half joking. In my experience, a good explosion went a long way to solving most problems.

After I choked down the rest of my meal—Patrick watched me eagerly to make certain that I loved it—I set about dismantling the camp. We'd done it hundreds of times before, so it didn't take long to take down the awning, store the hammocks, and smother the fire. In only half an hour, everything was packed away in *The Leviathan*'s expansive cargo bay.

We'd fully made use of it only a few times, so the space—which was bigger than the penthouse where I'd spent most of my childhood—was almost completely unoccupied. In one corner were a dozen huge crates of ammunition; I had a similar amount in my arsenal implant, which had expanded right alongside the growth of my [Cybernetic Mastery] skill, which had reached its final tier.

The other side of the cargo bay had only one occupant—a four-wheel vehicle the size of a hover car but with huge knobby tires and a sizable cannon mounted on its frame. Its official designation was ATAV—all-terrain assault vehicle—but Patrick always referred to it as the Buggy. And considering that it was usually him driving it, it was his right to name it.

Other than a few piles of supplies and my weight training apparatus, the cargo bay was completely empty, which gave it a bit of a depressing feel. After all, *The Leviathan*—designation C-L3411S—had originally been built as a military transport ship for some galactic empire whose name I couldn't remember. The shipwright who'd modified it had brought it to Earth's Bazaar in hopes of selling it to one of the alien forces who wanted to circumvent the quarantine. However, he hadn't had any takers, and when Patrick had come around, the alien had been on the verge of giving up. So, seeing that the shipwright was eager to get a deal done, Patrick had gotten the ship for far less than it should've been worth.

The net result was that *The Leviathan* was likely one of the most advanced ships on the planet. She wasn't particularly fast—relatively speaking—but she was incredibly durable, fuel efficient, and most importantly, stealthy. Because of the modifications the shipwright had made, it was a perfect vessel for smuggling, which meant we had little trouble flying under the radar when we wanted to.

It also had the distinction of being huge, which gave us plenty of space to stretch out. Or more importantly, enough room for us to have a little bit of privacy. In addition to the cabin we shared, there was a common area where we usually ate—when we weren't camping out on the beach—and a couple of fully equipped bathrooms. Finally, Patrick had his workshop, and I had a room dedicated to my training.

After everything was stowed away, Patrick and I went in separate directions. He wanted to refamiliarize himself with his old schematics so that, when we got the circuits he needed, he would be ready to start putting things together. Of course, he said he needed many other resources—metals and the like—but we had enough money that we could source raw materials fairly easily. For my part, I went to my training room.

It was a simple room—just a cube with bare walls and a steel floor—but that was just a facade. Once I was inside and the door slid shut behind me, I said, "Activate training protocol two-two-seven."

"Affirmative," came a robotic voice.

One of the walls shimmered, and a familiar scene came into being. Three featureless dummies faced me, and I immediately embraced my Misthack ability. In seconds, I'd torn through the first dummy's defenses and uploaded a Ghost. Two more seconds, and I'd infected the other two. Once I did, the dummies flashed, then disappeared. A moment later, they were replaced by three more. But when I dove into the first of this group's defenses, I found them to be slightly stouter.

That was the point of the training protocol, which had cost me almost as much as my entire arsenal, including the value of my Cutter. Each respawn would come with slightly more difficult opponents until, at some point, the dummies' defenses would become so complex that I couldn't overcome them.

It really wasn't so different from the training programs I'd used before, save that even after eighteen months, I still hadn't exhausted its capabilities. More, when I failed, I suffered the same backlash I would if my efforts were rebuffed in a real situation. So, not only did I train Misthack, but I also put my Mistwall to the test, and with each failure, it grew marginally stronger.

Over the next two hours, I forced myself through the program. The slightest slip of concentration, and my mind would be fried by the backlash. But by this point, I was well used to maintaining my focus. Still, I eventually reached the point where the defenses became far too complex, and I failed.

That's when the backlash hit me.

"Ugh," I spat, sinking to my knees and clutching my head in my hands. I'd had more than one doctor assure me that the backlash had no lasting consequences—other than augmenting the Mistwall ability—but as I was subjected to the blinding pain of that headache, it was easy to imagine that my brain was being irreparably damaged.

It took an hour for it to pass.

I wasn't a masochist. I didn't seek out pain. But as far as I could tell, it was the only easy way to train my Mistwall. Sure, I could've found another Mistrunner to put my defenses to the test, but I didn't know any of those. And besides, I had no intention of letting anyone take free shots at my system. Weighed against the dangers of that, a little bit of pain didn't seem so high a price to pay.

Once I'd recovered, I said, "Protocol nine-two."

"Affirmative," the same robotic voice said.

A moment later, a pillar rose from the center of the room. It only stood about three feet high, which meant it was reasonably comfortable for me to stand before it, extract the black-and-gold cord of my personal link from the Hand of God, and jack into the port in the center of the column.

The second I made the connection, the familiar menu associated with my Mistwalk ability appeared on my interface. I chose to challenge the system and was immediately thrown against a set of defenses that reminded me of the aural sensor net I'd fought against outside of my second Rift. There were plenty of differences—chiefly, that I was hardwired into this set of defenses—but the difficulty was similar.

I tore through it in only a few minutes, but just like was the case with the Misthack training protocol, it was immediately followed by a more difficult version. I defeated that one, as well, and was confronted by a third. Then a fourth. On and on I went until three hours had passed; by that point, the defenses had grown so complex that they weren't even represented by logic puzzles or equations. Instead, I was forced to read the symbols and glyphs directly, and though my Universal Language ability helped quite a bit, I still couldn't really understand them. They were too alien, and they represented concepts I couldn't hope to comprehend. However, I could still follow the patterns.

Mostly.

I made plenty of mistakes, and as a result, I was subjected to a number of miniature backlashes. However, I was still able to keep going until the defenses finally toppled. But I knew that was my limit. Still, I forged ahead, assaulting the eleventh iteration of the program.

I lasted thirty seconds before the backlash overwhelmed my mind and rendered me insensate. I only blacked out for a few minutes, and when I forced my eyes open, I was assaulted by yet another intense headache that took another hour to subside. When it did, I sat up and asked, "Score?"

"Forty-one-point-seven percent on protocol two-two-seven, making for a two-tenths of a percentage point improvement," the voice answered. "For protocol nine-two, you reached thirteen-point-seven percent, a three-tenths of a percentage point decline from your last session. Would you like to try again?"

"Ugh. No," I muttered. "I think I'd get a brain hemorrhage if I did."

"Your brain is functioning at one hundred percent efficiency" was the program's unhelpful reply. That was the other function that made it so valuable—not only was it equipped to train my abilities better than any other training program, but it could also monitor my vitals and, according to Dex, even enact certain protocols to ensure my survival should I overstep my abilities. I was a long way away from that kind of danger, though.

The program boasted a thousand protocols meant to train Misthack and five hundred for Mistwalk. I'd barely scratched the surface of what it could do, but eventually, I'd reach a point where there was very real danger in failure. I hoped that my high Constitution attribute would help mitigate some of that risk, but I wasn't sure. And there wasn't anyone around who could guide me.

I massaged my temples, but it didn't really provide any relief for the phantom pain that came after my training. Normally, I'd have gone straight into physical training, following it up with weapons drills—that always helped—but as late as it had gotten, I didn't really have the time. Still, I sat down and took a moment to pull up my status. It had been quite some time since the last time I'd looked, but I didn't expect it would have changed much. Even so, the slightest improvement would be a nice surprise.

At my command, the familiar menu appeared on my interface:

Select one:
Status
Skill trees
Certifications
Equipment
Conditions
Upgrade modules

As usual, I checked my conditions first, and I found a distinct lack of injuries. Once, walking around with broken bones, multiple contusions, and mild concussions had been commonplace for me. However, the combination of my climbing Constitution as well as playing things much more safely had pushed those days into my past.

Hopefully.

Certainly, I still got injured from time to time, but it was nothing compared to what I'd gone through during my various training missions or when I'd waged my one-woman war against the whole of Nova City. It almost felt like I wasn't pushing myself hard enough.

Perhaps I was a masochist, after all.

I shook my head before moving on to the fun stuff.

CHAPTER FOUR

STATUS REPORT

I didn't intend for anything to happen with Cy. But after Mira and I went our separate ways, she was the only person I could turn to. She welcomed me with open arms.

—Patrick Ward

With some anticipation, I navigated through the menus of my interface, settling on the one dedicated to my overall status. Once it flashed before my eyes, I couldn't help but look upon it with a mixture of satisfaction and regret. On the one hand, it was nice to see a verifiable measure of my progression. Watching those numbers go up was satisfying in a way few things could match, and I knew I'd long since become addicted to seeing the steady uptick of my quantifiable progress.

But on the other hand, I knew I hadn't pushed myself to my limits. In a lot of ways, I'd squandered my potential when I'd chosen not to seek out new Rifts. But while that was objectively true, it also wasn't the whole story. As much as I didn't want to acknowledge it, I was also painfully aware that if I'd kept going the way I was going, I'd have died in the first year after Nova's fall. It was almost a good thing that Patrick and I had come so close to death, if only because it had served as a reminder that I wasn't even close to invincible.

Sure, I'd come close to dying before, and more than once. But in that Rift, I was confronted with a level of danger I could scarcely comprehend, let alone defeat. We had barely escaped with our lives, and even then, we'd been forced to spend more than a month in recovery. I still bore the scars, both on my body and my psyche. So, as much as I wished I would have pushed myself a little harder, I was self-aware enough to recognize that doing so would have been a recipe for disaster. And given that it wasn't just my life on the line, I couldn't in good conscience take that sort of risk.

Not again.

Not unless I had no other choice.

Shaking my head, I studied my status:

NAME	Mirabelle Lisa Braddock		
CLASS	Mistrunner		
LEVEL	38 (14%)		
CONSTITUTION	231/276		
MIND	252/276		
MIST	207/276		
SKILLS	7/7		
SKILL NAME	Skill Tier	Modifiers	Abilities
CYBERNETIC MASTERY	Tier 5 (71%)	300% Efficiency	10 Cybernetic Slots
COMBAT	Tier 5 (42%)	+75% Damage (All) +100% Speed (Melee) +60% Accuracy (All) +50% Range (Firearms) +75% Reload Speed (Firearms) +25% Damage (Small Arms) +25% Range (Small Arms) +25% Accuracy (Small Arms) +50% Damage (Heavy Weaponry) +15% Range (Heavy Weaponry)	Empowered Shot (D) Double Shot (D) Combination Punch (D) Pummel (D) Engage (D) Disengage (D) Mark Target (E) Barrage (E) Explosive Shot (E) Multishot (E) Shatter Shot (E) Instant Reload (E) Riposte (E) Execute (E) Double Jump (D) Teleport (D)

		+50% Rate of Fire (Heavy Weaponry) +25% Damage (Melee) +25% Accuracy (Melee) +25% Movement Speed +25% Jump Height	
INFILTRATION	Tier 4 (97%)	+95% Effectiveness (Stealth) +25% Effectiveness (Deception) +15% Effectiveness (Charisma) +15% Effectiveness (Mimic) +25% Effectiveness (Bluff)	Stealth (D) Camouflage (D) Deception (D) Mimic (D) Observation (D) Charisma (E) Interrogate (E) Distraction (E) Vanish (E) Bluff (F) Chameleon (D) Sense Deception (E) True Sight (E)
MISTRUNNER	Tier 5 (33%)	+75% Speed (Misthack) +75% Processing Speed (Mistwalk) +75% Strength (Mistwall) +15% Ghost Strength +25% Ghost Stability +25% Infiltration Stability +50% Processing Speed +50% System Defense +20% Damage (All)	Mistwalk (C) Misthack (C) Mistwall (C) System Redirect (D) Disable Cybernetics (D) Overcharge (D) Surge (E) Plague (E) Rewind (E) Skeleton Key (E) Backlash (D) Mental Fortress (E) Assassinate (F)

FIELDCRAFT	Tier 5 (95%)	+50% Combat Effectiveness +50% Effectiveness (Triage) +50% Recovery Speed +25% Medication Effectiveness +25% Less Food/Water Required +25% Less Sleep Required +50% Endurance +25% Effectiveness (Combat Focus) +25% Effectiveness (Regeneration) +25% Explosives Yield	Triage (D) Basic Explosives Handling (C) Combat Focus (C) Pain Tolerance (D) Resistance (D) Foraging (D) Improvisation (D) Regeneration (D) Universal Language (E) Stabilize (E) Mend (E) Bastion (D) Tinkering (F) Share Map (D) Waypoint (E) Combat Map (D) Secure Connection (C) Ignore Injury (E) Focused Will (D)
DEMOLITION	Tier 5 (99%)	+50% Explosive Radius +50% Explosive Strength	Blast Shield (C)
ACROBATICS	Tier 5 (99%)	+100% Proprioception	Balance (C)

There was definitely a lot to take in. One of the major reasons I hadn't inspected my status in quite a while was because it took a significant amount of time for anything to progress anymore. Once my various skills had reached Tier 5, their progression had slowed to an absolute crawl. If I had to guess, it would probably end up taking just as long to reach the end of Tier 5 as it had to reach my current level of progress. That meant that it would take years to see the end of that journey.

But then what? If [Demolition] and [Acrobatics] had taught me anything, it was that there was nothing after Tier 5. Both of those Rank 1 skills had been stuck at ninety-nine percent progress for more than eighteen months, and I suspected that something drastic would have to happen if that was going to change. I'd thought about seeking that information out in the Bazaar, but at the end of the day, I'd grown even more paranoid as the years went on. I'd angered a lot of people by facilitating Nova City's fall, not to mention the fact that I'd made a habit of hunting aliens and stealing their Rift Shards. No—going up to the Bazaar and asking a bunch of questions would just paint an even bigger target on my back.

One thing that did please me was the fact that I'd finally crossed the two hundred threshold in all my attributes. Sure, it hadn't come with the significant increase that crossing the one-hundred-point mark had, but it was still nice to see. If things kept going the way they were going, I would reach my potential in a few more months, even if I managed to gain a couple of levels along the way.

Once again, I couldn't help but wonder what I would do then. Go out and actively seek levels? Maybe. I knew of a few sizable herds of powerful beasts I could hunt. Perhaps that was the answer. One thing I knew for certain was that I couldn't stop training. I'd be lost without the constant drive to improve.

"Maybe I could pick up a hobby," I muttered to myself.

But I knew that wasn't going to happen. Nothing could compare to the visceral cycle of training and quantifiable improvement.

I moved on to look at my abilities, and I couldn't help but blanch at the sheer number of possibilities. Some of them, like Mark Target, Barrage, Pummel, and Bluff, often went completely unused. Over the last couple of years, I'd made a point to train them as often as I could, but I almost never used them in actual battle. As advanced as my Mind attribute was, I tended to fall into patterns of thinking. I knew I wasn't getting the most out of my skills, but I also knew I couldn't really change that. Perhaps I just needed to try a little harder.

Thankfully, the use of the various abilities was usually clear. For instance, Explosive Shot was an ability much like Empowered Shot in that it added an augmenting effect to my shots. However, the key difference was that it could be used on an entire magazine, which meant that it was very useful for enhancing the power of my assault rifle. That ability alone was one of the reasons I hadn't bothered upgrading the weapon.

The other reason was nostalgia. The R-14 had been with me for a while, and just the thought of getting rid of it twisted my stomach into knots.

Multishot, by comparison, was clearly intended for weapons with slower rates of fire. It had a long charge—five seconds—but it had the distinction of giving me the ability to shoot multiple targets at once. My record was four, but I felt that if I could upgrade the ability to the next grade, I could move that needle a bit further. Of course, each shot was about ten percent weaker than the last, but with my modifiers as well as my powerful weapons, that wasn't such a problem.

Shatter Shot was like the heavy-weapon version of Empowered Shot in that it simply improved the damage of a single shot from my BMAP. And given the already devastating power of that weapon, the ability was almost scary to use. Not that that stopped me. When I'd first gotten the ability, I'd gleefully used it to turn an entire alien encampment into a crater, which was more than a little satisfying. Terribly wasteful, though. By the time I was done, there was nothing left to steal.

Instant Reload was exactly what it sounded like; it allowed me to use Mist to instantly reload my weapons. However, it had the downside of being almost as Mist hungry as Balance, which meant that I had to use it fairly sparingly. It had definitely come in handy a couple of times, though, and I knew its usefulness would only increase as I continued along my path.

Riposte and Execute were both very situational. Riposte simply allowed me to parry and return an enemy attack with one of my own. It wasn't a flashy ability, but it had its uses. Execute was simple, as well, even if it was wildly different. So long as I was undetected, it gave me the capability to increase the damage of a single strike by five hundred percent. Most of the time, that was more than sufficient to kill just about anything I'd seen. However, its limitations made it difficult to use except at the beginning of a battle.

Finally, the movement abilities were just as self-explanatory. Double Jump allowed me to leap into the air, then, at the apex of my jump, spring off a platform of Mist to propel me much higher. Not complicated, but useful all the same.

Teleport was a bit more complex. On the surface, it seemed simple. Using the ability, I could just move myself from one place to another. But in practice, it was extremely situational. For one, the range was only about ten yards, which meant it was useless for travel. For another, it was extremely disorienting, even after spending hours on uncomfortable practice. Still, I was determined to make it work in combat, though I hadn't quite cracked the code yet.

All in all, I was satisfied with most of my [Combat] abilities, even if I knew I had a long way to go before I'd integrated all of them into my fighting style.

[Infiltration], by contrast, hadn't seen quite as much growth, and it still hadn't ticked over into Tier 5 yet. None of its branches had, either, so its ability list wasn't quite as long. In addition to the holdovers from before I'd become a {Mistrunner}, I'd gained Charisma, Distraction, Bluff, and Sense Deception.

Charisma, when used on someone, made them more apt to trust me. However, it didn't work so well with people who already knew me. And besides, it made me feel a bit gross to manipulate people's minds. So, I rarely used it, save in the interest of training. Distraction was better in that it created, well, a distraction. Sometimes, it was a noise. Other times, it was a flash of light. Whatever form it took, it would briefly draw the attention of my victim. That, combined with my already impressive Stealth and Camouflage, meant that I had an even easier time infiltrating behind enemy lines.

Bluff fell into the same category as Charisma, but instead of increasing a target's perception of my trustworthiness, it made me far more intimidating. I used it a lot more often than Charisma because it was meant for my enemies. I had fewer qualms about messing with their minds.

Finally, there was Sense Deception, which was a passive ability that gave me some insight into whether or not someone was concealing something. The only problem was that I had no indication as to whether someone had beaten the ability or was simply being honest. Still, it was a nice ability to have on my side.

My third—and probably my favorite—skill was [Mistrunner], which gave me a few newer abilities, as well. Surge gave me the capability to enhance the power of a single Ghost by a significant amount. I'd tested it a few times, and as far as I could tell, the augmentation clocked in at about two hundred percent. That meant that my Ghosts could be incredibly powerful. The only limiter was that it was my most Mist-hungry ability, and using it tended to drain me dry.

Rewind gave me the ability to reverse a failed infiltration, letting me escape any resulting backlash. I could only use it once a day—I'd tested it, and it reset twenty-four hours after the last usage—but I'd already put it to good use on more than one occasion. By contrast, Backlash allowed me to counter any attempted infiltration of my system with a vicious attack.

But as useful as those abilities were, for [Mistrunner], the real gems were in the fifth tier.

First up was Plague, which functioned a lot like *Time Bomb (Mk. IV)* in that it could infect large groups with a debilitating Ghost. However, unlike *Time Bomb (Mk. IV)*, its gestation period was counted in moments rather than hours, and it was even more deadly. The only limiter was that it cost a ton of Mist, and it was only usable once per week. Still, it was a great card to play in an emergency.

Skeleton Key was similar to Rewind in that its use was also limited. In its case, its cooldown period was a week. It was incredibly useful, though, because it could effortlessly bypass anything with less than B-grade defenses. I rarely had occasion to use it, mostly because I relished any opportunity I had to test myself against a powerful Mistwall, but it was nice to have it in my back pocket in case I ran up against something I either couldn't or didn't have time to overcome.

The last ability on the [Mistrunner] list was Assassinate. True to its name, it was a simple ability that allowed me to kill anyone whose system I could infiltrate. I hadn't encountered anyone who could resist it, either. I only had to Misthack them, then, once their system was laid bare, I had the option to kill them. Once I used it, they just dropped dead. No long death scene. No gasping for air. Just death.

But as useful as the skill was—and it was incredibly powerful—there were three limiters associated with its use. First, it took every last ounce of Mist in my stores. It didn't matter how much or how little I had available. It just drained everything, leaving me incredibly vulnerable to retaliation. Second, it had a monthlong cooldown associated with it. That limitation was only helped by the fact that, as far as I could tell, the number of times I could use the ability seemed to roll over month to month. So, if I went an entire month without using it, then when the next month rolled around, I would have two uses available. At present, I could use the ability six times, so long as I had the Mist to support it.

But the final limiter was the fact that the ability scared me a little. Sure, I had no issues with killing people, but there was a marked difference between shooting someone and just seeing them drop dead for seemingly no reason. Those reservations wouldn't stop me from using the ability, but they definitely made me think twice.

Shaking my head, I moved on to [Fieldcraft], looking over my newest abilities. Stabilize allowed me to help someone in critical condition by keeping their wounds—or sickness—from getting any worse. It only lasted about twenty-four hours, but for me, it was invaluable. In a day, my other abilities could carry me away from the brink of death, so long as I didn't die before they had a chance to work their magic. If I used it on other people, it might just give me the opportunity to get them to a proper doctor.

Mend was a bit more active in that it could seal wounds. It wasn't quite as good as a foam bandage—or even crude stitches—but it was still nice to have in case I didn't have any supplies available.

In the Survival branch, the first ability I'd gotten was Bastion, which had seen copious use because it allowed me to specify a location and protect it with powerful Mist defenses. I usually only activated it at night when Patrick and I were asleep, but I'd used it a couple of times in battle, as well. And while the shield wouldn't last under concentrated fire from a powerful enemy, it was enough that it gave me plenty of options.

By comparison, the Tier 5 ability in the branch was one I'd rarely used at all. On paper, Tinkering sounded great in that it allowed me to improvise various weapons and explosives from mundane materials. However, it was limited in that the results were less powerful than what I could easily buy. Still, I expected it would be valuable if I ever found myself without my equipment.

In the Communication branch of the [Fieldcraft] tree, I'd gained various map-related abilities that made navigation much easier. For instance, setting a Waypoint on my map would give me some guidance in the form of a wisp of Mist that directed me along the appropriate path. Combat Map highlighted enemy positions and orientation, even going so far as to help me detect concealed foes.

But the real jewel of the tree was Secure Connection, which gave me a completely untraceable and incredibly difficult-to-hijack connection that I could extend to up to five people. Usually, I only used it on Patrick, but even that gave me peace of mind that few other abilities could have rivaled.

The last branch, Utility, gave me the ability to Ignore Injury, which was pretty self-explanatory. Using it allowed me to not only ignore the pain, but also to function normally until the ability ran out. It typically only lasted about an hour—less if the injury was severe—but that was usually enough.

Focused Will was probably my favorite ability in the branch, though. True to its categorization as a Utility ability, it allowed me, through intense focus, to rapidly regenerate my entire pool of Mist. I could only use it once every few days, but even that was invaluable, given the Mist-hungry nature of many of my abilities.

For [Demolition] and [Acrobatics], not much had changed, save for the fact that they'd both grown more powerful. One day, I hoped to have the opportunity to improve them in some way, as I had with my other skills.

But that was a worry for another day.

For now, I needed some sleep. So, after rising from my seated position, I headed to one of the ship's bathrooms, where I took a shower before heading to the quarters I shared with Patrick. I climbed under the covers next to his sleeping form. He mumbled something in his sleep, and I couldn't help but smile.

As rocky as our start had been, things had definitely improved. Against all odds, life was pretty good. Not perfect by any stretch of the imagination, but I really couldn't complain.

Still, in the back of my mind, I couldn't help but wonder how long it would last. Our world was one of conflict, and whether it was this latest job or when the aliens came in force, I knew we wouldn't be able to steer clear of the fray for much longer.

CHAPTER FIVE

MEETING THE CREW

Mira has told me a little about what she did while we were apart, though I feel sure she's kept the worst of it to herself. I get it. After Nova, she was broken, and no matter how much I tried, I couldn't fix her. Because she didn't want to be fixed. She didn't think she deserved it.

—Patrick Ward

I lay on my side, my hand resting on Patrick's bare chest, the rise and fall almost hypnotic in its simplicity. Slowly, his eyes fluttered open. Once he was completely awake, he turned to me, let a slight smile play across his face, and said, "Good morning, you."

"Morning," I replied, returning his smile with one of my own. In times like that, I sometimes questioned what I'd done to deserve happiness. Certainly, I hadn't earned it through my actions. I'd done horrible things, and though I didn't necessarily regret them, the guilt still weighed me down.

"What's wrong?" he asked, reading my emotions like a book. My expression hadn't really changed much, aside from my smile fading away, but for Patrick, that was enough to paint a clear picture.

"Just thinking," I said, shifting closer. He lifted his arm, letting me rest against him, and hugged me tight. "About everything. About how lucky I am."

"I agree. You're extremely lucky to have such a supportive, handsome, and understanding partner," he said. "And did I mention handsome?"

I playfully slapped his stomach. "Shut up. That's not what I'm talking about," I said. Though that wasn't really true. Without Patrick, I never would have climbed out of my malaise. Absent his anchoring presence, I probably would be dead somewhere after having picked a fight I couldn't hope to win. I was functionally immune to inebriants—and God knows, I tried to challenge that—but there were plenty of other forms of self-destruction, and I'd sampled them all.

"I know," he said. "I look back at everything, and I'm sometimes amazed at how we're even alive. One little change, and everything would be different."

"Yeah."

For a while, we just lay there, enjoying one another's closeness, but then I said, "So, you really think they'll betray us?"

"Probably. It makes sense," he said. "Once they get what they want from us, they'll turn on us. Probably try to take *The Leviathan*, too."

"I was thinking the same thing."

"Do you not want to do it?" Patrick asked. "We could head out right now and be on the other side of the world by tomorrow. You remember that mountain town we visited a few months back? The one with the monks? You liked it there, didn't you? Isaac and his people wouldn't be able to follow."

"But you wouldn't get your circuits," I said.

He gave a slight shrug, then said, "I've gone this long without them."

"You really want them, though," I countered. "You're not really good at hiding excitement."

"Wasn't trying."

"Right. But I can tell how important this is to you," I said. Indeed, Patrick loved to tinker with various machines and cybernetics. In the beginning, I thought he was just trying to advance his [Cybernetic Engineer] skill, but over time, I'd come to realize that he truly enjoyed the process of creation. That wasn't really my thing, but given my work creating various Ghosts, I could understand how rewarding such a process could be. Besides, his hobby had often proved useful.

"I'd be lying if I said it wasn't," he stated. I started to respond, but he cut me off by saying, "But it's not as important as other things."

"Like what?" I asked.

"Like staying alive" was his response.

That much was true. I was reasonably certain that I could survive just about anything Isaac and his crew could throw at me, but I wasn't invincible. More importantly, neither was Patrick. In fact, he was downright squishy next to me. Sure, he had some nice equipment to shore up some of his weaknesses, but the best equipment in the world was useless in the face of overwhelming power.

"Still. I think we should do this," I said. "If they turn on us, we'll just be ready. Then, we'll take their stuff."

He sighed, closing his eyes. When he opened them again, he said, "Guess that's that, then. May as well get ready to go."

With that, we both got out of bed and got dressed. I started with my infiltration suit; I still hadn't found anything better, regardless of how hard I'd looked.

I wasn't disappointed with that, though. It just proved that I had the best available. Still, I was hoping that, someday soon, I'd be able to find an upgrade.

My Sheath, by contrast, had seen a couple of updates. Neither were game changers or anything—just a couple of enhancements that made it more durable—but I was more than happy with my subdermal armor. Patrick had even gotten something similar, though his was of lower quality. Not because we didn't want to spend the money but, rather, because Dex had been unable to find anything as good as mine.

Over my infiltration suit, I donned a pair of tight-fitting black pants, a black top, and a short red jacket that didn't even reach my waist. Next came my gun belt and Ferdinand II. Finally, I slipped on a pair of heavy black boots that laced up to midcalf.

Patrick, by comparison, wore his own version of the infiltration suit—again, not quite as high-quality as mine, but it was probably light-years ahead of anything Isaac and his ilk would have. Over that was a white tee-shirt emblazoned with a logo I'd never seen before, a pair of blue pants, and a yellow jacket.

"Lookin' good," I said, grinning as I saw him strap a holster to his own belt. In it was his Tergan Tactical pistol. "You look like a real swashbuckler."

"Wouldn't I need a cutlass for that?" he asked.

I shrugged. "You would look pretty dashing with a sword," I said with a small grin. "Would probably be awkward to sit in the pilot's chair with that, though."

"See? That's why I keep you around. You think of everything," he said with feigned earnestness.

I stepped forward and put my arms around his neck. "Is that the only reason?" I asked, looking up into his eyes.

He swallowed hard. "I can think of one or two others," he admitted, pulling me close. Then, he leaned down and kissed me. It only lasted a few seconds before I pulled away, and he asked, "What?"

"If we start going down that road, we'll be late."

"I can be quick," he complained.

"Not really what a girl wants to hear," I said with a shake of my head followed by a light chuckle. Then, I pulled out of his embrace and added, "Come on. They're going to be waiting for us."

He let out a dramatic sigh, but he said, "Fine. But I reserve the right to ravage you later."

I winked, asking, "Who says you're the one who'll be doing the ravaging?"

With that, the pair of us continued making the final preparations for our departure. Most of *The Leviathan*'s vital systems were automated, but Patrick was a stickler for his processes. So, even though doing so wasn't entirely necessary, we went through his preflight checklist before finally getting underway.

I settled into the navigator's chair beside him and shared my map with his interface via the Secure Connection we'd established. On it, I'd placed a Waypoint for our destination, which was a midsize town nestled high in the nearby mountains.

"And off we go," he said after firing up the Mist reactor. Because the ship was fueled by Rift Shards, even starting *The Leviathan* up was an expensive prospect, but flying it was enough to bankrupt a small town. We could afford it, though, if only barely. If worse came to worst, we could've just run a Rift.

I shuddered as the memory of my last attempt at delving a Rift came to mind. No—I didn't want to risk that unless absolutely necessary.

The Leviathan lifted into the air, rocking a bit as it fought against the planet's gravity. After only a second or two, it stabilized, and then, we were on our way. The ground sped by beneath us; the ship was capable of going much faster, but doing so would have drained our fuel extremely rapidly. The ship wasn't designed for terrestrial travel—instead, it was meant for space flight—so it took a lot of power to make up for its unsuitability. As a result, we kept our speed low enough to minimize the fuel consumption.

Still, it was fast enough that it only took us about an hour to reach our destination.

One thing I'd learned soon after Nova's fall was that airships were not nearly as rare as I'd expected. Most were cobbled together versions of pre-Initialization vessels, but there were plenty of newer ships around, too. Because of that, most important settlements were equipped with some version of an air dock. Our destination was no different.

The city was called Abernathy, and as far as I knew, it hadn't even existed before the Initialization. That meant that the city had been built with modern issues in mind, so its air dock was fairly advanced, if a bit small.

The dock itself was a series of circular spaces enclosed by high walls, and after communicating with the Abernathy authorities, Patrick settled *The Leviathan* into an assigned slip. Once we'd set up the automated defenses—and I'd used Bastion to augment those defenses—we disembarked the ship. Immediately, we were greeted by one of the city's officials.

She was a small, nervous woman with dark skin and vivid pink hair. "What brings you to our great city?" she asked in accented English.

"Meeting friends," said Patrick. "Maybe picking up some cargo. Depends on how the meeting goes."

"Then you need to be aware of the tariffs on exports," the woman said before explaining that anything leaving the city was subject to a tax. That wasn't abnormal—most towns had a similar system—but it didn't worry me. With Patrick's [Smuggler] skill, he could easily get around such things.

Unless someone had a skill to counter it, but that rarely happened.

Once we'd finished with the official, we headed through the slip's gate and into the town itself. Like most cities, it was constructed of durable materials and protected by a Mist shield—though not a powerful one. Still, we hadn't seen any particularly noteworthy wildlife on our way in, so it was probably sufficient.

That was one thing I'd learned since leaving Nova behind. The wilderness was dangerous—even more so in some of the untamed regions we'd visited in the past couple of years—but there were pockets of stability where habitation was fairly safe. Abernathy had clearly been built in one such area.

Certainly, nowhere was completely safe. Danger could spring up out of nowhere, and I was sure that Abernathy was not completely protected. Still, it was safer than most places, which meant that it could afford some level of stability.

The architecture could be categorized as what I had come to recognize as influenced by an Eastern style. With sweeping tiled roofs, the buildings combined with the gardens to evoke a sense of serene stability. As if neither time nor danger would ever touch the place. Cherry blossoms lined the road leading away from the air dock, enhancing that atmosphere.

"Not a bad place to settle down," Patrick said, looking around.

"I'm sure it's hiding something below the surface," I responded. My cynicism had died down a little since what had happened in Nova, and I recognized that my perception of the city had been tainted by my mindset. However, no amount of personal growth could mask the notion that people were, by and large, self-interested. And where there was selfishness, there existed a seedy underbelly of crime and corruption. It was an inevitable part of human nature. So, when I saw a beautiful town like Abernathy, I recognized it for the facade it was.

"Might just be a nice place," he said. "Everywhere isn't like Nova."

I shrugged. I didn't want to argue with him. As well as we got along, his mindset was fundamentally different from mine, and I didn't think we'd soon bridge that gap. Even so, we didn't need to agree on everything, so we hadn't let it affect our relationship.

We continued on to the meeting place—a tavern called the Wandering Duck—and as we traversed the town's streets, I used Observation to get a better sense of the place. And just as I'd expected, I saw precisely the corruption that infected every other human settlement. I saw pickpockets, more than a few addicts, and shady businesses that were obviously fronts for less-than-reputable activities. However, I was pleased to note that the local constables—as recognized by their bright-red uniforms—seemed to be doing their jobs. I didn't notice a single undeserved beating, which was a rarity when someone gained even a modicum of power.

Gradually, we crossed the town, and eventually, we reached the Wandering Duck, which was a three-story structure following the same architectural pattern as the rest of the city. We went inside, and I let out a sigh of relief when I saw the familiar confines of a bar. No matter where else I went, they were always the same—a comforting through line that connected everything.

Sure, details changed. Decor might be different. But the atmosphere? Or more importantly, the people—they remained consistent. In this case, the furnishings reminded me more of a spacious teahouse than a pub. Still, the feeling was the same as any other bar.

As I searched the area for threats—there were at least four people in the tavern that looked like they had the attributes to handle themselves—and potential escape routes, Patrick told the host, who was a small man with sharp features and slick-backed black hair, that we were there to meet our friends. He seemed to have been prepared for our arrival, and he quickly led us into a private room upstairs.

That's where we were reunited with Isaac, Huascar, and four other people. The first was a tall, broad man wearing a wide-brimmed hat and a sleeveless shirt sporting a logo I'd never seen before. The second was a pretty, petite woman—a girl really—with stark-white hair streaked with green and a pair of pistols strapped to her hips. Third came a sloppy, rotund man who looked as if he'd never participated in a physical activity in his life. His hair was a thin fringe of fuzz, and even from a distance, I could smell the stink of excess sweat and sour beer. Rounding out the group was an incredibly handsome man with high cheekbones, lavender eyes, and blond hair that hung down to his shoulders.

And he had pointed ears. It actually took a flare of Observation for me to notice them, but they were there all the same.

I had Ferdinand II out in the space of an instant, and it only took a fraction of a second longer before I had the barrel pointed in the intruder's direction. "Alien," I muttered, locking my eyes on his.

I'd encountered plenty of aliens in my young life, but aside from a few merchants in the Bazaar, I'd never had what anyone would consider peaceful relations with them. They were invaders, after all. And there was only one thing to do with those sorts of people.

Everyone erupted into motion. Patrick drew his own pistol, getting it out almost as quickly as I'd drawn mine. The pretty girl did the same, and though she couldn't match our speed, she still managed to arm herself in a flash. The big man pushed himself from the table and promptly tipped over onto his back, cementing my impression that he wasn't a real threat. Huascar bent over, covering his head with his hands as he tried to make the smallest target possible while his brother held up his hands in a gesture of placation.

Meanwhile, the alien just smiled and said, "Impressive. Very perceptive."

"Give me a reason not to kill you or I'm going to start painting the walls," I growled. Then, I felt someone smash against my Mistwall. They were rebuffed by my defenses, and I counterattacked with Backlash. Immediately, the fat man started to convulse. "And if big boy there tries to attack me again, I'll drop him without a second thought."

"Very impressive," repeated the alien.

"Everybody just calm down!" hissed Isaac. "We don't have to fight."

"Tell that to the invader."

"Mira . . ."

I didn't turn to look at Patrick—I had no intention of taking my eyes off the enemy—but I could hear the plea in his voice. So, I said, "Explain. Quick. Or—"

"You will paint the walls, presumably with our blood. A very visceral description," said the alien. "I promise, I mean you nor the inhabitants of this world any harm. In fact, our interests are far more aligned than you know."

"Yeah? Gonna need more than that," I said. If I had to go on the attack, I'd take out the alien first. I had a hard time getting a read on his power level. Then, I'd hit Isaac. After that, the girl. The man in the hat still hadn't moved. Instead, he seemed entirely disinterested as he took a sip from his mug of dark beer. Yeah—he'd be next. Then, Huascar. Finally, the fat man. I could manage that, so long as none of them displayed any particularly impressive abilities. Not a guarantee. Plus, I'd have to get Patrick out of harm's way. No—a fight was a bad idea. Maybe necessary, but still not smart.

"This doesn't change anything," said Isaac. "Askar is part of the team."

The alien spread his hands and smiled. I had to concentrate to see that the tips of his incisors were slightly pointed. "Indeed. Just a cog in the machine."

"We need an explanation," said Patrick. "Now. Or we walk."

Isaac looked from me to Patrick, then back at me. After a second, he sighed and said, "Very well. At least have a seat. This might take a few minutes."

I nodded before pulling out one of the chairs and taking a seat. I kept Ferdinand II out, and out of the corner of my eye, I saw that Patrick hadn't holstered his weapon, either. Finally, once we were seated, I said, "Okay, talk. And make it convincing."

CHAPTER SIX

MAKING AN EXAMPLE

I'm not powerful. In Earth terms, I'm a little above average. But on a galactic scale? I'm nobody. I can overcome that, though. It'll be difficult, and I have to think outside the box, but it's possible. I have to believe it is.

—Patrick Ward

I kept my pistol trained on the alien—Askar—as I said, "Okay. Go ahead. Make me believe I don't need to kill this asshole right here and now."

"You say that so confidently," the alien said with a shake of his head that sent his fine blond hair swishing back and forth. "I am not your enemy."

"Yeah? Prove it."

"Askar has been working with us for years," provided Isaac. "Tens of jobs. He's personally saved my life multiple times."

"Mine, too," squeaked the girl. Her voice reminded me of a chirping bird, but I didn't fail to notice the slight quiver in her tone. "Twice."

"So? That's not the convincing argument you think it is," I stated. "For all I know, you're all traitors, and you're working for the aliens. You wouldn't be the first, and I know you won't be the last."

Askar held out his hand, his motions slow and precise, presumably so I wouldn't interpret it as a threat. Then, a holographic display appeared above his upturned hand. The hovering depiction of his face was instantly recognizable, and my Universal Language interpreted the glyphs beneath, giving me the gist of what I was looking at.

"What is it?" asked Patrick.

"A wanted notice," I said. "Mr. Askar here has been a very bad boy."

Indeed, the list of crimes was extensive. Theft was the least of them, but it also seemed that he'd committed numerous other offenses, all targeted at his own people. It painted a vivid picture of his own opinion of his race.

"Care to explain?" I asked, nodding slightly. I still didn't trust him, but I did respect him a bit more. Anyone who'd killed that many aliens was worthy of my regard.

"My planet was invaded, just like yours," he said. "It was centuries ago, well before I was even born, but the result was a dystopian world where every natural resource had been stripped clean. We had no choice but to leave because the environment had grown so hostile. I was born on a giant space station in a dark, mostly forgotten corner of the universe. My people, they were barely surviving off whatever scraps our overlords deigned to grant us."

"Sounds familiar," I said.

"No. It isn't. This planet is a paradise compared to most recently Integrated worlds," he explained. "That will not last."

"I'm aware," I said. "Hence the reason I'm holding a gun on you. In my experience, most aliens are here to ensure Earth ends up like your home planet. That's why I make it a point to kill them whenever possible."

He raised his perfectly arched eyebrows as he asked, "Have you encountered so many?"

"I've seen my fair share. Now, keep going. I'm getting a little twitchy. Who knows when my finger will slip and make a mess of this nice private room."

"Very well. I recognized the situation for what it was before I'd even reached maturity," Askar went on. "And after I realized that my pleas for change were met with disdain and hostility, I did what I had to do to escape. I left my home behind, and over the next few decades, I positioned myself to travel to a pre-Integration planet."

"Obviously."

"Right. Once I got here, I sabotaged the mining operation I was supposed to help guard and went rogue," he said. "Ever since then, I've been free. Isaac and I met on another job, and we decided to become allies. We've been together ever since."

"That's it?" I asked, a little disappointed. I'd half hoped he would prove to be some sort of freedom fighter. Instead, he was just another mercenary. "I . . . I don't know. I expected more."

"Like what?" asked Isaac, incapable of hiding his surprise.

"I don't know. Maybe that he was trying to organize a resistance or something," I said.

At that, Askar let out a sudden laugh. I reacted to the sudden change by raising my weapon a little, but he held up his hands in surrender as he said, "No. I'm not making a move. I just found it a bit . . . implausible."

"Meaning?"

"Resistance is futile," he stated. "The moment this world is Initiated, a swarm of powerful aliens will descend upon you. There is no chance of winning. Only survival until you can escape."

"Then why are you here if our situation is so dire?" I asked. My tone promised disbelief, but I knew how accurate his prediction was. My uncle had said the same thing.

"Credits," he said. "The whole universe isn't like these frontier planets. The core worlds are civilized. I intend to make enough money to get there where I can settle down for an easy life. Maybe raise a family if I can find a compatible mate."

It was such a simple goal that it should've seemed unbelievable to me. However, I had seen how desperate people could get when it came to what should've been a normal life. The fate of Askar's world was a peek into Earth's future, which made me somewhat sympathetic. Still, I didn't let my guard down.

"And you think this job will get you there?" I asked.

"No. But it is a step in the right direction," he stated. "One of many. These frontier worlds are dangerous and difficult to visit, but they offer incredible opportunities. Once the Initialization completes, the various powers will descend and monopolize the resources. We only have a couple more years to take advantage of this situation."

I didn't immediately respond. Everything seemed to have a proper explanation, but even so, I knew that I couldn't trust someone like Askar. He wasn't like Gala or Dex or any of the other merchants in the Bazaar. When he'd set foot on Earth's surface, Askar had established himself as an enemy of humanity.

But just because he was the enemy didn't mean I couldn't work with him, at least until he and the rest inevitably betrayed me. I glanced at Patrick. Betrayed us, rather.

"Fine," I said, lowering my pistol to the table. The tension remained, but the others visibly relaxed.

The man in the hat chuckled, saying, "I was hopin' for a good tussle. S'pose I'll have to wait."

"Didn't catch your name, friend," Patrick said, his voice laced with uncharacteristic venom.

"Didn't throw it your way, did I, chief?" the man remarked.

That's when I noticed the barely visible seam in his right forearm. Otherwise, the limb looked entirely normal, but I could recognize high-end Realskin when I saw it. What sort of cybernetic did he have under there? That he hadn't visibly reacted to the tense situation only made me reassess and put him at the top of my list of threats. Nobody could be that calm in the face of danger unless they were used to such situations.

And unless they had a plan to come out on top.

"Don't be antagonistic, Rex," said Isaac. Then, he introduced the others. I already knew Huascar, who still looked like an extremely twitchy and colorful bird. The pretty girl was called Avery, the fat man's name was Paulo, and of course, there was Rex. As it turned out, Avery specialized in scouting, Paulo called himself a Mistrunner, and Rex was a demolitions man who claimed he was handy with a pistol, as well. Askar was a jack-of-all-trades, and Huascar fancied himself a pilot. Or a driver, perhaps.

Finally, Isaac was the group's leader, and he was the one who'd come up with the plan we would follow. Which was both simple and more complicated than I expected. One thing I'd learned since my Awakening was that complex plans tended to go wrong. Sure, it was tempting to create intricate plans where everything fit together like a well-made puzzle, but the reality of it was that simpler was almost always better. Complicated looked good on paper, but in practice, the more moving pieces a plan had meant that there was just more that could go wrong. And inevitably, it would. And when everything started to unravel, it opened the door to terrible consequences.

No—simple was definitely better, especially if, as was so often the case with me, you had the skills to back it up.

"So, let me get this straight—first, we need to hijack a train," I said, once Isaac had gone over the basics of the plan. "Then, we have to get it into position so it blocks the route the gnomes—"

"Dengyts," interjected Isaac.

"Right. Them," I said. "Anyway, we've got to block the path their convoy's going to take. Once they're stopped, we hit them hard and fast, take what we can, jump in *The Leviathan* and be on the other side of the world before they have a chance to respond."

"You're missing one step," said Paulo, mopping the sweat from his face with a less-than-clean handkerchief. "I need to get into their systems so I can identify the one carrying the goods."

"Right," I said. I could have done it, and probably better, but I didn't want to give away too much about my abilities. After all, I fully expected to be betrayed, so it wasn't wise to show them too many of my cards. "Which requires another stop."

"And Rex has to set the explosives to disable the extraneous vehicles," added Askar. "Even then, we'll have a firefight on our hands."

"Do you really think we can do this?" asked Patrick. He was always the cautious one, but I had to agree that the question needed to be asked. Because from what I'd seen, the group of would-be hijackers was destined to fail.

It was telling that, if it was just Patrick and me, I felt better about the heist than if the others were included. I was fairly certain that I could rival any of the specialists in their specific jobs, and I knew for certain that I was a better

Mistrunner than Paulo. After all, my Backlash had completely incapacitated him, and that hadn't required any real input from me. If I truly flexed my abilities, he would have died in an instant.

"All you gotta worry 'bout is flyin'," said Rex. "Just be where yer s'posed to be, and we'll do what we're s'posed to do. No muss, no fuss."

To accentuate his statement, he tilted his head to the side and spat on the floor. My dislike for the man grew.

"Yeah, if we agree to do this, I'm not sitting out," I said.

"And you think you kin keep up?" Rex asked, leaning forward and smiling broadly. "Or are you just gonna be our eye candy? Huascar told me about that little getup you was wearin' when they found you. Put that little number on and I'll be right fine with you taggin' along."

I sighed.

Back in Nova City, I'd gotten into the habit of hiding my face behind Mimic. Rare was the occasion when I'd left our compound without wearing some sort of mask. However, in the years since the city's fall, I'd worn my own face far more often. And during that time, I'd come to realize that men and women were very appreciative of my looks. I knew I wasn't the most beautiful girl in the world, but I was definitely a cut above average. Combine that with a body that I'd spent quite a bit of time training, and I'd endured my fair share of romantic overtures. In the year when Patrick and I were apart, I'd even given in to many of them.

But there was a time and place for that kind of thing, and in the middle of a clandestine meeting concerning a potential job was neither. Especially from someone like Rex, who, though he was a decent looking man, certainly wasn't my type.

So, I knew I needed to make another example. And judging by Huascar's cringing expression, he knew what was coming, as well.

In a lightning move, I exploded from my seat and reached out to grab the back of Rex's head. He tried to react, but he was far too slow. With measured force, I yanked his head down, and a moment later, I was rewarded by the sound of cracking bone. He flailed in pain and surprise, and I released him.

That's when his arm opened up, and a long, thin blade jutted up and out like the claw of a praying mantis. Before he could bring that cybernetic weapon to bear, I had Ferdinand II's barrel pressed to the side of his head.

"Nuh uh, buddy," I growled. "One wrong move, and your head's a canoe."

The others didn't even have a chance to react, everything had happened so quickly. But already, Patrick had his gun in hand, and he was more than ready to do whatever was necessary.

A long moment of silence stretched between us, with each member of the group on the verge of attack. But then, a small, high-pitched voice interrupted, asking, "What's a canoe?"

I glanced at Avery, who had a quizzical expression on her face. I answered, "Type of boat. They used to make them by hollowing out tree trunks."

Her face squinched as she gave it some thought, and then recognition dawned. "Oh! I get it!"

Askar locked his eyes on me. He still hadn't drawn a weapon. "If you're going to kill him, let's get it over with."

"Don't want to. But I couldn't let that kind of thing go," I said. "Slippery slope and all that."

He seemed to understand my issue. If I let Rex act that way, he would keep pushing until he went too far. By taking care of it now—just as I had with Huascar during the first meeting—I'd cut that kind of thing off at the source. Perhaps Rex would harbor some resentment, but given his attitude, that was unavoidable. Men like him only understood one thing, and peaceful coexistence was never in the cards.

"If you let him go, we can work together," said Isaac. "Kill him, and . . . Well, things are going to get messy."

"I want an apology."

Isaac demanded, "What?"

"Fuck you!" spat Rex, his voice nasal from what I thought was a broken nose. "You let me up, and I'll—"

"Know when to shut up, Rex," interrupted Askar. Curiously, the other man snapped his jaws shut. Askar continued, "Apologize. Promise not to say anything offensive. And maybe we can get this thing back on track. Just think of the rewards, if it makes you feel any better."

A long, pregnant silence blanketed the room, but it only lasted a few more seconds before Rex muttered, "Sorry." When I didn't immediately let him up, he shouted, "I'm sorry, aight? I didn't mean it. Just foolin' about is all. Don't pay it no mind."

After a couple of moments, I withdrew my pistol. I didn't holster it, though. Instead, I remained wary as Rex pushed himself up. His nose was a misshapen ruin of blood, though I suspected it wouldn't be long before it healed. The resistance I'd felt when slamming his face into the table told me all I needed to know about his Constitution, and though it didn't compare to mine, it was still high enough that a little broken nose wouldn't be more than a minor annoyance.

"So, do you want to do this?" asked Patrick via our Secure Connection. He hadn't spoken out loud, so none of the others were aware of his question. "Or do we just leave?"

"You think they'll let us?" I asked in the same way. "If we refuse, they won't let us leave this room alive. We'll have to subdue or kill them. They can't afford us getting out and warning the gnomes."

"Dengyts," he said.

"Whatever. My point is that we either join them, or we hash it out right here and now. I think I can take a couple of them out before they have a chance to react, but that still leaves—"

"Let's just go along with it," he said. "If we feel the pressure, we do what we need to do."

I resisted the urge to nod. We'd already discussed contingencies, and we'd made preparations for betrayal. So, we'd mitigated most of the risk associated with joining the group. It wasn't safe, but it was as close as we could make it.

"Fine," I said aloud. "So, let's go over the details. And no—I'm not staying in the ship. I know you only wanted Patrick and *The Leviathan*, but we're a package deal. And if I'm coming along, I'm going to make sure we don't screw things up."

Isaac glanced at Askar, who gave him a slight nod. If I hadn't been looking for it, I might've missed the subtle movement, but it was more than enough to tell me who was really in charge. "I think . . . I think we can all agree to that," he said. "You seem competent enough that we'll find a use for your . . . ah . . . skills."

CHAPTER SEVEN

RECONNAISSANCE

I've given a lot of thought to the question of my own identity. After Mobile, I latched on to Mira and just went along with whatever she wanted. But when we were apart, I was forced to chart my own course. I'm still not certain as to the shape my life might take, but I do know I'm not content to ride someone else's coattails.

—Patrick Ward

I knelt in the ditch, staring through the binoculars as I watched the Dengyt satellite compound. Strictly speaking, I didn't need the visual aid—Observation was plenty powerful to see what needed to be seen—but I didn't want to give away too many of my abilities. Already, my so-called allies had seen too much for my comfort, and I didn't want to give them any more ammunition for their inevitable betrayal.

Beside me sat Avery, the diminutive girl with the streaked hair. She couldn't stop fidgeting, as if she was unused to sitting still for longer than a couple of minutes. Or perhaps I had a skewed perspective; after all, we'd been sitting there for the better part of the day, so it was possible that she was simply reacting as anyone would have. Still, it showed a lack of professionalism.

To the rear was a supremely uncomfortable and corpulent Paulo. I didn't need to look to know that he was drenched in sweat. The smell of his body odor gave that detail away, and I couldn't help but wonder if his stench would alert the gnomes, even from almost a mile away. I was self-aware enough to recognize that his discomfort was probably as much due to my treatment of him as because of the overbearing heat.

"I've got everything I need," he said, his voice soft. "I don't know why we needed to stay here this long."

Every so often over the past few hours, he'd said much the same thing. It seemed that he was content to take his readings of the Mist shield and leave. Predictable, given that his life wasn't the one on the line. He was willing to exert the minimal effort needed to do his part of the job. Everything else was someone else's problem.

Sheer idiocy. It was no wonder he hadn't taken advantage of his opportunities and enhanced his physique. He was lazy and stupid.

Or maybe my assessment was too harsh. For all I knew, he was decent enough at his job. My perspective was just skewed by my own power. Not everyone had been through what I'd endured, and I'd long since discovered that the vast majority of the population hadn't even bothered to gain any levels. Even among mercenaries like Isaac and his group, only the frontline fighters would've done enough to raise their potential by any appreciable degree. In fact, I would have been surprised if any of them possessed classes at all.

That was one thing I'd been more than a little shocked to discover after Nova City's fall. Many people had no idea that classes were even a thing. They just gained their skills and progressed them, never killing anything. As such, their stats were woefully underdeveloped.

Sure, some people—especially in the circles I traveled within—knew. But the general population? They were woefully ignorant. In that way, the residents of Nova City had been lucky. Because of the constant tribal conflict, enough Operators had progressed to the point of gaining classes that it had become common knowledge. But the city had always been isolated, and other settlements had managed to keep that kind of information from the general population.

And I understood why, as well. Information was power, and even if I now recognized that the world wasn't quite as dreary a place as life in Nova City suggested, I wasn't so blind that I couldn't see the benefit of keeping the population from becoming too powerful. After all, there was a very real risk of some madman with a decent tier gaining enough power that the authorities—whoever they were—would be completely incapable of containing him. I only had to remember the damage I'd left in my wake, and the possibility grew even more plausible.

I lowered my binoculars and said, "I think I've got what I need. What about you, Avery?"

I could practically feel Paulo bristle at my refusal to acknowledge him, but he didn't say anything. He knew better. The Backlash he'd experienced when he'd tried to probe my Mistwall had frightened him to the point where he couldn't look me in the eye, much less verbalize any disagreement with my choices.

"I was done ages ago," she huffed. "This is all pointless. I could get in and out of this place in my sleep."

"Maybe. But you'll only get one chance to be wrong," I stated.

"These guys, though? The Dengyts are harmless without their machines," she stated. "They're like little kids."

I just shook my head. She had no idea that the gnomes were almost assuredly equipped with classes, which meant that, regardless of their diminutive size, they had the inflated attributes that came with advanced levels. While the people of Earth might be largely ignorant, I couldn't imagine the aliens would be.

Glancing at the girl, I gave her some advice that had been drilled into me by my uncle and the Amigos. "Never underestimate your enemy," I said. "In this world, appearances can be deceptive. Those little gnomes are probably twice as strong as you. You have no clue what kinds of cybernetics they have available. Nor do you know what racial advantages they might have. For all you know, their muscles are denser and far more powerful than humans'. I'm surprised Askar hasn't taught you that much, at least."

"He's taught me plenty," she once again huffed, the tone making her sound like a petulant child. Or a wounded animal, perhaps. That could have been her youthful face and petite frame, though. Either way, she seemed a lot younger than she probably was. "I'm the best scout and infiltrator on this side of the world."

"Maybe," I acknowledged. I hadn't seen her in action, so I couldn't rightfully gainsay the claim. However, I suspected that it was little more than misguided bluster. "But you can always be better. Smarter. In fact, you need to be if you're going to make it out alive."

I could tell that my statement had fallen on deaf ears. It was possible that she wouldn't listen to me unless I'd proved my superiority. I had no idea. I wasn't particularly invested in any of it, though, and I certainly had no interest in mentoring her. If she wanted to be an idiot, I wouldn't worry myself with curing her stupidity.

"Whatever," she said, her hand finding the grip of one of the pistols at her waist. She had a habit of fiddling with them when she was nervous. "So, can we go?"

I nodded, and I heard Paulo sigh in relief and mutter, "Finally."

Clearly, he didn't think I'd heard, and I didn't give any indication otherwise. The more they underestimated my abilities, the better.

With that, the three of us retreated, climbing out of the ditch in the opposite direction of the Dengyt facility. As we moved, the air shimmered under the effect of the portable holographic display Paulo carried. A useful bit of tech, that. Even if it was nothing compared to Stealth or Camouflage, it was still convenient for those who didn't have the benefit of those abilities.

Once we were out of visual range, Paulo deactivated the display, and we continued along for another mile until we reached the vehicle they'd disguised beneath an earth-toned net. In the desert, it was sufficient to conceal the truck from anything but close scrutiny—which was unlikely, given our location.

After mounting up—I took the back seat while they sat up front—the three of us sped off toward *The Leviathan*. It took almost thirty minutes of cross-country driving, but eventually, we reached our destination. There, the team had set up a temporary camp beside my ship. It was composed of sturdy tents, but it at least had the benefit of a decent Mist shield.

Not that I cared about their defenses overmuch. Patrick and I had stayed in *The Leviathan*, which was virtually unassailable by anything but the most potent weaponry.

The truck pulled to a stop beside a few other similar vehicles, and we hopped out. Isaac and the others looked up from where they'd been sitting around a fire and enjoying some sort of stew. Patrick was with them, clearly having ingratiated himself to the others in a way I could never hope to match. He might not be as powerful as I was, but he definitely had other talents.

They were laughing at something when we approached, and Isaac asked, "So? You see what you needed to see?"

Before I could answer, Avery sat down and groaned, "We saw more than enough. We should've been back ages ago."

"Oh?" asked Isaac.

Taking a seat next to Patrick—he'd reserved a camp chair for me—I said, "Your people are too impatient. They're sloppy, and it's going to get them killed."

Avery rolled her eyes. "You're totally exaggerating. Those little—"

"So, you saw the concealed snipers?" I asked. I knew she hadn't. "What about the drone clusters? The combat bots? Or the patrols? Not the ones on top of the wall. I'm talking about the scouts that came within a quarter of a mile of our little nest?"

"What is that in kilometers?" asked Huascar. "I can never remember the formula for converting miles to a more civilized form of measurement."

"A little more than half," I said. "About sixty percent."

"Oh. Good to know."

"I saw the snipers," Avery announced. "And . . . And I'm sure I would've seen the others once I got close."

"Sure, sure. But by then, it would've been too late," I stated. "You've got plenty of ability. You just don't pay attention."

"It would've been fine," she muttered.

"Anyway," Isaac said, moving the conversation along. "Are we ready to start the plan?"

I shrugged. "I can't speak for anyone else, but I could get in without raising the alarm," I said. "But you won't tell me what we're after, so that doesn't really help us out."

"For our protection," he stated. "If you knew the whole plan, what's to stop you from doing it all yourself?"

"Oh, please," Rex blurted. "She ain't that good. The girl's got skills, I'll admit that much. But a few skills ain't enough to—"

"You have no idea who she is, do you?" said Askar. He looked at me, then added, "Oh, I looked into you. I'm not as isolated as you might think, and you're quite famous. It only took a couple of inquiries with my people to find out who you are, Mirabelle Braddock."

My fingers twitched. It would only take me a couple of seconds to mark them all with Multishot. It was best used with my sniper rifle, but I could still employ the ability using Ferdinand II. Or the BMAP, come to that—though that strategy would probably kill us all. I embraced the ability, charging it as I said, "Tread lightly, invader."

He held up his hands, saying, "I wouldn't dream of angering someone like you."

"What the hell's goin' on?" demanded Rex. "She ain't—"

"You ever hear of Nova City?" asked Askar.

"Course I have," he said. "Bunch of loonies who lived on platforms in the sky. At least until some crazy person blew it all up."

Askar nodded in my direction, and my heart jumped into my throat. "She doesn't seem all that crazy to me," Askar said.

It took Rex—and the others—a moment to catch up, but when he did, his jaw dropped. "Y'mean to say that this little girl blew up a whole damn city?" he grunted.

"Something like that," Askar said. "What's more, she's the daughter of someone I'm sure you've heard of. The Wraith."

The temperature felt like it'd dropped a dozen degrees, and inwardly, I groaned. The last thing I wanted was for my history to come out. It had happened before, and each time it had, the information had invariably changed everything. Most of the time, it was easier just to cut ties after that.

I said, "He was my uncle."

"So, it is you," Askar said, his grin putting his elongated incisors on display. The others couldn't see them, I was certain. Otherwise, they wouldn't have been so comfortable around him. Likely, he had some sort of ability that he used to mask his true nature. Sure, they knew he was an alien, but they probably thought he was just a human variant from another world.

"Is this going to be a problem?" asked Patrick. "Because we can take our ship and fuck off easily enough. Or better yet, I'm sure Mira could kill every one of you, then hijack your whole plan."

"Patrick . . ."

"No, Mira. These people have already violated our privacy," he said. "They asked us for help, and yet they don't trust us? Come on. We don't need them."

"It's fine, Patrick," I said, putting a hand on his forearm. With that touch, he could probably tell that I was charging an ability, though he had no way of knowing which one. "They just did a little research. I'd have done the same thing if I was as weak as they are."

It was a pointed reminder that, if it came down to a fight, I had no questions about who would come out on top. They weren't weak—at least not in terms of the rest of the world—but I'd already established that I was far enough ahead of them that the only way they could finish me off was if they took me by surprise.

And that wasn't going to happen.

The only one who worried me was Askar. He was an alien, so he probably knew more than I did about the system. He might even possess skills unique to his people. And as such, he was a bit of an unknown. Still, he didn't feel terribly powerful, so I was willing to bet on my own strength.

Abruptly, Askar laughed, and the sudden change very nearly prompted me to jerk Ferdinand II free of his holster and let loose with my charged ability. However, I caught myself just in time to hear him say, "But we're all friends here, aren't we? There's no need for all this hostility."

"I can think of a few reasons for a little—"

I cut Patrick off with a gentle squeeze of my hand. His forearm flexed beneath my grip, and I sent him a message via our Secure Connection. "It's fine. We just do the job, get the stuff you need, and get out. This might be a good thing, all considered."

"Yeah? How?"

"It might keep them from turning on us," I responded. "A little fear goes a long way."

And my reputation definitely warranted a bit of that.

"Or it might just make them more careful," he pointed out. "Which will, you know, make countering the betrayal that much more difficult. But whatever. If you think we're good, I'll trust your judgment."

"We can leave if you want."

"No. You're not worried, so I'm not either. Yet."

The conversation played out at the speed of thought, which meant that only a second had passed since I'd cut Patrick's statement off. Before any of the others could interject, I said, "It's fine. Like Askar said, we're all buddies here. We're on the same side. But I'll point out that, given my experience, you might want to listen to me when I say that, without my input, your little plan would've been doomed to fail before it even got started. These gnomes are smart, and their defenses are extensive. Even at that satellite facility. The main compound is probably impregnable."

"Which is why we're hitting them in transit."

"Right. But to do that, you need something inside this other facility," I stated. "Tell me what, and I'll get it for you. We move on to the next phase, and nobody has to get killed by tiny aliens."

"No. But you go in with Avery," Askar said.

"But I'm not—"

Askar interrupted Avery with a mere glare. She clamped her mouth shut as he went on, asking me, "Is that sufficient? Surely, with you along for the ride, she'll be fine. Maybe she'll even learn something."

I felt Avery's glare, but I said, "Fine. But I'm not babysitting. If she can't keep up, I'll leave her behind."

Or use her as a distraction.

"That . . . That is acceptable," said Askar. The others all agreed, and just like that, I'd inserted myself into the first part of the plan.

I pushed myself to my feet and said, "Give me twenty minutes and we'll head back. By the time we arrive, it'll be fully dark."

Avery rolled her eyes. "I could do it in the middle of the day," she muttered.

I ignored her, then asked Patrick to accompany me back to *The Leviathan.* Once we were inside, I shook my head and said, "She's so young."

Patrick laughed, and I raised my eyebrow, which cut him off before he got out more than a chuckle. Coughing, he said, "Wait, you were serious? She's probably the same age as you. Maybe even a little older."

"Doesn't act like it," I said, already stripping out of my clothes. For the mission, I intended to wear only my infiltration suit. Once, I might've shied away from going out in public in the skintight outfit, but I was far more concerned with keeping a slimmer profile than adhering to some misguided sense of modesty. After I'd discarded my overclothes, I rewrapped the gun belt around my waist and holstered Ferdinand II before putting my nano-bladed sword on my back. A few minutes later, I'd checked all my other weapons, ensuring that everything was loaded and ready for battle.

I didn't intend to fight, but things didn't always go according to plan. So, it was better to be ready and not need it than to need my full arsenal and find that I wasn't prepared.

With that, I took a few more minutes to center myself before giving Patrick a kiss and telling him that I'd be careful. As if there was any other option. Finally, I stepped out of *The Leviathan* and summoned my Cutter.

I hadn't intended to reveal the existence of the hover bike, but I refused to ride that truck back to the compound. It was too loud, and because of its bulk, it was difficult to hide. No—using the hover bike was a strategic decision, and it was in no way motivated by my vanity. Still, it was nice to see Avery's jaw drop at the sight of the sleek black-and-gold bike.

I mounted and looked back at her, saying, "Hop on."

CHAPTER EIGHT

MAKING A MOVE

Initially, I didn't want to go back to her. Back then, it was a toxic, unequal relationship where I fully believed that what she wanted was more important than what I needed. But the moment I saw Mira again, I knew I couldn't resist diving back in. Not because I needed her. I did, but I could stomach staying away. Rather, I went back because I saw how lost she was without me. It might be distasteful to admit, but there's a certain satisfaction in knowing someone else would fall apart without you.

—Patrick Ward

This is the coolest bike I have ever seen," breathed Avery, running her hand along the Cutter's sleek fuselage. We'd pulled to a stop a little more than a mile away from the enemy stronghold, giving her a chance to examine my hover bike. And she was more than a little impressed. "I need one of my own. Where did you get it?"

"It was a birthday present from my uncle," I said. Then, I decided to reveal a little information so I wouldn't have to answer more questions about the bike. "I didn't get it until after he died, so I have no idea where he acquired it."

A notification flashed across my HUD, telling me that Patrick was trying to contact me via the Secure Connection I'd established. I accepted it, opening the line of communication, and he said, "You sure that was a great idea? They know about the Cutter now."

I resisted the urge to shrug—it would've been weird, considering that Avery couldn't hear the conversation between Patrick and me—and mentally replied, "It's not a big deal. They would've found out at some point. Besides, it makes the job easier."

Indeed, the biggest reason I'd chosen to use the Cutter was because I didn't want to run the risk of leaving one of the trucks out in the open. The hover bike functioned as a cybernetic, and as such, it had its own dedicated storage space tied to a bracelet around my wrist. Once I dismissed it, there would be nothing for the Dengyts to discover.

"Fine. Whatever. Anyway, the reason I contacted you is to let you know that there's a storm coming. A big one, too. You might be able to use that for cover or something," he said.

"Maybe. I'll have to see," I said, looking back the way we'd come. With Observation flared, I could just make out some dark clouds on the horizon. And if there was one thing I'd discovered about desert life in the past few years, it was that, while it didn't often rain, when it did, it came in a downpour. Soon enough, we would be drenched.

"What are you doing?" asked Avery.

"Huh?"

"You were just staring off into space for a couple of seconds," she said. "Is it some kind of ability or something?"

"Something like that," I acknowledged. "There's a storm coming. I'm thinking of hunkering down for an hour or so and letting it mask our approach."

Avery crossed her arms. "Do you think that's necessary?" she asked, a pout on her face. God, she was young. "I mean, you acted so high and mighty back there, right? Surely you can get in without a little rain to cover your tracks."

I shrugged. "Maybe. But I'll never turn down an advantage, even if it's unnecessary," I stated. "Perhaps you should adopt that same attitude. Or not. Dying young isn't so bad, I hear. Maybe somebody will tell stories about you or something."

"I'm not going to die," she argued.

"Not if you follow my lead, you won't," I said. "Now, sit down for a few minutes. Rest. Relax. Twiddle your thumbs. I don't care. Just stop talking."

With that, I dismissed the Cutter, and Avery stumbled slightly because she'd been leaning against it. At least she had sufficient attributes to catch herself before she tumbled to the ground, so that was something.

In any case, I settled down on the leeward side of a craggy slope, then cast my mind inward. I kept Observation flared, which was a slight drain on my Mist, but my attributes were high enough that it wasn't terribly impactful. Besides, it would have been stupid not to keep an ear on things while I worked on my latest Ghosts.

None of them were the breakthroughs I'd hoped to create, but they were still light-years ahead of my first attempts. In terms of potency and efficiency, there was no comparison. Still, I wasn't happy, so I set about tinkering with them. I knew I wouldn't make much progress in the time we had, but—

"What are you doing?" asked Avery. I had my eyes closed, but with Observation working at full tilt, I knew she was kneeling beside me. For a moment, I considered lying, but the reality of it was that I'd taken her measure, and I didn't think she would pose much danger to me, regardless of how much information she had. As for the rest of her team? I suspected that Askar already knew most of what I could do. Even if he didn't know the specifics, his research into my history would've told him enough that he could fill in the blanks well enough.

"Creating Ghosts," I stated. "They're like hostile programs meant to do very specific things when I deploy them."

"Wait, what? You're a {Mistrunner} like Paulo?" she asked, obviously surprised.

"Paulo is no {Mistrunner}," I stated, opening my eyes and giving her a steely glare. "He's an amateur masquerading as a professional. He knows some tricks, but he's not a real {Mistrunner}. I am."

"So, you . . . like . . . You hack into systems and stuff?" she asked. "But you have combat skills, too. I'm sure of it."

"That's the difference between a real {Mistrunner} and an amateur like Paulo. I'm sure he can be effective at whatever it is he's asked to do, but I can assure you, I can do whatever he can do, and I guarantee that I can do it better."

"But that doesn't make sense," she said. "There has to be some sort of . . . I don't know . . . balance or something."

"Does there?"

"Of course! Otherwise, everyone would . . . I mean . . . Some people would just be so far ahead of everyone else that they could do whatever they wanted," she said, obviously distressed.

"You're not wrong. About being able to do whatever I want," I said. "Most of the time, at least. There are plenty of people out there that could probably take me out, and that's not even considering the aliens. But . . . Well . . ."

I let the statement linger. After a few seconds, Avery said, "I don't believe you."

I shrugged. "I don't need you to."

"So, prove it. Show me you're so much better than me," she said, her hands on her hips.

I sighed, knowing that she wasn't likely to drop it anytime soon. So, I pushed myself to my feet and, like lightning, clamped my hand around her slender neck. Then, I lifted her off the ground with one hand. I could barely even feel her weight. Of course, she clawed at my hand—stupid, really, when she had a pair of pistols at her hips, but a panicked mind doesn't always pick the best course of action. Either way, neither tactic would do her any good. Her fingers could no more hurt me than a grain of dust could knock me over.

After a couple of seconds, I released her. She fell to the ground, gasping for air. I hadn't held her for long, but the adrenaline probably exacerbated her situation. I asked, "Happy?"

"W-what . . . What did you . . . How?" she breathed. "Was that a skill?"

I shrugged. "Not really," I said. "I mean, some of my modifiers might've applied. That part's a bit fuzzy, if I'm honest. But no abilities. Just pure Constitution."

"How?"

"Tell me—how high is yours?" I asked.

"Thirty-two," she said, puffing up with pride. Another bout of silliness, considering that she'd just been so thoroughly manhandled.

"Well, mine is quite a bit higher than that."

"But how?" she asked.

"Training."

"No—that's not enough. You should've hit your potential a long time ago, and . . ." Her face went white. "W-what level are you?"

"Thirty-eight." I saw no real reason to conceal it. Not anymore. Sure, she'd probably tell Askar, Isaac, and the others when we returned, but I hoped that would just make them hesitate before turning on me. If I was lucky, I could show enough of my power to dissuade them from betrayal altogether. After all, I had nothing against them, really. It was just a job.

"But that means . . . H-how many people have you killed?" she asked.

"Directly? Thousands," I said. "Indirectly? A lot more."

"How many, though?"

"I don't know. And the number's even higher if you count wildlings. Or aliens, come to that. My point is that if you want to get stronger, you've got to put in the work," I said. "And judging by your face right now, you don't really have it in you. My advice? Hunt animals and the like. It's a lot slower than people, but you'll make some progress."

With her Constitution, she was probably somewhere around level seven. Not bad, given her age, but she was still three levels from gaining a class. Likely, she hadn't even maximized her skills. No—she had a long way to go before she could threaten anyone important.

"If it makes you feel any better, I was right where you are not that long ago," I stated. "Seven . . . maybe eight years ago, I was looking up at my uncle the same way you're looking up at me."

"What happened to him?" she asked.

"He died," I stated simply, and in a tone that said I wasn't going to offer any more information on the matter. "We all die sooner or later, Avery. Nobody's invincible. No one is immortal."

"But—"

Just as Avery began to speak, the deluge hit, drowning out her voice with the sound of rain. It came like a great sheet, and in mere moments, visibility was cut to almost nothing. Even with Observation, I could only see a dozen feet or so, which made me feel strangely claustrophobic. Normally, even in the dead of night, I could see for hundreds of yards, so having my sight so thoroughly obstructed was a bit disconcerting.

I reached out and gripped Avery, pulling her close. With my mouth only a few inches from her ear, I said, "Tell me what we're after. I don't think you can keep up."

"I . . . I can't do that . . ."

"Sure you can. It's easy. It can be our little secret," I said.

"But—"

"Or you could have an accident out here," I interrupted. "With these conditions? Who knows what would happen, huh? Besides, don't you trust me?"

"Uh . . . No . . ."

"Good girl," I said. "Still, tell me what we need in there. I'll head in, steal it, and then we can head back to camp. Everyone will think you did it."

She clearly didn't know what to do. I'd already demonstrated how easily I could kill her, so she knew that my not-so-subtle threat wasn't idle. Which meant that she had to weigh the personal danger against following her orders. I knew which one would win out, so I wasn't surprised when she said, "It's an information packet. It should be in one of their security terminals. I'm supposed to use this." Avery held up a small box with a jack on one side, then continued, "It'll give Paulo access and—"

"Not necessary. What's on the information packet?" I asked.

"An itinerary," she answered quickly and with a slightly quivering voice. I could barely hear her over the rain. "A schedule for when they're transporting the goods from the main compound to the city. Also, it'll contain a manifest that will detail what's in which vehicle in the convoy. Without it, we might destroy the wrong trucks."

"I see," I said. "Well, that simplifies things. Anything else I need to know?"

"There are robots in there," she said. "Big combat bots that are as big as an exosuit. If you trip an alarm, they'll wake up and kill you."

"I'm pretty hard to kill," I said. Of course, I'd come across more than a few combat robots that could rip through me with ease, but I had plenty of advantages if it came to that.

"These are top-notch, according to Askar," she explained, wringing her hands. "Like, if we wake them up, the mission's over. Askar said they're more advanced than anything else on Earth."

Well, that was interesting. But given what I knew about the Dengyts, it tracked. They were a technologically advanced race that leaned on their creations for combat effectiveness. So, it only made sense that they would possess top-grade robots. Still, it didn't worry me.

"Anything else?" I asked.

"Uh . . . No?" she said.

"Good enough. Wait here. If I'm not back in two hours, you should probably vacate the area," I said.

"You don't want me to rescue you?"

I gave a soft chuckle. "If I get caught, I doubt you can rescue me," I said. More, I didn't think she would risk it. "But if it comes down to it, Patrick's going to bring *The Leviathan* over and start blowing stuff up. So . . . you'd better get out. That's all the warning I'll give you."

Then, without any more conversation, I slipped away, disappearing into the rain as I activated Stealth. With that, as well as the darkness of night, covering me, I knew just how undetectable I could be. However, I did cast out my senses—using Observation and the unique perception granted by {Mistrunner} that allowed me to sense nearby systems, I searched for anything that might give me away.

And it didn't take me long to find a web of sensors. They were at the edge of Misthack range, but given the feeling I got from them, I didn't dare progress any farther. If I was right—and I usually was—they were cameras that used thermoception to detect enemies. And while I thought that my infiltration suit would mask the bulk of my heat signature, I didn't want to chance it. So, using Misthack, I dove into their systems, toppling their defenses one by one until I could upload a Ghost.

Upload Ghost. Options:
Time Bomb (Mk. X)
Cascade
Destroy
Confusion (Mk. IV)
Blind (Mk. III)

I chose the second option, which would send a rolling pulse of Mist through the web of cameras, temporarily disabling everything connected to the system. It would only last for about five minutes, but that was plenty of time for me to do what I needed to do. Once I was inside, I could find a security terminal and deactivate things more permanently.

Once I'd uploaded *Cascade*, I waited for a few seconds before sprinting ahead. I reached the wall in only a few moments, and I jabbed my consciousness into the Mist shield, deactivating it via brute force. It was quick and dirty, and it wouldn't last long, but it allowed me to leap onto the wall and vault into the compound before it shimmered back to full strength.

And just like that, I was inside.

Unfortunately, I found myself face-to-face with a hulking monstrosity of metal and Mist.

My heart jumped into my throat, and I very nearly leaped into combat. However, my brain soon caught up to the situation, and I realized that the combat bot was completely inert. It had yet to activate. Which meant that, so long as I didn't do anything stupid—like start hacking at it with my sword, which was precisely what I'd intended to do—I would be fine. With a force of will, I mastered my breathing and slowed my heart rate enough that I could take stock of my situation.

The layout of the compound wasn't complicated. Just an outer wall, a few outbuildings, and a main structure bearing a huge antenna. Doubtless, it was meant as some sort of satellite command post. I didn't really care, so long as I got the information I needed.

I knelt, looking around for threats. I knew from our reconnaissance that there were only a handful of gnomes stationed in the facility, and I felt certain that they would remain inside during a storm. So, aside from the combat bot in front of me—and the four others positioned throughout the compound—I was completely alone.

Which put my hackles up.

It had been too easy. These Dengyts were supposed to be equipped with top-tier equipment, which meant that the defenses I had seen so far were almost assuredly just the tip of the iceberg. There was more I wasn't seeing.

So, wrapped in Stealth and Camouflage, I flared Observation.

It only took a few seconds before I had to suppress a gasp. Clearly, the defenses were much more advanced than even I had expected. For one, cameras were everywhere. For another, there was a flock of concealed drones floating in the air above the main building. And finally, there were multiple patrols of stealthy gnomes, one of which was almost on top of me.

There were three of them, all armed with rifles that looked at least as big as they were. I couldn't see much more detail than that; their stealth abilities were predictably high-quality. But I didn't need to see anything else to know I didn't want to get into a fight against an enemy with unknown firepower.

Besides, I wasn't there to start a war.

I just needed a little information.

So, I quickly reactivated Misthack, targeting the combat bot in front of me. Once I'd torn through its defenses, which were weaker than I had expected, I uploaded one of my favorite Ghosts.

I'd initially created *Rage* to help infiltrate Elysium back in Nova City, but in the years since, I'd found that it was quite versatile. Most of that was due to the fact that it left no traces behind. To any investigator, it would appear that the victim had just gone crazy. Or in the case of a combat robot, that there was a glitch in its system. Either way, the effect was simple: it just increased the target's aggressive tendencies by a significant degree. For a person, that meant they'd probably start a fight with anyone who looked at them funny. But for a bot? Well, it would start to see everyone as an enemy.

I grinned as the Ghost finished uploading. Then, I backed away, leaping to the top of the wall so I'd have a good, safe view of what would come next.

CHAPTER NINE

AMID CHAOS

Though I have the skill, I'm not a real cybernetic engineer. That much became obvious the longer I tried to learn the ins and outs of the skill. From a rational standpoint, I understood it well enough, but I knew from the very beginning that I was missing something vital. That little spark that separated someone meant for a skill from everyone else. Cy had it. And so does Mira with her skills. But me? I was meant for something else.

—Patrick Ward

It only took a moment for me to realize that I might've bitten off more than I could chew. As the combat bot rose to its full fifteen-foot height, I raced along the top of the wall. It was only six inches wide, but with the proprioception modifier associated with [Acrobatics], it might as well have been a sidewalk for all the narrow width affected me. By the time the combat bot came fully online, I was almost forty feet away, but I still questioned whether it would be enough.

Nearby, the patrolling gnomes dropped their concealment and whirled around, looking for an external threat. They were truly tiny creatures—maybe three feet tall—with bulbous noses, huge pointed ears, and broad faces. They might've passed for tiny humans if it weren't for their wide eyes, each of which bore twin irises of varying colors. Arrayed in concentric circles, they made for a truly disconcerting sight that marked the creatures as the aliens they were.

As they searched for whatever had tripped the alarm and activated the combat bot, the huge mechanical figure took aim and opened fire. Thunder filled the air—both the natural sound of a lightning strike as well as the rattling report of the huge Gatling guns that were the bot's main weapons.

The Dengyts never stood a chance.

I watched in mingled horror and satisfaction as the first two patrols were ripped to shreds, their crimson blood misting as their flesh flew in every direction. One reacted quickly enough to avoid the first burst of gunfire, but a second later, it met the same fate as its comrades.

For a moment, a heavy silence filled the air, broken only by the sound of the Gatling guns winding down and the heavy whir of the bot's servos. It rotated, looking for any additional threats, and when its perception passed over me, I couldn't help but hold my breath. Maybe I would survive such a barrage, but I suspected I wouldn't fare much better than the gnomes. No—I needed to avoid notice.

That's when I detected a tiny hitch in the robot's whirl. I knew what that meant. It had noticed me. Perhaps it wasn't sure, but then again, under the effect of *Rage*, it probably wouldn't care so much for certainty. It would likely adhere to the fire first, look later mentality. So, right before it would inevitably open fire, I used Distraction.

An instant later, a high-pitched sound not unlike a woman's scream echoed from the opposite direction. And the combat bot reacted just as I'd hoped, wheeling around and opening fire on what it deemed a much more obvious threat. It didn't bother aiming. Instead, it blanketed the entire area in concentrated gunfire from its twin Gatling guns. Even as bullets ripped into the buildings, sending concrete and plasti-steel flying, I leaped from the wall and ran deeper into the compound.

My heart was beating out of my chest as I turned a corner and sprinted down a narrow corridor before turning again. And again. Before I knew it, I was on the other side of the facility, my breath coming in ragged pants. In the distance, the combat bot continued to fire, but the other combat bots had finally responded, and the atmosphere was filled with the deafening sounds of their explosive battle.

I knew it wouldn't last long, though. The combat bots were doubtless very durable, but with four going against one, the one I'd hijacked would soon be cut down to size. So, I quickly calmed myself and moved on, creeping along the side of the main building until I found a door. Once I had, I used Misthack to open it, then darted inside. Fortunately, no gnomes were present in the entryway. Still, I maintained my Stealth as I slowly made my way through the compound.

It had been built with the short Dengyts in mind, so I was forced to crouch—especially as I passed through the doors—but I was fortunate enough that I didn't run into any of the occupants. As I moved, I cast my {Mistrunner} senses out, looking for the security terminal as well as any surveillance or security devices. I found none of the latter, but after only a few seconds, I found a signal that I expected was the terminal.

It was on the second floor, so I wasted no time before finding a stairwell that took me to my destination. Unfortunately, that's where most of the Dengyts were stationed.

Cursing my bad luck, I slowed down and positioned myself in a corner where I hoped my abilities would keep me unseen. None of the passing gnomes were paying attention to me, though. Instead, they were wholly focused on the catastrophe outside. My hijacked combat bot still hadn't gone down, apparently, and the gnomes were panicking.

"What happened?!" screeched one as it raced by. Its voice was high-pitched and whiny, reminding me of a petulant child. "Those things are supposed to be foolproof!"

"I don't know, Garix," grumbled the one trotting alongside the first. "I've told you that a hundred times. I won't know anything until we take it apart. I think . . ."

Their conversation faded away as they turned a corner, and I took my chance to dart down the hall. I didn't stop until another set of gnomes barred my way, but they didn't stay in one place for long. Like Garix and his companion, they were in crisis mode, and they had jobs to do. So, I waited until they had passed along before I continued my creeping journey deeper into the facility.

I was tempted to explore, to see if I could pick up anything of note. These aliens were clearly advanced. Even without their reputation, the quality of the combat bot was proof that they had high-grade technology at their disposal. Who knew what I could find if I poked around a bit? However, I knew that the crisis would soon pass—if it hadn't already—and so, my window to acquire the information I'd come to retrieve was quickly closing.

Still, I was sorely tempted, even if I had the self-control to keep my avaricious tendencies in check.

Like that, I kept going, leapfrogging between different groups of gnomes. Thankfully, I remained completely undetected all the way up to the room that was my destination. Less fortunately, it was locked, and I could tell that there were at least two gnomes inside. Grinding my teeth, I considered my options.

I could go in, guns blazing, and I felt certain that I could win the battle. However, coming out on top of one fight wasn't really the goal, and it would almost assuredly leave me vulnerable to a response. As effective as my distraction had been, I didn't think I could get away with gunfire within the facility. And besides, I needed to remain in the shadows; the plan was for the infiltration to go undetected. Anything else would likely result in the gnomes changing their plans, rendering the information I'd come to steal ineffective.

So, an assault was probably out of the question. I wouldn't kill anyone unless it became absolutely necessary.

That left me with two options. The first was to upload one of my Ghosts and hope I could put the gnomes down for long enough to do what I wanted. The problem with that plan of action was that I had no idea what kinds of personal defenses they had in place. For all I knew, they had Mistwalls as thick as mine, which would mean trying to Misthack into them would take time I didn't think I had.

The other option was to find somewhere to hide, observe the gnomes, and pounce when I thought I saw an opening. They weren't infallible. Nobody was. And over the course of the last three years, I'd assaulted a number of alien bases. During that time, I'd learned many things, but the one takeaway that had stuck with me over everything else was that the invaders really weren't all that different from humans. They got bored. They lost focus. They slacked off. And I was positive that the Dengyts were no different.

So, with that in mind, I retreated from the door to a ventilation duct I'd passed a few dozen feet down the hall. Once I'd found it, I summoned a wrench from my arsenal implant and removed the bolts, then the vent itself. I leaped, grabbing hold of the duct's lip, and hauled myself inside. Once I was securely in place, I replaced the vent and awkwardly reattached it.

Then, I let out a sigh of relief that I quickly cut off when I heard footsteps echoing down the hall I'd just vacated. A moment later, three gnomes marched through, obviously in a hurry to get somewhere.

I shifted backward, slithering along until I reached an intersection. Then, I turned in the appropriate direction as I tried to make my way back to the room containing the security terminal. It took a while, as well as quite a bit of backtracking, but eventually, I reached my destination. And just as I'd feared, when I looked down at the room's occupants, I saw a single guard and a technician of sorts. The warrior held a rifle that looked huge in his hands while the technician was plugged into the security terminal via her personal link. Neither noticed me perched in the duct above.

So, I settled down to wait.

Over the years, I'd been forced to surveil hundreds of targets. Back in Nova City, I'd spent days just watching Nora from a neighboring building, and in the time since the city's fall, my attacks on dozens of alien encampments had always been accompanied by a good deal of reconnaissance. After all, preparation was the best way to ensure survival, and preparation was nothing without proper intelligence. So, my patience had been trained nearly as thoroughly as the rest of my abilities, and lying there in a too-small air duct, I exercised that patience to its fullest extent.

For hours, I remained completely motionless, watching the pair of gnomes. A few times, the guard shifted his position, but the technician remained almost sedentary. I'd experienced much the same thing when jacked into a terminal; in those situations, it was so easy to lose track of the rest of the world.

After a few hours, Patrick checked in via our Secure Connection, and I sent a message to him that I was fine, adding, "Everything's going according to plan."

He knew me well enough that he could tell that I had little interest in holding a conversation. I could have done it, but I didn't want to lose focus for more than a few seconds. If I did, I'd run the risk of missing my opportunity. I knew myself well enough to recognize the risks of distraction, so it was easier to cut that off before it had a chance to bloom.

So, I continued to wait. And watch.

Eventually, the female gnome—or at least that was my assumption, based on her long pink hair and feminine figure—disconnected with a sigh, saying, "I need to use the facilities, Dig. You want to come with?"

"We're on duty, Gretha."

She batted her eyelashes at him and said, "I won't tell if you don't. Come on. All that commotion got me all worked up. Just a quickie in the bathroom. Nobody ever has to know."

In my experience, men were fairly simple creatures, and rare was the man who'd turn down an offer like that. And it seemed that male gnomes weren't so different from their human counterparts, at least in that respect. So, it didn't take much more persuading to get poor Dig on board, and in only a few seconds, the pair scurried off on their amorous adventure.

I Misthacked the door, commanding it shut before I quickly unbolted the duct's vent and descended into the room. In seconds, I'd retrieved the black-and-gold cord of my personal link from the Hand of God and jammed it into the security terminal's access port. Instantly, I saw the system's security looming before me, represented by a series of nodes containing a wide variety of puzzles and equations I'd have to solve before gaining access.

I tore into the first layer of defenses, and when it only took me a few seconds to break through, I couldn't help but smile slightly. A couple more seconds, and the second node toppled. Then, the third. On and on I went until I'd overcome all fifty, and in only a minute or so. Still, I knew I was up against a time limit, so I wasted no time in self-congratulation before diving into the system and navigating to the information packet I needed to steal.

That took another minute or so, and I knew my time was growing shorter by the second. I had no idea how quick a quickie really was, but I suspected I didn't have much longer before the two returned to their post. Finally, I downloaded the appropriate packet—along with a couple of others that looked interesting, sequestering them in a quarantine corner of my interface before climbing my way back into the duct. I'd just attached the final bolt when the door slid open.

"Did you close the door?" asked Gretha, looking flustered. Her clothes— which consisted of a purple jumpsuit—were rumpled, as well.

"Maybe?" mumbled Dig. "Probably. Yeah, no—I'm sure I did."

"Oh. Okay," Gretha said, shaking her head. "Don't do that next time. It's against protocol."

"Affirmative, you saucy little reakinx," he said with an exaggerated wink of his off-putting eye. Gretha clearly appreciated it because a blush that came close to matching her hair bloomed on her cheeks.

As the two settled back into their roles—after a little more flirting—I slowly inched my way to my original access point. Once I saw that it was clear, I descended from the vent and slowly returned through the halls and out of the building. It was more than a little nerve-racking, and I was forced to stop more than a few times, but I still managed it without being detected.

By the time I was outside, the rain had ceased, which meant I'd have that much less cover. No matter—I could just vault to the top of the exterior wall, Misthack the Mist shield, and then be on my merry way.

As it turned out, things were a bit more complicated than that because I had to avoid a few patrols, as well as a couple of drone swarms, but I managed it all the same. Along the way, I did catch a couple of glimpses of the wreckage my distraction had left behind. Whole buildings had been destroyed, and the walls that were left standing were pockmarked with bullet holes. The destroyed combat bot was being examined by a few technicians—all wearing the same purple jumpsuits Gretha had worn—but I felt confident that they wouldn't find anything. Once my Ghosts ran their course, they were undetectable.

At least as far as I knew. Perhaps there was something out there that would prove to be the exception to the rule, but I'd yet to encounter anything of the sort. And until I did, I felt confident in banking on my Ghosts' undetectability.

Once I got over the wall, it was child's play to retrace my steps back to where I'd left Avery. Sure enough, she'd remained encamped in the same hollow, and though she looked miserable, she was unharmed.

Once I got close, I dropped Stealth and said, "You really should pay better attention to your surroundings. Someday, somebody with ill intentions will sneak up on you and make you pay for your lack of attention."

As she flinched away from my voice, her hands twitched to her guns. However, it only took a moment before she settled down. Trying to pretend that she hadn't lost her composure, she pushed a lock of hair behind her ear, asking, "Did you get it?"

"Of course," I said. I was a little annoyed that she hadn't followed my instructions and gone back to the camp after two hours, but I didn't mention it. Likely, she had different orders from her own leaders. "And I'll go ahead and tell you right now—if you'd have gone in there, you would have died."

"I think you underestimate me."

I shrugged. "Maybe. Maybe not. Either way, there's no way you get to that security terminal without raising the alarm," I said.

"I disagree. I've snuck into better-secured compounds," she stated.

"Sure. Keep believing that. But if you want some advice—"

"I don't."

"Well, you're going to get it anyway. My advice is to stow your pride and try to learn," I said. "Maybe you're as good as you think you are, but I doubt it. At some point, you're going to trip on something you can't handle. If I wasn't here, that's what would've happened in there. That combat bot would've ripped you to shreds."

"I can handle myself," she huffed.

I looked at her for a few silent seconds, then realized that nothing I could say would get through to her. She'd already made up her mind, and there was little I could do about it. It seemed that some lessons needed to be learned firsthand. I just hoped she had the ability to survive when she found her limits.

"Fine. Whatever," I said, summoning my Cutter. Once it had materialized, I threw one leg over the fuselage and added, "You coming? Or did you want to walk back?"

I didn't need to flare Observation to hear the grinding of her teeth before she took a deep, steadying breath and climbed on behind me. Once she had her hands on my waist, we took off across the muddy desert.

The first part of the plan was in the books. Now, we just needed to execute the remainder.

CHAPTER TEN

PRESSURE POINTS

The day we hit that Rift, we had no idea that it was going to change everything. At the time, we'd been riding high off of a few victories, and Mira was still running away from what happened in Nova City. Maybe that's why we failed so horribly. For months, that's what I told myself. But in the end, I had to admit that if I'd been able to pull my own weight, things might have turned out differently.

—Patrick Ward

The moment we arrived back at *The Leviathan*, I knew I had some explaining to do. I'd expected as much, but I definitely didn't enjoy having a rifle trained on me. I pulled to a stop only a few feet from Askar and glanced at Isaac, who was perched atop a nearby dune, his rifle pointed in my direction. Then, I locked my eyes on the alien's, saying, "We have a problem?"

"You tell me," he said smoothly, pushing his fine yellow hair back with one hand. "You didn't follow the plan."

As he spoke, Avery hurriedly dismounted, but before she could get too far away, my hand found her slender wrist. Without breaking eye contact with Askar, I said, "You really shouldn't be communicating without a secure connection of some sort."

"Who says we don't have one?" he asked as Avery tried to pull herself free. I tightened my grip—not enough to break her wrist, but plenty to tell her I meant business.

"I do," I said. "You could've jeopardized the whole mission."

"I could say the same thing to you," he stated. "After all, you're the one who went off script. I've already got one cowboy in the crew." He nodded toward

Rex, who was leaning against one of the trucks, his fingers drumming against his pistol's grip. "I don't need another."

"Good."

"So, you're not a cowboy?"

"Well, I'm a girl, so . . . No?"

For a moment, he just stared at me. I didn't make a move for Ferdinand II, but I kept my R-14 on the edge of summoning. With only a moment, I could have it in hand and laying waste to the entire group. I didn't want that, but I wouldn't shy away, either. In some company, showing weakness was tantamount to offering yourself up for slaughter. And I had no intention of being anyone's prey.

Finally, he shook his head in resignation. "My point is, we had a plan," the alien stated. "A good one, too. Avery is one of the best at what she does, and you sidelining her could have blown everything up."

"If I'd let her tag along, she'd have probably died," I pointed out. "And even if she hadn't, I'd have had to go loud. Then, your precious plan would've been useless. Who provided the intel on that facility, by the way? Because the defenses were a lot stouter than the information you gave me indicated."

"How so?"

"Stealth patrols, advanced combat bots, and concealed drone swarms," I said. "That's in addition to the other stuff we already knew about. The place was a fortress."

"And yet, you got in there just fine, huh?" drawled Rex. "Convenient."

"You want to say something?" I asked. "Or do you want to just have it out, right here and now?"

"I'm game."

"Me, too," I said, releasing Avery. She staggered away, gripping her wrist. I hadn't exerted enough pressure to break those delicate bones, but it would definitely bruise.

Before I could distance myself from the Cutter, Askar dropped his rifle to hang from the strap over his shoulder and stepped between us. With his arms stretched toward either of us, he said, "Calm down! Nobody's . . . having it out, okay? This doesn't have to go bad."

"Then put a muzzle on your dog," I said, nodding toward Rex. The comment only drew a grin from the man.

"Rex . . ."

"Aw, come the fuck on!" he growled, pointing his finger at me. "That little cunt's gonna get us all killed, and you know it! She ain't a team player, and that's a goddamn fact."

"Neither are you," Askar said. "And if you don't keep your mouth shut, I'll shut it for you."

"But—"

"I said shut up!" Askar bellowed, for once losing his composure. Rex shrank away, looking somehow smaller. "This doesn't have to be like this, and you're just making everything worse." He regained some of his calm, adding, "So please, Rex. Just keep your mouth shut. For once in your life . . ."

"Whatever," the man spat. Then, he once again resumed his position leaning against one of the trucks. With Observation, I could tell that he was mumbling something under his breath, but it was low enough to evade even my enhanced senses.

"Now," said the alien. "Did you at least get the information packet?"

"I did."

"And will you share it?" he asked.

"Sure," I said. Then, I initiated a data transfer. Fortunately, his interface was advanced enough to receive the packet intact. Otherwise, I'd have had to upload it to some sort of physical media. He accepted the transfer, and by his glassy expression, I could tell that he was looking it over. Slowly, a smile spread across his face, and I asked, "We happy?"

"Oh, yes. Very. Good work."

"She blew stuff up!" interjected Avery. I noticed that she was just out of reach. If she thought that would protect her, she was sorely mistaken. "Like, it sounded like a full-blown battle. There's no way they don't know that someone—"

"I was undetected," I stated.

"Oh?"

"One of their combat bots had a malfunction," I said. "Glitches happen every day, I'm told. They won't look any deeper than that. And if they do, they won't find anything. I guarantee it."

"Well, then . . ."

"You don't believe that, do you?" asked Avery. "She was—"

It was Askar's turn to interrupt her, and he did so by saying, "I believe her. Already, the facility is back to normal."

That's when I realized that there was one person missing. Well—other than Paulo, who probably spent as little time outdoors as possible. "You had us followed," I said. "Huascar, huh?"

"Like a guardian angel," Askar said. "Another layer of surveillance."

"That you told me nothing about."

He shrugged. "I don't know all your secrets, do I?" he said. "I can't show you my entire hand. Besides, he had orders to help if things went wrong. That little distraction almost had him running in, guns blazing, but then he saw that you'd left Avery behind."

I shook my head, guessing, "And he wasn't so worried about my safety, huh?"

"Well, you did shoot him."

"Just a little," I said with a small smile. "Barely a flesh wound. So, are we good?"

"We are," Askar answered.

"Good," I said. Then, I sent a message to Patrick, who'd been inside *The Leviathan* the whole time. The cannon noisily retracted into its turret atop the fuselage. "Probably for the best, all said."

Askar glanced at the cannon, then back at me. "Would he have shot?" the alien asked.

"Who knows? He's very protective of me," I answered. "And he's seen me survive worse than a little cannon fire."

He swallowed hard. "How powerful are you?" he asked.

"Oh, you're just going to come out and ask, huh?"

"I did."

"I'm strong enough to survive a point-blank shot from a cannon that could, with only a couple of shots, take out a megabuilding," I said. "It wouldn't be pretty, though. I'd probably have to spend a few weeks in recovery. You would fare much worse."

Indeed, I felt confident that I could survive such an attack—mostly because I'd done it before, albeit in a Rift. It had nearly killed me, and Patrick had come out of it even worse. But in the end, I hadn't even picked up any new scars. So, as much as I didn't want to go through that kind of thing again, I appreciated Patrick's willingness to bathe the entire region in fiery devastation.

In his own way, he really was protective of me.

"You're way worse than I am," Patrick said via our Secure Connection. "Just in case we're keeping score."

"Noted," I replied in a virtual mumble.

"Get some rest. I want you to help Rex set up the killing field," Askar said. "You can keep each other in line."

Rex clearly didn't like that idea, but he'd already been put in his place, so he didn't argue. Instead, he just ambled off toward one of the tents, disappearing inside a moment later.

"I don't think he likes me," I remarked.

"He doesn't really like anyone" was Askar's response. "But he's one of the best demolitions experts I could find. Unless your expertise extends to blowing things up, as well."

"Well . . ."

"Really?" asked Avery, whose presence had been wholly forgotten. She just didn't rate as a threat. "Is there anything you can't do?"

I tapped my chin as if lost in thought, then answered, "I can't really dance."

"What?" Avery and Askar said at the same time. It was only then that I noticed just how similar the two looked. And were Avery's ears a bit pointed?

Were her teeth slightly sharper than normal? Or was my mind playing tricks on me?

"Dancing. Never really got the hang of it," I said. "I think it's because I'm shy by nature."

Both of them looked at me like I'd gone insane. And in a way, I understood their confusion. After all, I took great pains to put forth a confident, self-assured foot. And standing there in my skintight infiltration suit that left almost nothing to the imagination, I could see how my statement would be a bit incongruous with the image I'd established. Still, that didn't make my words any less true.

I'd never liked attention, and I didn't think I would ever grow fond of it. And as I'd said, that made dancing—especially in public—an exercise in torture for me. I could manage, but I'd been told that, even with the body control that came with [Acrobatics], my movements were far from graceful.

It was annoying, really—I could do gymnastics across a thread-thin tight-rope, but the moment I tried to move with any sort of rhythm, I felt like a clumsy oaf that everyone was—and should be—laughing at.

"But everything else . . . Yeah, I'm pretty good at most other things," I finished. "Except cooking. I don't really cook."

Neither of them knew what to say to that, but I did notice that Isaac had finally lowered his rifle. I didn't recognize the type, but I suspected that it wasn't advanced enough to do much damage—unless I just stood there and took it, which wasn't likely to happen. It was yet another piece of evidence that, while they weren't amateurs, none of the others were blessed with very much power.

Still, there was Askar who, as an alien, was a bit of an unknown. I had no idea how long he'd been on Earth, and even a modest talent could accomplish a lot if he came with a certain degree of knowledge. Even if he was only Tier 3 or 4, he was probably strong enough to threaten me.

I had no intention of giving him that chance, though.

After a little more conversation, during which I learned that Rex and I were intended to set out at dawn, I returned to *The Leviathan*. The moment I stepped inside, I felt an enormous weight slip from my shoulders. I sagged and let out a long, deep breath as I leaned against one of the bulkheads, my head tilted toward the ceiling. I remained in that position, just letting my mind unwind, until I heard Patrick approach.

"You alright?" he asked. I opened my eyes to see that he was offering me a steaming cup of something that smelled delicious. I took it with both hands and breathed in the aroma. Patrick grinned. "I've been saving this one. I got it back in South America. I can't remember the town."

I took a sip of the beverage, and then let out a moan of appreciation as the coffee splashed across my tongue. He'd prepared it precisely how I liked it. A little sugar. Some cream. And a lot of real coffee taste. It was perfect.

I swallowed and said, "I'm fine. It was just tense out there. Really tense."

He took my hand and led me to the ship's common area, where he sat on a couch. I laid down next to him, putting my head in his lap as his fingers twined through my hair. I'd kept it short lately, with one side shaved while the other side and the top were arranged in thick curls. I liked it, but at times, I missed letting it grow out.

Lying there, I recounted my experiences in the gnomes' facility, going over everything from my ingress to the sabotage of the combat bot. I told him about my trek through the main building as well as my experiences crawling through the air ducts. He found that improbable, remarking that air ducts weren't supposed to be that big, but I had no response, save my firsthand experience.

When I'd finished, I asked, "You wouldn't have really fired the cannon on us, would you?"

"What? No. I wouldn't waste the ammunition. You know how expensive those Mist-infused artillery shells are," he answered with a grin. "But seriously—I'm pretty sure you wouldn't need my help. They're not exactly the cream of the crop."

"Except Askar. He's a question mark."

"I was thinking the same thing," Patrick agreed. "Do you have any idea what his skills are?"

"Not really. But he doesn't know what I can do, either. They'd have to be stupid not to suspect, and I let Avery know a few details," I said. "I don't think she's experienced enough to put any of it together, though. But maybe Askar could figure it out if given the chance."

"Why tell her?"

I sighed. "I guess I felt sorry for her," I admitted. "She's so clueless. Like a baby, you know?"

"She's probably older than me," he said. "Maybe older than you, too."

"Not where it counts," I stated. And I believed it. Patrick and I had packed more into our years than most people thrice our age. By comparison, someone like Avery was a child. "Speaking of her, have you noticed a slight resemblance between her and our fearless leader?"

Patrick was silent for a moment, then asked, "You don't think . . ."

"I think they might be related," I said. "Maybe a daughter."

"Is that even possible? Can aliens . . . You know . . ."

"No clue," I admitted. "But probably? So long as the equipment's the same, I mean. Last time I went into the Bazaar, I visited Anaseteramanimix, and—"

"Ugh. That's a mouthful," he interrupted. "Just use the shortened version like everybody else."

"She only uses Ana because she feels bad making us pronounce her real name. But she does prefer her full name, even if she would never say as much,"

I said, referring to the skillsmith who'd created my [Demolition] and [Acrobatics] skills. Each time I visited the Bazaar—which was less often than I would have liked—I made a point to stop by. She appreciated the company, and I wanted to keep an open line of communication with someone who could be a very valuable commodity sometime in the future. After all, I'd learned that classes were not static, and that, so long as certain prerequisites had been met, they could evolve. If that happened, I suspected that some of my skills would merge, and I would need to fill any open slots.

"Probably safer if I just use the shortened version," he said. "I don't want to offend her by mispronouncing it."

"Sure. That's your reason," I said. "And it's totally not that you just don't want to make the effort."

"See? I knew you'd see it my way."

"Anyway," I said, dragging out the word. "What I was going to say was that Anaseteramanimix told me that a lot of the aliens are human variants. Like, they've taken a different evolutionary path, but a lot of the important stuff stays the same. So, if that's the case—and given that Askar looks pretty human—he might be able to mate with somebody from Earth. God knows he's handsome enough to have them lined up."

Patrick let out a dramatic gasp. "My pride! My vanity!" he exclaimed, clapping a hand over his heart. "My woman is looking elsewhere for male companionship!"

"Your woman? Ugh. That sounds so . . . Just . . . Ugh."

"Well, you are my woman," he said, his smile widening. "And I'm your big, strong, and incredibly muscular man."

"Oh, yes. That's you, alright."

Patrick was fairly muscular, but he was only a couple of inches taller than me. Not that it mattered. I didn't care how tall he was. Or how powerful, really. I had enough strength for the both of us. All I really needed from Patrick was for him to do precisely what he was doing. Anything else was just icing on the cake.

He said, "We can still get out of this. I could fire up *The Leviathan*, and we could be gone in a flash."

I gave him a slight shake of my head and said, "No. Nothing's really changed. In fact, if Askar steps out of line, we now have a pressure point to exploit." He narrowed his eyes, and I added, "Not that that's our primary plan or anything. I'm not a monster, Pick."

"You know I hate when you call me that."

"No, you don't," I said.

He didn't respond, but when he leaned down and kissed me, I took it as confirmation.

CHAPTER ELEVEN

THE DRAGON ROARS

I don't think what happened in Nova really hit Mira until she discovered that her favorite band had been one of the casualties of the city's destruction. Obviously, from a rational perspective, she knew. She had to have known. But it didn't hit home until someone told her Leviathan's fate. After that, our ship got a new name, and Mira truly started down a dark road.

—Patrick Ward

I gripped the strap, the wind whipping through my hair as *The Leviathan* sped along. Through the open cargo doors, I could see the long, snaking form of the train stretching toward the horizon, and I knew that if I could see in the other direction, it would look much the same. The train itself was around nine miles long, and it sped along at a velocity *The Leviathan* struggled to match, especially so low to the ground. If we'd climbed higher into the atmosphere, it wouldn't have been difficult, but doing so would have negated the plan. So, Patrick maintained our altitude, skimming along only fifty feet above the train's sinuous form.

"Deploying signal blockers now," said Isaac through the communication device I wore in my ear. I could've established a Secure Connection with the rest of the team, but I didn't want to reveal that particular back channel to them. Besides, I still wasn't entirely sure of their capabilities, and giving them a potential back door into my system would have been sheer idiocy.

Isaac stepped up to the open cargo doors, his long coat snapping back with the wind. He wore a harness around his chest, which was connected to a nearby hook on the bulkhead, but he still looked a little nervous. Not surprising, given that if he fell, he probably didn't have the Constitution to survive. I was reasonably certain that stood for the entire team, save for Askar, whose abilities were still something of a question mark.

He raised a curious weapon to his shoulder—it looked a little like my BMAP, though with a longer, thicker barrel—and fired. It discharged with a thump, sending a cylinder flying from *The Leviathan*'s open cargo doors. For a moment, it sailed in a long, slow arc, but then a tiny jet of flame erupted from its rear, guiding it to the train below. It landed a moment later, embedding itself in the roof of the train car.

Then, it unfolded, releasing dozens of tiny, spiderlike robots that skittered in opposite directions. They moved so quickly that I needed Observation to track their progress, and only fifteen seconds later, Isaac announced, "Signal blockers in place. Communication is jammed. Remember, it'll only last about twenty minutes, so we need to get this done in a hurry."

Askar's voice came over the communication channel, asking, "Everyone ready? We all know our jobs?"

Everyone said that they did, which was my signal to move. I released my grip on the handle, flared Balance to keep from falling over, and sprinted forward. Only a moment later, I leaped from the cargo bay, fell for a brief second, then hit the train's roof. Rolling to disperse my momentum, I found my feet a second later, my R-14 already in hand.

"The Eagle has landed," I said via the Secure Connection I shared with Patrick.

"That's not what we agreed on," he said. "You were supposed to be—"

"If you call me what I think you're going to call me, I'm going to be very angry with you, Patrick," I said. He'd wanted me to use a different code name, but I'd objected because I found it mildly offensive.

"But you don't even fly! If anybody's the Eagle in this scenario, it's me," he complained. "There's nothing wrong with being called Cupcake. A lot of girls would find it endearing."

As I stalked across the roof of the train, leaping from one car to the next, I asked, "And what about me suggests I'm like other girls? If I can't be the Eagle, at least give me something cool. Like Cobra. Or Lioness." I thought about that one for a second, then said, "Ugh. Scratch that one. I don't like it."

"How about Sparrow? You can still be a bird, and—"

"If you call me Sparrow, I'm going to shoot you down," I said as calmly as I could.

"Alright, alright. Uh . . . What about Rhino? It fits because you're tough and strong—"

"You're terrible at this. You realize that, don't you?" I muttered.

"Yeah, well, I don't hear you suggesting anything."

He had me there. For the life of me, I couldn't think of anything appropriate. Not that it really mattered. Nobody except Patrick and me would ever hear it. Still, I couldn't stomach the idea of my partner calling me Rhino.

"How about Baby Wraith?" he blurted.

"That's worse!" I exclaimed, leaping across another gap between cars as I sprinted along the length of the train. "Nothing says awesome like evoking the memory of my dead uncle, right?"

"Yeah—didn't really think that one through. Give me a second," he said. Then, he rattled off a few more options, each one somehow worse than the last. As he did, I kept Observation active as I raced across the metal roof of the train. Without Balance, I could never have kept my footing, but flaring it every now and again, I had no difficulty adjusting to the rushing wind.

When I finally reached my destination, I dropped into a feetfirst slide, saying, "I think we're just going to have to chalk the whole code name thing up as a loss."

"I've almost got it figured out!"

"You really don't," I said, my foot finding the lip of an access hatch, which I used to pop back up. Reaching down, I pulled the handle free and twisted. With an outrush of air that I couldn't hear, the seal was broken, and I threw the hatch open. As I summoned a flash-bang from my arsenal implant, I heard a few shouts of alarm that I ignored, and I tossed the grenade into the car. I cut Observation off just in time to avoid the explosion of sound and light, then reactivated it before leaping into the open hatch.

"I'm in," I muttered, switching over to the communicator I had in my ear. "Neutralizing hostiles."

I swept the R-14 around, finding a cluster of men and women wearing red-and-blue uniforms and carrying substandard weaponry. To an amateur, they would probably look impressive enough. But to me? I could see that their rifles were only slightly better than the mundane weaponry I might have found in the hands of a run-of-the-mill bandit. Hopefully, whatever armor they possessed—if any—would be just as outdated.

The flash-bang had done its job, and the entire crew—fifteen of them, all completely outfitted for battle—was in a state of disarray. A few of the would-be guards clutched their deafened ears, a couple blinked in unseeing confusion, and one even sported terrible scorch marks on her face.

I almost felt sorry for them.

They were just people, after all. Each of them had probably taken the job because they couldn't find anything better. And as far as I knew, they weren't terrible humans like the Enforcers back in Nova. But I couldn't afford pity. Nor could I afford to hesitate.

So, I opened fire.

The R-14 barked, sending concentrated bursts of superheated plasma at my targets. Their armor was completely incapable of stopping the ordnance—especially when augmented by my significant modifiers—and my gunfire tore through them with ease. None had even recovered from the flash-bang before I cut them all down. In seconds, they were all dead, and none had even gotten a shot off.

"Hostiles down. Moving to cut distress signal," I said. Then, I flipped over to my Secure Connection and said, "Well, that was horrible. This better be worth it."

I'd never shied away from killing, and that had become even more true after Nova City. However, I much preferred targeting invaders over fellow humans. I would do what I had to do. Obviously. But that didn't mean I was happy about it.

"It will be," he assured me. It didn't help, but I was committed.

I spotted a security terminal across the car, which was pretty bare-bones and lined with benches meant for the soldiers. Likely, they never expected anyone to drop in on them in transit. Instead, they were meant to guard the train in the event that it had to stop for whatever reason. There were six other guard cars throughout the train, but this was the most important because it was the only one equipped with a security terminal that had access to the long-range communications system. There were other short-range communications stations in the train, but the others were taking care of those. Or that was the plan, at least. I was a little skeptical that they could get it done.

"I wonder what they'd have done if I wasn't here," I said, retrieving my personal link from the Hand of God and jamming it into the terminal's port. As I tackled the defenses—which were less than stout—I went on, "I mean, can you imagine them dropping Paulo from *The Leviathan*? Could he even fit through that hatch?"

"That's not fair. He told me he has a glandular problem," Patrick stated.

I didn't believe that for a second, mostly because that very morning, I'd seen him scarfing down enough food to feed six people. He was fat because he ate too much and didn't exercise. Which was fine, if that was a choice he wanted to make. Good for him, living his life on his terms, but it clearly had its downsides.

"Sure. Whatever. I'm in. Disabling communications . . . now," I said, having torn through the Mistwall with ease. For such an important train—it connected two huge cities—the defenses really were laughably weak.

No sooner had that thought crossed my mind than an explosion rattled the car and nearly derailed the train.

"What the hell . . ."

"Back of the train. The one where they sent the cowboy. Some kind of explosion, but . . . No communication from our guy," he said. "You want to check it out?"

"Not sure. Give me a sec," I said, switching back over to the communicator. "What's going on, guys?"

"Fucking Rex . . ."

"Goddamn it. Every time!"

Askar cut through the traffic, saying, "Rex blew something up. Before communication cut off, he was in trouble."

"Disconnect the cars," said Isaac.

"What?" I asked. I didn't like Rex very much, but he was part of the team. And I wasn't in the habit of abandoning my allies.

"You should have access from that terminal. Just cut everything from car six-thirty-eight back. It's the simplest solution," Isaac said.

"You can't do that!" screamed Paulo. "He's an asshole, but he's our asshole!"

"Unless somebody wants to physically go back there and deal with the problem, I don't see a choice."

I sighed. "Fine. But if I save this idiot, you all owe me," I said, already moving. I leaped to the hatch and yanked myself back onto the roof. The wind hit me like a brick wall, but I managed to maintain my footing. Then, I started sprinting, switching back to the Secure Connection. "I'm about to do something stupid. Wish me luck."

Patrick sighed. I have no idea how he did that considering we weren't really communicating audibly, but that's definitely what it was. Then, he said, "Isaac's freaking out up here, by the way. Just so you know."

"Whatever. He's not the boss of me."

"Askar isn't happy, either."

"He's not my boss, either."

"Isn't he, though? Like, he's kind of in charge of this whole thing."

"Yeah. Sure. Doesn't matter. None of them can stop me from doing what I want, so . . . Yeah. Not the boss of me. Anyway, keep an eye out for me, okay? Rex might be a bit of an idiot, but he struck me as pretty capable. Something's a bit off with this whole thing."

Indeed, my own part of the mission had been a little too easy. Sure, maybe I was lucky and the people in charge of the train were stupid, complacent, and overconfident, but I didn't really want to put my faith in that—especially now that things had started going wrong. The thought had just crossed my mind when two things happened concurrently.

One was Patrick's shout. "Look out!"

The other was Observation picking up the sound of heavy footsteps behind me. I whipped around just in time to see a huge combat bot sailing through the air, propelled by rockets in its feet. At the apex of the bot's jump, the rockets cut off, and it plummeted from the sky.

And its trajectory was aimed directly at me.

I took a quick instant to catalogue its characteristics. Two legs. Four arms. Shiny yellow paint job. And a sword bigger than my whole body. More, that weapon glowed with blue energy, announcing its status as a nano-blade.

I dove forward in a roll, but I knew I wasn't going to make it. So, I used Teleport to speed me another dozen feet away. It was just enough to take me out of the combat bot's range, and its sword crashed down behind me, cleaving the roof of the car in two.

I twisted, coming up with my R-14 at my shoulder, and I fired. The first three-round burst took it in the chest, and I was dismayed to see the super-heated plasma splash harmlessly across the heavy armor. So, I used Explosive Shot, augmenting the remainder of the magazine. I felt my Mist drain at a precipitous rate, but I could tell that holding back was a bad idea.

I fired, aiming at the combat bot's comparatively vulnerable leg. Its programming had clearly dismissed my weapon as too weak to threaten it, so it made no attempt at avoiding the resulting burst of fire. That was a mistake.

The superheated plasma rounds erupted from the R-14's barrel, huge and angry, and this time, instead of splashing ineffectually against the metallic armor, they exploded upon contact. Three rounds. Three hits, each tearing into the joint that, on a human, would have been its knee. By the third, the limb was hanging on by a couple of cords. I fired again, and to similar effect.

As the bot's leg was torn out from under it, it teetered in place for a long second before tipping over the edge. It fired its remaining rocket booster, but without the second, it was off-balance. It wouldn't take it long to adjust, but it was still too long. The thing hit the desert ground, tumbling with the inertia of the train's momentous speed. It would recover, but on one leg, it stood little chance of making it back on the train.

Still . . .

I fired again, my shots tearing through its remaining leg. It clattered to the ground, disappearing behind a sand dune as the train's path left it behind.

"Abort mission!" screamed Isaac. Idly, I realized that he'd been shouting that same sentence over and over again.

"Cool your jets," I grumbled. "The threat's down."

"Uh . . . Mira," cut in Patrick's voice, the first time he'd spoken over the shared connection with the rest of the group. "You got one. That's great. Awesome job. But . . . What about the others?"

I turned, seeing a half dozen more combat bots alternating between running and hopping, courtesy of their rocket boosters, from the front of the train.

"Crap."

"I'm going to swing by," Patrick said. "Just be ready to jump!"

"Negative."

"What?"

"Not going to happen," I said with a determined sigh. "I guess it's time to bring out the big guns."

"Do you mean . . .?"

"No—the other big gun," I said.

"Oh. Are you sure?" he asked.

I nodded, though I knew he couldn't see me. He knew as well as I did that I wanted to keep some of my arsenal hidden. I didn't trust our companions farther than I could throw them—which, given my Constitution, was probably an inaccurate saying—and I wanted to keep a few cards in reserve, just in case.

But I also wanted to win.

Badly.

And I supposed I wanted to get those circuits for Patrick, too, and without the train, the plan would be completely spoiled. Yeah—that was definitely the reason I didn't want to retreat. Not because of my fundamental incapability to admit defeat. Never that.

Whatever my reasons, I stowed my R-14 back in my arsenal implant. As I did, the Mist required to augment the rest of the magazine with Explosive Shot flowed back into me. I wasn't running low, but given what I had planned, it was a welcome addition. Then, I summoned my newest weapon from my recently unlocked fifth weapon slot.

The Dragon was a visually impressive weapon, and ever since I'd seen it, I'd wanted one. Sure, the BMAP had suited me better back when I'd first been offered the choice between the two, but I'd never forgotten Gala's description of the powerful weapon. So, a couple of years after the fall of Nova City, I'd returned to the Bazaar and persuaded the minotaur woman to accept far less than the thing was really worth.

Ever since, it had become my favorite weapon.

Narrowly, sure—the BMAP was still up there—but there was just something about the Dragon that made it a pure joy to use.

Probably the carnage that always followed in its wake.

The weapon itself—dubbed the DR-4 EMG—was a little more than four feet long, with a casing as thick as my waist and a corrugated barrel that gave it an incredibly aggressive look. Designed to be held by the handles atop the casing and fired from the hip, the Dragon was far from a precision weapon. But given the size of the enemies bearing down on me, that was a perfect fit for the situation.

I squeezed the handle—the thing didn't even have a trigger, instead using a lever embedded in the back grip—and the Dragon roared. A ten-foot flame erupted from the barrel, reddening my cheeks with the sheer heat, propelling its ordnance at a two-thousand-rounds-a-minute rate of fire. In fact, without the built-in spatial storage for its ammunition, it would have been largely useless. Thankfully, that space held about ten thousand bleedingly expensive rounds.

And I couldn't keep the grin from spreading across my face as I sent as many as I could down the length of the train.

Some of the shots went wide. Others tore through the train. But I managed to keep the grouping fairly tight as I swept the weapon through my enemies' paths. The unenhanced R-14 might not have been capable of doing much damage to the combat bots, but the Dragon was a very different beast.

The destruction was glorious.

The rounds, even unenhanced by Explosive Shot, tore through them like they were paper. I only held down the weapon's lever for a couple of seconds, but in that time, the rounds had torn them to pieces. Whole limbs were destroyed, thick armor was obliterated, and the machines' progress was stopped cold.

I released the lever, and the Dragon went quiet.

I panted from the excitement of it, but I still heard Isaac's voice echo through the communicator, "What the fuck was that?"

I ignored him. Instead, I switched back to the Secure Connection but still said aloud, "I've decided what code name I want. From now on, I want to be the Dragon."

Once again, Patrick sighed, saying, "Of course you do . . ."

CHAPTER TWELVE

HEIST

Cy got out of Nova City before we even returned from our delve into the spider Rift. Didn't leave a note. No communication whatsoever. Just escaped the city and fled across the country without so much as a goodbye. I should have expected it, really. Our situation was so complicated, and I'd already made my feelings clear.

—Patrick Ward

Just so you know," said Patrick. "I'm definitely not calling you that."

"Oh, come on!" I said, sprinting down the length of the train. A low-slung drone that looked like a giant metal millipede skittered out from the gap between one car and another, and I barely managed to dodge its oversize pincers. I returned its attack with one of my own, bringing my nano-bladed sword down on its midsection and severing it into two pieces. That didn't stop the thing; in fact, I'd probably made it more dangerous because I now had to deal with two attackers instead of one. But it did delay it for a moment, which allowed me to race past it. I leaped, bridging the gap between cars, landing, and continuing my sprint without breaking stride. "Dragon is so cool, though!"

"If anyone should be the Dragon, it's me," Patrick said. The voice over my interface was punctuated by the sound of *The Leviathan*'s cannons firing. Or guns, really. It only had one cannon, and nothing big enough to require its use had appeared on the battlefield.

Yet.

"You already took Eagle," I pointed out.

"Well, you can have that now," he said. "I'm taking Dragon."

"You can't do that!" I said aloud, dodging another drone—this one looking like an oversize spider, which sent a shiver of remembered fear up my spine. At least they weren't mind spiders. Instead, this one sported a gun barrel attached to its bulbous abdomen, which it discharged at point-blank range. I couldn't dodge the fire. Instead, I only had enough time to turn so that I took the bullet in a nonvital area. The round exploded into my shoulder, tearing a neat hole in my infiltration suit. However, it didn't get past my subdermal Sheath, which meant that I'd only get a surface wound and a sizable bruise for slow reactions.

It did pack enough force to send me spinning around, though, and I nearly went tumbling off the narrow train car. Activating Balance, I turned the spin into a round kick that took the spider drone square in the thorax. My Constitution was high enough that the attack sent the mechanized arachnid flying off the side of the train, where it hit a dune in a spray of sand.

Regaining my footing, I resumed my sprint, saying, "You can't have all the cool nicknames. We've talked about this, Pick!"

"Then stop picking flying animals. You don't fly. End of argument."

"You also can't just declare that an argument's over!"

"I just did."

"Agh!" I growled. "You are so frustrating!"

"That's why you love me, though," he said, his voice far calmer than the situation called for. Even as he finished the statement, a deafening thump sounded, and a moment later, an explosion erupted somewhere near the front of the train. "Oh, that's not good . . ."

"What?"

"Nothing. Just focus on your thing," he said. *The Leviathan*'s cannon fired again. "Everything's completely under control up here."

I had to force myself not to look back. I trusted Patrick, and not just because every good relationship was built on that sort of foundation. Sure, that was part of it. But I also knew just how good of a pilot he was. I'd seen him navigate through swirling Mist storms and fight off a flock of monstrous reptilian birds that gave off an intimidating sense of power, even to me. He could handle whatever was going on back there.

Probably.

Or maybe I'd have to save him.

"You'd better not hurt my ship," I mumbled, though not through the interface. He didn't need to hear my every thought, after all. In any case, it was just as much his ship as it was mine. We'd established that soon after getting back together.

Regardless, I had other things on my mind because a trio of new arrivals—all drones in various insectile forms—crawled up from the sides of the train about thirty yards in front of me. With my speed—even with the not-inconsiderable wind of the train's passage slowing me down—I was on them in seconds. Using my sword with one hand, I aimed a backhanded slash at the one on my left while yanking Ferdinand II from his holster with my right hand.

Without looking, I fired, and the pistol roared to life. I'd loaded him with heavy subsonic rounds that had enough mass to pack a real punch, and it was enough to send the praying-mantis-shaped drone skittering backward. Still, out of the corner of my eye—and with Observation enhancing my sense of sight—I saw the thing latch on to the edge of the train with barbed claws. It barely managed to stop itself from skidding off the side of the train.

Not an ideal situation, but it was still enough to put the drone out of the fight for a second or two. Which was all I needed to finish my backhanded swing at a beetle-shaped drone. It didn't bother dodging, its programming telling it to rely on the thick armor of its shell to keep it safe. It wasn't enough, though, and the nano-blade bit deep into the thing's body, the thin layer of Mist on the edge of the blade ripping through the armor with ease.

I must've hit something vital because the bot went haywire, half of its legs going limp as the other half convulsed erratically, knocking it off-balance. A quick kick sent it flying away, but by then, the third drone was upon me.

More than anything, it looked like a metal cockroach, which made me wonder why anyone would ever create such a horrifying thing. Roaches were already bad enough, but when they were the size of adolescent children, they were absolutely terrifying. Even knowing that it was just another robot, I couldn't suppress the tremble of fear in my mind—especially when it brought its whirring buzz saw of a mouth to bear.

Again—I had no idea what kind of twisted mind would design something like that, but I didn't have the time or the inclination to figure it out. Instead, I raised my forearm to intercept the lethal mouthparts, and I suppressed a scream when the teeth bit deep into my muscle. It bypassed both my Sheath and my infiltration suit with relative ease, so I knew if I didn't get rid of it soon, it would sever my entire arm.

Fortunately, with Pain Tolerance blunting the agony, I was clearheaded enough to bring Ferdinand II up to its robotic head and fire. Once. Twice. Three times, all in quick succession. That was more damage than the creature could take, and with the last shot, the head blew apart with a shower of circuits and metal as well as a puff of Mist.

By that point, the praying mantis drone had recovered and was almost on top of me. With my sword, I parried its first scything claw while dodging the second, countering with a lightning-fast thrust that speared through its body. It ignored the wound, aiming another descending blade at my chest. I dodged to the side, and it ripped a long cut in my infiltration suit. It bit into my skin, as well, drawing a line of blood, but the sheath stopped it from going any deeper.

The drone was clearly unprepared to miss, and the momentum of its blade sent the scything claw spearing into the train. It yanked, but the blade was stuck fast—at least for the moment—so I had the thing at a disadvantage. That was all I needed.

My blade became a blur as a storm of attacks fell upon the stuck drone, and I severed its legs in only a moment. Then, with it helplessly rolling around on the train, I finished it off with a quick lunging strike to its head. After that, I kicked it free of the train.

"Patrick, is—"

"Under complete control!" he shouted, the cannon firing again. It had continued its barrage throughout my short fight, and I didn't think it was going to stop anytime soon. Accompanying the sound of the cannon was a steady staccato of gunfire—probably *The Leviathan*'s other guns. Or maybe the other members of the crew were putting up a fight, as well. Everything was slightly muffled by the rushing sound of the wind in my ears, making it feel so very far away.

"Cowboy, you still alive?" I asked after shifting to the open channel.

"I ain't a cowboy," he growled. "And I'm fine. Just a bit of—"

He grunted over the channel, a sound followed by an explosion toward the back of the train. I heard coughing, then his gravelly voice came through, "Just a bit of unexpected resistance."

"Hang tight," I said, resuming my sprint. I was about a mile from his position, and I knew I could cover that ground in a blink. "Coming to help."

"Don't need your help, girl," he spat with enough vehemence that the connection crackled.

"He does," came Askar's smooth voice. "He really does."

I heard Isaac agree. If Avery, Paulo, or Huascar hadn't been busy in other parts of the train, I felt certain that they would have, as well. They were tasked with taking the control room, which was supposed to have been lightly guarded. Judging by the gunfire I kept hearing, that wasn't necessarily the case, but then again, those three weren't exactly powerful, so it was entirely possible that the situation was precisely as Askar's intelligence had dictated, and they just weren't strong enough to take advantage.

Either way, I couldn't worry about them for now. I wasn't all that concerned about Rex as a person. I didn't like him, and after the job, I wouldn't care if he ended up buried in the desert. But for the job at hand, we needed him—or at least Askar and the others thought so. If I wanted the plan to go ahead without unnecessary delay, I needed to make sure he was alive to do his part.

So, I sprinted to his rescue.

I didn't encounter any other drones for the next few cars, but after that, I was forced to wade through a sea of mechanical attackers. At first, it wasn't so bad. Even if the drones were technically capable of killing me, in practice, they just weren't strong enough, fast enough, or deadly enough to make it happen. Still, they were more than able to slow me down via sheer numbers. To counter this, I raced through them, dispatching them where I could, but mostly just shouldering them aside.

Meanwhile, the battle reached a crescendo, and somewhere at the head of the train, *The Leviathan*'s cannon continued its thumping reports. The intensity of the smaller-arms fire increased, as well, and more than one explosion threatened to dislodge that half of the train. But with the Mist keeping it attached to the tracks, that was an unlikely prospect.

I ignored it all, focusing on moving as quickly as possible. And against all odds, I made decent time, even if I did so while trailing a veritable army of insectile drones. I would deal with them later, though. First, I needed to rescue the cowboy.

An explosion of fire erupted about a hundred yards ahead of my position, marking Rex's position as well as a waypoint on my map, and I pushed myself to even greater speed. As I did so, I summoned my R-14, mostly because it was my most versatile weapon. The Dragon was great, and it was perfect for mass destruction. The BMAP served a similar purpose, though it was better for destroying vehicles and buildings than the more personnel-focused Dragon. Neither would be good to use in an enclosed space, though.

Ferdinand II was limited by the size of his drum, and the nano-bladed sword suffered from the same disadvantages typical of every melee weapon. The sniper rifle had the opposite problem, and its fire rate was so low that it was really only suited for fighting at a considerable distance. Finally, my scattergun was ill-suited for fighting bots, so by process of elimination, I was left with the familiar assault rifle. I wasn't going to complain about a weapon that had served me so well.

When I reached the appropriate car, I slid to a stop, reached down, and yanked open the access hatch. The sound of a pitched battle nearly overwhelmed me, but I suppressed Observation, retrieved a very special grenade from my arsenal implant, and tossed it inside.

The overload grenade was my own invention, and I'd created it specifically to combat robots and drones. Its design was simple, and when it activated, it sent out a pulse of Mist-infused lightning that was perfectly suited to stunning mechanized foes. It wouldn't last long, and it would only give a biological entity a bit of a headache, but considering that the entire train was protected by drones and robots, it seemed appropriate.

The grenade exploded, and ignoring the sharp spike of pain that I knew would quickly disappear, I leaped down into the train car. The scene that greeted me was very gratifying.

Seven humanoid robots occupied the car, each one sporting a series of scuff marks that might've been the result of Rex's gunfire. There were also scorch marks aplenty, and a few destroyed bots decorated the floor. Each of the standing robots twitched as if under the effects of a seizure—which, for them, wasn't really that inaccurate of a description. Whatever the case, they were helpless to defend themselves against me.

I heard Rex shout something, but I ignored him as I opened fire. I didn't dare use Explosive Shot—not in an enclosed space—but it didn't matter. The R-14 ripped into the robots, dislodging bits and pieces with every shot. Still, they were durable, and I had to use Instant Reload to eke out as much damage as I could in the short amount of time I had left. It was enough, and by the time the stun wore off, there was only one robot still standing. That lasted for maybe a second before I finished the job.

An eerie silence filled the air as smoke and clouds of Mist drifted to the top of the cabin. In the distance, I could still hear the muffled sound of the battle at the front of the train, but it was muted by the car's soundproofing.

"What the hell you doin' here, girl? I said I had it!" growled Rex.

"You're welcome," I said, leaping to the hatch and pulling myself up just in time to see the horde of drones bearing down on me. I grinned as I once again switched weapons, exchanging my R-14 for the Dragon.

By the time the small army of insectile drones drew within fifteen feet, the Dragon had already started to spit Mist. The next moment, it roared to life, and my fire scythed through them like so much wheat. The burst only lasted for a few seconds before the weapon went silent, the last of its ammunition spent, but it had done its job. Aside from a couple of quick-processing drones that dove to the sides of the train, the horde of robots was gone, their parts flying off the train as the Dragon tore them to pieces.

I dismissed the heavy weapon and drew my sword before dispatching the stragglers with practiced ease. Behind me, Rex had paused halfway out of the hatch, and he stammered, "What the . . . Who the fuck are you?"

"You know my name," I said without looking back. I wasn't sure if he heard me or not, but it didn't matter. He'd seen enough to know just how easily I could kill him. After a moment, I looked back to see that he'd made his way to the roof of the car, and I asked, "Did you finish your part?"

He nodded. "Took care of the backup-comms car pretty quick," he said, his voice losing a bit of his trademark swagger. Fear would do that to a person. "Didn't run into trouble till I started movin' forward."

Sheathing my blade, I said, "Same. Almost like they were expecting us."

"No," Rex said, stepping up beside me. I saw that he was clutching his hat to keep it from blowing off. "If they knew . . . It would've been worse."

"Saw worse back toward the middle of the train," I said, referring to the combat bots I'd taken out after taking care of the main communications car. "But that might not be too unusual for a train this size. Who's it belong to, anyway?"

Rex shrugged. "That don't matter," he said. "This ain't the main target."

"But once it stops, we're not going to just leave whatever they're hauling alone, right?" I asked sarcastically. "Might be smart to know who we're stealing from."

"Maybe so, but that ain't my thing," he said.

"And what is your thing?" I asked. His explosive battle had been loud, but he hadn't proven himself to be a particularly deadly combatant. Then again, maybe my perspective was a bit skewed. Still, even Patrick could have taken care of that car of robots.

"I blow shit up," he said. "B'lieve me, I'll show my worth when we hit the convoy."

I just shook my head. I had no doubts that I could do his job at least as well as he could, but maybe I would end up surprised for once.

"Whatever. I'm just tagging along, anyway," I said. Then, I added, "C'mon. Let's go see if there's anything left to fight up front."

"I don't—"

Just then, the gunfire ceased, and I felt the train start to slow down. A moment later, Patrick's voice came through my interface as he said, "Told you I could handle it."

"Never doubted you for a second."

"Sure you didn't, you control freak," Patrick said, and I could practically see his grin in my mind's eye. "Everything fine back there? Askar seems worried."

"Everything's good," I said. "Cowboy's fine. Bots are dead. And the train's ours. Seems like it worked out pretty well."

But in the back of my mind, I knew I'd shown way more of my capabilities than was probably wise. Logic said I should've just let Rex die. There were reasons to save him, but in my mind, the most important one was that he was part of my team. Saving him was just the right thing to do.

I just hoped it wouldn't end up biting me in the ass.

CHAPTER THIRTEEN

TO THE VICTOR

For the longest time, I didn't think happiness was really possible. With what was coming, everything looked so bleak. But then I saw that Nova City wasn't really representative of the entire world. Sure, there were other places like it. Most of the biggest cities in the world were under the aliens' thumbs. But a different kind of life was possible. Of course, I knew it was all going to end soon enough, but at least it gave me some hope.

—Patrick Ward

As the train slowed to a stop, Rex and I swept through each car with practiced ease. I knew he wouldn't have had as much success without me, but he seemed reasonably capable so long as he didn't encounter overwhelming odds. For those instances, I was there, and I'd already established that the drones and combat bots that constituted the bulk of the train's security were completely incapable of stopping me. And as we progressed through one car after another, no new threats presented themselves to disprove that assumption.

At the halfway mark, we ran into Avery. About a hundred cars later, we picked up Huascar. And finally, after traveling the length of the miles-long train, we found Isaac and Askar in the control room. Bodies littered the floor of the car, ignored and seemingly forgotten.

"I hope these were bad guys," I said through the Secure Connection.

Patrick responded, "Me, too. Body count's at about three dozen."

I didn't mind killing people. I'd done it often enough that, even when it was someone undeserving, it wouldn't keep me up at night. No more than all the other innocent lives that could be laid at my feet, at least. What were a few more to add to the total, after all? I was already a mass murderer, and even if I suddenly changed my ways, it wouldn't change the things I'd already done.

I didn't consider myself a villain. Not really. But I was self-aware enough to recognize that I wasn't a hero, either. And besides, there was a part of the world that very much disagreed with my own self-assessment. Back in the region surrounding the ruins of Nova City, the population definitely wasn't going to be throwing me any parades. Part of that was my fault—after all, I had done what I'd done, and there was no taking it back—but the aliens had also made sure that everyone knew just who was ultimately responsible for Nova's fall.

That was why I had no intentions of ever going back.

Still, even if I had come to terms with my nature as a killer, that didn't mean I wanted to engage in the wanton murder of innocents. I might've been a bit of a villain, but I wasn't evil.

"Who owns this train, anyway?" I asked aloud, directing the question toward Askar, who was busy fiddling with a security terminal. Paulo hovered nearby, clearly having facilitated the alien's access. It had taken a few seconds for me to even notice him, which, given his bulk, was quite surprising.

"Nobody important," he replied without looking up. "We're not taking much, anyway, so they probably won't care enough to come after us."

Probably. That sounded far too uncertain for my taste, but I'd known the plan going in. And as much as I hated leaving an enemy at my back, it wasn't unreasonable to suspect that whoever owned the train would be incapable of finding us. The world was a big place, after all, and we'd taken great pains not to leave any witnesses. With the communications having been jammed, they'd have no way of knowing whom to even pursue.

Besides, *The Leviathan* gave us the advantage of mobility. In a day or so, we could be halfway around the world, enjoying some tropical beach. There were plenty of ways for people to get around, but few people on Earth had the kind of mobility afforded by *The Leviathan*. I wondered how Askar and the rest of his crew intended to avoid pursuit.

Not that it mattered. That wasn't our problem. Patrick and I would do our jobs, reap the rewards, and get out. Every other detail represented pointless complications that were beneath our concern. Askar had been on the planet for almost a century, so it was reasonable to assume he knew how to take care of himself, so even if I could bother myself to worry over his and his crew's safety, it didn't seem necessary.

Without responding to Askar, I stepped up to a different terminal, retrieved the cord of my personal link from the Hand of God, and jacked in. Paulo said something that I ignored as I tore through the flimsy defenses in only seconds. Once I was in the system, I turned my head to him and said, "Don't worry about me. I know what I'm doing."

He sputtered some sort of objection, but by that point, I'd already dismissed him as completely useless. For the group, he was probably necessary, but to me, he was just redundant. I dove into the system, searching for the cargo manifest. On my way through the train, I'd passed one car after another, all filled with crates of various sizes, and it only took a cursory search through the manifest to learn that most of them contained foodstuff. Or medicine, which was valuable enough in the right hands. I had no interest in going through the hassle of fencing it, though. After a couple of minutes, I chanced upon a listing that interested me.

Through the foodstuffs, I said, "Car two hundred and twelve. Refined metals. Listed as high priority in the manifest."

"Oh, that sounds interesting," Patrick replied. "Do you think it's gold or silver?"

"I literally have no idea, Pick," I answered. "I'm looking at a single line on an inventory list."

"Don't you want to guess?"

"Not really."

He huffed and said, "You're no fun. I think it's gold. You remember that guy in the mountains? The one that had the huge collection of gold bars?"

"Edgar."

"Yeah. Him. I bet he'd buy it," Patrick said. "How much is there?"

"Seventeen crates, so probably a ton. Maybe a little more," I said. "What do you think he intends to do with all that gold, anyway? It's practically useless."

"It's a good conductor that doesn't degrade," Patrick remarked. "Some cybernetic engineers use it for wiring and circuitry."

"I bet he just likes looking at it," I said. "You saw it in his eyes, didn't you? Wasn't gold, like, super valuable back in the old world? They used it for money, didn't they?"

"Some places still do," Patrick pointed out. "And it is kind of pretty. People love using it for jewelry."

I sighed. I liked pretty things as much as the next girl, but gold had never really done it for me. It was one reason I'd insisted on repainting *The Leviathan* so many times. Sure, the original black-and-gold design had a certain regality to it—as did the Hand of God beneath the faux flesh that covered my arm—but it really wasn't my style. "Takes all kinds, I suppose," I said. Some people did go crazy for the shiny metal, and who was I to judge them for it? They had the right to like the things they liked.

"No point in speculation, though. We'll find out soon enough," I added.

Patrick voiced his agreement, and I continued searching through the manifest for likely fodder for my larcenous tendencies. I found a couple of stores of high-quality food, spirits, and some medical gear that I felt would prove useful, and I marked what needed to be marked. As I scoured the inventory list, Askar and Paulo presumably did the same as the train gradually slowed to a stop. It had been going more than two hundred miles per hour, so it took quite a while for all that momentum to dissipate. When it finally coasted to a stop, Patrick said, "Meet you at the first car on the list."

"How long?" I asked aloud, glancing at Askar.

"Moving out in an hour," he answered without looking up. Instead, he continued to stare at the security terminal's tiny screen, presumably poring over the inventory just as I had.

The goods in the train were first come, first served according to our agreement. His support personnel—people I'd never even met—should have been arriving any second with cargo trucks, but they weren't of interest to me. Patrick and I had our own transport, and *The Leviathan* was more than capable of carrying whatever we chose to steal.

With thievery on my mind, I left the control hub behind and climbed a ladder between cars. Once I was atop the train, I beheld the damage we—well, mostly I—had caused. The cars were pitted with gunshot holes, and more than a few cars were still smoking from the explosions I'd affected.

Clearly, Patrick was thinking the same thing, and his voice came over my interface, saying, "You really did a number on this train, Mira. I thought you were going to try to keep the collateral damage to a minimum."

I looked up as *The Leviathan* flew overhead, settling in at the first car I'd marked as a target. It contained a shipment of top-tier med-hypos that, given my penchant for injury, could always come in handy. "Yeah, well—nobody told me there would be high-grade combat bots, either," I replied.

"That was a bit of a nasty surprise," he agreed. "You should've seen the fliers."

"You didn't mess up my ship, did you?"

"Our ship. And no. The Mist shields held. It was close, though. And it probably cost us more than we'll make off this train heist."

"Then those circuits you want better be worth all the trouble," I said.

With that, I jogged forward. Calling it that was a bit of a mischaracterization because, with my Constitution attribute enhancing my body, I could trot faster than most people could sprint. And if I really went all out? I could give some hover cars a run for their money. Still, I kept my pace measured—for me—and I quickly found the appropriate car. It helped that Patrick had piloted *The Leviathan* to hover directly over it, with the cargo bay's ramp extending to within a foot of the car's roof.

"Show-off," I muttered with a slight grin. He really was an exceptional pilot, and he was familiar enough with the big ship to bring all his skill to bear. In anyone else's hands, *The Leviathan* would've been a lumbering beast of a ship, but in Patrick's, she was as light and nimble as a wasp.

Over the next twenty minutes, I raced down the length of the train, loading the goods I'd marked for procurement into *The Leviathan*'s spacious hold. There were medical supplies, crates of fresh fruit, and more than a little alcohol that I hoped would fetch a bundle of credits. I passed over the few cars holding weapons and ammunition. None of it would be all that useful for me or Patrick—we used better-quality stuff—and pound for pound, it just wasn't as valuable as some of the other goods I'd found.

Eventually, I reached the final car on my list and descended into the interior. Like all the other cars, it was entirely dark, but with Observation on my side, that wasn't much of a detriment for me. I could see clearly with only scant illumination, and where my eyes failed, my other senses could easily pick up the slack.

Soon enough, I found the right group of crates. There were only eleven of them, all stacked neatly against the wall. The boxes were about three feet tall and twice as wide, and when I opened one, I let out a sigh, saying, "Well, it's not gold."

"What is it?"

"If I'm reading this right, it's called carbonatium. Mostly, it's in black bricks that . . . Well, they look really dull. Like, they absorb rather than reflect light," I said. "But I'm mostly in the dark here, so that might be an optical illusion."

"It's . . . It's not."

"What? You've heard of this stuff?" I asked.

"I have. How much is there?"

"Uh . . . One sec," I said, reaching out to pick up one of the bars. When I tried to lift it, I got a bit of a surprise. The ingot was only about eight inches long, five inches wide, and about as deep, but it must've weighed a hundred pounds. Maybe more. "If each crate's the same . . . Maybe two thousand pounds?"

"I think I know why the security was so tight, then."

"This stuff?" I asked, hefting one of the bars. Now that I was prepared for the weight, it wasn't difficult to lift, but the density was definitely noteworthy. "What's it for? Where'd it come from? And why do you think—"

"That little cache of ingots is probably worth more than everything else in this train combined," Patrick stated, and he did so with enough confidence that I could tell he'd had some dealings with the metal. "And that's if you could find someone willing to sell it. It's not just useful. It's rare, too. You need to get that loaded as quickly as possible."

"But—"

"No more talk, Mira. Seriously. Not even over the Secure Connection. Wait until we're in the ship and you've got Bastion running, okay?" he breathed, his voice quivering slightly. "Wars are fought over that stuff. The implications of finding it here . . . Just . . . Let's just hurry, Mira."

Patrick didn't really get spooked very easily, so I had no issues with trusting his judgment. Following his instructions, I hefted the first crate and, with a grunt, threw it over my shoulder. It didn't really challenge my strength, but the box was awkward enough to make getting it out of the train and into *The Leviathan* more than a little annoying. Still, I managed it well enough and quickly made the requisite trips to collect the other crates. By the time I was finished, my allowance of time had elapsed, and Askar's voice crackled over the communication channel reserved for the crew. "Time's up," he said. "Everyone to your positions."

Fortunately, my position was in *The Leviathan*'s cargo bay. Unfortunately, that was also true for everyone but Isaac, who was tasked with piloting the train to its destination. I climbed into the ship, then cast a glance at our surroundings. The trucks carrying whatever Askar and the rest of the crew had stolen were already speeding away, presumably to some sort of hidden location.

After confirming that I was on board, Patrick maneuvered the ship back to the front of the train, where the others all boarded. Once they were loaded up, the train resumed its journey down the tracks with *The Leviathan* following from far above.

"Get what you were looking for?" asked Askar, glancing at the pile of crates. I'd taken a few extra moments to position the boxes containing the carbonatium behind the medical supplies, but I was well aware of just how poor of a hiding place it was. Still, there hadn't been enough time to do anything else, so I had no choice but to accept things the way they were.

"Mostly medical supplies and booze," I said, nonchalantly flipping my hair out of my eyes. It was just long enough that it was becoming annoyingly difficult to wrangle. Perhaps I needed a haircut. Or maybe a different style. "You?"

"Mostly food," he admitted. "My people need to eat."

I didn't know if he meant the crew, his support personnel, or a group I'd never met, but it didn't really matter to me. He could be supporting an entire town of innocents, for all I cared. It wouldn't affect my choices.

As our brief conversation lapsed, I glanced at the rest of the crew. They were all giddy with relief after the first stage of the heist had gone so well. They seemed to have no idea just how screwed they would've been if I hadn't been around. None of them—save for maybe Askar, whose capabilities were still an unknown—would've been able to handle those combat bots I'd destroyed with the Dragon.

Askar probably knew. I think Rex did, too, judging by the way he kept looking at me with a curious mixture of awe, respect, and resentment. Of course, the others kept glancing in my direction, as well, but they hadn't seen what the cowboy had seen. So, they almost assuredly underestimated me.

Which was more than fine by me.

Others had fallen into that trap, and most of them were now dead.

Over the next hour, the train slowly made its way into position. On the surface, it looked like an unimportant stretch of desert, save for a barely visible bit of road that crossed the tracks. That was the route the Dengyts would take, according to Askar. So, the plan was to simply block the road, then hit them hard, take what we needed, and get out.

"This is your stop," Patrick said over the Secure Connection. I could hear the anxiety in his voice. He had plenty of confidence in me, but he wasn't immune to worry.

"Think of it," I said through my interface. "This time tomorrow, we'll be back on a beach somewhere, kicking back while I drink more of your . . . uh . . . interesting concoctions."

"You said you liked it!"

"I say a lot of things, Pick."

Before he could respond, Askar stood and said, "It's time. Everyone knows their jobs, so don't screw it up, and we'll be fine."

"Inspiring," I muttered. He cut his eyes at me with a murderous glare. I didn't even flinch. If he wanted to escalate things between us, I was more than willing. Besides, I knew he wouldn't make his move until after the job was done. I just hoped I'd be ready when the time came.

CHAPTER FOURTEEN

FALLIBILITY

For a while, I thought it was love. Cy treated me like an equal. We talked. We had things in common. We were doing great, important things. But Mira was always in the back of my mind. The moment I admitted that to myself, I realized that I could never have a future with Cy. For both our sakes, it had to end. I just wish she'd seen it that way.

—Patrick Ward

N ot bad," I said, kneeling atop a sand dune and watching Rex plant his explosives. He clearly knew what he was doing, and I recognized a fellow enthusiast in the man. There was a difference between someone with a skill and a job and someone who truly enjoyed his work. With Rex, that difference was obvious in the care he took with each charge, in how precisely he placed them upon the would-be killing field.

He stood, taking off his broad-brimmed hat and wiping his forearm across his head. With a long exhale, he squinted toward the horizon where the sun had begun to set. It cast the sky in a spectrum of colors ranging from orange to purple. I didn't think I'd ever get tired of such sights.

That was one of the advantages of being away from civilization—I got to see wonders I'd never thought possible. Sure, sunset was a thing back in Nova City, too, but it wasn't nearly as impactful as it was in the wilderness.

"Glad to have your approval, your majesty," Rex muttered, sweeping his hat down and across his waist before bowing. His attitude had softened since the train heist, probably because he was well aware that I'd probably saved his life. Maybe he could have made it out alive on his own, but I doubted it. Clearly, he did, too. He grinned, adding, "I'm guessin' you know your way 'round a bomb, eh? Course ya do. Ain't there nothin' you can't do?"

"I don't really cook," I said, rising to my full height. I held the R-14 with the stock against my waist. "But if it involves killing or blowing things up, I'm probably your girl."

"That an offer?"

I snorted a laugh. "That's a big negative, cowboy," I said.

His face wrinkled in distaste. "Don't have ta sound so dismissive," he muttered, climbing the dune to join me. He replaced his hat on his head and squinted toward the horizon.

"You're old enough to be my father," I stated, following his gaze. There was nothing there, but soon enough, a caravan of trucks would appear. Once that happened, the job would start. Hopefully, it would go off without a hitch, but I couldn't help but expect a few surprises. After all, Askar's and Isaac's intelligence seemed incomplete when it came to the train; who was to say that wouldn't be the case with the caravan? I had plans for most possible scenarios, but even I couldn't think of everything.

Rex went on, "Is that what you like? You got daddy issues, eh?"

"Not even remotely. I barely knew the guy," I answered with another laugh. "You're barking up the wrong tree here. Not interested. Will never be interested. And if you keep going the way you're going, I might shoot you. Where that shot goes depends on how annoyed I am."

He raised his hands in surrender. "Just offerin' is all," he said. "Can't blame a fella for takin' a chance, yeah?"

"I can if that fella keeps it up."

"Alright, alright. I get it," he said.

I nodded, then said, "Guess we should get back to the others. What's your range on the charges?"

"S'posed to be up to three hundred meters, but I keep it down to two hundred just ta be safe," he said. Then, he grinned, conspiratorially offering, "Plus, that's close enough to feel the shock wave."

Definitely a man who enjoyed his work. I could relate. There was nothing like being buffeted by the wind of your own shock wave.

After that, the two of us headed back, giving the field of buried explosives a wide berth. The last thing I wanted was to set them off early because I stepped on the wrong spot. That wasn't supposed to happen, but bombs were notoriously finicky. Sometimes, they went off for all the wrong reasons, and every bomb maker learned early on not to tempt fate with disrespect or inattention.

Soon enough, we reached our assigned position, which was a hole that had been dug in the coarse sand and concealed beneath a few layers of subterfuge.

The first was a simple earth-colored tarp, the second was a layer of sand, and the third was a holographic display set up by Askar. In the field, it was just about as hidden as we could get.

Of course, my skills were probably better, but most people couldn't boast such powerful abilities as Stealth and Camouflage. As Rex and I ducked under the tarp, I saw the familiar forms of Askar and Avery resting with their backs against an earthen wall. They'd clearly been in the middle of a conversation, which cut off the moment they heard our approach. In that moment, I was shocked by how similar their mannerisms were.

It wasn't definitive proof, but the pair were clearly closer than they'd let on. The only question was whether they were lovers, kin, or just a pair of close friends. Any of the options were possible, but I hoped it wasn't the first. If Avery was more than twenty years old, I would've been surprised, and given that Askar, despite his appearance, was at least as old as my uncle had been, that sort of situation just struck me as wrong.

Not uncommon, but wrong all the same.

I hoped they were somehow related, though that seemed unlikely, as well. By this point, Askar was exiled from his people, which meant that finding a mate among the others who'd been sent down to Earth was extremely unlikely. And I wasn't sure if his kind could mate with humans.

But what did I know? The universe was a vast place, and there was every possibility that such a human-seeming alien could do just that. Either way, Avery represented a pressure point that, if necessary, I could needle. I still didn't know Askar's capabilities, so cataloging every avenue of potential attack was just smart.

"Hot as balls out there," Rex growled, grabbing a bottle of water from the small cache of supplies sitting nearby. Next to it was a portable security terminal.

"Are the others in position?" I asked, ignoring the cowboy.

Askar answered, "Ready and waiting. The bombs set?"

"Them bastards won't know what hit 'em," Rex answered before taking a long, deep drink. Water splashed down his chin, but he didn't care, so long as most of it went into his mouth.

Askar continued to stare at me, and I said, "Everything's set. Your plan should go off without a hitch."

"Good. Very good," he said. "And you two know your roles, right? You know the plan, don't you?"

"Convoy passes us by," I said. "We blow the explosives once the last few trucks are in range, blocking retreat. Train's blocking the way forward. We swoop in, disable the defenses, and take what we need. Patrick lands *The Leviathan*, we load everything up, and then we retreat."

"Skeedaddle," said Rex, slapping his hands together with a grin. "No trace, no pursuit. Like ghosts in the goddamn wind."

Askar nodded. I had to respect his plan, if for no other reason than because of its simplicity. Sure, there were a few moving parts, but he'd taken as many variables as possible into account during the plan's formation. Hopefully, that would be enough.

For the next few minutes, I remained outwardly silent while talking to Patrick over the Secure Connection. We didn't discuss anything important—just idle chat to distract us from our impatience to get things started. Waiting was always the worst part for me. I was so used to moving. To acting. To making things happen. So just sitting still and waiting for my target to come to me was an exercise in torture. Patrick's voice helped mitigate some of that, but the wait was still more than a little frustrating. Over the years, I had learned to deal with it, but that didn't mean I enjoyed sitting still and waiting.

Soon enough, the sun set, and night fell over the desert.

"Wish I could see the stars," I said, glancing up at the tarp.

"Me, too," Patrick answered, his voice full of awe. He'd often spoken of leaving the planet, of traveling through space and seeing all the amazing things he'd read about. Apparently, astronomy was one of his other hobbies, and given half a chance, he would wear my ears off with tales of supernovas and comets. For my part, I didn't much care about any of that. Sure, it was all probably amazing, but I was more interested in traveling to other settled planets.

Partly, I wanted to take the fight to the aliens' home turf. They'd invaded my planet, so it was only right to return the favor. However, even I knew that was a route to ruin. I couldn't stand up to whole civilizations. Instead, my desires were mainly influenced by a need to leave Earth—and its wholly disappointing populace—behind. I didn't hate my own people. But I was frustrated with them. Perhaps I could find somewhere better out there.

Somewhere I could fit in without feeling like a freak.

Because, on Earth, that's what I was. If there were more than a hundred people on the planet—not including the aliens—who could rival my power, I would've been surprised. The combination of my advanced skills and inflated attributes sometimes made me feel like a wholly different species. Most of the people I met would be dead in a few decades. But me? I'd live for hundreds of years. Maybe indefinitely. That made friendships a tricky prospect.

More, it made it easy to understand why my uncle had kept himself separate from everyone else. Aside from Heather, Nora, and me, he hadn't really been close to anyone. And I understood it. Getting close to someone meant enduring the pain of inevitably outliving them.

"It's time," said Askar, yanking me from my thoughts. I blinked, and he looked up from the security terminal, adding, "The convoy is a little bigger than expected."

I sighed. "And let me guess, the defenses are stronger."

"There's no way to tell for sure," he answered.

"That's a yes," said Rex, checking the hand cannon at his hip. Avery was doing the same with her dual pistols.

"Shit," I muttered. "How many more trucks?"

"Nine extras. Two have profiles that suggest armored—"

"Damn it!" I growled, slapping my hand against the ground. Then, I forced myself to calm down. I pushed myself to my feet, saying, "Okay, here's what's going to happen. I'm going out there. I'll take care of the extras. The rest of you follow the plan, okay?"

"You do understand that they probably have—"

"I understand perfectly well," I spat, interrupting Askar. I jabbed a finger at the alien, saying, "You've had bad intel from the very start. If I wasn't here, your little heist would have already failed. So, if you'll kindly just step the fuck back and let me do my thing, I'll pull your ass out of the fire. Then, we can go our separate ways. Got it?"

I hardly wanted to take over. I had fully intended to simply play my part and hope for the best. But that wasn't really in the cards. The problem was that I'd assumed Askar knew what the hell he was doing just because he was an alien. Clearly, he was just as amateurish as the rest of his crew, and he covered that up with his backstory and cool demeanor.

But if I wanted this thing to happen, I needed to take control.

Which meant showing my cards.

"Goddamn it," I growled into the Secure Connection. "New plan, Pick. When shit goes down, I need you to swoop in and open fire with the cannon."

"Uh . . . On who?"

I loved him for not arguing with me. He trusted my judgment, God bless him.

"You'll know it when you see it," I said. I had an inkling of what to expect, but only because of some of the files I'd glimpsed during my infiltration of the Dengyt satellite camp. I'd hoped I wouldn't need the information, but now, my hopes seemed silly. From the moment I'd discovered its presence, I knew I'd end up facing it.

A part of me even looked forward to it.

But if any of the others faced off against what I suspected was coming, they'd end up dead before they even had a chance to react. If they were going to survive, I was their only real chance.

Patrick and the others confirmed that they were on board, and I slipped out from underneath the tarp. Immediately, I embraced Stealth, masking my presence in the process, and started moving forward at a jog. I knew that an observant watcher would notice my passage, but I trusted that none of those were around. Soon enough, I reached a short cliff overlooking the would-be site of the ambush. Once there, I pulled my Pulsar out of my arsenal implant and extended the stabilizer arms. With that done, I took a prone firing position and searched the horizon for the dust that would announce the convoy's arrival. I had to flare Observation, but I found it a couple of seconds later.

"Half a mile out," I said over the communications channel reserved for the crew. "ETA forty-five seconds."

"Understood," came Askar's terse response.

I could practically see Rex's grin as he pulled the detonator from his pocket. At least I'd get a good view of the fireworks while he was tucked away safe and sound under a giant tarp. Silver linings and all that.

The caravan's lead truck came into view, and I was a little surprised to see that it had Mist vents where I'd expected wheels. Keeping that stable must've cost a fortune. I knew because I'd had to feed my Cutter a handful of Rift Shards every time I wanted to take it out in a Mist-dense territory. Doing so for a truck the size of the one slowly closing in on my position had to have been incredibly expensive.

A second truck followed the first. Then a third. And a fourth. In the end, almost thirty trucks had come into view, speeding across the desert. The last nine trucks were subtly different from the others. Reinforced frames gave them a much bulkier appearance, and I could see that they were equipped with thick armor that would stop anything short of my BMAP.

The sight of those bulky trucks verified that my prediction had been correct.

"This is going to get really messy," I said over the crew's channel. "I can't guarantee everyone's going to make it through."

"They're just gnomes!" came Huascar's voice. A couple of others agreed.

"Yeah. Sure. I just thought I'd give you fair warning," I said, resisting the urge to argue. They had no idea what was coming. For my part, I had only read a few lines on a file, but even that was enough to tell me not to underestimate what was in store. The crew had no such warning, and even if they'd seen what I had, I suspected they wouldn't have reacted appropriately. They just weren't serious people. "Heads up. Arrival in five, four, three . . ."

I finished the countdown, and a second later, the lead truck in the convoy passed the explosives. The others raced along behind it, and soon enough, the tail of the caravan moved into position.

Suddenly, a series of explosions rocked the desert, sending sand and bedrock flying into the air. Trucks were torn asunder, flipping onto their sides as the explosions ripped their occupants to shreds.

Or that's how it should have gone.

But the back nine trucks were too heavily armored to succumb to the explosions. In the wake of the blast, I heard tiny, high-pitched shouts of alarm, pain, and despair. I ignored them as I watched the mostly unharmed trucks, hoping against hope that I had been mistaken.

As I watched, Rex let out a crow of victory that carried over the communication channel. The idiot had no idea that his actions should have signed the entire crew's death warrant.

"Are those trucks moving?" asked Patrick over the Secure Connection. "How are they still standing?"

"They're not trucks," I said.

"What?"

Just as he asked the question, one of the trucks flipped over on its back and sprouted a hundred metal appendages. It skittered toward the next truck and, through some mechanical process I could scarcely track, attached itself to the other. The new, much larger vehicle repeated the process, absorbing the next truck in line before moving on to the next. And the next after that. In less than half a minute, the nine vehicles had combined into a huge clump of mismatched metal parts.

And then it started to shift.

First came the legs, retracting into the thing's bulk. Then, it folded in on itself. Once. Twice. Three times. Over and over until only a cube remained.

"What the fuck is that?" cried Huascar over the communication channel.

I ignored him as I watched the thing sprout a pair of arms. Then legs. The cube slimmed out into a torso, and a head emerged from the body. In only a few seconds, a sleek, humanoid form stood in the center of the battlefield. Composed of shiny metal, it looked like a featureless mannequin. But I knew that, beneath that mostly benign exterior was the most advanced combat bot I'd ever beheld.

"Don't worry about it," I said, taking aim with my Pulsar. I embraced Empowered Shot. "I'll take care of it."

A second passed, and I squeezed the trigger. A moment later, a ball of superheated plasma tore into the robot's chest, melting through it with ease. And just like that, the battle was joined.

CHAPTER FIFTEEN

A CHALLENGE

Sometimes, I wonder what would happen if Mira and I just settled down somewhere. I can't help but think neither of us would be particularly happy. I need my projects, and she needs adventure. Without those distractions, I'm sure we'd get tired of each other pretty quickly. Or maybe not. I don't know, and I'm terrified of the day I might get my answer.

—Patrick Ward

I continued to fire upon the giant combat bot at a rate of one round per second, which was as quickly as I could use Empowered Shot. Each shot tore into the huge robot's fuselage, melting the metal and sending it staggering. From experience, I knew that each one of those shots was enough to tear a hole in a tank; with my modifiers and the extra oomph added by the ability, my sniper rifle could rival some artillery for damage.

But when I fired the last round in the magazine, I got a nasty surprise.

The bot straightened to its full height, and even without flaring Observation, I could see almost liquid streams of metal flowing back together as the thing repaired itself. I growled, "Shit. Pick, it's got regenerating armor."

He swore over our Secure Connection, then said, "Cannon's online. Firing."

Just then, a huge explosion tore across the sky, disintegrating the clouds to reveal *The Leviathan*, thousands of feet in the air. A massive blob of liquid blue Mist descended from its cannon, making a beeline toward the recovering bot. Without skipping a beat, it raised one of its arms just in time to intercept the cannon's issue. Another explosion roared into being, kicking up a cloud of billowing dust.

"Direct hit," Patrick announced.

But I wasn't optimistic about the viability of *The Leviathan*'s cannon. In most situations, it was more than enough to do the job. This combat bot was not an ordinary opponent, though, and I suspected the cannon would be insufficient in the task of defeating it. Fortunately, I had a lot more firepower at my disposal, and I knew exactly how to beat the thing.

The dust settled, and sure enough, the combat bot was entirely unscathed. The blue sheen of a Mist shield formed a canopy above its raised arm, and though it flickered a bit, it seemed strong enough to take a dozen such shots.

That was the problem with the cannon, really. It could pack quite a punch, but the projectile—a ball of roiling Mist—was slow-moving and, for capable enemies, easily mitigated. Luckily, most of my weapons had no such issues.

While Patrick brought the cannon to bear, I'd reloaded the Pulsar. So, with a fresh magazine, I kept firing. This time, the bot didn't just stand there and take it. Instead, the moment I unloaded that first round, it started scanning the area for my location. I still had Camouflage active—as always—but it was a poor screen when I was steadily firing upon the bot, and it didn't take long before it zeroed in on my location.

By that point, I'd already fired most of the magazine at the thing, so I shouted into the Secure Connection, "Relocating!"

Stowing my weapon, I sprang to my feet and sprinted away. It was just in time, too, because only a second later, the shallow cliff exploded into an eruption of rocky shrapnel as the sound of gunfire filled the air. I glanced back to see that the bot's arms had transformed into a pair of heavy machine guns, which it was steadily firing at my previous location.

I kept going, and the moment I was clear, I embraced Stealth and slowed to a light jog as I slipped behind a dune. The bot continued to fire, but for the moment, I was safe.

"Is it following yet?" I asked.

"Still sitting still," Patrick responded. "Want me to hit it again?"

"No. The ship's too big of a target. If it thinks you're the primary threat, it'll bring out the big guns," I said.

And nobody wanted that.

The specifications I'd read had designated the combat bot as a fully adaptable combat system—or a FACS—and it was entirely capable of destroying an entire city if it was pushed far enough. Obviously, I wanted to avoid that, so my goal was to slowly drain its energy reserves until I could get close enough to disable its systems via Misthack. If I went in too early, its Mistwall would adapt to my intrusion and lock me out. If I went too late, it would calculate that, with its energy reserves getting low, it needed to end the threat in the most efficient way possible.

Which would mean blowing everything up, including me and everything in a three-mile radius.

Yeah—not exactly a good outcome for anyone.

I relayed my plan to Patrick, and he said, "Walking a fine line there."

"What's new?" I asked, settling into a new position. This time, I'd chosen to leave the Pulsar in my arsenal implant. It was reasonably effective, but I'd run out of ammunition before accomplishing my goal. Instead, I needed something bigger. Something that could rapidly drain those reserves.

I needed the BMAP.

As my fingers closed around the familiar grip, I checked that it was loaded with the appropriate ammunition. After confirming that it held explosive rounds—my favorite, if I was honest—I crested the dune and took aim. Then, I used Shatter Shot. The ability was similar to Empowered Shot in that it enhanced a single discharge from an appropriate weapon—in this case, the BMAP—but it differed in the manner of enhancement. Empowered Shot simply charged a round with Mist, making it more powerful. Shatter Shot was a little more complicated.

Once three seconds—the charge time for Shatter Shot—had passed, I squeezed the trigger. The BMAP discharged the bulky round with a thump, and I restarted the process. As I did, I watched the miniature artillery shell arc through the air, a sense of anticipation dancing in my mind. When the round came within twenty feet of the target, it seemed to suddenly split into a half dozen copies, and when they hit, they did so with seven identical explosions that not only tore a massive hole in the FACS's torso, but also sent the huge combat bot flying backward to land on its back.

That was the beauty of Shatter Shot. For a bit of Mist and a slight charge time, I could effectively turn one round into a tight grouping of seven, and though each individual copy didn't pack quite the same punch as the original, it was enough that I judged the overall effect to be five times more impactful than if I hadn't used the ability. That kind of force multiplier—especially with my modifiers—was enormous.

The moment the next round was charged, I fired again, and to similar results.

Idly, I was aware of the chatter coming across the crew's communication channel. Someone chastised Rex to focus on what was important instead of ogling the pretty explosions, and Askar continued giving instructions, but none of it was important to me. I continued my bombardment until the drum went empty, and the moment I fired that last shot, I sprinted away to relocate.

And it was a good thing, too, because only a few seconds later, I saw a beam of pure Mist descend from the sky and obliterate the dune. It didn't just explode. Instead, it melted the sand into a molten slurry that, when it cooled, would no doubt become glass. Thankfully, I was already a few hundred feet away and reloading my BMAP with another cannister.

I repeated the same pattern three more times until I'd used all the appropriate ammunition in my arsenal implant. I had a few drums loaded with nonlethal rounds meant to disperse various gasses, and I had a couple of drums that would blanket an entire area in a raging inferno. But those weren't really useful against a cold, unfeeling combat bot like the FACS.

While I did that, the crew continued to plunder the convoy. I still had no idea what Askar and the others had targeted, but at that moment, I didn't really care. I'd already established—at least in my own mind—that I could handle them if it came down to it, so I wasn't terribly worried about them.

The combat bot was a completely different story.

It had taken everything I could throw at it—and it was enough ordinance to turn a sizable town into rubble—without skipping a beat. If I stood still for longer than the time it took to discharge an entire drum of the BMAP's ammunition, that sky beam would descend upon my location and roast me. I still didn't know where it had come from, and even Patrick couldn't find its origin, claiming that it looked like it came from the upper atmosphere. *The Leviathan* could have gone up there, but the quarantine meant that, without significant preparation, that would result in censure from the system.

Which meant we were at the bot's mercy. For now.

"How much power does this stupid thing have?" I growled into the Secure Connection. "Are the others finished?"

"Just about," answered Patrick. "They've got one more truck."

"Alright. When they're done, I want you to swoop in and get them out," I said. "I'll meet you at location three as soon as I'm done with this thing."

"But—"

"It's the only way," I interrupted, anticipating that he didn't want to leave me behind. "The bot's going to hit you as soon as you come into range. We both know that. And it has enough firepower to tear through the ship's shields in a second. I'll keep it distracted, then go in for the kill when it's depowered enough. Once it's done, I'll head out on the Cutter. In this terrain, I'll be there in less than an hour."

Patrick wanted to argue, but in combat, we both acknowledged that he would follow my lead. Sure, I made plenty of mistakes, but it was important that one of us had the final say. Anything else, and indecision would get us both killed. Due to my experience and training, I was the obvious choice. By contrast, on the ship, he was in charge.

It was a good system, but it did rankle on both our nerves. Still, it was necessary, so we had long since accepted it.

"Fine. I'll relay that to the others," he said.

"And Pick?"

"Yeah?"

"Keep them locked in the cargo bay until I get there," I said.

"At least we can agree on that," he responded. Then, he added, "Stay safe."

"Don't I always?"

"No. No, you do not."

I left the conversation hanging there and sprinted to my next location. I'd tried leading the FACS away from the battlefield, but it had stubbornly resisted. If I'd continued, it would have turned on the others and destroyed them.

Setting up a hundred yards away, I re-summoned my Pulsar and took aim. I only got one shot off before it found me, and I had to scramble down the dune to avoid a barrage of gunfire that preceded yet another beam from the sky. I was close enough to feel the uncomfortable heat as I scampered away, using Stealth to mask my progress.

It didn't help.

Something had changed. The bot had adapted to my tactics, and though it couldn't home in on my location with perfect accuracy, the usefulness of Stealth had begun to decrease with every passing second. I ran like my life depended on it, zigging and zagging to make myself a less predictable target. Every now and then, I'd get a free couple of seconds to take aim, use Empowered Shot, and fire my Pulsar, but it grew increasingly infrequent the longer the battle continued.

Fortunately, only a couple of minutes later, Patrick announced that the others had completed their heist, and he was descending to pick them up.

That was my cue.

I dismissed the sniper rifle and summoned the Dragon. Propping it on my shoulder, I continued to sprint as I used Explosive Shot on the entire store of ammunition in the weapon's spatially enhanced magazine. Mist drained out of me in a moment, leaving only dregs behind, but that was expected. Once the ability took hold, I settled my sights on the target and let the Dragon loose.

The weapon roared as I continued to move, hip firing at a rate of two thousand rounds per minute. Most of those rounds found their way to the combat bot, predictably ripping it to shreds. Liquified metal splattered onto the ground as it stumbled from the sheer force of impact.

"Go!" I screamed at Patrick.

In the distance, I saw *The Leviathan* drop like a rock, its descent so fast that it looked like a falling meteor. However, in a well-practiced maneuver, Patrick slammed on the Mist thrusters, slowing the huge ship to a dead stop only a yard or two above the ground. Then, he settled it down, and I saw a few trucks racing forward loaded with crates. The crew didn't bother unloading the trucks. Instead, they simply raced up the ship's ramp and into the cargo bay. In seconds,

The Leviathan rocketed back into the sky, and just in time, too, because that's when my ammunition ran dry.

I quickly stowed the Dragon and took stock of the situation. The FACS had been reduced to a pile of molten slag, but already I could see it starting to pull itself together. The regenerative capabilities of that metal were absolutely off the charts, and I figured it must be swimming in Mist. How could the gnomes even afford to deploy such a weapon in the first place? Why would they bother? It was almost assuredly expensive enough to bankrupt a host of small towns, and it made the expenditure Patrick and I had made to keep *The Leviathan* in the air look like spare credits.

Even as I raced across the battlefield, leaping over the huge divots the Dragon had left in the terrain, the combat bot continued to remold itself. I poured on the speed, using Balance sparingly to keep from tipping over into the craters. My Mist was running low, but there was nothing to be done. I needed to get closer.

Foot by foot, I covered the ground, and bit by bit, the bot reformed. By the time I drew within range, it had taken shape, and I found myself staring down the barrel of an enormous cannon. It ignited with a puff of Mist and fired an instant later.

On instinct, I used Teleport. My dwindling supply of Mist drained away, and faster than I could process the change, I found myself atop the combat bot's shoulders.

"Well, that wasn't what I was aiming for," I muttered via the Secure Connection. I reached into my arsenal implant and retrieved a Mist booster. A moment later, I jabbed it into my hip, and a small supply of Mist came flooding into my system. I let out a sigh of relief.

Patrick, in a panicked voice, shouted, "What? What happened? Are you okay? I'm turning back!"

"No. Don't," I said, already activating Misthack and diving into the machine's defenses. Its Mistwall was complex, but after I had spent hundreds—if not thousands—of hours training the ability against tougher defenses than the bot possessed, I found myself more than up to the task. Especially since it had drained a good portion of its available power reserves rebuilding itself over and over again. Still, I was on the clock; my Teleport had confused the thing, but I knew it wouldn't be long before it noticed me. By that point, I needed to have finished it off. "I got this."

Over the next few seconds, one defensive emplacement toppled after another until, soon enough, the system was spread out before me. And it was glorious, complex, and sophisticated, and I had no issues with saying that I'd never seen anything like it. Whoever had built the thing had really accomplished something extraordinary.

It was a shame I was going to tear it all down.

First, I used Surge, which would enhance the next Ghost I uploaded. Once that was done, I looked at the menu on my interface:

Misthack successful. Options:
Reboot system
Overcharge
Disable cybernetics
Upload Ghost

I was tempted to simply reset or overcharge the system, but given the sophistication of its layout, I suspected that it wouldn't take long for the FACS to recover. Thankfully, I had an arsenal full of Ghosts at my disposal. I selected the final option, which opened a second menu:

Please select deck:
Assassination
Infiltration
Robot Disposal
Mass Murder
Annoyances
Wild Cards

Soon after the fall of Nova City, I'd discovered a problem with relying heavily on Ghosts. Basically, the system only allowed me to equip, at most, five options at any given time. For a few months, I'd been distraught—what if I loaded all the wrong Ghosts and didn't have access to the perfect one for whatever mission I'd found myself on? However, my despair was soon dispelled when I mentioned the issue to Dex and he'd helped me reconfigure my interface to add another step to the process.

Basically, I had to arrange my Ghosts into premade groupings that I'd labeled decks. That allowed me to skate in under the system's restrictions while giving me access to almost thirty Ghosts. It seemed a bit of a cheat to me, but Dex claimed it was common practice, at least among the few actual {Mistrunner}s in the universe. In any case, it had solved my problem.

I selected the third option, Robot Disposal, and I was given five options:

Select Ghost:
Scramble (Mk. XVII)
Explode (Mk. CXII)
Melt (Mk. XVI)

Cascade (Mk. XXIV)
Drain (Mk. VII)

Looking at the options, I desperately just wanted to blow the thing up. I'd spent far more time working on *Explode* than any of the other options, and I knew it was the best-formed Ghost in the deck. However, I didn't think it was appropriate for the situation. So, I selected the one that would give me a chance to win: *Drain*.

The Ghost wasn't complicated, really. It just caused the system to rapidly expend its power stores. For most bots, that was a blend of electricity and Mist, but the FACS was almost entirely powered by Mist, which was one of the reasons it was so potent. I uploaded the Ghost.

Instantly, the thing went wild, rapidly changing shape with every passing second. I held on, but I had to flare Balance to keep from being thrown aside. Then, a moment later, a beam of light hit the ground about fifty feet away. It was followed by thirty or forty more. Over and over, the waist-thick bars of light slammed into the ground, melting sand and sending molten rock flying into the air. The first had been the closest, but the others were close enough to send the temperature skyrocketing past the realm of discomfort and into painful territory. Without my abilities and high Constitution, my skin would have probably boiled off. As it was, by the time the barrage ceased, I had a few blisters on any bits of exposed skin.

But I was alive.

So was the combat bot, though its erratic movements had become sluggish. I pulled Ferdinand II from his holster at my hip, aimed at the thing's head, and squeezed the trigger. The bullet tore a huge hole in the robot's head, but it didn't seem to notice. Instead, it continued to spin around, firing random shots in every direction.

So, I shot it again.

And again. Over and over, I fired until Ferdinand II was completely spent. Rather than waste more ammunition, I holstered him and yanked my sword from its sheath on my back. Then, I went to work. My attacks weren't graceful. In fact, they probably had more in common with a lumberjack's technique. But over the next few minutes, I hacked the thing to pieces. Eventually, it stopped trying to flow back together, and I felt the last of the Mist drain away.

I let out a deep, shuddering breath as the robot collapsed into a pile of half-formed bits of metal.

I'd been in control of the fight the entire time, but if I'd have slipped up even a little bit, it would have ended me. It'd been a while since I'd fought something that strong. Maybe I never had. And it resulted in a feeling that was equal parts excitement, fear, and anticipation.

I ignored it, sliding into the Secure Connection and telling Patrick that I'd finished the thing off. He implored me to collect as much of it as I could, so I dug into the pile of now-scrap metal and found its central processor. After that, I gathered as much of its metallic body as I could fit into my arsenal implant— which must have been a couple of tons, at least—before I heard the sound of hover cars in the distance.

That was my cue to leave.

So, I summoned my Cutter, mounted up, and sped away. As I raced across the desert, I started to prepare myself for the inevitable betrayal coming my way.

CHAPTER SIXTEEN

PREDICTABILITY

Mira always thinks everyone is going to turn on her, and more often than not, she's been right. And I think that's a terrible tragedy because the entire world is not the mob of self-interest that she thinks it is. There are good people out there. She just doesn't let herself see them.

—Patrick Ward

The passage of the hover bike kicked up a rooster tail of dust as I guided it through the desert. For the most part, I kept to a straight line, often ramping high into the air after ascending the steep slope of a sand dune. However, on more than one occasion, I was forced to skirt around them. So, it took a little longer than I expected to reach the rendezvous point. All the while, I kept tabs via the Secure Connection I shared with Patrick, and what I'd heard so far wasn't good.

As I crested the last hill and looked down upon *The Leviathan*, Patrick said, "They're arguing, and Isaac is demanding that we go."

That didn't surprise me. Not really. Even if they weren't planning on betraying us, we were supposed to be on a schedule, and we were already running late. Soon, the Dengyts would figure out that something had gone wrong—if they weren't already aware—and the search for the hijackers would begin. Obviously, the plan was to be well out of the area before that happened. There was still some time left, but we were cutting it close. So, it wasn't shocking that they wanted to leave me behind.

The moment I entered into communications range, I announced my arrival by saying, "You didn't leave me. Surprising."

"You made it!" Avery half shouted.

"Knew you'd take care of it," said Rex.

"Is it gone?" asked Isaac. Paulo added something, but it was lost amid a burst of static.

Askar was the only one who'd remained silent.

I told them that I would arrive in thirty seconds, which was met with a few sounds of relief. The alien still hadn't said anything, which remained the case until I reached the ramp leading into the cargo bay. Once there, I saw that no one had escaped the hijacking unscathed. Avery bore a wound on her shoulder that looked like a plasma burn, Rex was holding an arm over a foam-bandaged gut wound, and even Paulo had a bloody cloth wrapped around his head. Isaac lay on the floor, his torso held upright by a huge crate. His lower half didn't even twitch. Askar was standing near the stairs that would lead toward the cockpit, an angry expression marring his sharp features.

"Where's Huascar?" I asked, glancing at the dozen other nondescript people in the cargo bay. Wearing black coveralls, they looked like hired laborers, which was probably accurate. Someone had to do the heavy lifting, after all. The results of their labor had been pushed to the edges of the spacious cargo bay, where each crate had been stacked neatly and secured in place.

Except the big one in the center of the bay.

"Didn't make it," grunted Isaac, his voice strained. "Took a plasma bolt to the face. The idiot never did know when to take cover."

I hadn't expected that. In fact, according to all the intelligence the others had gathered, the convoy was supposed to have minimal security. That the FACS had been there should have been an indicator that the information was faulty, but I'd somehow convinced myself that its presence was the only alteration. Clearly, I was wrong.

"Heavy resistance?" I asked, glancing at Avery. Paulo hovered over her like an overprotective parent. Judging by the fact that she kept trying to edge away, his was an unwanted presence. Not surprising, given that where he went, an unpleasant odor usually followed.

She answered, "That's an understatement. Those little gnomes were supposed to be pushovers, but—"

Just then, *The Leviathan* trembled as it lifted from the ground. Most of the gathered people grabbed something to keep from falling over, but I easily maintained my balance. As we rose, the ramp retracted, and the cargo bay closed soon after. Before long, the bay was sealed, and the inertial dampeners had engaged. They were a necessity, especially in Earth's atmosphere. Without them, we'd all have to be strapped in.

"Waited as long as I could," Patrick said over our Secure Connection. "If they try to pull anything, I'll disengage the dampeners. Should give you an advantage."

"Understood," I said. That was the first—and probably most important—part of our contingency plan. If it came down to it, I trusted my [Acrobatics] skill to give me an edge. Even so, the moment I'd stepped into the cargo bay, I'd activated Multishot and selected my targets. Askar would get the original round. Then Rex. Avery. Isaac. Finally, Paulo. After that, I'd deal with the laborers. It split my concentration a half dozen different ways, but with my Mind attribute as high as it was, I could handle it.

I still didn't draw my weapon, though. I wouldn't, so long as they played nice. Once any of them stepped out of line, I'd do what I had to do, even if I regretted the necessity.

"So," I said, stepping up to the big crate. It was a good foot and a half taller than I was, and it was at least as big as a cargo truck. I slapped my hand against the metal exterior, asking, "This is what all the fuss was about, right? What's in it?"

"That's not your concern," said Askar, finally turning to look at me. He looked angry and annoyed. "Tell your pilot to open the cockpit. He has no idea where we're going."

"No."

"What?"

"You heard me," I said, resting my hand on my pistol's grip. I knew I could draw it in less than an instant, and so long as I got one shot off, everyone in that cargo bay would be dead. I saw the crowd of laborers out of the corner of my eye and amended that to everyone that mattered. "Tell me what's in the box."

"Or?"

I sighed. "Or I'll get angry. I might kill everyone in here," I said. "Or I might just accept it as none of my business. I haven't decided yet. But what I do know is that every piece of intelligence you provided was wrong, and without me, every last person in this ship would already be dead."

"So, you think we owe you?" asked Askar.

"I think I deserve to know why your threat assessment was so horribly wrong. You underestimated your enemies at every turn," I said. "First, if you'd sent Avery into that compound, she would have died. Full stop. I don't care what skills she has. If it pushed me even a little bit, she would've ended up as a bloody splatter on the wall."

"I disagree," he growled. I could hear his teeth grinding in frustration. Or anger, maybe.

"It's not an opinion," I stated. "It's fact. The same with the train. Those combat bots? Yeah—you and your merry band of amateurs might've taken a few of them out, but the whole horde? And that's saying nothing about the drones. Again, without me there to pull you out of the fire, dead."

Before he could object, I went on, "And then the convoy is guarded by the most advanced bot I've ever seen. If I hadn't pulled its specs from the security terminal back in that satellite compound, even I would've ended up dead. None of you would have stood even the slightest chance. So . . . Invader. Tell me what the hell is going on."

"Just show her," growled Isaac.

"What?" barked Askar.

"You've seen what she can do," the injured man stated. "If you push her, she'll kill every single person in this ship. Easily."

"Not before I—"

"And we'll all still be dead!" Isaac spat, slapping his hand against the floor. The movement cost him, though, and after a second, he doubled over in a coughing fit. I'd had internal injuries before, so I knew just how unpleasant that could be. A moment later, he croaked, "Just tell her. Or I will."

Askar looked as if he was going to argue, but then he glanced at Avery. It was just a moment, and then his eyes were back on me, but it was enough that I knew precisely what he was thinking. I didn't know their relationship, but I did know that he cared about the girl. He was probably willing to roll the dice and risk his own life. Most of his crew, too. But Avery? He couldn't stomach that.

The fire drained from his expression, and his shoulders sagged. "Very well. You want to know? Then know you shall. But I warn you right now that you'll regret it," he stated.

"In my experience, knowing is always better than ignorance" was my response.

He gave a slight shrug, then descended the steps. His footfalls clanged against the corrugated metal, loud in the mostly empty space. Everyone else was silent, save for Isaac, whose breathing had become labored. My Triage ability told me that unless he was treated soon, he would almost assuredly die.

To keep my eye on him, I circled as Askar approached the container in the center of the hold. He didn't seem to notice. Or he was just too stupid to care. Instead, he stepped up to a security terminal on the crate, retrieved his own personal link, and jacked into the terminal. For about thirty seconds, nothing happened, but then, the crate trembled. A second later, the metal sides began to retract, folding into the four corners and revealing a glass case.

Inside was the most adorable child I'd ever seen.

"What the fuck?" I breathed.

"That is the granddaughter of Duke Arbolex of the Dengyt Confederation," Askar said. When I clearly didn't understand what that meant, he went on, "Arbolex is the second in line for the Dengyt throne, which means that if his brother were to die, he would rule an entire solar system of habitable planets."

"Pick, we've got a huge problem," I silently said through the Secure Connection.

"What happened?"

"I don't know yet, but Askar might have just put the biggest target in existence on our backs," I answered.

Meanwhile, Askar continued, "The Dengyts aren't just some backwater frontier power, either. They are a core system."

"And you chose to kidnap the ruler's granddaughter? Why? More importantly, why the hell is someone like her on Earth?" I demanded.

"It's a long story."

"I'm not going anywhere," I said. "And neither is anyone else. Not until I know what the hell you dragged me into. So, get to talking."

He sighed. "I haven't been completely honest with you," Askar said.

"There's a shocker," I muttered.

"I didn't choose this world by chance. Instead, I chose it because I knew the Dengyts would come here," he said. "I've been targeting them since the very beginning. More precisely, I was waiting for this very situation. The child is the daughter of Duke Arbolex's second son, who was sent here to oversee their operation. He's dead now."

"In the convoy?"

"No. A month ago. He had an accident," Askar said. "The little girl, who was born here on Earth, was on her way to the closest Bazaar access point, which was the first step in her journey back to the rest of her family."

I nodded. "I'm guessing you engineered all of this?"

"I did. I ensured that the gnome was surrounded with beautiful females, and once he finally got one pregnant, I kicked off my plan," he explained.

"Why? What do you hope to gain?"

"I intend to ransom the girl back to her family, of course," Askar said. "No—I don't want credits. I want authorization to settle in the core."

"I assume you'll be taking your . . . daughter with you?" I could tell by his change of expression that I'd gotten it right. "Right. I get it now. Do a bad thing to an innocent child so you can ensure that your own kid has a better life, right?"

"Mira," Patrick said. "My long-range sensors are picking up multiple ships. Evasion has failed. What do you want to do?"

"Shit!" I spat. I knew what I had to do. Before any of them could respond to my outburst, I said, "Look. You've got two options here. One ends up with you dead. The other doesn't. I'm good either way, but I'll admit that I don't want to kill the girl."

"Hey! What 'bout me?!" Rex demanded. "I thought we had a connection, you and me."

"Fine. I don't want to kill the cowboy, either," I admitted. I nodded toward the group of men and women in coveralls, adding, "Them, either. You and Isaac I'm fine with putting down, though."

I hadn't mentioned Paulo, but I didn't feel one way or another about him, so I didn't much care about the omission.

"And what determines the outcome?" asked Askar.

"You. I'm going to take the gnome girl," I said. "Chances are she's got a tracker on her, so there are two ships following our every move. We're not getting away from them. And even if we do, I'm pretty sure this ultrapowerful Duke What's His Name has enough gnomepower to send more. Our only option is to give her back."

"What? No!" Askar shouted, and I nearly shot him right then and there. "I've spent decades putting this together. I won't let you—"

I yanked Ferdinand II from his holster and shot him between the eyes. The entry wound was a neat hole that only leaked a little blood, but the exit was a different story altogether. Skull, brains, and blood exploded from the back of his head, and a second later, he fell.

But nobody else got hit because I'd canceled Multishot at the last second.

Even as Askar crumpled to the ground, I raised my voice and said, "Not a debate, people. Be happy I'm not killing the rest of you. So, here's the deal—I'm going to take the girl away on my own. Patrick is going to drop you all off somewhere reasonably safe. And then, we'll never see one another again, okay?"

"What 'bout the loot?"

"Take half," I said. "No more, no less. And if those circuits aren't here, I'll hunt each and every one of you down and kill you. Slowly. Got it?"

I didn't get any more argument from the crew. So, I told Patrick what was going on, and predictably, he objected to me going off on my own. "I can get away from them, Mira!" he argued. "Just—"

"I know you can," I said. "But this problem isn't going away. I can almost guarantee that if we keep this girl, we'll end up being hunted from one end of the planet to the next. Our only option is to give her back."

"And how do you plan on surviving the handoff?" he asked.

"I don't know yet. I'll figure it out when I get . . . Wait, what's the name of the nearest town with Bazaar access?"

"New Cairo," he said. "Two hundred miles or so northeast. You'll see it from a good ways away. Apparently, they have pyramids."

"Pyramids? What kind?"

"Big ones. It's, like, their whole thing," he said.

"We know anyone in the area?" I asked.

"Yeah, but you're not going to like it," Patrick answered. "You remember Vanna and Simon?"

"Ugh."

I definitely remembered the pair. They'd handled different parts of my training back in Mobile, so I didn't really consider them hostile. However, the last time I'd seen them had been during the year after Nova's fall, and I had not acquitted myself well. They'd tried to help me, but I've always had a bit of a stubborn streak, so it didn't really end the way anyone wanted it to.

"You want me to contact them?" asked Patrick. He'd seen them more recently, and apparently, they'd known his stepfather, Remy. So, that reunion had gone much better than my own meeting with them.

"No. Where can I find them?"

"They own a club," he said. "Called the Palace. I don't know anything else."

I sighed. "Fine. I'll figure it out."

With that, I turned to the stunned onlookers and said, "Alright. If anybody has any objections to what I just did, speak now. If you try anything after I'm gone, just know that *The Leviathan*'s security system is capable of killing each and every one of you. The only reason Patrick hasn't already done it is because I didn't want to spend the Rift Shards to power the system. But he's not quite as frugal as I am."

It was a lie. The ship didn't really have any internal security, aside from a few cameras throughout the ship. But they didn't need to know that.

Rex said, "We'll behave."

That's when I noticed that Isaac had bled out. He hadn't even uttered a death rattle. I glanced toward Avery and saw that she was shaking. I had just killed her father, so I guess it was understandable. For a moment, we locked eyes, and I saw that she was weeping. Suddenly, she stepped forward, her arms out wide, and the movement surprised me so thoroughly that I didn't even react when she wrapped them around me in a tight hug.

"Thank you," she muttered, burying her head against my chest. "He . . . He did . . . things . . . I don't . . . I didn't know how I was going to get away. But . . . T-thank you . . ."

She continued to sob as I connected the dots. As I did, my stomach churned. I didn't know the details, but then again, I didn't need to. Whatever he'd done, whatever abuses he'd subjected the girl to, it had been a horrible experience. That was enough to assuage any guilt I might have felt. My only regret was that I couldn't kill him again, and more slowly.

"You're welcome," I managed to say before pushing her away.

Then, without another word, I retrieved my personal link from the Hand of God, then headed over to the cubicle's security terminal and jacked in. In only a few seconds, the glass—or whatever clear material comprised the container— slid aside with a puff of air. The girl, who was the size of a toddler but with more maturity in her eyes, glared at me.

She immediately started crying.

I sighed and rolled my eyes. "I really don't want to do this," I muttered.

CHAPTER SEVENTEEN

PYRAMIDS ON THE HORIZON

Shoot first, ask questions later. That's Mira's motto. I don't know if she got it from her uncle or if it's the result of a mountain of experience, but I sometimes wish she'd just stop and think things through. Of course, her general policy has saved my life more times than I can count, so maybe I'm the one who needs to change.

—Patrick Ward

Look," I said, locking my eyes on the little girl. Because of her diminutive size, I had no real context for how old she was. If she'd been human, I might've pegged her as three or four years old, but because she was a gnome, my perception was probably a little skewed. I just hoped she was old enough to understand logic. I knelt in front of her, continuing in as calm of a voice as I could muster, "I'm going to take you home, okay? I'm here to . . . uh . . . rescue you from the bad guys."

"Y-you are?" she sobbed, fixing me with a wide-eyed gaze. The little girl sniffed loudly, then wiped her nose on her sleeve. Maybe she really was just as young as she looked. Who knew how Dengyts aged? The girl looked around at the other people, then her gaze found Askar's dead body, and the sobbing intensified.

Suppressing an eye roll—why did I have to deal with an annoying little kid?—I hooked my hands under her armpits and picked the sobbing mess of gnomehood up. That proved to be a mistake because she immediately stabbed me in the shoulder. The blade only got a quarter of an inch before it hit my subdermal armor, but the fact that it had gotten that far—through my infiltration suit, no less—was surprising enough that I let out a yelp.

I pushed her to arm's length only to see a snarling face that held none of the innocence of a moment before. In her flailing and tiny fist was a dagger that looked more like an ice pick. It sizzled with Mist, telling me that it was no mundane blade.

"What the hell?!" I spat, resisting the urge to toss her across the cargo bay.

She screeched again and tried to stab my forearm. That was far as her reach would allow. Otherwise, she might've attacked my face. Now that I was on guard, I was able to twist just enough to send the blade skittering off my infiltration suit's armored surface, but she was undeterred, aiming another attack at whatever piece of me she could find.

I wasn't in the mood to endure any longer, so I quickly shifted so that my grip found her upper arm. Then, I slammed my palm into her throat and latched on. Releasing my other hand, I grabbed her wrist and twisted. The dagger clattered to the ground.

I growled, "If you'd stop trying to kill me for just one second—"

She screamed like a wild animal and tried to claw at my arm. Her efforts were ineffectual, but they were more than a little annoying. Besides, we didn't have time for the little girl to throw a tantrum.

With an annoyed sigh, I said, "If you don't stop, I'm going to knock you out. It won't really hurt that much—not until you wake up. But when you do, your interface will be completely inert for at least a day. Maybe longer if it's poor quality."

She didn't give an answer—or at least not one I could interpret as anything but a feral scream—so I shrugged and used Misthack to infiltrate her system. I found it odd that a little girl would have an interface at all, which suggested that she was older than she looked, but I quickly discovered that she had a Nexus Implant, too. So, unless the Dengyts did things differently than everyone else, she was technically an adult.

Which made me feel a lot better about what I was about to do.

Her interface was more complex than average, and her defenses were stouter than what I usually encountered, but I still tore through them with frightening speed. My constant training, it seemed, had borne fruit. After only a few seconds, the last node fell, and I was able to upload a Ghost I'd fittingly named *Knockout*. It only had one purpose, but it did it extremely well, knocking the victim unconscious for a period of time that varied based on Constitution. So long as the subject had less than a hundred attribute points in the category, they'd be out for about a day. Over that, and the duration rapidly decreased. If I used the Ghost on someone with attributes similar to my own, it wouldn't last more than a few seconds.

Still, judging by everything I'd seen, the little girl would be out for quite some time.

I used the Ghost, and after only a few seconds, she went entirely limp.

"What did you do?" asked Avery, a bit of surprise and horror in her voice.

"Just knocked her out. She'll be fine."

"How, though?"

That's when I realized how it must have looked. To them, I'd only stared at the girl for a few seconds before she fell unconscious. It must've appeared like magic.

"A girl's gotta have her secrets," I said. Then, I looked the others over before my gaze settled on Rex, and I asked, "Any other questions before I go? No? Okay, then. Hopefully, we'll never see one another again."

With that, I threw the little girl over my shoulder and walked toward the opening cargo bay. Once there, I summoned my Cutter, mounted up with the Dengyt girl draped over the fuselage in front of me, and sped off. Before I'd gone even a dozen feet, *The Leviathan* lifted off, and within a few seconds, it had started moving in the opposite direction. Soon enough, it disappeared over the horizon as I sped toward New Cairo.

After a few minutes, during which I hit a dry riverbed that was straight and flat enough that I could push the Cutter to top speed, Patrick's voice came over the Secure Connection. "They changed direction," he stated. "It looks like they're coming for you."

I resisted the urge to swear. I'd expected that they were tracking the Dengyt girl somehow, but I'd hoped that it was tied to the container in which she'd been traveling. To combat that, Patrick was going to dump the box over the ocean. But it looked like that strategy would do little good.

"Guess the tracker's in the girl," I said. "I'll lose them in New Cairo."

"You sure?" asked Patrick. I could hear the other unspoken question in his tone. I could just dump the girl in the desert and get away. However, I suspected that if I didn't smooth things over, the Dengyts would continue to pursue the people stupid enough to have stolen the granddaughter of one of their leaders. It would be infinitely better to frame myself as a rescuer.

And if that failed to do the trick, I had no issues with going full scorched-earth on the gnomes. I'd done it before, and I wouldn't lose a bit of sleep if I had to do it again. Still, that was definitely not plan A, if only because I'd gotten a glimpse of their combat capabilities, and I really wasn't sure if I could kill them off without incurring massive collateral damage.

Or ending up dead myself.

"Yeah. I'm sure," I said.

Then, I continued on my way, tearing through the desert at speeds that would have been impossible without the increased reflexes I'd gained via my inflated Mind attribute. I'd seen fighters who'd ignored that attribute, focusing instead on their bodies. Doing so had hamstrung their progress because their brains simply couldn't handle their physical potential, except in short bursts.

Some had chosen to shore up that weakness via various cybernetic enhancements to their minds, but even that strategy had its limits. I preferred the more natural approach. Sure, I loved my Hand of God and subdermal armor, but I wasn't completely useless without them, either. A few times, I'd been forced to do without, and though it was uncomfortable, I could make it work.

Most serious warriors couldn't say as much.

After a couple of hours' worth of speeding across the desert, I saw a river glittering on the horizon. It flowed northward, and because of my map, I knew that it would lead me to my destination. As I approached the bank, flora began to appear, and with every few hundred yards, it grew thicker until it became a veritable jungle of vegetation.

I continued north, passing various crumbling ruins and some wildlife that never had a chance to react to the speed of my passage. As the sun began to set, Patrick announced that he'd hit the ocean and dumped the crates; apparently, Avery, Rex, and their nameless henchmen had been busy unloading and sorting the stolen goods. The fact that they hadn't found any obvious trackers put my mind at ease.

I wasn't exactly happy with being tracked, but it was better me than Patrick and *The Leviathan.*

Just before the sun set, I got my first view of New Cairo.

And it was breathtaking.

Huge pyramids reached for the sky, glittering in the dying sunlight. At first, I wasn't sure of their construction, but as I drew closer, I realized that they were built entirely from gleaming metal and reflective glass. There were other, much smaller pyramids nearby—three of them, in fact—but these were clearly far older and made of stone. They made even the ruins I'd already passed look new, which was impressive enough all on its own. Not only had those stone pyramids survived the Initialization, but it looked as if they'd managed to endure thousands of years before that.

Not for the first time, I realized that humanity was far more complex than I knew, and I found myself wondering just how much history and culture we had lost when the Mist descended upon the Earth. In a lot of ways, it was a depressing thought, but in others, it filled me with hope. If even ancient humans could build something as impressive as those pyramids, even before all the technology that came with our inclusion in a wider universe, then we were capable of just about anything.

Even resisting the incoming invasion.

Or at least, I hoped that was true. My uncle hadn't believed it, but then again, he'd always been a pessimist. Most of the time, I was, too, but I wanted to be better. I wanted to be different. I wanted to hope, to believe in the human spirit. I just hadn't seen much evidence to support that faith in humanity.

I slowed a little, mostly because it probably wasn't a great idea to try to get into the city at full speed, especially given that explaining the presence of the childlike Dengyt in front of me was going to be a bit tricky. As I cruised through the area, I saw a few of the residents. Some were out on the river, where they were fishing; most had deployed some buoys nearby. I'd seen their like before, and I knew that they would agitate the Mist to warn large predators off. They weren't perfect, and they tended to make fishing a bit more difficult—after all, many of the smaller fish were frightened away, too—but it was a necessity for any fisherman.

The people themselves were predominantly dark of skin, with thick, curly hair much like my own. However, there were plenty of other ethnicities apparent, as well. Most were fisherman, but there were people gathering fruit from the vast orchards on the other side of the river, too. I expected that somewhere nearby, there were farms where they grew grain and corn. A city the size of New Cairo couldn't survive without it, regardless of how many fish they managed to catch.

Slowly, I made my way across the terrain until I found a wide gravel path that looked like it would lead me to the city. Once there, I was forced to slow even further by the flow of pedestrians, hover bikes, and other vehicles. Like everywhere else in the world, the people were eager to return to the city before nightfall.

Because I was getting quite a few covetous looks, I dismissed the Cutter and threw the Dengyt girl over my shoulder. Then, I started jogging ahead, weaving through the traffic for a couple of miles until I finally reached the city gate. It was a massive thing, set in the center of a giant concrete wall that must have been at least a hundred feet tall. I saw the telltale shimmer of a Mist shield dancing along its surface, and there were turrets—not the automated kind, either, but rather the sort that required operators—every fifteen yards or so. I had never encountered their specific kind of gun, but I could recognize quality when I saw it. Finally, patrols with a mixture of combat bots, drones, and human guards walked along the top of the wall.

It was a fortress.

But it was one I needed to infiltrate. So, I found the line for entry into the city and waited a few minutes until it was my turn. When it came, I stepped forward and smiled at the bored-looking guard. He was wearing a deep-purple uniform trimmed in gold, and he wielded a sleek assault rifle that looked as if it probably packed a pretty good punch. If I'd had to guess based on the feeling I got from him, I'd have put him at around Tier 4, and with a little Mist accumulation to back it up. A dangerous opponent, and he was only a random guard? New Cairo definitely took its security seriously.

The man looked me up and down, then asked, "Not from around here, are you?"

He'd clearly spoken another language, but my Universal Language ability had saved me from an awkward situation by translating his words in real time. So, I said, "No. Just visiting some friends."

"With a little girl?" he asked, nodding to the unconscious Dengyt. Thankfully, he hadn't looked too closely, or he'd have seen her slightly too-large eyes and pointed ears.

I shrugged my unencumbered shoulder, saying, "She got a headache, so I gave her a med-hypo. She passed out straight away, so I've been carrying her ever since."

He poked her back, and she stirred slightly before saying, "She's not contagious, is she?"

"Just a headache," I assured him. To drive it home, I used Charmisa. I saw it take hold immediately, and his eyes went slightly glassy before he nodded.

"Okay. Sounds plausible. Who're you here to see?" he asked.

"Old friends," I said, using Charisma again. I had no intention of telling him any more than that, and if it came down to it, I'd knock him out the same way I'd disabled the girl. Then, I would sprint through the gate and disappear once I reached the other side. With Mimic, Stealth, and Camouflage, they'd never find me.

He blinked, and for a moment, I thought he was going to resist the effects of Charisma. Some people could, but only if they'd worked on raising their Mind and Mist attributes. Clearly, this guard had, which spoke well for his competence. But in the end, whatever resistance he'd managed melted away, and he nodded again.

"Alright. Carry on, then," he said, waving us through.

I didn't hesitate to do just that, and I hurried through the gate. As I passed through the gap in the wall, I couldn't help but notice just how thick it was. It was almost thirty seconds before I found the other side. Thankfully, it was just in time, too, because through Observation, I noticed that someone—a supervisor, perhaps—had taken issue with how the guard had done his job, and she was berating him for it.

Before she could chase me down, I ducked out from the passage and into New Cairo.

In a lot of ways, it was a city like any other. But even the small glimpse I'd managed was enough to tell me it had a flavor all its own. Because there were pyramids everywhere. Sure, there were the massive ones I had seen from a distance, but there were only a dozen of those sprawling creations. Between them were smaller pyramids. Some were the size of single-family dwellings, but others were quite a bit larger than that, too. For someone who'd grown up in Nova City, where all the buildings were rectangular, it was a bit jarring.

But I regained my wits quickly enough that I managed to duck into an alley, where I embraced Mimic, changing my face to one of my standbys—a Tier 2 dark-skinned woman with long, flowing braids—and used Stealth. Camouflage came next, and finally, I deployed a tiny holographic display that I hoped would hide me from the authorities.

A moment after I'd finished my preparations, the objecting guard appeared at the head of the alley. She took a moment to scan the area before moving on. Still, I chose to wait another twenty minutes before I gathered my holographic display, returning it to my arsenal implant before boldly striding out of the alley.

I was ready to fight a battle, but thankfully, nobody was there. I'd made it inside. Now, I just had to find Vanna's bar. Hopefully, she could help me get my bearings so I could set up a safe house. If not, my meeting with my Dengyt pursuers would probably be very unpleasant.

And from what I'd seen so far, I liked New Cairo. Its architecture was weird, but it seemed peaceful enough. It would certainly be a shame if I had to start blowing stuff up.

BURNED BRIDGES

I want to see the stars. Right after my mom died, I would spend hours just lying atop The Jitterbug *and looking up at the night sky. If I could have, I would've gone right then. No looking back. No regrets. Just me and the heavens.*

—Patrick Ward

I walked through the open-air market, cradling the Dengyt girl in my arms. As I did, I studied my surroundings. In a lot of ways, New Cairo reminded me of a hundred other cities I'd visited. The architecture, which tended toward the almighty pyramid, was certainly unique, but the market stalls were no different than those in parts of Nova City. Or Mobile. Both of which brought back memories I didn't really want to confront.

Aside from stopping a few times to peruse goods—just like every other shopper within the market—I didn't linger, and after finding the location of my intended destination on the local intranet, I made my way to the Palace.

When Patrick had first mentioned it, I'd expected that it would be a bar like any other. And given the nature of the proprietors, I thought I knew what I'd find when I finally reached my destination. And in a lot of ways, it was exactly what I'd anticipated. Despite her job as an infiltrator, Vanna had never been much for lying low. Simon, her partner, was the opposite, but he tended to follow her lead.

So, when I looked upon the Palace, I just shook my head in resigned expectation. It was a grand, asymmetrical building with an elongated, conical tower on one side. Every inch of the building looked like it had been carved in minute detail. Unlike most of the buildings within the city, it was obviously very old and had clearly existed well before the Initialization.

And it was bright purple trimmed in gold.

I sighed as I beheld the sign labeling it as my destination, then joined the lengthy line of people waiting to get in. As I did so, I listened to the thumping music emanating from the Palace's interior while I looked around at the would-be patrons. Each of them was dressed for a night out, which meant most were wearing tight, revealing clothing and copious jewelry. That also meant that I stood out like a sore thumb.

So, when I finally reached the front of the line and encountered the door-man—a big, beefy fellow who probably appeared a lot stronger than he really was—he looked me up and down and shook his head before saying, "Not a place for kids, lady. Move on along."

"It'll be fine," I said, using Charisma. I hated relying on the ability so much, but I had neither the time nor the interest to get into the building the normal way. My choice was a mistake.

The moment I used the ability, his eyes flared with red light, and I belatedly realized that they were cybernetic. More, Charisma clearly hadn't worked because he immediately pulled a pistol from his hip and pointed it in my direction. I shamelessly shifted the gnome girl to block any potential shot.

But thankfully, it never came. Instead, the doorman kept his cool and growled, "You could get arrested for using an ability like that."

"Wouldn't be the first time," I muttered. Indeed, during my darker months, I'd often been so inebriated that I'd made some truly terrible choices that had ended up with me in various jail cells. Of course, the moment I'd sobered up, I always escaped, but still—I didn't relish the opportunity to sample whatever incarceration New Cairo had to offer.

"Seriously, lady," he said, a bit of a plea in his voice. "Just go. Nobody here wants trouble."

That was more than reasonable. I knew it. He knew it. And given that he had a gun pointed at an unarmed woman who was carrying a child, he could probably sense that the crowd wouldn't approve of violence. He was between a rock and a hard place, and he just wanted to deescalate the situation.

So did I, if I was honest. If I hadn't been so off-balance from the fight against the FACS and the subsequent discovery that Askar's whole plan had been to kidnap a child, I probably would have come at the problem a little differently. It wasn't as if I didn't have the capacity to sneak in. It was a mistake I should have been well past making, and I mentally berated myself to be better.

Not the first time. Certainly not the last, either. I always wanted to improve, to make better choices, but in the heat of the moment, I tended toward my go-to strategy, which was to simply steamroll anyone in my way. Eventually, that would end up getting me killed, I was certain.

But knowing what you need to do to improve yourself was very different than actually putting those plans into action. I was only human, after all, and a particularly stubborn brand at that. Couple that with the power to keep my bad decisions from having lasting personal consequences like death, and it wasn't really surprising that I'd be a little set in my self-destructive ways.

Still, I managed to rein in my immediate impulses and said, "Vanna and Simon are old friends. They'll want to see me."

"Sure, sure. Let me just run along and get them," he deadpanned. "I'll—"

Once again shaking my head, I enabled the Ghost I'd uploaded the moment he'd pulled a gun on me. It was a testament to my training that I could infiltrate his system and launch a Ghost while having a conversation. Even as I patted myself on the back, he dropped unconscious. A few members of the nearby crowd gasped in surprise, but I paid them no mind as I stepped through the garishly painted building's massive front door.

Immediately, the overwhelming volume of the music washed over me, and I was forced to let Observation drop. What I wouldn't have given to be able to selectively enhance my senses as opposed to doing it all at the same time, but with my current skill set, that just wasn't possible.

I shouldered my way through the crowd, using my inflated Constitution to make a path. That strategy didn't come without consequences, and I got more than a few angry glares, but I had no interest in weaving my way through the mass of people. If they had a problem, they'd end up just like the doorman.

Eventually, I reached the main dance floor, but as I looked around, I saw no indication as to where I might find Simon of Vanna. The place was just too big, and I'd only visited a small portion of the first floor. No—if I was going to find them in any reasonable amount of time, I'd need help.

So, I made my way to the bar, where I was greeted by a pretty, dark-skinned girl with close-cut hair and a winning smile.

"What can I get you?" she asked, her eyes slipping from my face to the still-unconscious gnome. "And . . . Uh . . . We usually don't get kids in here . . ."

"Unavoidable," I said, shifting my burden a bit. "I'm here to see Vanna. Or Simon. It's important."

"Um . . ."

I felt a hand on my shoulder, and a polite voice said from behind me, "I'm going to need you to come with me, miss. Please don't make a scene. And don't try to resist. It won't go well for you."

"I don't know. It usually works out," I said, reengaging Observation. A wall of noise crashed into me, but I gritted my teeth and endured. More, I looked past it. Past the fog of odors wafting off the densely packed crowd. Past the seizure-inducing lights. And past the body heat of so many people.

Firearms have a very distinct smell. Most people don't know it, but it's there if you're looking for it. So, once I divorced myself from the tidal wave of sensory input that came with reactivating Observation, I could easily tell that there were no less than seven guns pointing in my direction. More, I could sense that each of my would-be assailants was equipped with a decently strong Mistwall. I could get through any one of them, but it would take precious time I didn't have.

I endured the unmistakable feeling of a gun barrel pressing against my back. "This time, it won't."

"You keep going like that, and I'm going to kill everyone in this building," I said calmly.

"You think you can do that?"

"It wouldn't be the first time," I stated, and without a hint of emotion. Three years before, I'd killed thousands of people with a single Ghost. And I'd gotten a lot stronger since then. If I really wanted to, I could bring the entirety of New Cairo down in the space of a few days.

"If you don't—"

"Look—just take me to your boss, okay?" I said, still looking at the pretty bartender. "That's all I want. Just let me see Simon or Vanna and nobody here has to get hurt."

"Is that a threat?" he asked.

"It definitely is," I answered with finality.

A few seconds passed, and I readied myself for a fight. I didn't have time to Misthack into their systems, but that didn't mean I was defenseless. My weapons were only a thought away, and I kept Teleport primed. Getting out of their line of fire would end the fight before it even started. Or so I hoped. If it came down to a prolonged battle, the body count would climb to an unacceptable number.

I couldn't imagine my old instructors would appreciate it if I murdered their clientele, after all.

"Fine."

"What?" I asked, surprised that he would see reason.

"I said it was fine" was the man's response. I still hadn't lain eyes on him, but his voice was pleasant enough. "I don't get paid enough to deal with this. Let Simon work it out. But if he doesn't know you . . . Well, let's just say you won't be anyone's problem anymore."

"Fair enough," I said, finally turning around. The man was not what I'd expected. For one, he was even shorter than me by a couple of inches, and his weight wasn't any more impressive. Finally, half of his face looked like melted wax. A curiosity, given the availability of decent-quality Realskin.

He seemed to notice my look and raised a hand to his face before cocking a half smile as he said, "Like it?"

"What happened?"

"I picked the wrong fight," he said. "It's a reminder to never repeat that mistake."

"I have a couple of those," I said, knowing precisely what he meant. I had a few scars myself, though I clearly hadn't taken the same lessons he had. Instead of prompting me to make better choices, my scars pushed me to keep training so that I would be strong enough to avoid getting more.

He responded with a grunt, likely because, in the realm of scars, he was the clear winner. To move on, I asked, "What's your name?"

"Husani," he said. Then, he chuckled. "Means 'handsome boy.' Used to be it wasn't so ironic. Come on, then. Let's get this over with. Hope I don't end up having to kill you."

With that, he led me along the outskirts of the dance floor. For their part, the club's patrons had no idea how close they'd come to being killed. As they danced in blissful ignorance, I followed Husani to a pair of doors that, in turn, led us to a stairwell. We climbed the narrow steps—Husani in front, his silent but probably deadly colleagues bringing up the rear, and with me in the middle—for a few floors until we left the stairwell behind. A short time later, we stopped in front of an unassuming door.

"Go on in," Husani said. "He's expecting you."

That wasn't surprising. Simon might've looked like an unintelligent thug, but he wasn't stupid. He'd probably known I was in the building before Husani had confronted me. But I felt certain that he had no idea who I was.

"Thanks for the escort," I said with a cocky grin. It felt a bit silly, given that, at that very moment, I probably had a few dozen Dengyt warriors homing in on my location. Times were desperate, and they were growing more so by the moment. So, without a minute to spare, I opened the door and strode inside.

Predictably, Simon, who was sitting behind a desk, was not alone. Vanna leaned against one wall, looking like she didn't have a single care in the world. I knew better than to accept her languid outward appearance as anything but a disguise. She was a capable infiltrator who saw far more than she let on.

"Simon," I said as Husani pulled the door shut behind me. I could feel the Mist swirling all around, heralding the pair's predictably stout defenses. I didn't know what form they might take, but I would have been a fool to underestimate them. I glanced at Vanna, greeting her, "Vanna. Nice to see you again after so long."

"Funny," she said, pushing herself from the wall. "I don't seem to recall ever meeting you. Guess you just didn't warrant notice."

I resisted the urge to roll my eyes. I didn't dislike Vanna. The opposite, really. During my training, we'd gotten along fairly well. However, I'd ruined that good relationship when I'd made a few mistakes during our last meeting. That said, I'd always found her demeanor a bit grating—especially when she wanted to seem more capable than she really was.

"Who are you, and what do you want? And for God's sake, why the hell would you bring a child into a place like this?" asked Simon.

"First of all, she's not a child," I said, gently placing the gnome on a nearby chair. "Second, I'm shocked you don't remember me."

I let Mimic fall away.

The results were predictable.

Vanna's eyes widened, and then a second later, she launched herself at me. I let her tackle me to the ground, but when she tried to bring her fingernails—claws, really—to bear, I clamped my hands around her wrists and grunted, "Nice to see you, too, Vanna. How have you been?"

She let out a wordless snarl, but she didn't get the chance to do anything else before her partner grabbed her around the middle and yanked her away. She tried to kick me as he pulled her free, and even when it was clear she had no chance of escaping his grip, she continued to struggle, spitting a hundred curses with every passing moment.

As I pushed myself up, Simon clamped his arms around Vanna in a tight bear hug. I said, "Simon. I see you're still the clearheaded one."

"Shut up, Mira," he said in an even tone. "Or I'll let her go."

"You do that, and I might have to stop her myself," I said. "This is me being diplomatic. You don't want the other way."

"That's how it always is with you, isn't it? My way or the highway, huh?"

"You know another way?"

"You could try, I don't know, thinking of how your choices affect other people for once?" he suggested. By that point, Vanna had stopped struggling. However, she hadn't stopped glaring daggers at me.

"Tried that a few times," I said, climbing back to my feet. I feigned dusting myself off. "Didn't work out. People got killed."

That wasn't really true. Everything I'd ever done, I had done for me. Or for my uncle, but even that was selfish. Although Simon and Vanna knew some of the things I had done, they had no way to know my entire history. Besides, it was better than admitting that I was just as selfish as the rest of the world. Maybe more so.

"Let me go," Vanna said, her voice icy. "I won't kill her. Yet."

Simon obviously knew better than to keep her restrained. I had no idea what kind of relationship they had—maybe she liked that kind of thing—but there was nothing about her tone that suggested she'd be okay with any objections. So, he released her. And to my surprise, Vanna didn't resume her attack.

"What do you want?" she asked. "Going to blow up the building again?"

"That was one time," I said.

"Once is already too much."

She had a point. But then again, I hadn't technically set the bombs off that destroyed their last bar. Sure, I'd made them, but still—I wouldn't have been so careless as to detonate them in a friend's place of business.

Of course, I hadn't exactly been in my right mind back then—various combinations of drugs and alcohol could still cut through my Constitution; it just took quantities that would kill other people a hundred times over—so it was entirely possible that I'd actually lit the fuse.

"Look, I—"

"Do you have any idea what you put us through? We had to come halfway around the world to outrun the problems you caused," she said, pointing an accusing finger in my direction. I didn't like that one bit, but I kept my cool. "And we don't have some fancy ship to ferry us around, either. We had to go the hard way. Public trains. Those horrible ships that take a month to cross the ocean, and that's if they're lucky enough to not be attacked by some ungodly sea monster. Oh, and the fliers? They're even worse. But only a few months after we get set up here in New Cairo, you show up. Probably to destroy everything all over again."

"That's not why I'm here."

"Yeah? Does it matter? Wherever you go, bad shit follows."

Again, I couldn't really dispute her point. Sure, I'd been to plenty of cities and towns where I hadn't even been noticed, much less blown anything up. But as she'd said, once was enough to give me a certain reputation. That it had happened more than that meant she was right to not want me around.

That notion sparked a few fires I thought had been extinguished, but I smothered them before they could take hold. I had no interest in going down that road of self-loathing. Not again. I'd barely made it out last time, and I wasn't sure I could repeat that feat again.

"By all rights, I should put a few bullets in you and call it a day," Vanna said. Then, she sighed. "Maybe I would if I thought it would do any good. But God knows if I have anything that could penetrate that thick skull of yours."

"Why are you here, Mira?" asked Simon.

"Okay, so I need somewhere to lie low," I said. "Just for a couple of days. Somewhere clean."

"I assume you don't mean clean as in sanitary?" Vanna guessed.

"Right. That little girl's got a tracker on her," I said. "I can't disable it, either. So, I just need it blocked for a day or two. Probably less."

"Kidnapping?" asked Simon, frowning.

"Originally, yes," I answered. Then, I held up my hands. "It wasn't me, though. I'm the good guy here. I just want to give her back. I don't want there to be any misunderstandings that end up with me in the ground."

After that, I told them the full story. Both of them had participated in enough morally questionable activities that they didn't judge me for hijacking the train and participating in the heist. It could have just as easily been one of them. So, once I was finished, they agreed to help. For a fee.

"A hundred Rift Shards?" I muttered to myself as I stood in an elevator that would take us deep underground and into a bunker they'd set up for just such an occasion. Obviously, they couldn't have anticipated that they would need to hide from an army of gnomes, but they got into enough trouble that being untraceable had clear advantages. "Should've just killed the brat and moved on."

Neither Simon nor Vanna responded. After we finally reached the bunker—which turned out to be a fully furnished apartment—Vanna asked, "So, how do you intend to do this?"

I started to respond, but she cut me off by saying, "Without blowing everything up."

"I don't always do that," I mumbled. Then, I told them my plan. It wasn't complicated, but that was true of most of my ideas.

When I'd finished, they both agreed to stay out of the way while I set things up. That's when I woke the little girl up, and before she could speak, I said, "I need to know how to contact your guardians. My goal is to get you home safe, but before I do that, I need to make sure I don't end up dead just for being in the wrong place at the wrong time. So, spit it out."

That's when she started screaming unintelligibly, and she didn't stop until I knocked her out. "Guess we do this the hard way, then," I groaned.

CHAPTER NINETEEN

THE EXCHANGE

I've never had a normal life. Not really. Even when I was with Cy—brief though our relationship was—I was just looking for a way out. So, when Mira came back, I was more than ready to believe that she had turned a corner. Now, I wonder if I was just being optimistic. Had she come to terms with what happened in Nova? Or had she just buried her feelings beneath a new facade? She always was good at pretending to be other people. In fact, playing a role—whether it's the cocky mercenary or a regular person—is the only way she's ever really comfortable.

—Patrick Ward

How have you been?" asked Simon, sitting next to me as we waited for the call to come in. I'd already used Bastion, which meant that whatever tracker they'd implanted in the gnome child was useless. Her pursuers probably knew we were in New Cairo but nothing beyond that. And it wasn't as if they could just start asking questions, what with the quarantine and all. It was one thing to smuggle in a small force, but it was something else altogether to flaunt it in front of everyone. I wasn't sure exactly how censure worked—I never could get a good answer from my friends in the Bazaar—but the aliens seemed to prefer to stay under the radar. In any case, I felt confident that we wouldn't be found.

I glanced at Simon and answered, "Fine. You know, toppling alien operations and killing people who probably deserve it. The usual."

"Probably?" he asked.

I shrugged. "You can never be completely sure" was my answer. "But as far as I know, I haven't killed any good guys lately."

I'd long since abandoned the notion that I was one of those good guys. At best, my life was stranded in a morally gray abyss. Sure, I'd helped people. I'd saved a few lives, even. And I tried not to make evil choices. But nobody with a body count as high as the one that followed me around could ever truly be considered virtuous.

The best I could do was try to keep myself from sliding into the other end of that spectrum. I think I had been mostly successful, but every now and then, I slipped up. The problem was that it was so easy to be the bad guy. After all, who was there to stop me from taking what I wanted? From killing whoever crossed me? There were people out there that could stand up to someone with my power, but there weren't a lot of do-gooders among them.

It all came back to one simple tenet: People looked after themselves first, their friends second, and everyone else a distant third. And the existence of that last bit was questionable at best.

"Well, that's a start," he said with a good-natured smile. He knuckled his thick mustache, then took off his bowler hat. "What's taking her so long?"

Vanna had gone out to get the lay of the land, so to speak. I was reasonably certain that we wouldn't be found—not with Bastion running and whatever defenses Vanna and Simon had erected around their safe house—but it was always better to confirm that kind of thing with your own two eyes. And Vanna was more than capable of doing so without raising any suspicion. Not only was she a talented infiltrator, but she was a respected resident of the city. So, she was the natural choice to investigate the situation.

"Are you sure they got the message?" Simon asked.

"I'm sure," I said. I'd contacted Gala via Secure Connection, and the minotaur arms dealer had in turn contacted an intermediary she knew. That go-between had sent the Dengyts my terms. They were simple enough. Framing myself as a rescuer, I only wanted to give the girl back. In return, I wanted to avoid any reprisal.

Sure, I could've probably demanded a ransom, but I truly didn't want anything else from them. The Dengyts were smart enough to recognize that I'd probably had a hand in the kidnapping, but I hoped my cooperation would keep them from doing anything vindictive. If they took the other route, I would have to do some things I really didn't want to do.

Only an hour after making contact with Gala, she'd responded with the Dengyts' agreement to the exchange. Or handover, really. I wasn't getting anything back, after all. And now, we were just waiting. At least, Simon and I were. Vanna was out in New Cairo trying to gauge whether or not I'd have to murder a bunch of gnomes.

On the surface, I didn't so much mind taking out another alien settlement. They were invaders, just like any others. However, I wasn't so bloodthirsty as to completely ignore the threat such a mighty civilization might pose to my continued survival. Soon enough, the quarantine would lift, and when that happened, I didn't want to find myself on the wrong end of a galactic manhunt.

Of course, that might still happen regardless of how the gnome issue turned out. It wasn't as if I'd done a thorough background check on any of my previous victims.

"So, you and Vanna settling down for good here?" I asked.

He shrugged his heavy shoulders and leaned back. "I have no idea," he admitted. I'd always had a much easier rapport with him than with Vanna. "Maybe. Probably not, though."

"Why?"

"Other than old friends dumping a mess on our table?" he asked with a wide grin.

"We're old friends?" I countered.

"Something like that," he said with a sigh.

"But seriously—why not settle down? Seems like you have a good thing going," I said. And I meant it. The Palace was obviously successful, and from what I had seen, New Cairo wasn't such a bad place. Certainly, it was better than Nova had been. Of course, I hadn't seen enough to make a real assessment.

"We do, we do," he said. "But Vanna doesn't really like to sit still. She'll manage it for a bit, but then something will come up. And then . . . Well, things happen, and before I know it, we're headed to a new city."

"Sounds hard."

"You would know as well as I do," he said with a twinkle in his eye. "Like back in Chicago. We could've smoothed it over with the Capelli gang. Even with what you did—"

"That was an accident. And they were as much to blame as I was!"

"Maybe. But they're the ones who ended up with a destroyed warehouse," he said. "My point is that we could've probably figured out a way to make it work. But Vanna, she took it as an excuse to move on. That's who she is. Always looking at the next adventure. Always headed toward the horizon."

"Are you saying I'm the same way?"

Again, Simon shrugged. "If the shoe fits," he said.

Was that how he saw me? Sure, I'd never really tried to settle in anywhere, but that was because I'd never had the chance. The moment my uncle had given me a Tier 7 implant, my fate had been sealed. Or maybe the true decider had been when I'd learned that aliens would soon descend upon our planet and enslave us all. How could I live a normal life with that hanging over my head?

How could anyone?

Thankfully, Simon let the topic drop, and I spent the next hour or so mindlessly going through my old mental-training program. It wasn't a challenge, but it was a comforting way to pass the time. Or to avoid thinking about things I couldn't change.

Eventually, Vanna returned and, once she had settled in on one of the chairs, said, "Well, they're looking for you."

"More for the kid than me, I think," I responded.

"Same difference."

Then, she proceeded to outline an infestation of gnomes that had descended upon New Cairo. Most were cloaked in various holographic displays meant to conceal their identities behind facades of immaturity—more evidence of their advanced technology—but Vanna had seen through their disguises. According to her, they looked like children, but anyone with half a brain could recognize their adult mannerisms.

"It's actually a decent disguise," she went on. "Nobody really pays much attention to street kids, so they kind of fade into the background unless you're specifically looking for them."

Simon asked, "Where are they set up?"

"By the river," she said. "An old warehouse. It's swarming with bots now. Probably other defenses, too. And there are cloaked drones searching through the city."

I sighed. "I just want to give the girl back," I muttered. "Why is this so hard?"

"You poked the bear," Simon said. "They can't let it stand."

I hadn't told them everything, but I'd said enough to give them an idea of what had gone down. They knew the situation well enough that I could agree with Simon's assessment. In attacking that caravan, we'd thumbed our noses at an established power. By now, anyone who mattered probably knew about it. So, the Dingyts had no choice but to respond with at least a show of force. Otherwise, people might think they were vulnerable.

"Well, the handoff is still on," I said.

"And you're sure they'll just let you go?" Vanna asked.

"I don't really know," I admitted.

"Such confidence," she deadpanned.

"Vanna, stop. She's just trying to work with the hand she was dealt."

"A hand she chose."

"Be that as it may—"

"And you know we're going to have to move now," Vanna went on. "I've already talked to Eko about buying the Palace."

"You think that's strictly necessary?" Simon asked.

Vanna nodded at me, saying, "She might be an idiot sometimes, but if she's worried about them, then we should be, too."

"I'm not an idiot," I protested, though I instantly regretted it. As both of them fixed me with withering stares, I said, "Fine. Shutting up now."

The pair of them continued to go back and forth about the future, and for a moment, I actually felt a little guilty about dumping my issues on their doorstep. However, I soon remembered Simon's assertion about Vanna's inability to stay in one place. Likely, if it wasn't for my interference, she'd have found some other reason to abandon New Cairo.

Probably.

Still, I couldn't escape some feeling of responsibility.

Soon enough, I excused myself to go look in on the still-unconscious Dengyt child. She hadn't moved from the bed we'd given her, but that wasn't unexpected. Looking down on her tiny form, a different sort of guilt assailed my mind. Sure, I hadn't picked the target. I hadn't even known what Askar and the others intended to steal. But I couldn't disregard my own culpability in her kidnapping.

For a while, I just sat there watching her. Until, at last, my interface's alarm sounded, telling me that the time had come. Pushing extraneous thoughts out of my mind, I focused on what I needed to do. Gathering the girl in my arms, I marched back into the safe house's common area and announced, "It's time."

"You sure you don't need any more help from us?" asked Simon.

I shook my head. "No. You've done enough," I answered. Then, I retrieved a small crate of Rift Shards from my arsenal implant and set it down on the table in the center of the room. "Should all be there, but I won't be offended if you count them."

"We trust you," he said.

Vanna snorted. "I don't."

"She's joking," Simon stated.

"I'm really not," she countered.

"Whatever. Thanks for your help," I said, not wanting to deal with any more snark. "If you ever need me . . ."

"I intend to lose your contact information as soon as you're out of the building," Vanna said.

Simon rubbed his eyes and added, "Just be careful, Mira."

"I always am."

With that, I left the safe house. I quickly ascended to the surface via the elevator and made my way through the club and into the streets of New Cairo. As I went, I couldn't help but stare at every child I saw. Could they have been gnomes in disguise? Maybe. But none of them seemed to notice me.

Throughout my trip through the city, I continuously backtracked and changed identities. For a while, I was a short, nondescript man. After that, I was an old crone. And after that, I was a teenage girl. On and on it went until I'd used almost a dozen different identities. I also took great pains to hide any time I saw a group of children.

Thankfully, their tracking system wasn't terribly advanced. Or maybe it sacrificed some utility for undetectability. I really don't know. But as I went, I came to realize that it only gave them a general idea of the girl's location. So, as long as I kept moving, they couldn't find us. Still, I caught sight of the disguised Dengyts on more than a few occasions, and just like Vanna had indicated, they stood out under any kind of close scrutiny. They looked the part, but the way they moved labeled them as impostors.

Predictably, I also saw evidence that New Cairo was afflicted with a similar disease that seemed so prevalent in any sizable city. The inequality—and human suffering—wasn't as dramatic as it had been in Nova City, but it was still there all the same. In the shadow of those grand pyramids were ruined hovels filled with addicts, the destitute, and those driven to apathy by an unfair world.

In the years since Nova City's fall, I had seen much the same in dozens of other settlements. For a while, I'd even joined them in their misery.

But there was some hope, too. For every lost cause, there were people just living their lives. Shopkeepers. Tradespeople. Workers of every sort. I saw families with their children in tow, lovers holding hands, and friends laughing and smiling together. Perhaps those same things had been present in Nova and I'd just been too blinded by my quest for revenge to acknowledge their existence.

Eventually, I reached my destination.

I looked around the park, seeing only the expected sights. Trees. A few small fountains. Plenty of people lounging about. There were children there, too, but none were unaccompanied by adults. The gnomes had yet to arrive.

Of course, that wasn't unexpected. I'd spent hours setting up a daisy chain of locations meant to slowly guide them to the park. Hopefully, it would be enough to keep me out of their sights.

After crossing the park, I found my way to a secluded section characterized by well-cultivated gardens. There, I deposited the girl behind a hedge and promptly vacated the area. However, I didn't go more than a mile before I climbed an ancient wall and drew my Pulsar. There, I waited for the gnomes to arrive.

I'd chosen the area for two reasons. First, the garden was fairly isolated, so I hoped to avoid civilian intervention. Second, the wall—which was avoided by the locals—offered great sight lines so I could observe the pickup. And, if it came down to it, kill a few gnomes.

As anticlimactic as that would be, I hoped it wouldn't come down to that.

So, I was more than a little surprised when a high-pitched voice came from behind me. "I hope you don't intend to use that on my people," it said. I started to turn, but I was brought up short by the barrel of a gun pressed against the back of my head. "Drop the rifle, please."

I knew better than to disobey, so I pulled my hands away from my weapon and raised them. Already, I'd started to prime Teleport.

"Turn around," my assailant ordered.

I did, and predictably, I saw a gnome. He was a bit taller than the others I'd seen, but he had the same characteristically wide eyes, pointed ears, and diminutive stature. He also had a head of wild white hair that stuck up in all directions. Couple that with a truly stupendous mustache, and he cut quite a striking figure.

"How did I screw up?" I asked.

"You didn't," he said. "In fact, you proved quite slippery."

"Then how did you find me?"

"Superior technology" was his only answer. I knew I wouldn't get an elaboration.

"What do you want? I didn't kidnap the girl. I went to a lot of trouble to put things right," I said. "None of this was my plan."

"Oh, I know. That's why you're still alive," he said. "For now."

"What do you want?" I asked. Even as I uttered the question, I engaged Misthack and got another big surprise when I tried to infiltrate his system. I came up against a completely solid Mistwall. There were no defensive nodes to assault. Nothing to bypass. Just an error message that said:

Misthack failed.

There was no elaboration, but I must've shown some of my surprise because the gnome said, "Not what you were expecting, was it? After what happened in the beta-three satellite compound, I suspected there was a {Mistrunner} involved. So, I took certain precautions."

My mind whirled. His precautions made him completely immune to a big part of my arsenal, but I knew from experience that something like that had to come with a big downside. I just had no idea what it was, and judging by his smug expression, the gnome wasn't keen on revealing his secrets.

"I thought we might come to an arrangement," he said.

"What kind?" I asked, resisting the urge to put a few plasma rounds in his face. But I knew that would be counterproductive. It was one thing to shoot some nameless thug like Huascar, but doing so against someone like the Dengyt would have lasting consequences.

"The kind where you do a few jobs for us," he answered. "No questions. No complaints. And no refusals. I point to a target, and you do what I say."

"And why would I do that?"

"Two reasons," he answered. "One, refusing this deal will bring attention you don't want. You may not be aware, but my people are not like the chaff that usually visit worlds like this. We are well funded and, as anyone in the galaxy can tell you, very vindictive."

He left that threat hanging for a few seconds. It was a simple concept. Do what he wanted me to do or I'd get precisely the attention I'd hoped to avoid. Perhaps it wouldn't be that bad for now, but the moment the quarantine lifted, there was every chance I'd have an army of gnomes following my trail.

I had no notion of the state of galactic politics, so his threats might have been empty. But Askar had believed the Dengyts were major players, and so, I had to, as well.

He continued, "And second, you'll get to do exactly what you've been doing all along."

"What's that?"

"Killing aliens, of course. Isn't that what motivates you, Mirabelle Braddock? Oh, yes—I know who you are. I know what you've done. And most importantly, I want you to keep doing it, albeit with a little direction from yours truly," he explained.

I hesitated only for a moment before I said, "Three jobs. That's it. You pay me in useful metals. And only aliens. I have no interest in killing my own."

"And yet you do it so well."

"That's in the past," I stated.

"Indeed," he said, stroking his mustache with his free hand. Then, the little pistol in his hand disappeared. "Then we have a deal?"

I knew I didn't have much of a choice but to agree. Perhaps I would back out when I had some room to maneuver, but for now, he had me right where he wanted me. "Yeah. I guess we do," I said.

"Good."

Then, the air shimmered, and a full dozen gnomes came into view. They were all dressed in skintight infiltration suits similar to my own, and each one carried a gnome-sized rifle, each trained on me.

"Very good. I didn't want to do this the other way," he said.

Only then did I realize just how close I'd come to getting myself killed. Still, I didn't let my own fear make its way to my expression as I said, "You know my name. Only polite if you tell me yours."

"Kargat," he said. "Alistaris Kargat, at your service."

CHAPTER TWENTY

LIFE GOES ON

Mira and I don't always agree on everything, but I think we understand each other. We've both lost so much, and I don't know how I would function without her. I tried it, and looking back, I know I wasn't happy. So, as much as she sometimes frustrates me, I can't imagine a world where we weren't together.

—Patrick Ward

I didn't even know they were there, Pick," I said, still shaken up after the encounter with the gnomes. "It's like they were ghosts. No Mist signature. No noise. I couldn't even smell them with Observation going. And I was paying attention, too. It wasn't like they snuck up on me when I was distracted by something else. I was on guard."

Patrick sat across from me, his elbows on *The Leviathan*'s galley table, his brows creased in frustration and concern. I couldn't blame him, either. Usually, I did my best to cultivate an aura of power and, most of all, confidence. Sometimes, it was just a facade to cover up real fear, but I rarely let it drop, even with him. My encounter with Alistaris Kargat—and his troop of invisible warriors—had knocked me more than a little off-kilter. I wasn't used to being on my back foot, and usually, on those rare occasions when I was forced off-balance, I had the skills to turn the situation around. This was not one of those cases.

And it had left me shaken to my core.

"Did they say what they wanted you to do?" he asked. "Like, did they give you a mission?"

"No. But he said they'll be keeping an eye on me," I answered. That had creeped me out more than anything. I was used to being the watcher, not the watched, and I didn't like the reversal. Not one little bit. "He said I have to do three jobs. That's it. And once I'm done, we'll be square."

"He didn't want the circuits or the other stuff back?" Patrick asked.

"Never even mentioned them. I got the feeling he only cared about the girl," I said. "Or maybe he was just using the situation to back me into a corner. I don't know, and he wasn't really eager to give me a lot of extra information."

"It's probably a reputation thing. He has to do something, or people will start thinking the Dengyts are weak," he said, and I couldn't help but see the logic behind it. Then, Patrick asked, "Do we run? Go to one of the safe houses?"

"You think it'd work?" I asked. "I mean, I never could find the tracker on the kid. Neither could you. For all I know, they put one on me, too."

"That shouldn't be possible."

"Like that ever stops anything from happening," I said, remembering the host of things I'd seen that defied logic, physics, and my overall understanding of the world. Atop that list was the planet-sized space serpent I had seen in my second Rift. Even in a world where miracles happened every day, that stuck out as particularly noteworthy. "I'm not saying they're tracking me right now, but I'm pretty sure they can find us whenever they want."

Otherwise, they wouldn't have found me in that park, much less had the ability to surround me. It was as if they could find anyone, anywhere. Perhaps that was my new reality, having to walk on eggshells while I waited for Alistaris Kargat to call due on what he considered a debt. That I didn't think I owed him anything was irrelevant.

The reality was that I was outmatched and powerless, and there was nothing I could do about it.

"What do you want to do?"

"About this? I don't know. I don't think it would be a good idea to go to war with the gnomes," I said. Even if I managed to win—and maybe I could kill the contingent of Dengyts on Earth—what would it accomplish? I'd just mark myself as their enemy, and the moment the quarantine on Earth lifted, they would deal with me accordingly. "I'm open to ideas if you have any."

Patrick shook his head, then muttered something about being hunted down by Dengyt assassins. Clearly, he was thinking along the same lines as I was. He then added, "What if they want you to do something you don't want to do?"

"I don't want to do anything at all for them."

"You know what I mean, Mira. I know you act like you don't have lines you won't cross, but we both know that's not even close to true," he said.

And he was right. I would kill without a second thought so long as I thought it was justified. However, there was no guarantee that the Dengyts would only send me after people who deserved it. What would I do if they wanted me to destroy another city? Could my conscience take that hit?

"I don't know, Pick. I'm flying blind here," I said. I'd never really been in a situation where I wasn't in charge of my own life. Not since my training, and that didn't count, largely because I'd trusted my uncle. I couldn't say the same for Kargat or the gnomes, so it was a wholly different sort of situation. "What I really want to do is go find their base of operations and blow everything up."

"Mira . . ."

"I know. Not really a productive thought," I said, leaning back in my chair. "For now, I think we just go on like normal."

"How?"

With a target on our backs—or mine, at least—it didn't seem possible. But we were nothing if not adaptable. Hopefully we could get used to the idea of an unseen gnome looking over our proverbial shoulders.

I shrugged. "Same way as always," I said. "Just put one foot in front of the other."

"That's your answer to everything."

"It's worked so far," I said. "So—change of subject. What did you do with the others?"

"Dropped them off a few miles from Boston," he said.

"Ugh. Never want to go there again," I said. Indeed, I'd only been in that area a few times, but I would never forget it. The entire region looked like a war zone, and there were more than a few bombed-out craters reminiscent of the one I'd encountered on the way to my second Rift. The memory of all those infected wildlings still caused nightmares more than three years later. That had been the motivating factor behind at least a few inebriated nights.

What civilization was left in that region had been built on the ruins of something far grander. I'd even visited the remnants of a huge city composed of enormous buildings that made anything else I'd seen look small. Of course, that destroyed city, with its crumbling architecture, was also populated by hordes of roaming wildlings and ravenous, territorial beasts that looked like a combination of some kind of prehistoric lizard and a hover-car-sized scorpion. Needless to say, I didn't stay long, and I had no wish to return.

"I don't envy them," I added with a shiver.

Patrick shook his head, saying, "I tried to warn them, but that's where they wanted to go. Well, they wanted to stay with us . . ."

"But you rightly refused."

"I did. But it wasn't easy. I'm glad I didn't have to do it face-to-face."

"Wait—you didn't even leave the cockpit?"

"No. I didn't think it was safe," he said. "I just opened the bay doors and shooed them out over the intercom system. They tried to argue, but I threatened to take off and shake them out. They left pretty quick after that, but the girl tried to leave a tracker behind. I held on to it just in case you wanted to—"

"We can toss it out over the ocean," I said. "I don't ever want to see them again."

"Mira, we talked about this . . ."

"Are you seriously going to say that I need to make friends with the people who were planning on turning on us? The ones who lied to us about what we were doing?" I asked.

"That's just part of the game, and you know it. If we cut contact with everyone who ever lied, we'd have a pretty lonely road ahead of us," he pointed out.

"She's half-alien. And the cowboy's a pig . . ."

"Seemed like you two were getting along just fine," Patrick said. "Besides, you're the one who saved him when you didn't really have to."

"That's only because—"

"I mean, who knew that was your type?" he needled. "Here I was thinking that you'd never even look at another man, and just like that, you're leaving me behind for some idiot in a cool hat."

"His hat wasn't that cool. And he's old."

"Experienced. And there's no way you actually believe that about his hat."

I sighed, then rolled my eyes. "If you're angling for a compliment or something, we really don't want to get distracted right now," I said.

"Don't tempt me with a good time. Distraction sounds just about right," he replied with a self-assured smirk. He wasn't necessarily wrong—God knows I could have used something to take my mind off the past couple of days—but we really needed to make a plan before getting into said distractions.

Of course, I wasn't always terribly rational about that kind of thing, and in the end, I made a host of nice-sounding excuses for why we had plenty of time to worry about the future later. So, I shouldn't have been surprised when we ended up going to bed early. Of course, Patrick nearly ruined it all when he tried to imitate Rex's drawl. But even so, we pushed through and released all sorts of tension before falling asleep, satisfied and briefly relaxed.

The next morning dawned, and we were once again forced to confront our circumstances. Regarding the Dengyt situation, there didn't seem to be much we could do about it—aside from going full scorched-earth on them, which I didn't want to do for a variety of reasons. First on that list was the fact that I didn't think it would solve the problem. Instead, it would probably just make things worse for us. And second, it wasn't as if the gnomes had really done anything terrible to me. In fact, they had more reasons to kill me than I did to kill them. Outside of them being invaders, of course. Either way, murdering hundreds of them didn't seem like the right response—especially when they'd had mostly peaceful interactions with me.

So, by the time I'd finished making a breakfast of powdered eggs and synthetic toast, we had decided to simply go about our lives like normal. But that begged the question of what that meant.

"We could go back to that mountain from last year," I said. "The one with all the snow."

"You hate snow."

"But you like it," I said. "And I can deal with a few cozy nights by the fire."

"I have another idea," Patrick stated. "But I'm not sure you'll like it, so I'm a little hesitant to bring it up . . ."

"Oh, that sounds juicy," I said, leaning forward and grinning broadly. "Now you have to tell me. What is it? Who do you want me to kill?"

"Uh . . . It's a little distressing that that's where your mind goes."

"Oh, come on. It was a joke," I said, clutching my hands to my chest. "You wound me."

But in the back of my mind, in the deepest parts of my thoughts, I recognized that it wasn't really much of a joke. After all the people I had killed—both deservedly and not—it was more reality than fantasy.

"Sure it was. But this isn't that kind of trip," he said. "So, while you were in New Cairo, I did an inventory of the stuff we . . . uh . . . confiscated from that train, and I kind of hoped we could go somewhere I could work on my mech suit. I mean, I have all those fancy alloys, and with the circuits, I think I can make it all work. It'll take a little while, though."

"None of that sounds unreasonable to me," I said, a little confused as to why he'd hesitated to bring it up. "So, why did you think I wouldn't like the idea?"

"It's not really the idea, per se. It's more the company I thought you might find objectionable," he said. Before I could ask for more information, he went on, the words tumbling out of his mouth like a verbal avalanche, "Just to be clear, it's not that I want to see her again. It's just that she's probably the most qualified person I know when it comes to cybernetics. And she's got a fully equipped workshop. And she knows more than I do about those circuits. But it's not because I want to see her. Not at all."

"I don't . . ."

Before I got another word out of my mouth, I realized whom he meant. Cirilla Montague. She'd actually been the one who'd installed my cybernetics, including my interface, and the fact that my uncle had chosen her to do the job was evidence enough of her competence. So, on the surface, everything Patrick had said made perfect sense.

Except one little thing.

"So, you want to go shack up with your ex, huh?"

"It's not—"

"Maybe you're hoping we become friends and then you can have the best of both worlds, right? I mean—"

"It's not like that, Mira!"

For a second, I didn't respond, and he used that opportunity to hastily explain all his reasoning. Most of it was just a variation of what he'd already said, but I let him keep going. Finally, by the time he'd repeated—for what felt like the hundredth time—that his interest in a reunion was purely professional, I could no longer contain myself.

I burst out in laughter, which cut him off short. His brows furrowed, and his eyes narrowed as he said, "This isn't something to laugh about, Mira."

"I'm sorry!" I said, catching my breath. "It's just that you were so worked up. Seriously, Pick—I'm fine with it. We're all adults here, and she has something you need. There's no reason we can't all get along. Even if she is a cradle-robbing bitch."

"She's not—"

"Joking!" I reiterated. "Just joking. Geez, Pick—I'm not completely unreasonable."

He just shook his head. Then, he said, "If you're at all uncomfortable with this, I'll figure out another way."

"But this is the best option, right? To getting that suit done, I mean."

"It is."

"Then that's what we should do" was my response. In truth, I didn't like the idea of seeing Cirilla again. But that had nothing to do with the fact that she'd tried to snake Patrick out from under me. Well, maybe more than nothing. In my defense, though, I hadn't had a great impression of her since our first meeting, and nothing she'd done since then had changed that. She was prim, proper, and worst of all, condescending. She'd even looked down on my uncle, a man who could've twisted her into knots without an ounce of effort. To say she was arrogant would be an understatement.

But she had something Patrick needed for his progression, and that was what really mattered. I could put aside my misgivings if it meant that he'd be safer in the event that one of our enemies—well, mine really—came calling.

"Okay," he said. "But if you want to leave at any point . . ."

"I'm a big girl who can use her words," I assured him. "I'll tell you. Or I might just do that whole murder thing we were talking about earlier."

"Mira . . ."

"Fine, fine!" I said, holding my hands in surrender. "No murder. But I might slap her."

"Please don't—"

"Okay! No violence. But I might glare at her really aggressively."

"Maybe it would be best if you stayed in the ship or something," he muttered.

"And leave that cradle robber alone with you? Nope. Not a chance. I'll be watching her like a hawk," I said, pointing to my eyes, then at him.

"Totally reasonable," he deadpanned. "That's my Mira. Completely logical at all times."

I let that go without a response. Otherwise, we'd have kept going back and forth indefinitely. Instead, I changed the subject, saying, "Vanna and Simon said hello, by the way."

"How are they?" he asked.

"Angry. Well, Vanna is. Simon's just . . . Well, he's Simon. He doesn't let much get under his skin," I explained. "They're going to have to leave New Cairo, though. For some reason, they wouldn't tell me where they're going. As if I'm going to just barge in and destroy everything."

"Well . . ."

I fixed him with a glare, and he cut off. I knew what he was going to say, though, and if I was honest, I'd have admitted that he was kind of right. By going to Vanna and Simon, I'd probably involved them with enemies they couldn't hope to defeat. If I couldn't do anything against the gnomes, then they certainly couldn't. The only difference was that I had proven myself skilled enough that the Dengyts thought they could get something out of me. Vanna and Simon, as talented as they were, weren't unique enough to garner alien interest.

So, they were forced to leave and hope that the Dengyts would overlook their involvement. Or at least deem tracking them down and taking care of them to be more trouble than it was worth.

"I'll find out where they're setting up," Patrick said. "Vanna likes me."

Patrick had never even met the pair back in Mobile, but our paths had crossed a few times since the fall of Nova City. For some reason, they were always happy enough to see him—a stark contrast to how they reacted when I showed my face.

"Another older woman? You've definitely got a type. I guess I could use Mimic to do a little role-play . . ."

He didn't dignify that with a response. Instead, he continued eating his breakfast. It wasn't very good, but at least we had some fresh peppers to liven things up. By the time we'd finished, we had a plan in place.

"Where has that old hag set up, anyway?" I asked.

"Cirilla is not an old hag."

"Whatever. She's old. That's all I'm saying."

"She set up in this town called Fortune," he said. "Western America, near the mountains."

"Ugh. I bet it's cold there."

"You said you didn't mind the cold."

"I lied because I thought it was going to be a fun vacation," I said. "I'm a tropical person, remember? Beaches and deserts are fine, but mountains and snow—or mountains of snow, like we ran into last year way up north—are not my thing. But it's fine. It'll be fun. I bet Montague chose the place so she could hide under a hundred layers of clothes . . ."

"Mira . . ."

"Okay. That's the last time I'll mention how old, ugly, and weird looking she is. After all, you'll see it with your own two eyes soon enough."

Patrick just rolled his eyes, clearly questioning whether or not it was a great idea to bring his girlfriend to a meeting with his ex.

CHAPTER TWENTY-ONE

FORTUNE AND GLORY

Cirilla begged me to stay. She said a hundred horrible things about Mira, some of which were objectively true. But I knew she just couldn't see past the person who'd brought Nova City to its knees. All she saw was the woman who was responsible for the deaths of thousands. I knew Mira was more than that, though. She was a good person, just one who'd been forced by circumstances to do a lot of bad things.

—Patrick Ward

The trip across the ocean was relatively quiet, save for a few hundred miles when we were chased by a giant squid whose tentacles could reach us even a few thousand feet in the air. We would have flown higher, but the quarantine might have interpreted that as us trying to leave the atmosphere. Neither of us wanted to chance that—Patrick had heard plenty of stories from Remy about people who'd been censured by the system for pushing the limits—so we were forced to outrun the monstrous thing rather than simply out-elevate it.

Still, even hamstrung as we were, we eventually outpaced it, though we had to burn quite a few Rift Shards to gain the necessary speed. Given that it was between spending a little money or being dragged into the watery abyss to be eaten by a creature out of myth, the choice was an easy enough one to make. Still, every second of increased speed came with a deep sense of annoyance. Not only were we wasting money, but I was impotent to affect the outcome. For all my abilities and skills, there was nothing I could do against such a creature.

After making it to the coast, we were assaulted by a few flocks of predatory birds, but with Patrick at the helm of *The Leviathan*, they didn't pose much of a threat. It was a testament to both his flying ability as well as the quality of the ship itself that, even if we were attacked by something like the condor that had very nearly downed *The Jitterbug*, it wouldn't have been terribly concerning. Not only could we outrun most birds, but *The Leviathan* was equipped with enough weaponry to make quick work of the vast majority of creatures.

Of course, there were always exceptions to that rule. Case in point, the giant squid. There were also plenty of airborne monsters that could, if we didn't take them seriously enough, bring the ship down. And that wasn't even mentioning the dangers presented by people. *The Leviathan* was advanced—maybe more so than almost any other ship on Earth—but that didn't mean we were invulnerable.

Thankfully, Patrick was more than a match for any other pilot we might encounter, so I knew the ship—and, by extension, our lives—was in good hands.

In all, the trip took almost an entire twenty-four hours. We set *The Leviathan* down a few hundred miles inland so Patrick could rest—he still didn't want me flying the thing—but we were back in the sky early the next morning. After that, we made great time on our way to our destination, which turned out to be a sizable settlement that wasn't quite as big as New Cairo but was much larger than Mobile had been.

There were enough commonalities that the comparison seemed appropriate, though. Like Mobile, the walled settlement had been built in the shadow of the crumbling ruins of a pre-Initialization city. Unlike the city where I'd spent much of my training, it was clearly more advanced, with the same prefabricated plasti-steel walls I'd seen in a hundred alien encampments. Likely, they'd consulted someone in the Bazaar to build it.

The buildings beyond those walls were a varied collection of disparate building materials. Brick, wood, and the more modern—and soulless, in my opinion—plasti-steel were all in evidence, but there was a decidedly workmanlike quality to the architecture. No frills. No flourishes. Just no-nonsense walls and roofs.

But they did have a dock.

Ever since leaving the region around Nova City behind, I had come to realize that the world was a little more connected than I'd previously thought. Not only were there plenty of ships—both airborne and the traditional oceangoing variety—capable of traversing the land and sea, but most cities had some sort of infrastructure to support such travel. That was how I'd gotten around during the year I'd spent apart from Patrick. Without him, what did I need with a ship? I could barely even fly the thing, much less navigate the many dangers associated with air travel.

No—it had been better to let him have it, even if I'd framed the arrangement as a loan.

In any case, just to the north of Fortune, the city's architects had created a dock meant to accommodate flying ships. In truth, it was little more than a walled field, even if said field was so well organized that it could house almost a hundred ships the size of *The Leviathan*. When Patrick set us down, I couldn't help but notice that less than a third of those berths were occupied.

"Not really a popular place, huh?" I remarked.

"It's a small city in the middle of nowhere," Patrick said. "Not a lot of reason for people to come here."

"Then why did Cirilla set up here?" was my next question.

"Family. She has a little brother who moved here for some girl," he answered. "The girl ended up moving on, but he stuck around. After Nova, Cirilla couldn't think of a better place to go. I think she'd had enough of big cities and all the other stuff that comes with those kinds of places."

"I can get behind that sentiment," I said. As much as I wanted to disagree with every facet of the woman's being, I'd found that larger cities inevitably bred corruption. Usually, that fire was stoked by alien interference, but even when it wasn't, human beings were more than capable of doing all sorts of horrible things to one another. No matter where in the world I went, I saw exploitation, oppression, and misery. There were other things present, as well—plenty of happiness and love—but it all seemed to pale in comparison to the negatives. Perhaps the aliens were right to invade and bring us to heel.

Once we'd settled into the berth, Patrick shut down the Mist engines and went through his postflight checklist. *The Leviathan* was a magnificent, well-made machine, but without proper maintenance, it wouldn't remain so for long. Or at least that's what Patrick insisted. He'd yet to find anything wrong, despite checking after every flight, but I left him to it, anyway. It made him happy—or failing that, it kept his compulsivity demons at bay—so who was I to judge the routine?

Finally, he announced that the ship was in perfect shape, and I used my Bastion ability. Normally, the ship's passive defense systems were more than enough to deter any criminal mischief, but like Patrick, I felt it was better to be safe than sorry when it came to something as valuable as *The Leviathan*. As the ability took hold, I felt the Mist stir and form into a potent shield. That wasn't the extent of its effects—it also restricted skill use to a certain degree—but it was the most important. Unless someone broke out some pretty big guns, they weren't getting through. And even then, doing so would alert me, which would in turn allow me to respond, probably with extreme prejudice.

"All buttoned up?" Patrick asked as we stood before the cargo-bay door. He'd stored most of the valuable materials in his skill-based spatial storage, so the cargo bay was once again mostly empty.

"Sealed tight," I said. "You want to take the Cutter? Or should we walk?"

"We could take the buggy," he suggested, glancing back at the wheeled vehicle. Then, he amended, "Probably not. The cannon might give the wrong impression."

"Or the right one," I said, winking at him.

"No explosions," he reminded me.

"Not unless absolutely necessary," I stated.

"None."

"You know I'm not going to agree to that," I said. "That's like asking me not to breathe. So, just drop it."

He sighed but nodded in agreement. I had no intention of seeking out conflict, but if it found me, I would respond appropriately. Or with overwhelming force, which always seemed appropriate from my perspective.

As we exited the ship, we were met by a uniformed functionary. He was a narrow-shouldered man with a bland face, a mop of brown hair, and a bored expression. Normally, people were impressed by *The Leviathan*, but he didn't seem to care that it was a clearly advanced ship that was at least twice the size of anything else docked there.

"Reason for visiting Fortune?" he asked, holding a tablet in one hand. He never even looked up at us.

"Visiting a friend," said Patrick. As captain of the ship, he liked to take care of the questions that inevitably came with every visit to a new city. For my part, I was content to stand to the side and hope not to be noticed. In the past, I probably would have used Mimic, but I had recently begun to realize that my reliance on wearing someone else's face as well as my habitual use of Stealth were both defense mechanisms. They were also largely unnecessary, given that very few people knew me by sight even if they were aware of my exploits, which was unlikely so far from Nova City.

"Anything to declare?" the functionary asked.

Patrick answered, "No. Not here to trade. Just visiting a friend."

There was a slight stir in the ambient Mist, which told me he'd used one of his abilities. I still wasn't sure of their precise names—it wasn't as if I could just ask him for a list—but I knew he had a few that would ease his entry into cities. He was a smuggler by skill, after all.

The man still didn't look up from his tablet; instead, he just pressed a few buttons on the screen before getting the ship's and Patrick's name. He never even acknowledged my presence, which was, despite my preference for anonymity, a bit disconcerting. Usually, people noticed me, especially when I wasn't trying to hide. That he hadn't was a bit of a blow to my ego.

Once we'd finished with him, the man quickly retreated to a broad, low-slung building at the edge of the dock, and we headed in the opposite direction. As we did, I noticed that a few of the other ships were either being loaded or unloaded with plasti-steel crates by burly men and women.

"What do they produce here?" I asked.

"Produce? Nothing. But there is a silver mine close by," Patrick said. "Supposed to be Mist infused, too. So, it's useful for all sorts of things. In fact, that's the origin of the name. Fortune and Glory—that was what the founder called it when it was just a mining camp. At some point, they dropped the Glory part and just went with Fortune."

"Probably a good call. The old name was a bit of a mouthful," I said as we strode toward a series of warehouses and traders' premises. No one paid us much attention, though I did notice that quite a few people had noticed *The Leviathan.* That was good. She was a fantastic and advanced ship, and she deserved a little attention. "This place reminds me of Biloxi. Did I ever tell you about that place?"

Patrick shook his head, saying, "You mentioned it, but you didn't talk about it much more than that."

"They harvested this weird red kelp there, and they had a bunch of warehouses like these. About half the workers were dust fiends, though," I said. "But the rich also had these huge boats that they used for casinos and stuff. It seemed a weird choice at the time, but it certainly made it memorable."

Indeed, I had seen dozens of cities and towns since then, and at first, I remembered them all. However, after a certain point, they had all begun to blend together. Only the ones like Biloxi, with some remarkable aspect, made it into my memory.

"Maybe we can visit it sometime," he said. "I'm not usually much of a gambler, but—"

"Probably best if I never go there again," I interrupted. "I didn't exactly leave on good terms."

"Oh. Okay."

It was telling that he didn't even question that. In truth, my time in Biloxi had flown completely under the radar, and as far as I knew, nobody had ever connected the Banshee I'd been impersonating with the woman who'd brought down Nova City. The real reason I had no interest in returning had to do with the details of what I'd done there. Not only had I ruined a mostly innocent man's life, but I'd done so without even a second's hesitation. As hard-hearted as I wanted to be—as I usually needed to be—that little mission had stuck with me and polluted my conscience to the point where I often found myself wondering how Calvin was doing. Had he kept along the path I'd put him on? Or had he broken free of the addiction I'd all but forced upon him?

I wanted to know, but I was afraid to search out the answer.

Eventually we reached the edge of the mass of warehouses to approach the city proper. Up close, it was easy to see that the wall wasn't Fortune's only defense. It was equipped with a decently powerful Mist shield, manned turrets every dozen yards or so, and enough security personnel—dressed in mundane black uniforms without any decoration to speak of—to put down a horde of wildlings. In all, I was fairly impressed with how seriously they took their city's defenses.

After being once again questioned about our purpose, we were ushered through the gates and into the city. Once inside, I found myself impressed by the level of order and cleanliness. There was no trash in the streets. No graffiti on the walls. Certainly, the architecture would never garner much attention—aside from an acknowledgment of the sheer utility of the structures—but what it lacked in originality, it more than made up for in practicality.

Just inside the gates were a few motorized rickshaws that were apparently driven by wheeled bots.

"That just seems wildly inefficient," I said, thinking about how pointlessly complicated such a design was. Lots of cities had weird quirks, but this one stuck out to me because it was so at odds with the rest of Fortune's workmanlike atmosphere. "Why not just make self-driving hover cars?"

Patrick shrugged, saying, "I don't know. I never really asked before."

After hiring one, we endured a featureless ride through the city. After a couple of minutes, I said, "Say what you will about Nova, but at least it had real personality."

"Yeah," said Patrick. "From what I understand, they took the whole mining-camp-efficiency idea and just ran with it when the city kept growing. Not that it's a bad thing, I guess."

I would have agreed if it weren't for the people. Just like the drab buildings, they seemed devoid of personality, often wearing colorless clothing and eschewing the fashion I'd grown accustomed to in my travels. No visible tattoos, dyed hair, or piercings were in evidence, which seemed incredibly odd to me.

"Seems like it'd fit her just fine, though," I said, referring to Cirilla. "She never had much personality, either."

"Don't be like that, Mira," Patrick said. "You said you'd be nice."

"I am being nice. You can tell because I'm saying this now rather than to her face," I stated.

"This was such a mistake," he muttered to himself. "I'm going to regret this. I know it."

"It'll be fine. What could go wrong when you bring your girlfriend to meet your elderly ex?" I asked cheerfully. Seeing him so uncomfortable made the entire trip worth it. Still, I hoped we wouldn't remain in Fortune for long, though I suspected it would take at least a few weeks for Patrick to work things out with the suit he was planning to build. From what I understood, it was supposed to be a very complex set of machinery, and that was even without the whole cybernetic aspect that would link it to his interface.

Patrick continued to mumble to himself—probably about how lucky he was to have such an understanding girlfriend—as we made our way to our destination, which turned out to be a mundane building that looked almost identical to its neighbors. The only identifying feature was a giant number that had been painted on the side, declaring that it was number fifty-one, whatever that meant.

I initiated a credit transfer to the self-driving rickshaw before leaving the vehicle behind. Soon enough, we'd stepped inside the building, and I was unsurprised to see that the interior was just as featureless as the outside. The only thing that could be said in its favor was that it was spacious and clean.

We rode an elevator up to the third floor, and upon our arrival, it announced, "You have reached the third floor."

Its voice was predictably boring.

Everything about Fortune was, which made me wonder why anyone would live there. Of course, Patrick knew me well enough to predict the question on the tip of my tongue, and he said, "Safety, cleanliness, and a fair government makes up for a lot."

"I didn't say anything."

"Your expression did."

"Whatever. Let's go do this thing," I said, slapping my hands together. "I'm super excited about seeing my old friend Cirilla again. Emphasis on old."

Patrick rolled his eyes, but he led me deeper into the building until we finally reached an apartment with a jarringly pink door. It was the only bit of color I'd seen since my arrival, which garnered a healthy dose of approval—at least until I remembered who was behind that door. Immediately, my attitude shifted, and I started grumbling about how she just had to do something to stand out.

After knocking on the door, Patrick took a step back and waited. There wasn't much of a delay, though, before the door slid open, revealing the familiar face of Cirilla. In my head, I remembered her as much older than she really was. Somehow, I'd added a host of wrinkles, a hunched back, and a bony, rather than slim, body. The reality was pretty far from the truth, and I had to begrudgingly admit that I understood why someone might be attracted to her.

Clearly, she was older than either of us but only by a decade at most. Which made my previous comments seem a bit ridiculous. Not that I'd ever admit as much to Patrick, of course.

Still, her appearance wasn't the most surprising part. Instead, that designation belonged to her desperate expression. The moment the door opened, she said, "Oh, thank goodness you're both here! We don't have much time!"

Then, before either Patrick or I could ask any questions, she had dragged us inside and shut the door behind us.

NOT MY PROBLEM

I only met Caden a few times, but it was clear from the very beginning that he didn't like me much. I think he was jealous of me, of his sister's affection. Or maybe he just didn't like the idea of seeing someone his own age actually succeeding. With me around, he had evidence that success was possible, and so, his excuses for why he'd never done anything noteworthy started to ring untrue.

—Patrick Ward

Cirilla Montague was a fastidious woman—normally. Patrick didn't talk about her much, likely because it would have been weird if he'd gone on and on about his ex-girlfriend to his current partner. But what he'd let slip definitely supported my first impressions of the woman. However, when she pulled us into her apartment, the first thing I noticed was that it was in a horrible state of disarray.

Empty food containers—that had once contained the sort of cheap stuff only the incredibly busy, lazy, or poor usually ate—decorated the counters, and there were piles of discarded clothing all over the floors. More, her appearance reflected the state of the apartment, and calling her disheveled would have been a generous assessment. Her pink hair hung limp and greasy, and dark circles stood beneath her eyes, hinting that she hadn't slept properly in quite some time.

Piles of junk, composed of disparate parts, wires, and raw materials meant for cybernetics, stood on shelves lining every wall. It appeared that the apartment was also Cirilla's workspace, and not a well-kept one at that.

As the door slid shut behind us, Patrick managed to say, "What's going on, Cy?"

I hated that he had a nickname for her.

"It's Caden," she said. "He's in trouble."

Patrick sighed. "What did he do this time? Another get-rich-quick scheme gone wrong?" he asked. "Or wait—he didn't fall in love again, did he?"

"No. Maybe. I don't know," Cirilla said, running her hand through her lank hair. She really was striking, though I never would have admitted as much out loud, especially not where she might hear. I hated her, and I didn't want reality to get in the way of my carefully constructed perception of her.

"Just tell us what happened," Patrick coaxed, reaching out to grip her shoulder. I flinched at the familiar, if innocent, contact. "Take a breath and go slow."

Cirilla did just that, taking a deep breath that came close to becoming a sob. Then, she just collapsed onto one of the apartment's chairs and buried her head in her hands. After raking her fingers through her hair, she gave a quivering sigh before speaking. "It's Caden, you know? He doesn't know the world. Not like we do," she said. Patrick sat across from her while I remained standing. Not only was there no room for me to sit—the place really was tiny, and the main room doubled as a kitchen, living, and dining area. It reminded me of the domiciles back in Nova—the really cheap ones where nobody lived unless they had no other choice. Clearly, she had fallen pretty far from the position she'd occupied back in Nova.

Was that my fault? Or was it a conscious choice on her part?

After composing herself, she said, "I don't know what got into him. One day, he was just gone, leaving only a note behind."

"What did the note say?"

"That he loved me and that he's fine," she said. "Just that he'd finally found his place."

"What does that mean?" Patrick asked. I remained silent, mostly because I had no idea what to say. I didn't know the backstory, so I didn't think I could offer anything of substance to the discussion.

"I don't know," she breathed. "He's run off before, but it's always because of a girl. Or some kind of job. This is different, though."

"How?" he asked.

"It's these people he's been hanging around," Cirilla said. "They're . . . They're not exactly bad. They help a lot of people around here. It's just . . . I just get this strange impression of them. It's like they have some ulterior motive."

"Like what?" Patrick asked, glancing at me. We'd seen a lot since branching out into the world, and one thing seemed almost universally true: if someone seemed like they had an ulterior motive, then they probably did. And chances were that it wasn't anything good. More than once, we'd encountered human-smuggling rings that duped impressionable young people into thinking they were going to escape their boring—or sometimes outright depressing—lives.

Only, when those young people reached their destination, they did so to realize that they were being fixed with a slave implant.

"They're called the Pillar of Heaven," she said. "I don't know what their doctrine is. Not exactly. But from what I understand, they preach collectivism. They've even established a city a few hundred miles from here."

"But you don't trust them?" asked Patrick.

She narrowed her eyes. "You know Caden," she said. "He's a lot of things, and I think he's a good person—under it all—but he's not really the type to work for the greater good. There's something weird going on with those people. I know it. And the worst part is that he completely cut contact. Like, he won't respond at all anymore. It's like he dropped off the face of the Earth. He's not—"

Just then, the door slid open. I reacted quickly, yanking Ferdinand II out of my arsenal implant and wheeling around to face what I thought was an attacker. As it turned out, the intruder was a teenage girl with vivid-blue hair and matching makeup. She was dressed in a pair of grease-spattered coveralls.

She threw her hands up, screeching, "Just take whatever you want! Don't resist, Cece!"

"Don't shoot!" Cirilla said at the same time as she reached for my gun. That was a big mistake, and she ended up with one of her arms twisted behind her back as I kept my weapon trained on the newcomer.

"What the hell is going on?" I demanded.

At the same time, Patrick asked, "Cece?"

Meanwhile, Cirilla whimpered in pain. I hadn't yanked her shoulder out of socket, but I knew precisely how much pain she was in. During my training, my instructors had favored pain as the best way to really nail a lesson down, and back then, I'd been taught plenty of those sorts of lessons.

"Ten seconds," I said. "That's how long you all have before I just cut my losses, start shooting, and leave this weird town behind. Ten. Nine. Eight . . ."

I didn't get any further before Cirilla hissed, "She's just my girlfriend!"

"Just?" asked the blue-haired girl. "I'm *just* your girlfriend?!"

"Cece?" muttered Patrick again.

That's when I let out a sigh of annoyance and let Cirilla go. As I did so, I said, "That was really stupid, you know. Never reach for someone's gun like that. You're lucky I didn't put you down by reflex alone."

"Can anyone explain why there are two strangers here?" interjected the girl. "And what the hell, Cece? Do you ever clean? I swear—"

"Stop," I said, still pointing my weapon at the girl. "Who are you?"

"I'm Tate," she answered. "And I should be asking you the same thing."

"Maybe. But I'm the one with the gun," I said.

"That's . . . a good argument," she admitted.

"So . . ."

"Oh. Right. I'm Tate. Cece and I have been together for . . . six months, maybe? But considering I'm *just* her girlfriend, that might change," she said. "That one little word has a lot of meaning behind it, doesn't it? *Just.* Like I'll never be anything else."

"That's not what I meant, and—"

"Stop," I said again. "I am not getting into your little relationship drama. What I will do is ask why any of this is our problem, though. I get it. Your brother up and ran off with some creepy people. But I really don't see why we should care."

Cirilla looked at me like I'd gone crazy and said, "Wait—that's not why you're here?"

"Uh . . . No?"

Before I could say anything else, Patrick said, "We'll look into it, Cy. I won't promise we'll find anything, but if we do this for you, I want your help with my project. You know the one. That's the deal."

"Of course. I'd have helped you regardless. You know that," Cirilla said, a shadow of her old composure returning.

At the same time, out of the corner of my eye, I saw Tate mouthing the word *Cy.*

"Pick," I said. "I don't think—"

He gave me a pleading look and said, "We'll talk about it in a little bit, okay? Just trust me."

Of course, that was easier said than done. I did trust Patrick, and more than anyone else I knew. However, doing so went against every instinct I had. Still, I just nodded and said, "Alright."

It was a simple response to what would probably turn out to be a complicated situation. But I owed him the benefit of the doubt.

After that, things settled down, and Cirilla gave us the rundown on the so-called Pillar of Heaven. There really wasn't much more to it, save the details of where they'd set up a small operation meant to cater to the dregs of any urban society. They offered counseling for drug addicts, free meals, and even a safe place for the homeless to spend a few nights. On top of that, they had a well-known slave-implant-removal operation, much like the Nats had cultivated back in Nova.

Once she'd finished, I said what I knew Patrick was thinking. "None of this seems bad," I said. "They kind of seem like the good guys."

"Except for the fact that people keep going missing," Cirilla said.

Tate, who'd decided to help herself to some questionable leftover food, gestured with a pair of chopsticks and said, "That's what I've been telling her. Caden was a screwup, but people change. They get better. Maybe he found a purpose."

"Caden doesn't care enough about anyone but himself to have willingly devoted his life to that kind of cause," Cirilla said.

Patrick added, "That's more like the guy I knew. Maybe he changed, but . . ."

"People never really change. They evolve, but they don't just do a one-eighty like that," I said.

Tate adopted a sullen expression, but she dropped the argument. Getting ganged up on by three other people would usually cut off any dispute. Finally, Patrick and I had exhausted the opportunity for more information, so after he and Cirilla made arrangements to work together on his project, we left the depressing apartment behind. The moment the door shut, I could hear the happy couple start shouting at each other.

That brought a smile to my face.

"She really does have a type," I remarked as we stepped into the elevator that would take us back to the ground floor.

"Huh?" he muttered.

"You and Tate," I said. "You have to have noticed the similarities, right?"

"She's a girl."

"So observant. That's why I love you," I said. "Nothing ever slips past those eagle eyes of yours. My point is that you're both young, pretty, and—"

"I am not pretty."

"I think you are."

"Men aren't pretty. I'm ruggedly handsome."

"Sure, sure. That's what I meant."

After that, we reached the ground floor and quickly found our way back to one of the robot-driven taxis, which took us back to the docks where we boarded *The Leviathan*. After seeing the state of Cirilla's apartment, I was very much glad to be back within the ship's familiar confines.

"So," I said once we were alone again. "Care to explain yourself?"

"Not really?"

"Well, do it anyway."

"Fine. So, when I contacted Cy, she was kind of . . . distraught," he explained. "And I might have offered to help. You know, in exchange for her help with the suit."

"So, she didn't demand it as payment?" I asked.

He shrugged. "Not as such, but I think she was going to," Patrick answered. "Like, I get it, too. Her brother's a screwup, but he's still family. That means something. Besides, it'll give you something to do, right? While Cy and I are working, you can look into the whole thing."

I sighed, but I didn't immediately respond. As much as I didn't want to leave Patrick alone with Cirilla, I knew I couldn't exactly hang around. For one, it would drive me insane from boredom. For another, me hovering over their proverbial shoulders would be terribly unproductive. And finally, I felt certain that Patrick would start to resent me for lack of trust if I insisted on remaining attached at the hip.

"So, what do you think?" he asked.

"That you shouldn't volunteer me for things without my permission," I said.

"Mira, I didn't—"

"I'm just joking," I lied. In truth, I was annoyed even if I knew the reasoning behind his actions. It wouldn't have been so frustrating if he'd just told me, but I knew making a big deal out of it was a good way to start an argument that would do neither of us any good.

"I should've told you," he said, guessing the source of my irritation. "It's just awkward, you know? I'm sorry."

"It's fine."

It wasn't, but I would get over it.

"We can go. We don't have to do this," he offered. "I can figure the suit out on my own. Jerry up in Vancouver has a solid workshop, and he owes us one."

"Jerry's an alcoholic with a gambling problem who's constantly in trouble with one group or another," I said. "Cirilla's a better option if you want to get this thing done without adding a bunch of issues."

"Like a missing brother and a creepy cult?"

"Are we sure it's a cult and not just a group of people who want to help their fellow humans?" I asked. He looked at me like I'd said the dumbest thing imaginable. "Yeah. You're right."

There were probably some such organizations out there, but in my experience, there was almost always some sort of nefarious purpose behind those sorts of groups. Individually, people were more than capable of kindness, but groups of people were far less inclined toward that sort of thing. Or maybe that was just my cynicism showing through once again.

In the end, looking into Cirilla's issue was probably a good way to distract myself while we were in Fortune. At worst, it would be diverting, but there was also the chance I would do some good. I'd certainly never claim to be a great person; I was just as selfish and self-interested as anyone else in the world, and my actions usually reflected that. But I tried to do the right thing whenever possible.

And looking into the Pillar of Heaven probably fell into that column. Hopefully, I'd find that they were just a charitable organization who wanted to make the world a better place, but I wasn't holding out any hope for that.

"I'll start the investigation tomorrow," I said.

"Just an investigation. No blowing things up."

"Hey—you're the one who dragged me into this. You can't tell me how to do my job now. Speaking of which, any chance Cirilla's going to pay me? Or am I doing this pro bono?"

"You saw her apartment. I don't think she's in a position to pay anyone any-thing," he said. "Which is weird because she lived in a much nicer place before."

"Maybe she's got a drug or gambling problem. She seems the type."

"No, she doesn't, Mira."

I shrugged. "You never know. A woman of her advanced age? She probably has to do whatever it takes to keep the existential fear of looming death at bay," I said.

"Mira . . ."

"Fine," I said, sitting down on the edge of our bed. "I'll keep the age com-ments to myself. But I reserve the right to go back on that if she annoys me in any way. Which is likely."

CHAPTER TWENTY-THREE

LOOKING INTO THINGS

Mira tries to be understanding. She wants to be a good person. She just doesn't really know how. She was raised by a man who saw only the worst in people. Jeremiah had his reasons for being the way he was—and he loved her in his own way—but he was ill-equipped to be a parent.

—Patrick Ward

greeted the next day with uncharacteristic enthusiasm. Part of that was because Patrick had spent much of the night trying to make up for his mistakes—both real and imagined—which was always a fun prospect. But mostly, I was excited because, as much as I saw the world for the cesspool of corruption it was, I was still always eager to see new places and experience new things. That the new experience in question was a boring place like Fortune didn't seem to matter. Every city had something to offer, and I was determined to find out what that meant for a town like Fortune.

Patrick was similarly excited, though he made it abundantly clear that his eagerness was due to the prospect of getting started on his armor, rather than being reunited with Cirilla. I let him sputter out one addendum to his enthusiasm after another until the discussion petered out over breakfast. For my part, I enjoyed hearing how uncomfortable he was with it all, if only because I knew that if anything was really going to happen, he'd have probably clammed up and tried to avoid the topic altogether.

If there was one thing about Patrick that I knew, it was that he was a fundamentally honest person. And on those rare occasions when he tried to lie, he usually did so poorly. That was comforting.

Finally, after breakfast, we went our separate ways. He headed to Cirilla's workshop—contrary to my first impression of her apartment, which was strewn with all sorts of parts associated with her work with cybernetics, she had an actual shop somewhere in the city. That was where she and Patrick would create his cybernetic mech suit.

As for me, I went in the opposite direction, heading to the headquarters for the Pillar of Heaven. It was located clear across town, so it gave me plenty of opportunity to take in the sights. And as I was supposed to be undercover, I made the trip incognito, having adopted a new persona via Mimic. I also bypassed the public transportation systems in favor of riding the Cutter, which had been suitably disguised, as well. So, as far as anyone in the city was concerned, I was just another unremarkable woman—this time, with light skin and muddy-brown hair—on an outdated hover bike.

Still, I stuck out.

The traffic in the city was so light that it offered very little protection from observation. On top of that, I didn't see more than a couple of other hover bikes, and the ones I did see were even more outdated than the disguise I'd adopted for the Cutter. And finally, my clothes were far too bright. In short, I was clearly a tourist, and everyone in the city knew it.

It took everything I had not to simply duck into an alley and let Stealth wash over me.

But I knew I couldn't allow myself to fall back into old habits. Not without reason. Stealth and Mimic had their uses, but they were just tools meant to help me accomplish my goals. Not a lifestyle. Still, all that attention made my skin crawl, so it took quite a bit of willpower to keep to the path I'd set for myself.

It didn't help that I couldn't even distract myself by taking in the sights—because there were no sights to see. Just a bunch of mundane buildings built with bog-standard materials and housing a bunch of people who'd never bothered to develop a culture of their own.

Or maybe they'd just lost touch with it.

That was one thing I'd noticed since leaving Nova City. The world had become a skewed and often distorted reflection of the past. For instance, I'd been surprised to learn that Nova had shared little more than a few names and a location with its predecessor, New Orleans. The culture that had suffused the region had mostly fallen by the wayside, replaced with something far more generic. Even the foods I'd always taken for granted were oddly different from those of the past.

And it was the same everywhere. In New Cairo, they'd latched on to those local ruins to establish their identity, but they'd completely lost any connection with the reasons those pyramids were important.

It wasn't really all that surprising, though. How many people had died directly after the Initialization? Billions, according to my uncle. And then, more than ninety years had passed, with entire generations growing up without the benefit of their elders passing down the culture.

Perhaps the people of Fortune, most of which had been displaced from somewhere else, according to Patrick, felt it more keenly. But whatever the case, to me, the city was nothing but an uninteresting mass of buildings populated by equally mundane people. So, I was more than a little relieved when my short journey ended before the building that was supposed to be the headquarters for the Pillar of Heaven.

Nothing really set it apart from any of its neighbors, though there was a decent amount of traffic coming in and out of the building. Most were clearly destitute, some looked like they hadn't had a decent meal in ages, and even more were clearly in the throes of withdrawal. The two guards—a man and a woman wearing identical light-blue outfits that looked like nothing so much as robes—didn't stop any of them.

I approached, and when I reached the pair, I noticed that they looked remarkably similar. Probably siblings, unless I missed my guess.

"Go on through. Food bank is the first door on the left. Addiction services are at the end of the hall. And relocation inquiries are on the right," said the woman.

"Oh, I'm not here for any of that," I said, cataloging the directions for later. If I didn't get what I wanted via straightforward inquiry, I would come back later with a different face. "I was actually looking for a friend of mine."

"We don't require identification," said the man. "Sorry. There's just no way for us to know if your friend's in there."

"He's not," I said. "He left me a note, actually. Said he was moving on. I'm guessing it has something to do with the relocation you just mentioned."

His eyes narrowed. "And you want to bring him back home, huh?"

"No—not at all. I'm just trying to make sure he's okay," I said, playing my role, which was based on Cirilla's situation. It might bring some attention, but given that I wasn't even wearing my own face, that didn't matter much to me. "Any chance you can check up on him?"

"Sorry, no. We have limited contact with the settlement," said the woman. Even their voices sounded similar, which was more than a little creepy. That's when I noticed the unnatural sheen of synthetic skin. It was high-quality stuff, but they were both covered in it. So, either they were covering up some pretty extensive cybernetics, or they'd both altered their appearances to an alarming degree. I'd seen plenty of that before—human vanity was boundless—but the fact that they'd chosen such similar appearances was extremely off-putting. And it made me realize that they probably weren't siblings after all.

I sighed dramatically, but I didn't push. If it was that easy, Cirilla wouldn't have needed my help. "At least tell me where he might have gone," I said. "Maybe I'll visit."

"Also not possible," said the man in his strangely androgynous voice. "For security reasons, only Heaven's Chosen are allowed inside the city."

"I'm not even allowed to know where it is?" I persisted.

He shook his head. "Not unless you want to join," he stated. "And given your attitude, I don't think you'd fit in."

After that, the pair continued to rebuff my every attempt to wheedle any extra information out of them. However, I couldn't help but notice that they didn't pay more than cursory attention to the steady flow of traffic entering the building. So, my way in was pretty clear, even if it wasn't one I really looked forward to taking.

Soon enough, I left the headquarters of the Pillar of Heaven behind and found my way to a market I'd passed on my way there. It was a depressing place filled with food carts hawking unappetizing fare, but it wasn't so different from what I'd seen in a dozen other cities. And certainly, I'd eaten worse, so I didn't hesitate to find one with food that looked mostly edible—some sort of meat on a stick—and settled in to think.

As much as I hated to admit it, I was inclined to take Cirilla's side regarding the Pillar of Heaven. In my experience, nobody was that secretive unless they had something to hide. Or protect, I amended. Perhaps that was what they were doing—protecting their people. But I suspected something more nefarious.

Because of course I did.

It was always something evil. No matter which stone I overturned, I almost inevitably found something terrible. Whether it was Heather's fate back in Nova or the slave ring I'd dismantled half a world away, there was no end to the human capacity for evil. So, as much as I wanted to believe that the Pillar of Heaven was just a well-meaning organization trying to make the world a better place, I knew that was too good to be true.

Or maybe I'd just seen too much human misery to believe that anything else was possible. Either way, regardless of my first impressions, I intended to get to the truth. And to do that, I needed to once again change my face. But that wouldn't be enough. I would have to completely alter my entire appearance. Otherwise, I'd never make for a convincing dust fiend.

So, once I'd finished the meat on a stick—which was surprisingly decent, given that I couldn't even identify what sort of animal it came from—I headed back to the dock. Once I reached *The Leviathan*, I started rummaging through my disguise kit. Normally, Mimic was enough to get me in wherever I wanted to go, but sometimes, I'd had to get a bit creative with my outfits. So, over the past few years, I'd built quite a collection of disparate clothing. I had ball gowns and dresses that looked fit for a princess, but right alongside those glamorous garments were dingy and decrepit clothes from the other end of the spectrum.

I knew which side I preferred; I wasn't exactly a fashionista, but I don't think anyone can put on beggar's rags and be happy about it.

I spent the next hour selecting a properly dull and distressed outfit, then another twenty minutes or so dirtying myself up. Once I was satisfied with my level of uncleanliness, I adopted a new persona via Mimic. For my latest foray into the Pillar of Heaven, I chose the face of a woman I'd seen on my trip through the city. She was probably twice my real age, but she looked far older, with creased skin and the sort of bony physique I'd attached to my image of Cirilla.

By the time I'd finished, I was unrecognizable, and I hoped I wouldn't garner much attention as I infiltrated the headquarters of the Pillar of Heaven. So, I threw on a thick overcoat—it was cold outside, and I needed to hide my appearance from anyone who might take note of someone who looked like a beggar leaving a clearly expensive ship. Then, with my identity properly concealed, I headed back into the city. As I did so, I sent a message to Patrick telling him that I might not return until morning. He responded by telling me to stay safe.

So, with that obligation seen to, I traversed the city on foot. Along the way, I noticed that my appearance garnered very little attention. The people were too focused on their own mundanity to even look up from the sidewalks, much less spend the brainpower to notice someone like me.

Instead of taking a taxi or the Cutter, I made the journey as a pedestrian. As I walked, I made certain to alter my gait so that I maintained the facade I'd built. In my experience, dust fiends tended to walk and talk a certain way, and over the years, I'd managed to craft a decent facsimile. It wasn't an enjoyable task, but it was a necessary one.

By late afternoon, I'd reached my destination once again, and as I'd suspected, the twins didn't even give me a second look as I stepped inside. The interior of the headquarters was mostly what I had expected to find, meaning that it followed the same utilitarian design that seemed so prevalent in the rest of the city.

There were little flourishes that set it apart, though. For instance, there were actual paintings on the walls. Not posters. Not prints. Real paintings depicting paradisial vistas that seemed like a promise of something better. It only took me a moment to recognize the Mist coating every inch of them. I had no idea what it did, but I suspected it had something to do with manipulating the people inside the building.

I had no evidence that that was the case, but experience had been a great teacher. The presence of that Mist put my guard up even further.

I quickly found my way to the food bank and partook of a surprisingly tasty meal. I couldn't identify much of what was served, but it was much better than expected. That shouldn't have been terribly surprising, though. If the Pillar of Heaven was as nefarious an organization as I wanted to think they were, of course they would serve good food. Doing so would make people that much easier to hoodwink.

After I'd finished eating, I lingered in the addiction-treatment center. I didn't approach any of the workers—all of which were dressed in the same light-blue robes as the twin guards; I also didn't fail to notice that they were coated in that same artificial skin—but that wasn't terribly out of place. Many addicts, even after making the choice to seek help, tend to be hesitant, so my demeanor didn't really stick out.

It also gave me plenty of opportunity to observe, and what I saw was actually pleasant. Whatever else the Pillar of Heaven had going on, they were capable addiction counselors, and they approached the subject with tact and kindness.

That alone put my hackles up.

For better or worse, very few people could look at someone in the throes of addiction and respond with absolute kindness. Most regarded dust fiends as lost causes, public menaces, or pitiful creatures who needed to be put out of their misery. I'd seen it enough that any other reaction made me wonder about ulterior motives.

It was like meeting someone who, on the surface, seemed perfectly pleasant and kind, but somewhere beneath the surface, you know there's a dark secret. The Pillar of Heaven counselors were like that, only I didn't see their facades slip even once. No annoyance. No frustration. Just endless patience and kindness.

"Hello, friend," came a voice from my side. I feigned a flinch, then looked in that direction to see a pleasant-faced man staring back at me. Like all the other workers, he was wearing the same blue robes and artificial skin I'd begun to associate with the organization. "I haven't seen you here before."

"I . . . Uh . . ."

He held up a hand, stopping me as he said, "No, don't mistake me. I'm not judging. We all come to Heaven's Path when it is appropriate to do so."

"Heaven's Path? I thought this was just . . . you know . . . for food and . . . treatment," I said.

"For some, it is," he admitted with a kind smile. It creeped me out something fierce, but I didn't let that show. "But for others, it can be so much more. Tell me—what are you looking for here?"

"A hot meal," I said without a moment's hesitation. "And . . . maybe to get clean . . ."

"We can help with that. It's the least we can do for our fellow humans," he said. "But what if I told you there was somewhere better than all this? A paradise on Earth."

"I'd say you was tryin' to sell me somethin'," I muttered. "Ain't no paradise here."

"That's where you're wrong, friend," he said. "So, so very wrong. It exists, and I think you'd be a perfect candidate for . . . relocation . . ."

At that, he cocked his head to the side, almost as if he'd only just noticed something peculiar. Then, without a moment's hesitation, his hand shot out as he lunged at me, intending to grab hold of my arm. But I'd recognized that look the moment it crossed his face, so I was ready for it.

Not many people could see through Mimic, but it had happened enough that I could recognize the signs—especially when they were as poorly concealed as they were with this mook.

But to my surprise, I wasn't quite quick enough to avoid his grasping hand, and when he grabbed me, he did so with a grip like iron. Clearly, he wasn't the mild-mannered counselor he was pretending to be. So, I didn't at all feel guilty when I reared back and punched him in the jaw. The sound of breaking bone should have been satisfying. And usually, it would have been. The only problem was that those breaking bones were in my own hand.

I grunted in pain, but I didn't let it stop me from summoning Ferdinand II from my arsenal implant and aiming it at the man's face. I pulled the trigger, and the sound of the gunshot sent the crowd into a panic. But unsurprisingly, my pistol's issue only ripped the fake skin from the man's face, exposing metallic subdermal armor.

So, I fired again. This time, at his eye socket. That did the trick, and he went down like a ton of bricks.

Unfortunately, by that point, I was surrounded by a dozen blue-robed guards, each one of which was pointing a rifle at me. That's when I noticed that the man I'd downed was already picking himself up. His face was almost entirely destroyed, but that didn't seem to bother him one little bit.

Which made me realize that I might've stepped into something much more complicated than I had expected. At that point, some people might have made some witty comment. Or maybe tried to talk their way out of the situation. But me? I'd always been a proponent of letting my actions speak for me.

So, I opened fire.

Yeah—that was exactly the statement I wanted to make.

CHAPTER TWENTY-FOUR

A BROKEN PROMISE

Mira believes the world is doomed. I hope she's wrong, but everywhere I turn, I see evidence that if the aliens don't get us, we'll just do the job ourselves.

—Patrick Ward

I stepped through nothing, using Teleport to avoid a hail of gunfire aimed at my previous position. Even as a wave of vertigo assailed me, I kicked off the ground and sprinted away. The pounding of my heartbeat echoed the sound of my feet hitting the tiled floor, and panic suffused my mind as I turned a corner just in time to avoid another series of gunshots. Behind me, I heard a few slower members of the crowd cry out. Had they been hit? Or were they just frightened? I didn't know, and I had no way of finding out as I raced down the hallway.

My broken hand throbbed, and with almost my entire store of Mist having been drained by Teleport, I had little choice but to effect an escape. Or try to, considering that the blue-robed guards were already hot on my heels. Usually, the skill left people momentarily confused as to my whereabouts, but my pursuers had reacted with terrifying alacrity. If I didn't move—and fast—they were going to close the gap. Never was that more apparent than when I reached the end of the hall and, before I could turn the corner, another barrage of bullets came. I managed to avoid most of them by dipping around the bend, but one lodged itself in my shoulder while another hit me in the hip.

It was all I could do to maintain my balance as fiery pain ripped through my body. Some part of my mind managed to catalog the fact that the bullets had made it through the high-quality infiltration suit I wore under my rags as well as the subdermal Sheath that was normally enough to stop gunfire. But even as I recognized those necessary bits of knowledge, I ignored them—because they wouldn't change my course. I was already committed to escape, and so, knowing that they had weaponry capable of penetrating my defenses was a confirmation I didn't really need.

Still, if there was a silver lining, it was that the bullets, while being capable of getting through my armor, were incapable of doing much else. My defenses weren't enough to stop the rounds cold, but the combined barriers of my Sheath and infiltration suit had robbed the bullets of much of their momentum. As a result, what should have been a pair of debilitating wounds was little more than an inconvenience.

But, even through my Pain Tolerance, an agonizing one.

Turning the corner gave me a precious second or two to take stock of the situation. There were at least a dozen blue-robed guards in pursuit, and stuck as I was on their home turf, I counted it an unlikely possibility that there weren't plenty more where they'd come from. On top of that, the guards were far and away more powerful than any random mook had a right to be. The one I'd shot had taken a bullet from Ferdinand II in the face—two of them, in fact—and I knew from experience just how powerfully destructive that could be. But he'd shrugged it off without any problems at all.

And then there was the result of my punch to worry about.

I was not the strongest person in the world. Certainly, my Constitution was high enough that I could hold my own, but most of my physical training was focused on speed, balance, and agility. And in those areas, I excelled. My raw strength lagged a bit behind, but it was still more than respectable.

So, the fact that the guard hadn't even been fazed by my punch was very concerning. The force I'd brought to bear wasn't the issue. Rather, it felt like I'd punched a Mist-infused wall. Or, belatedly, I realized another possibility.

"Uh, Pick—I think we've got a problem," I said through the Secure Connection. I hadn't contacted him since beginning my mission, but I thought it was more than appropriate to break the silence. "Like, a big one."

Only a second passed before he groaned, "What now?"

"I think I might've just punched a robot in the face," I said. It was the only thing that made sense. I'd fought plenty of cyborgs—Ashleigh, the so-called Red Terror, and Dierdre, Gunther's number one henchwoman came to mind— but none had taken a punch like that unaffected. That led me to the conclusion that either I'd met someone with incredibly advanced cybernetics or a robot. Neither was a comforting thought, but I was particularly distressed by the notion that some random guard would be equipped with enhancements that put mine to shame. So, I'd latched on to the more likely scenario—robots.

All of that flitted through my mind in the time it took Patrick to respond. When he did, it was with a resigned sigh. "You promised, Mira," he said.

Skidding around another corner and barreling through a crowd of dust addicts, I said, "Not my fault."

"How is it not your fault? You were the one doing the punching, right?" he asked.

I vaulted over another group, hoping that they would act as a barrier for my pursuers. When I landed, I responded, "They pointed guns at me. You know how much I hate that."

"Why did they . . . You know what? Never mind," he said. "What do you want me to do? I can be in *The Leviathan*'s cockpit in about fifteen minutes."

"Just hold steady," I said. "This isn't over."

Indeed, the mystery had only deepened. Cults were vile enough on their own, but the idea of an organization that had access to advanced robots that could mimic humanity? That was terrifying. And interesting. Suddenly, the disappearance of Cirilla's brother was a lot more intriguing.

With a moment to spare, I yanked a Mist booster from my arsenal implant and jabbed the needle into my uninjured hip. With a hiss, it discharged its payload, and I felt a surge of Mist suffuse my body. With that taken care of, I reached the building's lobby only to find myself facing off against another dozen blue-robed guards.

Which probably should have been a problem. But the fact that these were robots presented an opportunity, as well. After all, I had a Ghost deck built specifically for dealing with fully mechanical creatures. And without the use of one hand—it felt like I had broken every tiny bone in there—using my Ghosts was probably the best option. So, I embraced Misthack and targeted the centermost guard.

Like all the rest, she looked almost identical to the first couple I'd encountered. That, as much as anything else, suggested that they were artificial creatures. The moment I used Misthack, the familiar menu appeared. I selected the appropriate response, broke through the laughable defenses, and chose the intended deck. It all happened in less than a second—my processing speed was unreal, and it had been further enhanced by intense training—but in that time, the guards had already raised their weapons.

I let the Ghost loose as I once again teleported to the side, avoiding another hail of gunfire that instead ripped into the crowd of addicts. They'd barely begun to scream when the Ghost took hold. By that point, I'd infected the other guards, as well.

Robot Disposal, despite its mundane name, was a masterpiece. Aside from *Time Bomb*—and its various incarnations—it was the most complicated Ghost I'd ever written. Against humans—or mostly biological creatures—it was almost entirely useless. It would cause a bit of a headache, but beyond that, it had no effect at all.

But for robots and drones, it was an entirely different story.

One by one, the not-people dropped. Outwardly, there were no signs as to what had happened, but I knew the internals would tell a different tale. While writing the Ghost, I'd practiced its use on hundreds of cheap bots that Patrick had made, and in that time, I'd gotten a very good picture of what it did.

The basic gist of it was pure devastation. In the beginning, I'd been happy to fry a few key circuits, but the latest version wreaked absolute havoc on anything mechanical. I still wasn't sure why it didn't affect people—it would be an incredible boon if it did—but I wasn't going to complain too much. After all, I had plenty of other tools at my beck and call if I needed to deal with people.

I was just patting myself on the back when everything went wrong.

Not only had the other guards caught up, but I was distressed—and horrified—to see that my vaunted Ghost, tested hundreds of times and seemingly foolproof—only had a temporary effect on the robots. Were they, in fact, human? The fact that they were already picking themselves up from the floor suggested as much. But I had a niggling feeling that there was more to the story.

After all, I didn't know everything. In fact, I knew almost nothing about being a {Mistrunner}. It wasn't as if I had a teacher. Instead, I'd been making my own way after my uncle had died, and I was sure there was an entire galaxy of details of which I was not aware.

Thankfully, *Robot Disposal* had left the guards in front of me disoriented. Even as they tried to fight through it, I crashed through their ranks and through the building's front door. The moment I stepped outside, I summoned the Cutter, mounted it, and took off. By that point, the pursuing guards had caught up. As I sped away, I was further distressed to see that those guards—seemingly mundane—were capable of running almost as fast as I could.

Fortunately, the Cutter was leagues ahead in terms of speed, and I quickly left them behind. Over the next few minutes, I rocketed through the streets of Fortune, weaving between the self-driving rickshaws as well as the few hover cars on the road. I didn't return to *The Leviathan*, though. Instead, I made one haphazard turn after another before, almost twenty minutes later, I reached a dark alley in a less-populated part of town. Once there, I dismissed the Cutter and entered what appeared to be an abandoned building.

Inside, there were a couple of vagrants, but they were far too high to notice me—especially when I'd already wrapped myself in Stealth. It didn't take me long to find an out-of-the-way room. Inside, every surface—it had once been a domicile, I was sure—was coated in a thick layer of dust, so I felt confident that it was just as abandoned as my first impression suggested.

Reassured that I wouldn't have some junkie barging in on me at the most inopportune time, I engaged my defenses. First came a holographic display that I hoped would hide me from cursory examination. That, along with my Stealth and Camouflage abilities, would keep me hidden. Then, for good measure, I canceled the Bastion I had left around *The Leviathan* and activated it to protect my current position.

"Took Bastion down from the ship," I told Patrick. "Needed it more out here."

"Understood," he said, responding through the Secure Connection.

That was one of the things I loved about Patrick. He didn't complain. Nor did he ask stupid questions—not when it mattered, at least. Instead, he accepted that I knew what I was doing.

That made one of us.

Even in the best of times, my confidence was almost entirely composed of bravado. Certainly, I trusted my abilities as well as my training, but I always felt like I was scrambling and making things up as I went along. And I was constantly discovering just how much I didn't know.

Case in point, those guards.

Were they robots? Or the humans they appeared to be? Maybe they were just a different sort of cyborg. There was nothing to say that they all had to look like Dierdre, right? Some people probably preferred the flesh-and-blood aesthetic as opposed to the walking-tank look.

But I'd gotten a brief look at their systems, and I could say one thing for certain: they had Nexus Implants.

"Not that that means anything," I muttered to myself as I finished setting up my defenses. There was an entire universe of things I'd never seen, which effectively made my ignorance infinite. For all I knew, all the robots in the wider universe were equipped with Nexus Implants.

I cleared the dust from a patch of floor, then laid down a clean blanket for good measure. Finally, I commenced with my least favorite activity: cataloging and treating my injuries.

Curiously, the hand had gotten the worst of it. It was just further evidence that I needed to use the Hand of God for that kind of thing. Thankfully, though, only two bones were broken. Hopefully, my Constitution, combined with my abilities, would heal it fairly quickly. I'd also picked up a few abrasions I didn't know about, as well as a third gunshot wound in my upper thigh I hadn't even noticed.

After undressing, I inspected each wound, then applied foam bandages and a generous dose of antibiotics and anesthetic via one of my higher-quality med-hypos. It was telling that the entire process was mechanical; I'd treated so many injuries over the years that even gunshot wounds were uninteresting.

With that taken care of, I sighed and leaned back against the wall. Once again, I'd cut things incredibly close. And the worst part of it was that I hadn't even hurt my attackers. They'd shrugged off everything I could bring to bear.

Granted, I hadn't broken out the big guns, but still—it rankled on my pride that I'd left any of them alive.

It wasn't the first time I'd lost a fight. In fact, I wasn't even sure if I'd call what happened in the Pillar of Heaven headquarters a fight, per se. It was more like running away. Or a strategic retreat.

Yeah—that sounded so much better.

With my pride assuaged by self-delusion, I started to contemplate how to combat the situation. For the time being, I was safe enough. Hopefully, the guard hadn't truly seen through Mimic. Usually, that was the case. On the rare occasions when someone had recognized the ability, they hadn't actually seen my real face. Rather, they just knew the one I was wearing wasn't the real one.

If that was the case with the Pillar of Heaven guard, then I could keep going with my investigation. If not, then I'd probably have to leave the city. And given that Patrick had barely even begun his project, that wasn't what I wanted. Besides, the organization—cult, really—had garnered my interest. I didn't much care about Cirilla's brother, but a cult of robots? That was intriguing.

But I had no intention of heading back out until I'd had a chance to adjust some things. As proud of *Robot Disposal* as I was, I'd fallen into the trap of resting on my laurels. I'd made the mistake of thinking it was perfect just the way it was. And in most cases, it was good enough. I'd just had the misfortune of running into one of the few circumstances where it was woefully ineffective.

"Good is the enemy of great," my uncle had once told me, and never was that statement truer than when I'd found out that my Ghost was completely incapable of doing its job.

But that was fine. It simply gave me the motivation I needed for improvement. So, with nothing else to do, I dove back into *Robot Disposal*, searching out impurities in the structure. There weren't many, but with fresh eyes and proper drive, I could see precisely how inefficient the Ghost really was.

I'd gotten around the problem by simply throwing more power at it, but clearly, that wasn't always a viable solution. It was like trying to drive a nail into a board with a sledgehammer. Sure, it could work, but it wasn't the best way to go about doing the job. So, with that in mind, I went through the Ghost with a fine-tooth comb. And predictably, I found plenty of problems.

Hours passed as I continued to examine *Robot Disposal*, but my focus never wavered. In fact, I found the entire process oddly comforting—probably because it was a problem I could immediately work toward solving. The same couldn't be said for the Pillar of Heaven or their robotic guards.

Again, that was probably for the best. If I never encountered enemies that pushed me to my limits, I would never improve. And considering the impending alien invasion, improvement was probably the only way I could hope to survive, let alone thrive. There was an entire universe out there, and I'd barely scratched the surface of what was possible. The whole idea was a bit overwhelming, and I knew the only way to combat that was to continue working toward smaller goals, one step at a time.

For now, I would rewrite my Ghost. Then, I would solve the mystery of the Pillar of Heaven. After that, I would worry about the gnomes. And eventually, I would take on the entire universe.

One step at a time.

I sighed and got to work.

CHAPTER TWENTY-FIVE

INVESTIGATION

I've never seen someone work as hard or as long as Mira. Sometimes, I wonder how she does it, but then I remember who raised her. I remember the stories she's told me about her training. And then, it becomes all too clear.

—Patrick Ward

I spent two days in that disgusting room, and only once was I forced to dissuade someone from disturbing my privacy. Fortunately, dust fiends are particularly vulnerable to some of my more powerful Ghosts, so it only took one use of *Confusion* to send the pitiful woman on her way. A good thing, too, because if she'd made it even one step farther, she would have been forced to endure the effects of Bastion. And in her state, I suspected she wouldn't have survived.

The ability wasn't usually lethal, but dust seemed to compound its dissuasive effects. So, I was grateful that she stumbled down the hall when I was taking a break from working on *Robot Disposal*.

Interruptions notwithstanding, I'd made a ton of progress on the Ghost front. In doing so, I'd had to completely dismantle the Ghost and start from scratch. The foundations were flawed, and so if I kept going the way I was, the structure would always suffer. And as a result, so would the effect. So, I'd made the choice to rebuild it entirely. It would take a lot longer—weeks, if I was diligent—but I was certain that it would pay off in the end.

I would just be down one of my most potent tools in the meantime. Fortunately, I had plenty of abilities, other Ghosts, and weapons to make up for the lack. I hoped.

Whatever the case, those two days served another, arguably more important purpose in that they gave me the chance to heal. My Regeneration was powerful, and it was supported by the natural healing associated with my inflated Constitution. But even so, I couldn't heal broken bones overnight.

Instead, it took me two nights.

Of course, the bones weren't entirely mended. It would take about a week for them to return to perfection. However, by the dawn of the third day, I could use the hand, which was good enough. As for the gunshot wounds and other abrasions, they only took a day to scab over, so after a second day, I was as good as new. Without my subdermal armor or infiltration suit, that would not have been the case.

Muscle, fat, and skin were much easier to heal than internal injuries, I'd found.

During my convalescence, I'd kept in touch with Patrick, but we hadn't discussed much of consequence. So, I was a little surprised when he finally broke the news that I was a wanted woman.

"What?"

"Well, not the real you. The identity you were using for sure, though. They say you're a terrorist."

"Me? I didn't even do anything!" I insisted.

"Not according to the authorities," he said before explaining the story the Pillar of Heaven had fabricated, which consisted of me charging into the building and opening fire. According to the official statement they'd given, I'd indiscriminately killed every single dust fiend in the building. The only survivors were members of the Pillar of Heaven.

I sighed. It all made sense. They weren't going to very well tell the authorities that they'd killed a bunch of people who'd come to them for help. Even if they'd only done so accidentally, that wasn't going to garner much goodwill from the public. But being the victim of a terrorist attack? That simultaneously made them sympathetic while establishing the cult's importance. After all, terrorists didn't attack just anyone.

Making things even better for the Pillar of Heaven was the fact that their members had survived. The message of that was clear: the cult protected its people. That would be enough to get plenty of the city's population on board with a potential manhunt as well as painting their organization in a favorable light.

Whatever the case, it was annoying. I wasn't going to shy away from taking the blame for the things I had actually done. My self-recrimination included the events of Nova City as well as my actions leading up to its destruction. I had killed thousands of people, and the responsibility for many times that could rightfully be laid at my feet. But I hadn't killed a single person in the headquarters of the Pillar of Heaven, and the fact that they'd blamed me for their own actions made me incredibly angry.

If I hadn't already been committed to opposing them, I certainly was after that. Maybe they weren't evil—there was no telling without more information—but their actions certainly suggested as much. After all, they'd responded to a mere disguise with lethal intent, and when I'd escaped, they hadn't hesitated to mow down a bunch of innocent civilians. Then, they'd had the audacity to blame me for it. None of that said good guys, at least as far as I was concerned.

"Please don't blow them up," Patrick said.

"Huh?"

"No explosions."

"I wasn't going to," I lied. In fact, at that very moment, I'd been considering just how easily I could bring that building down. Robots or not, a few tons of falling plasti-steel would probably incapacitate them.

"I'm serious, Mira," he said. "Please."

I sighed, then said, "Fine. But just so we're clear, I really wasn't going to blow anything up."

"Sure, sure. So, what are you going to do?" he asked.

Even though he couldn't see me—after all, our communication was inaudible and long-distance—I shrugged. "Investigate, I guess," I said. "Now that I know they can see through Mimic, I know how to approach things."

Indeed, I'd given it a lot of thought, and I'd latched on to the simple fact that the guard hadn't immediately recognized my ability for what it was. Instead, he had led me all around the building, completely unaware that I wasn't what I appeared to be. That said that, so long as I didn't draw much attention to myself, I should be able to fly under the radar. That meant that Stealth would almost assuredly yield better results than Mimic.

"I think I'm going to have to go full cat burglar," I said.

"You think that's safe?"

"Probably not. But you're the one who told me not to blow them all up."

"Which you said you hadn't been planning to do, anyway," he pointed out.

"I don't always tell the truth. Keep up, Pick."

I could practically hear his sigh of frustration, but he didn't say anything else on the subject. Instead, he told me about his own progress. He and Cirilla had begun their examination of the Mist circuits, and though they didn't dare to use them—not yet, at least—they were well on their way to understanding how they worked.

"In a couple of months, we might be ready to start integrating them into cybernetics," he said. "Virtually, at least. Cy has this simulation program that we can run before—"

"Wait—a couple of months?" I exclaimed. I'd hoped to be done in Fortune after a week or two, and now he was telling me that they would be working on the project for at least two months? And that wasn't even considering the testing and implementation phases that would precede the final product. "How long is this thing supposed to take?"

"Uh . . . A year? Maybe a little less. I don't know yet because—"

"Ugh," I groaned. "You know what, just don't tell me. I'll do my best to stay busy."

"Mira, we don't—"

Once again, I interrupted him, "It's fine, Pick. It'll be worth it. Just concentrate on getting it done."

After that, our conversation slowly wound down. Even in the best of times, talking over the Secure Connection was a little impersonal, so neither of us wanted to discuss anything important like that unless necessary. Once he started to hint that he needed to get to work, I decided to do the same.

To that end, I left the room that had been my humble abode for the past couple of days. My trip out of the building wasn't eventful, but when I hit the streets, that changed. For one, most of the people I passed seemed incredibly anxious, and it didn't take me long to figure out why. From their perspective, some crazy woman had just shot up an organization whose only apparent purpose was to help the disregarded dregs of society. And given that I was currently in the least affluent part of town, it wasn't hard to see why the people were nervous.

Thankfully, I had the option of changing my face. It wouldn't do much to disguise me from the Pillar of Heaven, but for mundane people like the pedestrians I passed along the way back to the cult's headquarters, it worked fine.

Even so, I did get a dose of déjà vu as I trekked through the city. It wasn't really all that long ago that I'd seen those same nervous expressions on the faces of Nova City's citizens. And that had not ended well. Was I destined to have that effect wherever I went? Would Fortune soon descend into urban warfare?

I hoped not.

But I had to acknowledge that it was a distinct possibility. I didn't intend to go to war. In fact, I wanted the opposite result. However, things didn't always work out like I wanted them to, and I knew just how quickly a situation could careen out of control.

After all, I'd never wanted to destroy the whole of Nova City, either. I'd just been so focused on my goal that I never even considered what would happen if I pushed Nora into a corner. And I certainly didn't consider how my actions would affect the normal citizenry. They were just pieces of an overall puzzle and, thus, were beneath my notice.

That was then, though. Now, after spending three years in the world, I had a different perspective, and I could no longer ignore the consequences of my actions. As such, I couldn't simply do whatever I wanted to do; instead, I had to think of the repercussions.

So, I approached the building with appropriate caution. It was a hive of activity—far more than it had been a few days before—which supported my supposition that the "terrorist attack" had done wonders for the public's perception of the Pillar of Heaven. If the number of people heading into the building was any indication, my visit had been one of the best things that had ever happened to the cult.

After walking past the headquarters, I set off toward a cluster of buildings down the street so I could observe the comings and goings without being seen. Once there, I quickly made my way to the roof, where I settled in to gather information. I was an old hand at surveillance, but I wasn't immune to the boredom that inevitably came with it. Still, I only had to remember my previous encounter with the robots in human-face to keep that boredom at bay. I needed whatever intelligence I could gather if I was going to keep from repeating the same mistakes.

Over the next few hours, I grew ever more confident in my assertion that the blue-robed guards were all robots. They moved too predictably, like they were just following an established protocol. More, they never seemed to get distracted or bored. Instead, they just stood there, answered questions when they were asked, and otherwise acted as model guards.

They never even went to the bathroom, which, while it was possible they were just really good at holding it in, was improbable.

And that presented a host of problems, not least of which was that I had no real assessment of their capabilities. Were they really as durable as they'd seemed? I hadn't used any of my more powerful weapons—Ferdinand II wasn't even loaded with armor-piercing rounds—so I couldn't be sure of how vulnerable they really were.

On top of that, I had no notion of how many were there. Nor did I know what kind of support system they had. For all I knew, they had a thousand more guards of indeterminate power stashed away nearby.

The whole thing stunk of a death trap, and as reckless as I might sometimes seem, there was no chance I was going to rush in and get myself killed. So, even though I didn't relish the necessity, I continued to observe. And as the hours passed, I got few answers to my questions, and when I finally decided to head back to *The Leviathan*, I did so with many of the same blind spots niggling at my conscious mind.

By the time I returned to the ship, Patrick was already there. And he looked exhausted.

"Long day?"

"Long couple of days," he said, plopping down on the well-worn couch in the ship's common area. He wasted no time before lying down, his head in my lap. I snaked my fingers through his curly blond hair as he explained that his research into the Mist circuits had already hit a snag. Further complicating matters was that Tate seemed hell-bent on hanging around and, subsequently, getting in the way.

"It's not that she's useless," he went on. "She's smart and pretty capable. If I needed someone to fix *The Leviathan*, she'd be exactly the kind of mechanic I would turn to."

"But?"

"But she's a mechanic. She has no grasp of the theoretical concepts we're working with on the Mist circuits," he said. "If you want her to put something together or fix it, she's your girl. Otherwise, she's just in the way. I get being interested, but she's hurting us a lot more than she's helping."

I nodded along, but I suspected that she was hanging around not because she found the Mist circuits so intriguing, but rather because her girlfriend's ex was hanging about. I couldn't imagine there was a lot of trust in that relationship.

Or maybe I was just determined to see Cirilla in the worst light possible.

"And now she wants to see *The Leviathan*," he finished with a sigh. "She won't shut up about it, actually."

"I don't . . . I don't think that's a great idea," I stated, and that was the truth. I didn't like having other people on board, and not just because of the problems that might come with that sort of thing. It was also because *The Leviathan* was the home Patrick and I shared, and having other people poking around inside felt like an invasion of privacy.

"I actually agree."

"Actually? You say that like it's surprising."

"Uh . . ." I had to suppress a giggle as he quickly changed the subject. "So, how goes the cult business?"

"Frustrating," I stated. Then, I went on to explain my issues. First among them was that I had no idea how strong the robots were. Second, I didn't know the building's layout or how many fighters they could muster. Finally, I admitted, "And I don't know what'll happen if I push things. I really don't want another Nova on my conscience."

"So, don't attack the nest," he said. "Seriously—they're taking all those people somewhere, right? Just follow them. That way, they'll be out in the open so you can see what you're getting into. You can also see how they respond to any creatures that attack, which might give you some ideas as to their relative strength."

I started to respond, but then I realized that he was right. Normally, my go-to strategy was to attack every problem head-on. However, in this case, doing so would be a huge mistake. Attacking the issue from a different angle seemed so obvious that I wondered how I hadn't come up with it myself.

But then again, I had only slept about two collective hours over the past three days, so perhaps that was a good explanation. The moment that thought crossed my mind, I felt my eyelids drooping. My Constitution was high enough that I could keep going for quite some time yet, but there would always be consequences to ignoring my body's need for sleep. Finally, it seemed that it was catching up to me.

In my defense, sleeping in a den of junkies while I was being hunted by a bunch of androids probably wasn't the greatest idea in the world. But now that I was safe back in *The Leviathan*, sleep was definitely calling my name.

Still, I tried to resist. Unsuccessfully, as it turned out. I barely even remember going to bed—just that I woke up some time later to find myself in the comfortable and familiar confines of the bedroom I shared with Patrick. He wasn't there—regrettably—but I was still too tired to care that much. Before I knew it, I was back asleep; hopefully, my next encounter with the Pillar of Heaven would go a little better.

CHAPTER TWENTY-SIX

STALKERS

Pressure is a funny thing. For some people, it's a prerequisite for greatness. They can't thrive unless something is pushing them. But for others? That constant pressure is a detriment, preventing them from ever reaching their potential. And then there are people like Mira, for whom pressure is just a way of life. She barely acknowledges it, and it's gotten to the point where I'm not even sure she feels the weight on her shoulders.

—Patrick Ward

It took three more days of surveillance before the appropriate situation presented itself. In that time, I continued to work on the Ghost formerly known as *Robot Disposal*. With what I had planned, the name just felt a bit too silly, even if I was the only one who'd ever see it. As far as I knew—which increasingly didn't seem like all that much—no one else could see the names of my Ghosts, but on the off chance that I was wrong, I wanted to assign a more dignified name to my robot-murdering Ghost. Or failing that, at least something that sounded a bit more technical.

But that was a worry for another time because, at that moment, I had other things on my mind. First, I'd finally gotten what I'd been waiting for in that the Pillar of Heaven was on the move. At present, I was lagging about a half mile behind a caravan that had exited the city earlier that morning. In most ways, the convoy looked much like a hundred others I'd seen. Comprised of twenty vehicles which carried three dozen blue-robed guards as well as ten times as many refugees and addicts, it was an imposing force made even more dangerous by the fact that two of those vehicles were military grade, featuring powerful cannons that would probably be enough to down even *The Leviathan*.

The guards themselves were almost identical to the ones I'd seen back in Fortune. They wore blue robes, bore rifles, and even when they possessed plainly different characteristics, they struck me as identical. Like robots with different cosmetic features. It was as if some had chosen the blonde-female model while others had picked the brunette-male version. Underneath, they were probably all the same.

Which was terrifying, considering that if it had taken me so long to recognize it. Would normal people without my advantages ever see them for what they were? I guessed not, as evidenced by the fact that, according to Cirilla and Tate, they'd had a presence within the city for more than a year without much incident.

The convoy had stopped in the late afternoon and circled the proverbial wagons. Literally speaking, they arranged the various vehicles in a large circle, then enabled a portable Mist shield that I knew would do little to deter a determined predator. However, it was better than nothing and spoke highly of their competence. After all, potent Mist shields were both expensive to run and costly to obtain. It was unlikely they had access to anything better than the one they'd deployed.

Either way, the goings-on in the camp was only my first concern. The second was decidedly different but no less troubling.

Because someone was stalking me.

Poorly, too. I'd known they were there since the very beginning. They were using some sort of skill to mask their presence, but they'd forgotten to account for all the little things. Like the way the mundane wildlife reacted to their presence. Or the distinct lack of a smell where there should have been myriad aromas. They had even ignored the broken branches and disturbed rocks they left behind in their wake.

I wasn't sure whether or not I should be insulted or appreciative. It didn't take me long to decide it wasn't a gnome following me. The Dengyts I had encountered before had been entirely undetectable. So, at some point in Fortune, I'd clearly picked up a tail. They'd been following me ever since I'd left the city, and it seemed that they weren't going to give up the low-speed chase anytime soon.

And that meant that I needed to do something about whoever was brave enough to follow me around. So, as I lay on my stomach, watching the Pillar of Heaven camp, I kept Observation running at full tilt so I could keep an eye on my stalker.

As the night wore on, they crept progressively closer—emboldened by my lack of reaction, no doubt—and it wasn't long before I caught wind of their scent. As befitted someone who'd been outdoors for the entire day, it was not a pleasant odor. More, there was a hint of aromatic oils, suggesting that my stalker had a bit of a vain streak. Still, it wasn't overpowering, and without Observation, I never would have even noticed the smell.

Finally, once they'd gotten within ten feet, I decided to make my move.

Wheeling around, I summoned my oft-unused scattergun and trained it on my stalker's unseen form. Then, before they could react, I said, "You should really work on your stealth skills. Don't move or I'll put you down, tie you up, and torture you until you answer my questions."

"Whoa! Hold up! I didn't—"

"And keep your voice down," I spat, recognizing that my stalker was male—at least judging by his relatively deep voice, which was usually a good indicator. "Those robots down there probably have pretty good hearing. Or whatever passes for hearing for, you know, robots. Either way, use your inside voice."

"I don't—"

"Also, drop that skill. I don't like talking to a disembodied voice."

"Wait, you can't see me?"

At that moment, he tried to move away. To his credit, he was pretty good. He didn't make a sound. Nor could I see even a ripple to indicate his presence. But with Observation going, tracking him, especially when he was so close, was child's play. So, as he shuffled to the side, clearly intending to bolt, I followed him with the stubby barrel of the scattergun.

"I can smell you," I said. "So, let's not try to run, huh? I don't want to chase you through the forest at night. There are predators out there, you know."

"Huh? Of course . . ."

I used Teleport, draining my Mist in the process, but I didn't need skills or abilities to clamp the Hand of God around his neck. I squeezed. "I said to drop the skill," I growled in my best no-nonsense villain voice. It probably came out more as an annoyed squeak, but I hoped it would get the point across, anyway. "I don't usually like to repeat myself. If I have to do it again, I'm going to get angry."

"Ack," he choked, obviously trying to respond. Beneath my cybernetic fingers, I could feel his strength. His Constitution wasn't nearly as well-developed as mine, but he was no slouch, either. Perhaps I shouldn't have used the entirety of my Mist reserves to Teleport.

Finally, he let his skill drop. I noticed that the Mist swirled strangely when he did, but I was more concerned with the fact that, judging by his white robes, I'd captured myself a Templar. I released him the moment I saw his attire. He fell to one knee, massaging his throat. Maybe I'd gripped it harder than I intended.

"Why the hell is a Templar following me?" I demanded. "I've never done anything to you guys."

He held up one finger, then coughed a couple of times before rasping, "You really need to work on your people skills."

"You were stalking me. My people skills never came into it," I countered. "Now, tell me what's going on or, so help me, I'm going to start shooting, and I'm not going to stop until everything is dead."

He tilted his head up, and as he did so, I got my first good look at him. And I was struck by two things. First, he was young. Maybe sixteen, and that might've been a stretch. He had the gangly body of a youth who hadn't quite caught up with a growth spurt, and the soft fuzz on his cheeks seemed to support the notion that he was extremely young. Second, he would one day be quite a handsome man. For now, though, the combination of youth and his features gave his face a borderline feminine cast that was only accentuated by his long, curly hair, which he wore in a messy bun.

"You're staring," he said. "I know I'm a beautiful specimen, but I have to tell you up front—it's not happening."

"What?"

"You and me. I know it makes all the sense in the world after our little meet-cute here, but—"

"Shut up or I'm going to shoot you."

He grinned, making him look even prettier. And he was pretty. Not handsome. I'd decided that the moment I'd gotten a good look. "See? This is what I'm talking about. We already have the banter thing down. Before long, you're going to end up chasing me through the airport so you can profess your love. But like I said, I'm cutting that off right now. I'm already spoken for."

I was about to respond to his inane blather—what the hell was an airport, anyway?—but I stopped myself before falling into the trap. He was just trying to distract me and keep me off guard, and I wasn't going to let myself play into that ruse. Instead, I said, "So. Templars are following me. Why?"

"And if I don't answer?"

"That's when I shoot you and the torture starts," I stated. Realistically, I had no intention of following through with the promise—torture was a terrible way to get information—but he didn't need to know that. The threat of pain was usually just as effective as the real thing.

"You're really aggressive. You know that, don't you? And while I could see some men being attracted to that kind of thing, I'm just not—"

I pointedly raised my weapon and said, "Three."

"What are you—"

"Two."

"Wait!" he hissed, holding up his hands in surrender. "I didn't . . . I wasn't . . . I mean, I'm not even a Templar. Not yet. The only reason I was following you is because my master told me to!"

"And your master is?"

"Uh . . . He's friendly. He said he met you one time. Frederick Eagin. He's a master of the Templar Council, so you'd better—"

"Freddie's here?"

I'd only had a brief meeting with the man in question, but it had been a memorable one. Part of that was due to the nature of the meeting itself; he'd been in mourning over the transformation of his apprentice into a wildling, and I had just finished my first Rift. That was before the fall of Mobile, and back then, I'd actually believed the world was a fair place full of good people.

I had been wrong.

Of course, the opposite wasn't completely true, either, but that assertion might've had more to do with my resolution to look at things differently than it did with the reality of the world.

"Oh, I bet he hates that you call him that."

"I've only met him once, and I don't think either of us were in any state to judge the other," I said. "So, I'm wondering why he had me followed by a little kid."

"Little kid? I'm bigger than—"

"Shut up. Just tell me what's going on here and I'll decide whether or not to kill you."

Swallowing hard, he seemed to realize the gravity of the situation when he breathed, "But . . . I didn't . . . You would kill me?" Then, he remembered to bring his feigned bravado as he squared his shoulders and asked, "And who says you could? Maybe I'll be the one who . . . uh . . . takes you down."

He almost said it without letting his voice waver, which was more than I would've expected had I given it much thought. I rolled my eyes and said, "I'm game to figure out the answer to that question if you are. But I'll remind you that I'm the one with a gun pointed at you. It was built to be nonlethal, but aliens' perception of what constitutes lethality is kind of skewed. I've found that it rarely lives up to its intended purpose. Maybe you'll be one of the few who can take it. I don't know. But this conversation is beginning to annoy me, so if you want to figure things out, let's do it now."

For a moment, as his expression went from fear to annoyance and then to anger, I thought he might take me up on the offer. But then, he surprised me when he once again held his hands up in surrender before saying, "I'm here in peace. Master just wanted me to watch you and let him know if you get in trouble with the Pacificians."

"The who now?"

"Pacificians. You know, the aliens you've been following?"

"Wait, they're not robots?" I asked. Shaking my head, I said, "No. They definitely are. I saw the wires."

That's when he started laughing, stretching my patience to its limit. I didn't care that there was a lot more nervous giggle to it than outright mirth; I was getting extremely annoyed, and I wanted some answers. So, I shoved the gun in his face and said, "Explain. Now."

That certainly brought his laughter up short, and he tried to back away. I stepped forward, maintaining the barrel's close proximity to his dainty nose. Predictably, as he took another step back, he tripped over a rock and fell on his backside.

"Okay! Okay! I'm sorry!" he said. "I just . . . I don't know . . . The way he described you . . . Well, I just thought you'd know who you were following is all."

"And who is that? Pacificians. Aliens, not robots, right? What else?" I asked.

"Well, the line's kind of blurred, right? These guys are bad news. Everyone knows to steer clear of them."

I let it go that everyone didn't include anyone I knew, instead focusing on the relevant facts. "Why? They were actually doing some good back in Fortune," I said. "Helping addicts and feeding the poor doesn't really seem all that evil to me."

"Good and evil are manufactured concepts. There is only weak and strong. Everything else is just an illusion people cling to so they can feel better about themselves," he said, sounding like he was reciting something he'd memorized. Perhaps that was one of the Templars' tenets.

"I don't care. What makes people steer clear of the Pacificians?"

"Uh . . . Well, they kind of are evil," he said. "But don't tell Master I said that. We're not supposed to look at the world like that. Anyway, these guys are bad news. Like, they're kind of known for colonizing entire planets."

"So are most aliens," I pointed out.

"Not really. Some prey on newly Initialized planets, but most aliens are actually fine."

"And you've met a lot of aliens?"

"Well, no. Just one, and that wasn't in person. But that's what we've been taught," he admitted.

I glanced back at the circled vehicles in the distance. It was still quiet, so I focused on the conversation with my stalker. "Again," I said, my annoyance mounting. "What's so bad about the Pacificians?"

"They're kind of like an invasive species. Or at least that's how the rest of the universe sees them," he answered. "Like, they come in, and within a few decades, they've converted the entire population."

"How?"

"Social engineering, brainwashing, propaganda—that sort of thing. Oh, and they promise eternal life," he said. "And undiluted freedom from choice."

I gestured for him to go on.

"So, the social stuff comes first, right? They make promises, and they keep them. They feed people. They help them with their problems. And all the while, they make sure everyone knows just what they have to offer. The general pitch is eternal life, but there's also freedom from addiction. If you join the collective, you don't have to worry about food or shelter or anything else. You'll be just one piece of the whole, with a job to do and—"

"The collective. What is that?"

"Well, the Pacificians are a hive mind. Sort of. That's how they started, at least. In their native forms, they're, like, fish people or something. I don't know exactly because they left all that behind a long time ago. Now, they ride along in robotic bodies. And that's what they promise everyone who joins. State-of-the-art bodies. According to my teachers, the brains aren't even biological anymore. But I don't know how any of that works."

Suddenly, everything began to make sense. Before finding out that the members of the Pillar of Heaven—or at least the leaders of the organization— were aliens, I'd begun to wonder if my worldview was irreparably skewed. After all, they seemed like good people who just wanted to help. That they had an ulterior motive—to add to their collective—was comforting, in a way.

And wholly horrifying, as well.

But what really terrified me was that I could see the draw. If I understood the situation correctly, the benefits on offer were a powerful motivator. How many addicts would do anything—even giving themselves over to a hive mind—if it meant they could leave their habits behind? Making it even more attractive was that those people would never have to worry about where they might find their next meal. Or where they would sleep on a cold winter night. I'd met plenty of people who would have made that trade-off.

What's more, I had to wonder if it was necessarily a bad thing. Presumably, the Pacificians wouldn't provide all those benefits without getting something in return. Joining a hive mind likely meant working toward the greater good, which meant that a host of unproductive people would suddenly be forced to pull their share of the weight.

"And what makes them the bad guys? There has to be a catch if your teachers made a point to mention them as some great enemy, right?" I asked.

He shrugged. "I . . . Uh . . . We didn't get that far before Master brought me out here. He said that sitting in the temple was a poor education, regardless of how many facts they taught me," the boy said.

That seemed like a fair enough assessment. As far as I'd seen, experience was a much better teacher than listening to an instructor drone on and on. For one, my time in the classroom back in Nova had taught me only what they wanted me to know. By comparison, seeing something with my own two eyes was free of any bias other than my own. For another, things just hit differently when you experienced them yourself. I could hear descriptions of monsters all day long, but nothing could compare to finding myself face-to-face with an alligator the size of a small house.

"So, Master told me that if you saw me, I'm supposed to bring you back," my one-time stalker said. "So . . . Uh . . . You need to come with me."

"And if I don't?" I asked.

"I'm supposed to make you," he answered, his voice quivering with fear.

I sighed and rolled my eyes. Clearly, Freddie had a sense of humor if he thought the kid would be capable of forcing me to do anything. And in any case, I felt it was probably a good idea to reunite with my old Templar acquaintance.

But first, I had a question to ask.

"So, what's your name?"

"Brad."

"Uh . . . Just Brad? That doesn't seem very Templar-like."

"What's that supposed to mean?"

I shrugged and said, "Nothing. Just making a comment. So, lead on. Let's go see Freddie."

CHAPTER TWENTY-SEVEN

A REUNION

I don't think anyone would ever call Mira a people person. She would describe herself as no-nonsense, but I think prickly is probably a better word for it. Whatever the case, she often rubs people the wrong way.

—Patrick Ward

Freddie's camp was only a couple of miles away, and despite the untamed nature of the terrain, it didn't take us long to cover that ground. Not for the first time, I appreciated the fact that every region didn't feature the same thick vegetation of the area around Nova City. There, I'd have had to hack my way through a forest of vines to get any appreciable distance through the wilderness. In the more temperate regions of the world, the vegetation was much sparser, which made traversal far easier.

Still, as we made our way through the forest, I found that I was impressed by the young Templar. Brad wasn't the most skilled woodsman I'd seen, but he was far from the worst, either. So, we managed the trip without alerting any of the various predators native to the forest. When we arrived, I saw Freddie's familiar bearded face looking back at me from where he sat by the fire.

While his defining features were the same as what I'd seen when we had first met, Freddie was clearly in a better place from a psychological perspective. Of course, back then, he had just seen his apprentice become a mindless wildling, so I suppose his previous state was more than a little understandable. In any case, Freddie's hair and beard were neatly trimmed, and he actually wore a wide smile.

As we approached the fire, he rose to his feet. I didn't fail to notice that his robes, as they had been before, were completely spotless, and they stood out in stark contrast to the rustic atmosphere of his campsite, which consisted of a pair of small tents, a sizable fire, and a few stumps meant to act as stools.

"Welcome!" he said, his voice jovial. "I hope Bradley didn't give you any trouble, did he?"

I glanced at my escort, and I saw panic on his face. Doubtless, he expected me to tell Freddie about his antics. Or about his failure to remain hidden. I took pity on the kid, saying, "No. No trouble, except dragging me away from my mission."

"That's my fault," Freddie said. "I apologize for that, but I felt you needed to know what you were getting into."

"The Pacificians."

"Ah, so Bradley told you."

"Some," I admitted. Brad, for his part, remained silent, his eyes trained on the ground. "But not everything. I hoped you might fill in the blanks."

"That is precisely what I intended," he said, his smile widening. Then, he swept his hand to indicate the rounds of wood, adding, "Please. Have a seat. I was just about to cook supper. I hope you like grouse."

"I literally have no idea what that is."

"A bird. Like chicken. Tastes a bit like duck, if you ask me, but nobody ever does."

I certainly liked chicken, so I nodded and said, "Sounds great."

With that, he drew a whole bird out of nothing. I was well aware of the existence of various spatial-storage abilities and cybernetics, but they all required some expenditure of Mist. And in the past few years, I'd learned to notice such things. However, with Freddie, there was nothing.

Sensing what I was thinking—or maybe I hadn't schooled my expression well enough—he gave a little chuckle and said, "You young people are always so messy with your Mist usage. That's the hardest part about taking an apprentice." He tilted his head to the side and took on a thoughtful expression before adding, "Perhaps the second hardest part."

I knew precisely what he meant because I'd lost people, too. First Jeremiah, Jo, and all the other people in Mobile. Then Heather and almost everyone I'd known in Nova City. Though my count was doubtless higher than Freddie's, I couldn't help but wonder if his losses had been more impactful than my own.

Maybe.

Perhaps not.

Or maybe grief wasn't meant to be compared. Acknowledgment that it existed in different forms for different people was enough.

Freddie expertly plucked and cleaned the bird before putting it on a spit over the fire. The creature was enormous, at least three times the size of a chicken, which made me wonder if the species had always been so large; maybe, but it was just as likely that it had been transformed by the Mist.

Either way, it cooked reasonably quickly, and during that time, none of us spoke. Instead, Freddie busied himself with the bird while Brad tried his best to look unobtrusive. For my part, I was lost in thought as I considered what I'd already learned that day. The Pacificians were an insidiously dangerous race of aliens because, at their core, they gave people precisely what they wanted.

No accountability. Long, if not eternal, life. No more hardships. No more troubles. Just a life of service. To a certain kind of person, that sounded like heaven. For others, it was the opposite. I counted myself among the latter group.

Finally, Freddie finished with the grouse before pulling a sack of vegetables from nowhere, which he clearly intended to eat raw. That was fine by me, and soon enough, we were sharing a meal. As we ate, Freddie made polite conversation, asking how I was doing. Pointedly, he did not mention anything of import.

At last, the meal was finished—it was satisfying, if a bit plain for my tastes—and we could get down to business. So, as I wiped my hands on my pants, I asked, "So—what gives, Freddie? You're having me followed now?"

He chuckled. "Straightforward. I like that," he said. "But no. I merely wanted to warn you of the dangers ahead if you choose to oppose the Pacificians."

"Where do the Templars stand?" I asked.

"Firmly opposed," he said without a hint of hesitation. "But as you know, we have a policy of noninterference, at least on a global scale. If we get involved, the conflict will escalate, and this planet will eventually be destroyed. They would rather kill everyone here than lose out on so many new members of the collective."

"Brad said that they are universally considered an enemy in the larger galaxy."

"Universe."

"Whatever. Why does everyone hate them? I mean, from my perspective, what they're doing isn't that bad. I would never do it, but—"

"They are the single largest group of murderers to have ever existed," Freddie stated. "You believe yourself responsible for what happened in Nova City. You weren't. But even if you were, that would be a single raindrop to the oceans of deaths committed by the Pacificians. And they did most of it without even fighting."

"What are you talking about?"

"When these people upload their consciousnesses to new robotic bodies, what do you think happens to them?" he asked.

I shrugged. "I'm really not equipped to answer that question," I stated. I could guess, but I didn't have the background to understand what any of it really meant.

"They are killed, and digital copies of their brains are created. Those things . . . They are not people," said Freddie. "They are just machines with fairly advanced artificial intelligence. They are soulless facsimiles."

"I'm guessing they don't believe that."

Freddy shook his head. "No. They do not," he admitted. "But everything we know says that's how it is."

I sighed. "And what am I supposed to do with this information?" I asked. "I'm just doing a favor for a friend by trying to find her little brother. That's it. I have no intention of fighting a war against robots that might or might not be people."

"What you intend and what happens are often very different things, Mirabelle."

"Just because we met one time doesn't mean you know me," I stated evenly. I wanted to growl. Or shout. But I was trying to be civil; after all, Freddie had been kind to me so far, but he'd really begun to push my buttons. First, he'd had me followed, and then he had told his apprentice to drag me back to his camp if I refused to go willingly. Now, he was acting like he knew me? That was too far.

"But I do know you," he said, his voice mild. "After we met, I've made a point to keep tabs on you."

"You what?"

"Mostly, I just kept my ear to the ground," he elaborated. "But I did hear about what happened north of Nova City. You were lucky to have lived after running headlong into an irradiated zone populated by mutated wildlings. I fear what would have happened if Zachariah and Isla hadn't found you."

"I would've been fine," I lied. In fact, I would almost assuredly have died. And even if I had survived, I would have been scarred beyond all recognition. Perhaps crippled, too.

"Perhaps," he allowed. "But then you went back to Nova, and a short time later, the entire city falls."

"I didn't do that."

Again, that wasn't the whole truth. I'd made the choice to kill Nora, knowing full well that doing so would bring the city down. As far as I was concerned, that made me culpable for thousands, if not millions, of deaths.

"I am aware. But you pushed that woman into taking drastic measures. Even if her ploy had worked and you'd let her live, she would have ended up regretting the deals she made to obtain the means to beat you," Freddie said.

"How do you know all of this?"

He leaned forward. "Templars have a vast information network. I made it my business to follow your exploits," he said.

"Why?"

"At first? Curiosity. It's not every day you run into a teenage girl alone in the wilderness and wielding an arsenal fit for a Kaveki centurion," he said. "But then, as I watched you, I came to realize that you were much more than even I suspected. You're probably wondering why I would contact you now after so long, and the answer is simple—you are in more danger at this moment than you've ever been in before. And I don't want you to die."

"Again, why?"

Certainly, I didn't want to die, either, but having a relative stranger take such an interest in my survival definitely made the little hairs on the back of my neck stand up. From my experience, anyone who'd gone to the trouble Freddie seemed to have on my behalf did so with ulterior motives. Usually, nefarious ones.

I hoped Freddie's intentions were more righteous, but I knew better than to depend on hope. That was a path for fools who'd never felt the sting of betrayal or the devastation of absolute failure.

"Because you have potential."

I waited for him to go on, and when he didn't, I asked, "That's it? Just potential?"

"And a good heart," he added.

It was all I could do not to laugh out loud. A good heart? I'd spent the better part of a year seeking revenge at all costs. I'd killed more people than I could count, and I was responsible for even more deaths. I'd ruined lives. I had done despicable things, none of which originated with a good heart.

"I think you've got the wrong person," I stated.

"I don't believe that's the case," he said. "Besides, even if you're not who I think you are, you can still be what this world needs."

"And what's that?"

"A defender. Or failing that, an avenger," he said. "This is my home, Mirabelle. I was born here. I'm human just like you are. And I don't want to see this world overtaken by the coming tide. You're one of the few people on this world who can potentially fight back. So, I've taken it upon myself to help as much as I can."

"It would be a lot more help if you lost those white robes and remembered you were an earthling," I countered. "You say I can help. Maybe I can. But I saw what Zachariah could do. Same with Isla. And I get the feeling you're stronger than both of them combined."

"That isn't . . ."

He trailed off, which told me I was on the right track. "So, you say you're human, right? Well, fight for your world, then. Do that and you might convince me to join you."

He shook his head. "If I did that, countless millions would die in the war that would follow" was his response. "Universal politics are more complicated than you think. Whole galaxies could potentially be obliterated if I take one step too far. I won't risk that. Not even to save this planet."

I was more than capable of doing the math. Earth was home to maybe a billion people, and that might have been a generous estimate. Perhaps it'd been more populated before the Initialization, but the onset of the Mist—and the transformation of the world that came after—had killed billions. Compared to the trillions—or more—that would die in a universal war, his reasoning was eminently reasonable. Still, I resented him for it all the same. It felt as if he thought himself above the petty concerns of the world we both called home.

"Well, fuck them. I don't care about a bunch of aliens," I spat. "And neither should you. They're the enemy, remember? They've invaded our planet and intend to rip away every last resource before leaving for the next unlucky world. So, pardon me if I don't give a damn about whether or not they die in some war you've conjured in your head."

"You don't mean that."

I started to respond, but in the heat of the moment, a miracle happened. I actually thought about the consequences of running my mouth. Freddie might seem mild mannered, but would that change if I offended him? Besides, I didn't really believe what I'd said. I'd met a few stand-up aliens. Some of them I even considered friends. I wasn't nearly so prejudiced as I often pretended to be.

But still . . .

His attitude irked me.

"Yeah, maybe not. But I won't be shedding any tears over their deaths, I'll tell you that," I stated. "And if you think I'm going to stop killing them . . . Well, that's not happening."

"I wouldn't dream of telling you not to do what you think necessary," he said.

"Doesn't feel like that's the case."

"I just wanted you to understand how important you are to humanity's future," he said. "And as such—"

"Do you think I'm some sort of hero? If you do, you haven't been paying attention. I'm not some champion, and I don't intend to change that."

He shrugged. "Maybe not," Freddie said. "But circumstances have a way of changing attitudes. Just promise me you'll be careful with the Pacificians."

"I'm always careful," I said.

"That's blatantly untrue," he responded with a slight smile.

"You can be careful, and things can still go wrong," I countered.

"True. Very, very true."

Deciding to change the subject, I said, "So, tell me something, Freddie. You don't use Mist the same way I do, do you?"

"I do not."

"Can I learn how to do what you do?"

"Are you asking to join the Templars?" he asked, cocking his head to the side.

"No. I don't know. Maybe. What's your pitch?"

He shook his head. "To join our order, you would have to rip that Nexus Implant out of your skull," he said. "Then, if you managed to survive that, you would have to pledge yourself to us, foregoing all previous attachments and commitments. If you do all that, you'll be tested and sent to a Rift where you would more than likely die. If you don't, you'll go one of two ways: wildling or Templar novice. That's when your journey would begin. Are you interested?"

I shook my head. "No, thanks. I've already been through a hellish training regimen. I don't need another."

Freddie nodded. "Probably for the best. I believe your path will take you in a different direction."

"Yeah, me, too."

For all their power, Templars had far too many restrictions for my taste. Besides, I wasn't much of a joiner. Instead, I liked to carve my own path.

"I will tell you this, though. You are no less powerful for that Nexus Implant. It is restrictive at first, but the world will open up the further you progress," he said. "Eventually, there won't be much difference between you and someone like me."

"Templars, you mean."

"We're called mystics," he said. "Templars are just one organization among those who eschew Nexus Implants and manipulate the Mist directly. We're the only ones on Earth, though."

"That you know of," I reasoned.

He just nodded his agreement.

"Where do the Nexus Implants come from, anyway?" I asked, seeing an opportunity to gain a few more details about the world. My uncle had trained me well enough, but he'd never volunteered much information.

"Some are made. Others are natural occurrences in Mist-dense areas," he said. "I can't be certain, but I think the one in your head is one of the naturally occurring ones. That makes it special."

"And me, too, I guess."

He surprised me by shaking his head. "You know better than that, Mirabelle," he said. "Nexus Implants are about potential. What you make of that potential is up to you. I have known Tier 2s who have done great things and Tier 5s who have completely squandered the opportunities given to them. I don't think you'll be one of the latter, but I caution you not to think of your advantages in terms of absolute power. They are nothing without your will to improve and succeed."

That tracked with everything my uncle had told me, so I didn't really have anything else to say to that. So, Freddie went on, saying, "I won't tell you not to go after the Pacificians. That's up to you, and I suspect you wouldn't heed my advice anyway. But I will reiterate—be careful. They are dangerous foes."

"I've fought plenty of dangerous people, and I'm still alive."

"Indeed. But for now, I believe we should rest," he said, nodding toward Brad, who'd already nodded off. He was on the verge of falling off his stump, which definitely provided a bit of levity to the night.

Still, I shook my head, saying, "I'm going back out there. I don't want them disappearing on me."

"Just so."

And with that, I rose, thanked Freddie for the meal and the advice, and headed back to my perch where I could watch the Pacifician convoy. However, as I set about my surveillance, my mind kept wandering to the conversation we'd had. I didn't know what to think of it all, and I didn't think that was going to change anytime soon.

CHAPTER TWENTY-EIGHT

CITY ON THE MOUNTAIN

I've always liked to take things apart and see how they work. I think that's why Remy steered me toward the [Cybernetic Engineer] skill. Even if it didn't exactly work out how he wanted—he envisioned a future of me getting paid a fortune installing high-end cybernetics for the elite—I'm still grateful he put me on this path. Otherwise, I'd have never met Mira, and I certainly wouldn't have figured out my place in the world.

—Patrick Ward

As I followed the convoy for another forty miles or so, I continued to contemplate the information Freddie had revealed. In a lot of ways, I felt it was incredibly unfair that I'd never have a chance to be like him—or rather, like Zachariah or Isla, both of whom I'd seen in action. They had serious power, and they weren't reliant on cybernetics or implants to get them there. But the more I thought about it, the more I saw it as a challenge. Ever since the day my uncle had given me a Tier 7 implant, I'd been running a race with a head start. No matter what else happened, I had more potential than just about anyone else on the planet.

Sure—I needed to work extremely hard to realize that potential, but I was still special in a way nobody else was.

But now that I knew about people like the Templars—and whatever other groups counted mystics among their number—I could see that I had something to work toward. A goal that would take the entirety of my focus to achieve. I was behind now, but Freddie had given me hope that I could change that. With enough hard work, I could reach those same levels of power, albeit via a different route.

That was enough to banish any resentment I might've held on to.

Besides, who knew if I'd have survived becoming a Templar, anyway? Lots of people didn't, I was certain. And while I liked Freddie—and to a certain extent, every other Templar I'd met—I didn't want to be beholden to a group whose overall goals I didn't know, let alone understand. For all I knew, they were a murderous group of mercenaries who killed anyone who didn't agree with their dogma.

Or maybe they were just a bunch of cowards.

I still hadn't forgotten that they had all but abandoned Earth to the nonexistent mercy of the aliens. The Templars maintained a presence, but they were too frightened of the consequences to intervene in what amounted to an invasion. That was enough to make me suspicious of their motives, but not so much that I was going to label them enemies.

But I intended to go into any further interactions with my eyes wide-open. Anything else just struck me as naive.

My pursuit of the Pacificians continued until the convoy reached a mountain that, even in the middle of an impressive range, stood out. It was taller than any of the others surrounding it, and I could see the blue shimmer of a powerful Mist shield surrounding it. Moreover, I could also see the outline of a city at the peak.

In some ways, it reminded me of Nova, if only because it rested upon a giant disc that ringed the mountain's peak. But in every way that mattered, I could easily see—even from so far away—that it was very, very different. For one, there was only one platform. For another, it gleamed with expensive building materials that put even the wealthy districts of Nova City to shame. Gold, silver, and clear glass abounded, screaming the city's wealth to anyone who cared to notice.

The convoy pulled to a stop at the base of the mountain, where a small but well-fortified outpost stood. It was a little smaller than Biloxi had been, but where that town had been rife with the corruption I'd begun to take for granted, this outpost was in pristine condition and manned by the same blue-robed androids with which I'd grown familiar.

I watched as the convoy's passengers disembarked, and I was close enough that, with Observation, I could see the expressions of awe decorating their faces. Fortune wasn't a bad city, all told; it was mostly clean, and its citizens seemed as well-off as anywhere else I'd been. But the city atop the mountain was on an entirely different level, and even the drug-addicted and starving refugees could see it.

One by one, they were led into the outpost until the convoy was entirely empty. I noticed that none of the blue-robed guards spoke to one another, though. Perhaps they didn't need to. The Pacificians were noted for being part of a hive mind, so it wasn't out of the question that they could communicate telepathically.

Or maybe they were all equipped with abilities similar to Secure Connection.

Whatever the case, it struck me as more than a little creepy.

Once the convoy's cargo—because that's what those people were to the Pacificians, I was certain—had been discharged, the guards wasted no time before returning the way they'd come. I didn't follow, largely because I knew where they were going. Instead, I continued my observation of the city on the mountain and the outpost that barred entry.

Eventually, I saw a group of former refugees—I recognized a few of them from previous surveillance—board a ship that took them to the peak. However, there was another, much smaller group that was ushered into a separate ship that soon left the outpost and the city on the mountain behind.

There were a couple of key differences between the two groups. For one, the ones who'd been sent into the city all wore red robes that stood out among the blue-robed guards, while the ones who were sent away were dressed all in black. Pointedly, the red robes seemed much happier than the other group, many of whom looked like caged animals on the verge of an escape attempt.

The second thing I noticed was that the means of conveyance were also entirely different. The ship that went up to the city was just as bright and shiny as the mountaintop settlement itself, while the other ship was clearly meant for hard use that it regularly saw, judging by the fact that it was clearly made for practicality rather than to achieve some aesthetic standard.

That made sense. It was headed into the wilderness, after all. The dainty little white-and-gold ship that went up to the city would never survive in that environment. Still, it seemed important on a different level, at least to my eyes—even more so, considering that there were lifts leading up to the city that would have proved much more efficient. In any case, the people who had been sent away were clearly second-class. Perhaps they were even prisoners. Maybe slaves, for all I knew.

My initial plan had been to infiltrate the area, but seeing that Mist shield, along with Freddie's words of warning, had brought me up short. Hitting a Dengyt outpost was one thing, but sneaking into the main base of operations of a powerful alien faction was something altogether different.

For once, I chose the path of caution.

So, nestled in a crevice where I was certain I wouldn't be noticed, I utilized my various skills to conceal my presence before deploying my camouflaging holographic display. Then, I settled down to continue my surveillance.

And I saw nothing.

Even after an entire day of constant vigilance, I witnessed nothing of note. Sure, the way those blue-robed androids stood around without moving or talking to one another was unnerving, but given what I knew about their nature, I couldn't be surprised. Instead, I simply tacked that onto the list of suspicious activities and continued my watch.

By the second day, I was bored out of my mind, but I didn't dare cut my surveillance short. Too often, I'd jumped into the fire feetfirst, and inevitably, I'd gotten burned. Usually, I had the ability to survive, but I wasn't so naive as to think that would always be the case. If Freddie's warning was any indication, then I needed to alter my perspective, and quickly. Otherwise, I might run afoul of someone far more powerful than I could ever hope to be. If I found myself facing off against someone with Zachariah's power, I knew just how long I'd last.

And in the back of my mind, I had to acknowledge that human mystics were almost assuredly far less developed than those in the wider universe. My only solace came from the fact that it seemed that they kept one another in check. I didn't have the full picture, but it was easy to imagine that the Templars' main purpose was to keep other mystics from running roughshod over the rest of the universe.

However, there was a seed of hope there, too. Freddie had made it clear that I had the chance to reach as high as any mystic, albeit along a different, likely more difficult path. I was determined to walk it, though. A challenge was precisely what I needed to drive me forward.

Not that I really needed it. By now, I was addicted to my own progression, and I knew that, even without a proverbial mountain to climb, I would continue to improve. Not so that I could survive, which was a powerful motivator in and of itself, but rather, I would progress for progression's sake. I enjoyed it, and if I was completely honest with myself, I had to acknowledge that, without that constant quest for improvement, I would have no idea what to do with the bulk of my time.

Patrick might have his hobbies. But me? Everything else paled next to the constant and verifiable improvement I could see on my own status, as well as when my nature inevitably led me into fights with . . . well . . . everyone. Or at least that's how it felt. I'd never set out to be abrasive or combative, but that's how everyone interpreted my absolute refusal to let other people walk all over me.

And maybe I was a bit trigger-happy, but that was just a product of living in a combative world. Anything else would simply invite challenge, which would inevitably lead to death. Maybe not my own, but the people I cared about—like Patrick—weren't quite as durable as I was. It wouldn't take my enemies long to reason that, if they couldn't get to me, then those close to me would probably do just as well in getting me to do whatever it was they wanted me to do.

As I sat there, I sighed.

In the past few weeks, I'd discovered that I wasn't quite as powerful—at least in the grand scheme of the universe—as I'd thought I was. Earth—and its people—was in its infancy, and established powers like the Dengyts or the Pacificians were more than any of us could handle. Perhaps that was the source of my uncle's fatalistic outlook on the future. He'd seen far more than I had, and it was probable that he knew what awaited us in the wider universe. A bit of negativity was expected when that was hanging over your head.

But I wouldn't fall into that trap. I couldn't let myself. Not again. It had already poisoned my memories of Nova City—back then, I only let myself see the bad side of the city—and I wouldn't let it infect anything else. I didn't like the person I became when I looked at the world like that. No—I wouldn't let it happen. Not again.

Those thoughts—and many more—flitted through my mind as I watched the city. Eventually, one day became two, and two days became a week. Still, I watched, taking breaks only for necessities like food and sleep. Even then, I didn't let the mountaintop city out of my sight for more than an hour or two at a time.

And by the dawn of the second week, my vigilance finally bore fruit when I saw a transport descend from the peak to the outpost at the base of the mountain. There, I watched a group of brown-robed men and women—a first for that color—being ushered into a series of waiting trucks. Soon after that, the latest caravan set off from the city.

I followed, at least as much for the novelty as because I thought I'd exhausted the opportunities for new information to be gained by simply observing the city. So, I hopped on the Cutter, disguised it as a hover bike that looked like it could barely run, and began tailing the new convoy.

They led me on a twisting path through the mountains for half a day until, at last, they reached another camp. However, this one was unlike any of the others. Cut into the side of a mountain, it was guarded by high walls, a powerful Mist shield, and enough blue-robed guards to make even me blanch.

But what made it different wasn't the stout defenses. Instead, what alarmed me was the fact that all those defenses were faced inward, as if they were intended to keep something in, rather than out.

Had I stumbled upon a prison?

Or was something worse inside that mountain?

I watched as the convoy entered the high-walled settlement—it was a fortress, really—but I had to find a higher vantage point if I was going to see the goings-on inside. So, I retreated a bit, climbing a neighboring mountain before finding a cliff that gave me a good view. By that time, the convoy had already come and gone, but that was okay. I didn't intend to leave anytime soon, and I felt certain that another opportunity to find out what was going on would soon present itself.

So, after letting Patrick know what was going on via our Secure Connection—I really did take that ability for granted now—I settled in to continue my surveillance. As it turned out, the settlement was more of a slave camp than a prison, but the method of control was just as insidious as what I'd found outside my first Rift.

There, I'd found aliens that used a combination of slave implants, the positive reinforcement of chemical manipulation, and isolation to achieve total unthinking obedience. Back then, I'd considered it foolproof. Certainly, the unfortunate humans who'd been enslaved would have never considered rising up against their masters. But such a state was difficult to achieve, and it was only really possible when it started early. Trying to introduce an adult to such a method would inevitably result in less-than-optimal control.

I hated that I knew that, but aliens weren't the only ones who dabbled in slavery. I'd seen more than my fair share of slaves during the past three years, and I'd discovered that humans were just as prone to mistreating their own as the aliens were. Perhaps they were even worse.

In any case, the Pacificians seemed to favor a different method that hinged on leveraging their slaves' addictions to keep them in line. I saw more than one dust fiend stumbling around in a stupor. Clearly, they weren't intended to do anything that required fine motor skills.

As limited as the addicts were, their addictions dictated that they were easily controlled—provided the drugs kept coming. And for the aliens, dust was cheap and easily manufactured, with ingredients that were readily available. Was it foolproof? No. But it was inexpensive and easy to keep them coming back for more, which seemed to be what the Pacificians were looking for.

I also caught sight of a new robe color—a satiny gold—that seemed to denote someone of importance. I wasn't sure what that meant in an egalitarian society where everyone was part of a hive mind, but people seemed to treat the androgynous figure with borderline reverence. Still, they looked almost identical to all the others, so I had no indication of what made them special.

In the end, I spent almost a week studying the camp, and though I didn't really find anything else important, I did get a sense of the rhythm of the camp. Every other day, they received another shipment of would-be slaves. And more troublingly, I saw that, each day, they'd take a set of mangled bodies and burn them in a furnace that seemed dedicated to that purpose alone.

Whatever was going on in that mountain, it was deadly dangerous.

Was this what had happened to Cirilla's brother? Or was he back in that mountaintop city living the blissful life of someone who was about to be inducted into a hive mind and given a brand-new body?

I didn't know, but with my interest piqued, I needed to find out.

It seemed like the puzzle was coming together, but I still hadn't found Caden. Nor did I know if he was in that city on the mountain or the slave camp I had been watching for the past few days. Moreover, what did the different-color robes mean? Certainly, the gold robe seemed to signify importance, but what about the blue ones? The black? The brown? I had so many questions and not enough answers.

Part of me just wanted to sneak in, find the information I needed, and then take it from there. I'd done it before, after all. But my recent experience with the Dengyts haunted me. They had proven that I wasn't as infallible as I thought. And I suspected that if I stepped out of line with the Pacificians—especially on their home turf—they wouldn't react as well as the gnomes had.

No—I needed to keep watching. As boring as that was, I knew it gave me the best shot of accomplishing my mission. And, of course, staying alive.

So, I settled in and continued my surveillance.

CHAPTER TWENTY-NINE

SURPRISES AND ADJUSTMENTS

My pursuit of a proper cybernetic suit of armor came from Mira. Or more accurately, her hover bike. Until that point, I'd had no idea that external cybernetics even existed, but the moment she explained how it worked, my mind went wild with all the possibilities. But it wasn't until I started working with Cy that my plans really started coming together.

—Patrick Ward

That's it?" I asked, looking at the pile of metal, wires, and mechanical parts. I couldn't make heads or tails of any of it, and I certainly didn't think it looked like the precursor to an advanced suit of cybernetic armor.

"Do you have any idea how much work I've put into getting it this far?" Patrick asked, rubbing the back of his neck. His hands were covered in black grease, and he'd even picked up a few scrapes on his knuckles. His face was clean, but his neck bore a couple of black smudges. "And we're still working on integrating those circuits." He glanced over at Cirilla, who was bent over a workbench and fiddling with some complex bit of machinery, then added, "Well, Cy is. I'm more of a big picture kind of guy. That detail work just . . . Well, it's hard for me."

"It's the fat sausage fingers, isn't it?" I asked with a grin.

"My fingers aren't—"

"It is," said Cirilla without looking up.

"But—"

"It's okay," I said with mock sincerity. "I still love you even with your horribly bloated fingers."

He started to respond but thought better of it. In truth, Patrick's fingers were normal. Sure, he was a stout guy, and he had hands to match, but it wasn't like he was deformed or anything. He just didn't have the dexterity for delicate work like building nearly microscopic circuits from scratch. Not like Cirilla, whose slim fingers seemed to have been tailor-made for the task.

"Wouldn't be an issue if we didn't have to do it all by hand," he muttered, pointedly low enough that Cirilla couldn't hear him from across the shop. "But no—any Mist current, even if it's not even measurable, could foul the circuits. So . . . Here we are, with me sidelined."

I glanced at the pile of metal and said, "You seem to be keeping busy." I reached out to grab a shiny bit of armor plating and asked, "What's this going to be?"

Before I could finish my question, his hand shot out and clamped around my wrist. If I'd been in any other company, I probably would have responded with violence, but Patrick had my full trust, so all he got was a glare that made him release me a second later.

"Sorry," he mumbled. "I just . . . Just don't touch anything, okay? I have a system."

I rolled my eyes. As if me touching a bit of armor plating would screw everything up. I had half a mind to touch it anyway, but I restrained my childish impulses and asked, "How big is it going to be? Like, tank sized? Or just people sized?"

"Uh . . . Somewhere in between," he said.

"That doesn't sound very scientific," I stated.

"I haven't decided yet. I mean, part of me wants to go as big as possible. You know, a real walking tank. But . . . There are downsides to that, too," he explained. Unnecessarily. With my varied combat experience, I certainly didn't need anyone to explain the pros and cons of heavy armor. "But with a smaller suit, there's less protection and firepower. So . . . I'm kind of stuck, you know. I've been putting off finalizing the design until the absolute last moment."

I could understand his hesitation. This was Patrick's one chance to create something that would put him ahead of everyone else. Neither of us expected that whatever advantage the suit created would last forever. Once we made it off-planet, we'd both have to adapt and grow. But for now, it would let him keep up with me, which seemed very important to his self-esteem.

For my part, I was fine with the way things were. He had his areas of expertise—piloting the ship, dealing with various merchants, and keeping me sane—and I had my well-established talent for combat. So, I didn't feel nearly the same degree of urgency that he did regarding his combat potential.

But then again, maybe it was because I liked knowing that he was weaker than me. Perhaps I liked being the one expected to protect us from outside threats. And maybe I enjoyed his dependence on me. After all, his needing me kept him around, didn't it?

It didn't matter if it was true or not—it wasn't; he could be successful wherever he went. All that really mattered was how it made me feel. And I liked feeling needed. But then again, who doesn't?

"I don't know what to tell you, Pick," I admitted as I leaned over the table and pretended to study the various bits of machinery. I recognized some of it from Patrick's previous attempts to build various weapons and armor—some of which had been mildly successful, even if he couldn't see it—but the majority of the pile was completely foreign to me. "That's something you're going to have to figure out on your own, I think."

"What would you do?" he asked. "If I was building this for you, I mean."

"You're not, though."

"But if I was . . ."

I sighed. "I'd go big," I stated. "Like, full-on tank sized, with armor as impenetrable as I could make it."

"And your reasoning?"

I shrugged. "I'm already good at mobility," I said. "A tanklike suit of armor would fill a niche. Plus, the bigger the suit, the bigger the guns, right? Can you imagine what kinds of guns Gala could sell us if weight wasn't an issue? It would put the BMAP or the Dragon to shame."

He sighed. "It's always about the explosions with you."

"Not always. Sometimes, it's about sneaking," I countered. Then, I added, "But it usually ends with a big explosion, one way or another. I can admit that."

"You've got issues."

Shrugging again, I said, "My issues keep us alive, so I'll take it."

With that, the conversation petered out, and it soon became clear that I'd overstayed my welcome. Certainly, Patrick was fine with having me around, but he obviously wasn't going to get a lot of work done with me hanging around. For her part, Cirilla kept cutting her eyes at me when she didn't think I would notice.

But I noticed. And I stayed for about thirty minutes longer than I really wanted to just to annoy her. It seemed to work, too, so there was that to cheer me up. In the end, I gave one last look around the workshop—it was a spacious room the size of a small warehouse, and it was loaded with all sorts of materials that made it look like a well-organized junkyard to me—and then went on my way.

The moment I left the building, I switched gears and returned my mindset to one appropriate for an active mission. I pushed Patrick and Cirilla out of my mind and focused on the things I'd discovered during my weeks-long surveillance of the mountaintop city and the fortresslike prison carved into the side of a separate mountain.

Despite spending quite some time observing the two locations, I hadn't learned all that much new information. But there were a few tidbits I'd picked up—like the fact that there was more than one source of new recruits. It seemed that the Pacificians had a presence in other cities in addition to their operation in Fortune. I wasn't sure how useful that piece of intelligence really was.

What was useful was my observation of the various defenses in play. The Mist shields were almost identical, and though they were powerful, I felt confident that I could bypass them. However, I knew almost nothing about what lay inside either settlement's walls, and so, I couldn't make many plans to counter whatever other defenses they'd managed to erect.

For all I knew, once I bypassed the Mist shields and the guards, I'd be completely free to explore to my heart's content. But for some reason, I didn't think that would be the case. I wasn't dealing with a human-run city like Biloxi or Nova. These settlements had been built and were run by a race of powerful aliens; it would be the height of foolishness to assume that their defenses wouldn't be far more advanced than anything humans could create.

So, with that in mind, I decided that my best path forward was to return to its beginning. My reasoning was simple. The Pillar of Heaven headquarters had to at least appear to have been built by humans, and as such, any defenses would be hamstrung by the need to maintain appearances. I hoped that that would give me an opportunity to slip through the cracks and gather more intelligence on the pair of settlements I'd found in the mountains.

To that end, I soon found myself leaning against a wall a block or so away from the building in question. It looked much the same as it had when I'd attempted an infiltration a few weeks before. They hadn't even increased the guard presence, much less implemented any new defenses. Still, I chose to take things slow and continue my surveillance through the night and a few hours into the next day.

Even so, my cautious approach bore no fruit. So, after cataloging a new identity based on one of the guards, I retreated to a small market I'd seen on the way in. There, I spent way too long looking for a seamstress that could sew a set of blue robes styled after the ones worn by the Pacifician guards. Thankfully, the woman had some sort of skill that got the work done in only a few more hours. In the interim, I acquired some more rags and stored another identity for my infiltration.

The way I saw it, my first attempt at infiltrating the headquarters of the Pillar of Heaven had gone wrong for two reasons. First, I had underestimated them. That wasn't going to happen again, especially now that I knew I was dealing with alien androids that were connected to a hive mind. Second, I'd wandered around like a lost idiot, trusting my skills to protect me from detection. This time, I would be far more focused. That would be helped along by the fact that I knew the building's layout, and I had an idea of where I needed to go.

Was it a perfect plan? No. There were plenty of dangers that largely stemmed from the reality of my ignorance. I had no real notion of the Pacificians' capabilities, and so, I could only trust that my own skills and preparations would keep them in the dark. However, even if my attempts at espionage were to fail, I had plenty of contingency plans upon which I could call. I just hoped it wouldn't come to that.

However, as confident as I was in my plan, I spent another day waiting for the perfect moment. I wasn't in any hurry, after all. Patrick had barely scratched the surface of his own project, and so, there was nothing urgent about my mission.

Except maybe the fate of Cirilla's brother, which, if I was honest, didn't really rank very high on my list of concerns. Sure, if he could be saved, I would save him, but I'd only agreed to try to find him so that Patrick could get what he needed from his former teacher slash girlfriend.

That last bit brought a twinge of annoyance and jealousy with it. Here I was dressed in rags and pretending to be a dirty junkie while Cirilla was doubtless trying to once again insinuate herself into Patrick's life. Maybe even steal him away. I trusted him. I really did. But I definitely didn't trust her.

My only hope was that he'd aged out of her tastes, which, judging by her past and present partners, trended toward the younger side of things.

Damn cradle robber.

I pushed those intrusive thoughts out of my mind—or at least into a back corner where I hoped they would stay—and rose from the concealed alley in which I'd been squatting for the past couple of days. Wearing the face of a haggard addict, I garnered little notice as I ambled across the street—nearly getting hit by one of those automatic rickshaws along the way. I slurred a few curses at the driverless carriage, but quickly moved, mumbling to myself about "damn robots."

I got a few sideways glances, but that was the point. I'd tried skating in under the radar; now, I was going in another direction. I wanted attention. I wanted people to look at me and feel pity. Or frustration. Disgust, perhaps. If all they saw was an old addict, they wouldn't suspect my real mission.

I continued to stumble down the sidewalk, and the other pedestrians gave me a wide berth. Perhaps that was the odor; I'd taken quite some time to make certain that I smelled the part. It was disgusting, especially when I flared Observation, but I knew it was a necessary facet of the disguise.

I approached the entrance without hesitation, and when I reached the door, I gave the blonde-haired, blue-robed guard a glare and demanded, "Heard you got free food here, yeah?"

"We do," she said with a forced smile, but I noticed the slightest crinkle to her perfect nose. Not even androids were immune to the smell I had created, it seemed. Good. That made the disguise that much more believable. After all, the streets were a dirty place, and addicts weren't exactly known for their hygiene. "And showers, too. Fresh clothing, as well."

"You sayin' I stink?" I demanded, thrusting my finger into her face. To her credit, she maintained her placid expression. "I smell like petunias! Everybody says so!"

"Okay. No showers or fresh clothes, then. But food is available," she said, gesturing to the door. "Go right ahead. You'll see the signs."

I thought about telling her I couldn't read, but I didn't want to push things too far. Instead, I just nodded curtly—which came off as more pronounced than it should have been—before strolling through the door. I gave a little stumble, just to sell the disguise a little more.

Of course, that's when everything went wrong.

My fake stumble turned into the real thing as I collided with something solid. Blue light flashed in front of me as I caught my balance, and I wheeled around to run the other way. I didn't really know what was happening, but I'd told myself that, at the first sign of trouble, I would retreat.

The Pacificians had no intention of accommodating my plan, though, because I soon ran into another blue Mist shield. I twisted around, searching for a way out, but I found nothing. I was hemmed in by the entryway's thick walls, Mist shields on the other two sides, and a ceiling high enough I couldn't reach it. They had created a prison from which I couldn't escape.

"We knew you would return," bragged the blonde guard I'd just spoken to. She had her weapon trained on me. She was joined by her partner as the door slammed shut. On the other side, three more guards approached, their rifles trained on my position.

"How did you know?" I asked, dropping my act. Mimic remained in place, though. I still had no intention of letting them see my real face. Not unless forced to do so, which seemed increasingly likely unless I did something drastic.

That also felt more and more likely with each passing second.

"Recalibration of the Mist shield," she bragged. "A routine adjustment meant to counter spies like you."

I'd always known that Mist shields were far more versatile than most people suspected. For instance, *The Leviathan*'s shields could be adjusted in a wide variety of ways—most of which seemed useless except in very specific scenarios. So, I should have expected that the advanced Pacificians would be capable of something similar.

It was just one more reminder that my place on Earth wasn't indicative of my standing in the wider universe. I had skills, and I was capable enough, but when it came to advanced alien civilizations, I wasn't anything special. Not yet. I had potential, though, and I intended to see it reached.

The android raised a collar I recognized all too well from my own training. I used one just like the silvery hoop to restrict my attributes and skills so that I could get the most out of my physical regimen. So, I knew just how effective something like that could be.

"Resist and we will kill you," she said.

Then her partner added, "Cooperate and you will live."

Still another voice came from behind me, "You will be a strong addition to the population."

That was definitely not going to happen. I didn't care how good their people had it; I wasn't going to give up my identity or freedom.

Fortunately, I hadn't spent the past weeks idle. In addition to my surveillance, I'd spent quite some time working on my Ghosts. Specifically, *Robot Disposal*, which still hadn't gotten a new name. And the moment I'd been trapped, I'd used Misthack to tear through their systems and infect them with the latest iteration of the Ghost.

I'd rebuilt the Ghost from the ground up, and though I'd had to make some sacrifices in terms of its lethality, I was very happy with how it had turned out. The idea behind it was simple. Whereas the last version of the Ghost was meant to kill hostile robots, the newest iteration was intended to simply disable them.

Permanently.

This was accomplished by severing the tiny connections throughout the robotic body. It wouldn't kill them. I didn't have the Mist for that. Instead, it would make sending information—specifically, commands—from the brain to the rest of the body impossible. At best, those commands would be garbled and result in unintended movement. At worst, they would become paralyzed.

As I completed the process of uploading the Ghost into the last android, I hoped for the latter. Then, I activated it.

At first, the blonde android's fingers twitched, and after a moment, she dropped the collar. Then, the twitching became a seizure, and she fell to the floor. That's when she started screaming.

After all, the Ghost was intended for use on robots. But in every one of those androids was a sentient mind. And apparently, judging by those screams, losing control of one's body was a horrifying experience.

I ignored them, instead targeting a nearby security terminal that I hoped was meant to control the Mist shield. It was precisely what I was looking for, and even as those androids were continually beset by seizures—those weren't going to stop anytime soon, if ever—I ripped through the terminal's defenses and deactivated my cage. For good measure, I took down the cameras in the area, too. The Pacificians were smart, though. It was a closed, compartmentalized system, so the terminal was only connected to the immediate surroundings. If I wanted to affect wider changes, I would have to find another node. Still, for now, I was safe.

Once I was done with the security terminal, I disconnected and looked around. The lobby was deserted—everyone but the guards had fled the moment the cage had gone up—and so, I was free to leave if I wanted to. However, that wouldn't advance my plans, so I discarded that notion.

Instead, I used Mimic to adopt a new appearance and changed into the blue robes I'd had commissioned. Like that, I headed deeper into the headquarters in search of answers.

CHAPTER THIRTY

OLYMPUS

Overconfidence bordering on arrogance will always be an issue for Mira. She never sees a problem she doesn't believe she can overcome. And given her track record, she's probably right. But I'm terrified of the day she discovers otherwise.

—Patrick Ward

As I walked through the corridors of the Pacifician headquarters, I chose not to push my luck. Instead, I kept to little-used hallways and did everything I could to avoid notice, even going so far as to use Stealth and Camouflage to mask my presence. They might be capable of seeing through Mimic, but I suspected that it took the active use of a skill or cybernetic to do so. After all, they hadn't immediately figured me out before, and they'd taken the trouble of adjusting their Mist shield to better detect me. So, it stood to reason that they couldn't tell I was an impostor at a mere glance.

However, I also knew that they were all at least somewhat connected. Their society had been described as a hive mind, and the fact that they all looked and acted similarly seemed to support that. But there was some individuality there, as well, so I had to believe that they weren't always completely connected to one another.

Otherwise, I didn't stand a chance.

I had a plan for that eventuality, but considering Patrick's admonition not to blow everything up, I didn't want to resort to the utter mayhem that would follow copious use of explosives. Or at least that's what I told myself. In the back of my mind, though, I thought the world would be a better place if the entire Pacifician facility was swallowed by a giant ball of fire.

Maybe I really did have a problem.

I pushed those thoughts aside as I moved through the facility. Most of it was precisely what I expected to find. They had rooms set aside for housing the addicts, a couple of cafeterias, a huge kitchen, and the counseling center I'd seen on my first visit. And that was just the first floor. The rest of the headquarters was more of the same, and my cursory inspection suggested that it was precisely what it appeared to be. There was no evidence—aside from the androids who'd tried to take me into custody—that the so-called Pillar of Heaven was anything but a charitable organization whose goal was to help the less fortunate.

And the more I saw, the more I'd begun to doubt. Perhaps I'd misinterpreted the things I had seen outside of Fortune. Maybe Freddie and the Templars were mistaken. Or he could have simply been lying to me. It wouldn't be the first time, and I knew it wouldn't be the last, either. More, it wouldn't be that difficult to take advantage of my predilection toward cynicism to convince me that the good guys had evil motives.

Still, I continued my search until I reached the top floor, which was another set of domiciles occupied by homeless men and women. With my initial inspection done, I returned to the ground floor, where I found a hive of activity. The blue-robed guards had begun to swarm as they presumably searched for me.

More than once, I was forced to hide from particularly attentive guards, but for the most part, they ignored me. At the same time, I continued my search for anything out of the ordinary. Eventually, after I'd found nothing for hours, I started following a set of random guards as they combed the building. Predictably, they found nothing, and after a while, they led me to precisely what I was looking for.

I hid behind a corner as I watched the blue-robed-and-blond guards approach a blank wall. One of them stepped forward and placed her hand on the vertical, plasti-steel surface. The second her palm touched it, I felt a hum of Mist in the air. Then, a holographic display faded away to reveal a sliding door, which opened to reveal an elevator. The trio of guards wasted no time before stepping into the elevator, and once the doors closed behind them, the holographic display reengaged, presenting itself as an unmarred wall.

I found an out-of-the-way corner, engaged Stealth and Camouflage, then waited for another group to appear. About thirty minutes later, a pair of guards repeated the actions of the first trio, stepped into the elevator, and disappeared to wherever it took them. Presumably down, but I couldn't be sure. For all I knew, the building was dozens of levels taller than it appeared, and it was all hidden by an advanced holographic display.

Unlikely, given the practical issues with something like that, but I wasn't prepared to disregard the possibility.

Instead, I remained in place for another couple of hours, and in that time, I saw multiple groups use the concealed elevator. In addition, the guards' activity seemed to die down, probably because they assumed I'd run away. I was beginning to wonder if that would have been the right course of action.

Nothing said I had to actually find Cirilla's brother, after all. I could just tell her I'd tried and leave once Patrick finished his suit. Results were never part of the deal. So, it would have been much smarter to just cut my losses and head back to *The Leviathan* where I could spend my time on training instead of going up against an advanced alien civilization with unknown capabilities.

But I was too intrigued to stop short of discovering the truth.

That probably should have been an indication that my approach wasn't entirely rational, but I was well-versed in ignoring my own good sense. So, I kept watching and waiting until, at last, the headquarters returned to what I considered a normal state. Once it did, I dropped Stealth and approached the door. As I did so, I was careful to look like I belonged, and I copied the guards' mannerisms right down to the way they walked.

Or at least I tried to.

I wasn't a great actress, but I had still practiced enough that I considered my efforts passable. Even so, the guards had a subtly odd way of moving that I knew I couldn't completely replicate. Indeed—I couldn't even put my finger on just what made it stand out. I just knew that it was abnormal.

Whatever the case, I hoped I wouldn't garner too much interest if someone happened to see me. When I reached the concealed door, I was careful to put my hand in precisely the same place that the others had, but to my surprise, I got no response. I could feel something beneath the holographic display—probably a security measure meant to keep anyone but the Pacificians out.

So, I had another choice to make.

I could probably Misthack the system and open the door by force, but that would almost assuredly trip some sort of alarm. Even if it didn't, I couldn't be sure that the intrusion would go unnoticed. In fact, I couldn't be sure of anything; the Pacificians had already surprised me twice, and I didn't want to experience that a third time.

Which left me with my second option: abducting an android and asking some very pointed questions. Of course, that came with plenty of dangers, too. Aside from the obvious issues with subduing and interrogating someone without raising the alarm, I had to worry about the supposed connection they shared with their hive mind. I was already convinced that they weren't always in contact with one another, but I wasn't so naive as to believe that that wouldn't change the moment one of them was threatened. So, it was clear that I had some work to do.

With that in mind, I found an empty domicile, settled in, and got down to it. As was usually the case, my solution hinged on my Misthack ability. I had a few innate abilities that could mimic Ghosts—like Plague—but they were too broad for what I had in mind. So, I started building a new Ghost from the ground up. It was a tedious process, but it was one I'd grown accustomed to enduring. And in a lot of ways, I enjoyed it. Sure, there were parts I loathed, and it was often frustrating, but the sense of accomplishment I got when I finally created a working Ghost that did precisely what I wanted it to do was absolutely worth it.

And that wasn't even considering the positive reinforcement of seeing my progress on my status sheet, which was reward enough all on its own.

In all, it took me two more days to come up with a working prototype and another day after that to refine it to the point where I expected it to work flawlessly. In that time, I was forced to move a couple of times when various addicts or homeless people were assigned to the room I occupied, but that wasn't unexpected. It was why I'd continuously kept Stealth active.

Doing so for long periods of time gave me a headache, but at least my Mist reserves were more than up to the task. Credit to my constant training, I supposed.

In any case, while I worked on the Ghost, I managed to remain undetected. Moreover, the state of the facility seemed to normalize, giving me a better opportunity to affect my interrogation. So, it was with some optimism that I finally emerged from my Ghost-crafting session to select a target.

The problem was that they almost always moved in pairs. Or trios. So, I had to wait some time before the opportunity for abduction presented itself. Still, I remained patient, letting Patrick know what was going on every step of the way.

He inevitably told me to be careful, but I could tell by the tone of his voice that he never expected me to follow his advice. Which kind of annoyed me until I remembered that I was deep in enemy territory about to abduct and interrogate an android that was mentally connected to hundreds of others who possessed the firepower to do me in. So, maybe he was right to doubt my commitment to caution.

In any case, my opportunity came when, against all odds, I found a black-robed Pacifician tasked with cleaning one of the rooms that had been recently used by an addict who had since moved on.

I pounced, Misthacking the android in question and cutting them off from any nonverbal communication. The structure of the Ghost really was an ingenious design that featured an ability to search out any skills or abilities meant for mental communication and shut them down. I'd spent hours studying Secure Connection so I could get a sense of how such abilities worked, and it had paid off when I saw the panicked expression on the android's male face.

As soon as the Ghost took hold, my hand darted out, and my fingers clamped around his throat before I pushed him back into the room he'd just cleaned. Even as the door shut behind us, I pushed him onto the cot and growled, "Answer my questions and I let you live. Lie or refuse to answer and I'll end you. Got me?"

The black-haired man nodded. I hadn't even noticed the different hair color at first, but now that I had, it just looked wrong, especially considering that he otherwise looked remarkably similar to any of the others. Like his robes, the hair color seemed important in its distinction.

"Do you have any idea who I am?" I asked. I still wore the same face I'd used to impersonate a blue-robed guard.

He shook his head, then pleaded, "Please don't kill me. I'll do whatever you want."

That sounded remarkably human, which piqued my curiosity even further. So, I asked, "Why are you wearing black instead of blue? And why aren't you blond or brunette like all the others?"

"Uh . . ."

I hit him. Not hard enough to cause real damage. More to get his attention and show him that I meant business. Like I've said before, I'm not a fan of torture. I'll do it, but I don't consider it an effective means of interrogation. Now, the threat of death if someone doesn't answer my questions? That's better, but only marginally so. Still, I had to work with what I had.

"You know what? I'm not doing this," I said, realizing that I was being a little stupid. After summoning a pair of handcuffs from my arsenal implant, I bound his hands. Then, I pulled my personal link from the Hand of God, found the port at the base of his skull, then jacked in.

I immediately regretted it. The moment I tried to assault the defenses, I knew I'd made a huge mistake. In the split second before I felt my brain get fried by the backlash, I used Rewind, which allowed me to backtrack from the black-robed android's system without any repercussions.

I let out a gasp and muttered, "What the fuck was that?"

"Um . . . I don't know?"

"It's in your brain," I accused. "If anybody knows, it should be you."

"Uh . . . I don't . . . I'm not exactly used to this body, okay? I didn't think it would be like this . . ."

"What are you talking about?"

"I thought I'd hit the jackpot, you know? They told me I could get a new body without all my issues. I could live forever, too. But what they didn't tell me was that if I wanted to progress, I needed to give up more and more control. Like, I'm mostly still me, you know? Without the addiction. But if I wanted to get new colors, I have to—"

"New colors?"

"The robes. The hair. That kind of thing. There's brown, then black. We're about as low as you can get. But after that are the blues. The reds next. Then the silvers. And the golds. Finally, there's purple. Those are the real Pacies."

"Pacies?"

"The . . . uh . . . Pacificians. The aliens. Some of us are . . . You know . . . It's just a term of endearment. Like *buddy*. Or *friend*."

"Right. So, you made a deal with the aliens. They gave you a new body and everything. And what? You get to be their janitor?" I asked, remembering that I'd found him cleaning a domicile that had been recently occupied by an addict who was going through dust withdrawal. Not a clean proposition in the best of times.

"No. I mean, yeah. Sort of. I just have to do this until I can advance. But the problem is that when you do, you lose a little bit of yourself, you know? I had a buddy named Rix. He was like me. Good guy who'd give you the shirt off his back. But he found the Pillar of Heaven before me, and . . . Well, he's a blue robe now. Except he's not him. Not really. There's something missing."

"Like his humanity," I said, knowing precisely what he meant. It was the same with all the blue-robed guards I had seen. There was something altogether discomforting about the way they walked and talked. Even the way they looked at other people sent a chill up my spine. So, I knew precisely what he meant.

"I dunno about that. Can you help me? Get me out?" he asked.

"I don't think it works like that," I stated, and I saw his expression change. It had gone from hope to anger and then to resignation, all in the space of a second. Perhaps someone could have managed to extricate him from the Pacificians' clutches, but that was definitely outside my expertise. "I need some information. Like I said, if you give me the information I need, I'll let you go."

He sighed. "S'pose living as a damn robot is better than dying," he muttered. "Do you know what the worst part is? No more dust. Not that I'd feel like using it or anything. Those kinds of feelings are . . . gone. I guess everything else'll go when I get a better color than black. Least I'm not a brown. Those guys . . ."

I really didn't want to hear about the loss of his emotions, so I moved the conversation on to other topics. And I learned a few disturbing things. First, the city on the mountain was called Olympus, and it was populated by a rigidly delineated society. No one really wanted for anything, but life was definitely better for the gold robes than it was for the black robes. The ones in the brown robes were those who hadn't taken to their conversion quite as enthusiastically as the Pacificians thought they should. As such, they were removed from the city.

In addition to the basic structure of Olympus, the man gave me the information I really needed. Chiefly, that the Pacificians weren't without allies. They regularly traded with other aliens and had formed a strong alliance with a race of elfin aliens who had a Rift-delving operation nearby.

I also learned that Olympus was basically impenetrable. He didn't know the specifics, but according to everything he'd been told, the city was a fortress meant to withstand even other alien forces. After all, the Pacificians were not a popular race, largely because they existed by poaching the populations of other alien societies. That didn't endear them to anyone, and I was a little surprised that anyone would treat with them.

In any case, I'd learned everything I needed to move forward, so after knocking him out via another Ghost, I left him behind. It took a while for me to get free of the building, but I managed it via a generous application of Stealth and Camouflage. I abstained from using any other Ghosts, mostly because I didn't want to risk alarming the Pacificians. If they were on guard, the next part of my plan wouldn't work.

Eventually, I made it back to *The Leviathan*, where I found Patrick asleep on our couch. A few bits and pieces of machinery lay next to a couple of empty food containers. Clearly, he'd been working hard. Hopefully, that effort would pay off.

But in the meantime, I had another mission to plan.

CHAPTER THIRTY-ONE

RETURN

Many of the aliens I've encountered resemble creatures out of our mythology. From elves to gnomes and everything in between—I often wonder if there's some meaning behind that. Had they made contact well before the Initialization, and our myths were the result? Or was there some other explanation?

—Patrick Ward

You think it's safe?" asked Patrick, lying next to me in our bed. His head was cradled in his hands, and he wore a satisfied expression on his face.

I draped my arm over his bare chest and answered, "Probably not."

"Then don't do it," he advised. "I think I've got a good enough start to finish the armor on my own. We could head somewhere off the grid and—"

"No."

"Why not?" he asked.

"Aside from the fact that you'd be going back on your word and burning a bridge that doesn't need to be burned?" was my answering question.

"That's the pot calling the kettle black," he said.

He wasn't wrong. It sometimes felt like I was missing something necessary for maintaining relationships with other people. I managed it okay with Patrick, but it seemed like everything I did resulted in the alienation of people that should have been friends. Like with Simon and Vanna. If things had gone differently, I could have leaned on them. But every time I saw them, disaster followed. By now, they were probably on the other side of the world trying to set up a new life.

Because of me.

Still, just because I couldn't follow my own advice didn't invalidate it. So, I said, "You might need her sometime in the future. And besides, she has a state-of-the-art facility, right? And you said it yourself that she's a genius when it comes to this kind of stuff. If we want the best results, she should be involved. Plus, there's the other thing."

"What other thing?"

"I don't want to break the agreement," I said.

Patrick barked a laugh but cut it off as soon as he realized that he'd misread the situation. "Oh. Sorry. Thought that was a joke," he said.

"It wasn't."

"Yeah, no—I see that now," he said sheepishly. "But . . . Well . . ."

"What?" I asked, seeing him struggle to find the words for whatever he wanted to say. "Just spit it out, Pick."

"You've never cared about keeping your word before," he stated. "I've seen you lie through your teeth if you thought it could get you ahead. You've stolen. You've killed people for money. I mean . . . I'm not judging, but since when do you care about morality?"

"This isn't about morals," I said. "It's about trying to be better."

Indeed, my recent encounters with aliens had made it abundantly clear that I wasn't ready for life as a resident of the wider galaxy. I could easily stand up to the dregs that had found their way to Earth, but the moment I found myself facing off against any aliens that weren't two-bit smugglers who'd been pushed so far against the wall that they thought going to a recently Initiated world was a good idea, I had found myself at a distinct disadvantage.

For instance, I still had no idea how the Dengyts had even found me, let alone avoided my detection. It would have been so much easier to swallow if it had only been one. That was easily explainable by attributing it to an extraordinarily skilled individual. I had no doubt that Alistaris Kargat qualified. But it wasn't just him. It was an entire squad. So, either they were extremely advanced as a species—something I doubted based on my previous interactions with them—or I was missing something.

And then there were the Pacificians to worry about. I only had Freddy's word to go on, so I really wasn't sure who they were or what they were after. I liked Freddie, and the Templars had done right by me. Still, I had long subscribed to a trust-but-verify doctrine, and I wasn't going to stop now. As far as I was concerned, the more information I could get on them, the better off I'd be.

However, the simple fact was that I needed to be better in every facet of my life. I needed to stop relying on my skills as if they were foolproof. I needed to commit more to my training—even the parts I didn't like. And most of all, I knew I needed help. Maybe not immediately, but once the Initialization ended and the Integration began, I would need allies if I wanted to survive, let alone thrive.

And a few aliens at the Bazaar weren't going to cut it.

So, I'd decided that, going forward, I needed to be more cognizant of how I treated other people. Not because I thought they deserved my regard. Rather, because I thought I might one day need their support.

With that in mind, I had no intention of screwing Cirilla over. Or letting Patrick do so.

"Personal growth that doesn't have to do with your status readout?" he scoffed. "Who are you, and what have you done with Mira?"

"Ugh. That joke was old even before the Initialization," I groaned.

"I stand by it."

"Of course you do," I said with a slight smile.

"So—you want to go to the Bazaar, huh? Even with everyone gunning for you," he said.

I shook my head. I'd made a lot of enemies in the past few years, most of whom were aliens. And those aliens frequented the Bazaar. I didn't think they could actually hurt me up there—although, I'd recently discovered that what I thought I knew wasn't always based in reality—but the same couldn't be said for my friends. The last thing I wanted was to bring unwanted attention to Gala's or Dex's doorstep, so I'd refrained from visiting the Bazaar unless absolutely necessary.

"You could just call them," he suggested.

I shook my head. I'd discovered the hard way how easily communications could be hijacked. So, a call was fine if all I was doing was ordering ammunition or inquiring about mundane purchases. But for this? I needed to be face-to-face.

I explained my reasoning, ending with, "Besides, Ana has been begging me to visit for weeks now. I think she got a new poster, and she wants to show it off."

"She could just show some of her alien friends."

"I don't think they appreciate boy bands as much as she does," I said with a chuckle. "Come to think of it, neither do I. In fact, I don't think anybody appreciates boy bands like she does."

"I do believe you're right about that," he agreed. "But seriously, Mira—I'm fine with leaving all of this behind. This is a risk we don't need to take."

I just shook my head. As much sense as that made, I knew it wasn't the route I wanted to take. Besides, I was intrigued—and more than a little creeped out—by the Pacificians. I had gotten a brief look at the black-robed hostage's system before I'd been forced to use Rewind, and I was fascinated by what I had seen. So, I'd spent hours obsessively studying the little information I had. Maybe that colored my judgment more than I wanted to admit.

"It'll be fine."

"Every time you say that, something bad happens," he pointed out.

I shrugged. "Bad things are going to happen regardless of what I do," I countered. "I'm just trying to control what I can."

After that, we both went silent, and soon after, I fell asleep in his arms. I never felt safer than in little moments like that. It was nice, but it sometimes felt like the preamble to disaster. Or like the last meal of a prisoner meant for execution.

The next morning, I set about preparing for a trip to the Bazaar. The first item on my list was to determine precisely which Confluence I intended to use. Fortune simply wasn't big or important enough to warrant access to the Bazaar, so I would have to head somewhere else. To do that, I would need to pilot *The Leviathan*, which made Patrick incredibly uncomfortable.

"I could take a day off," he offered. "I think Cy's tired of having me around, anyway, and I could—"

"I'm perfectly capable of flying my own ship," I stated evenly.

"Yeah, but . . . Well . . . You do have a habit of running into things. Not that it's always your fault!" he was quick to add. But the damage had been done. Even if I'd been willing to entertain his offer, there was absolutely no way I was going to do so now. Not after he'd said that.

Even if it was kind of true.

In my defense, I didn't have a Pilot ability like him. Nor was I a [Smuggler], which meant that people noticed me when I landed. With Patrick at the helm, everyone just sort of ignored the giant, shiny ship. They knew it was there, but it wasn't noteworthy to them. With my lack of appropriate skills, things usually went a different way.

"Last time you took the ship off on your own, you started a gang war," he pointed out. "And you rammed a building."

"That building deserved it," I maintained.

And it had. Or rather, the people inside had. In any case, I wasn't going to apologize for doing what needed to be done. That gang had tried to steal *The Leviathan*; there was no way I was going to let that pass uncontested.

"You know the ship has a cannon, right? You didn't have to ram it."

"I can't use the cannon and fly the ship at the same time," I muttered, annoyed at having to point out my own deficiencies. Patrick's skills let him do lots of things all at once when piloting the ship. I had no such advantages. So, I'd used the tools I had at my disposal.

Chiefly, that I was in a giant ship that, so long as I kept the Mist shields running, wasn't going to even get a scratch from ramming a building.

"I'm going, okay? Even if I don't take the ship, it needs to be done. So, either I go in *The Leviathan*, or I use other transportation. Your decision," I said. I had no interest in using a train or hiring another pilot to fly me around, but I would do it anyway, if for no other reason than to make a point.

"Don't be like that. You know I'm not going to stand in your way if you really want to do something. I'm just pointing out that accidents tend to happen when you fly *The Leviathan*. That's all," he said.

I narrowed my eyes in annoyance. "Noted."

Patrick seemed to get the picture that he'd said the wrong thing—or many wrong things, really—so he quickly changed the subject to the armor project. He really hadn't made much progress that I could see, but he seemed happy with what he'd accomplished so far.

Soon after we had breakfast, he left for Cirilla's facility while I started researching Confluences I could potentially use. There was still one back in Nova City, but it was buried under a pile of rubble. I could probably still use it, and it had the added benefit of being completely under the radar. I'd have to dig it out, though.

And I'd have to return to the scene of my greatest regret.

My greatest accomplishment, too. While I hadn't set out to destroy the city, I had brought it to its knees. And through my actions, it had fallen. Dire though it was, that was an accomplishment.

Still, I wasn't quite ready to revisit Nova. Not unless I didn't have much of a choice.

As I went over my options, though, it quickly became apparent that it was the best solution to my problem. Every other potential choice came with a host of problems, most of which were my own fault. I had made a lot of enemies, after all, and most of them were congregated in the larger cities that just happened to play host to Confluences.

With a sigh, I realized that I was avoiding the city for all the wrong reasons.

Or maybe the right ones when I considered the effect it would have on my psyche.

Still, I made the right choice, and soon enough, I was piloting *The Leviathan* across the country. Thankfully, I didn't encounter any major threats, so I made it to the appropriate region in good time.

It wasn't the homecoming I'd expected.

The site of the city was nothing more than an overgrown mountain of rubble. The wilderness had begun to reclaim it, but it would take decades for it to complete the job.

In addition to the vegetation running rampant across the region, I also saw evidence of human habitation. Had some people survived the fall of Nova? Or had the people from the surrounding villages and towns recognized an opportunity for salvage? I didn't know, but I suspected I would soon find out for myself.

After circling the area a few times, I set *The Leviathan* down about forty miles north of the city's ruins. Then, I engaged Bastion before activating every security measure the ship had in its arsenal. Finally, I used Mimic to disguise my face. I didn't think anyone down there would recognize me, but I didn't want to take any chances. After all, any survivors had probably had family in Nova.

Family that I had killed.

So, with those precautions taken, I mounted the ATAV, opened the hatch, and started on my way. I could have used the Cutter, but I thought the all-terrain assault vehicle was a better choice. For one, it was equipped with a sizable cannon that might dissuade any would-be bandits from attacking me. For another, it was cheap to operate, and my stores of Rift Shards were running pretty low.

So, the ATAV was the obvious choice. And I had to admit that, while I preferred racing across the terrain on a cushion of Mist, there was something to the visceral sensation of feeling every bump along the way.

It took a couple of hours to reach my destination, but I quickly discovered that my caution was warranted. Because the ruins of Nova City were still populated. In fact, the mountain of rubble had become a veritable warren; it was invisible from the sky—probably by design—but it was evident the moment I laid eyes on it from the ground.

The people themselves reminded me of my time in Mobile. They were dressed similarly to what I'd seen in Nova City, but there was none of the bombast with which I was familiar. No garish colors. No outrageous cybernetics. Instead, everyone I saw looked as if they were prepared for a hard day's work.

The ATAV got a few curious glances, but it was a mundane enough vehicle—aside from the cannon—that it was easy for the population to ignore. So, I kept going until I reached a gate that protected a tunnel that led underground. Or into the ruins of the city I'd destroyed, rather.

It was manned by a trio of hardened warriors, each one armed and armored with serviceable equipment and better-than-average cybernetics. The leader asked, "Who are you, and why are you here?"

"Just passing through," I lied. "I had family who lived here, and when I found out the city had been destroyed . . ."

I left that hanging.

"You came running," she said, running a hand through her auburn hair. "Three years after the fact. You not like your family or something?"

I shrugged. "Came as soon as I could. There any survivors?" I asked.

"No. Not to speak of," she said. "A few made it out before the city came down, but they left the area. Everybody around here came from the surrounding towns."

"Why?"

"Salvage, mostly. There's a lot of valuable stuff in that pile of cement," she said, hiking her thumb backward to indicate the rubble. "Got to dig for it, though."

"Any of the old city still intact?"

"Just the Confluence. Crazy thing, that. We found it a month or so after the city came down. Completely undamaged."

The obelisks that allowed access to the Confluence, which in turn provided the ability to send one's awareness to the Bazaar, were protected by powerful Mist shields. Likely, that was why it had survived.

"Entry fee?" I asked.

"Three hundred credits," she said. "There's also a few information brokers inside who might can help you find your family. Like I said, there weren't any survivors, but maybe they got out. Can leave your . . . uh . . . vehicle here. It won't fit in the tunnels."

I nodded at that, then initiated the credit transfer, and once the lead guard accepted it, I navigated the ATAV to a nearby lot, where I left it under the watchful eye of a pair of other guards. Then, I was allowed through the gate. The tunnel beyond was just wide enough to accommodate a pair of people walking side by side, but it wasn't clogged with much traffic, so I had the space mostly to myself. The walls were lined with jutting and roughly cut rebar, and I could see huge cracks in the concrete. However, I could also sense the gentle hum of Mist in the air, telling me that everything had been reinforced.

After a few minutes, the tunnel led to a wide chamber that reminded me of the old city's underground society. Shops lined the walls, and the space was mostly populated with various booths where a wide variety of goods were sold. Most of it was clearly salvage, but there were also quite a few food stalls, as well. I didn't want to know which animals the meat they sold came from, so I passed them by without hesitation.

After wandering around a little, I surreptitiously asked where I could find the Confluence, and after handing over a few credits, I got the information I wanted. However, I didn't make it to my destination before I saw a familiar face.

Somehow, Gunther Gunderson had survived, and he'd clearly established himself as some sort of leader within the ruins of the fallen city.

CHAPTER THIRTY-TWO

FAMILIAR FACES

Sometimes, the only way to make sense of things is to take everything apart, figure out how it works, and then put it back together.

—Patrick Ward

I trailed my hand along the uneven concrete wall of the tunnel as I followed Gunther Gunderson through what was left of Nova City. Gone were the broad avenues and towering buildings, replaced by a series of underground tunnels dug through the rubble of what had once been a great city. Most of the time, it seemed like an entirely new place completely unconnected from the city where I'd spent most of my life. However, every now and then, I'd see something that sparked a memory. A holographic, neon-infused sign. A person wearing an old set of coveralls that had once belonged to a Silo worker. The smell of gumbo or the faux jambalaya I'd eaten so often in my youth. I even saw a few people sporting the colors or motifs of long-dead tribes.

But it wasn't the same.

Nova City was gone, and only the echoes of my former home remained.

And Gunther, of course. Like a cockroach, he had refused to die. I saw the telltale sheen of low-quality Realskin on his face, and I suspected that it had taken quite a bit of work to repair his skull. How his brain had managed to survive, I had no idea. But then again, I couldn't be sure if such a blow would kill me, either. Not with my Constitution and skills. Perhaps he had something meant to help him survive what should have been a deadly blow.

It was just further proof that, even though I sometimes felt like I stood at the top of the heap, I was woefully uninformed regarding what was possible. Before, I'd thought my ignorance was confined to aliens and the wider universe, but Gunther's continued existence was evidence enough that my lack of knowledge extended to Earth, as well.

I should have just left it at that, but seeing Gunther alive and well was enough to send my mission skittering to the back of my mind. Instead, I was almost wholly focused on following him.

I wish I hadn't.

Not because it left me open to ambush. It did, but that vulnerability never bore fruit. Instead, I wish I hadn't followed Gunther because I got a good look at how pitiful his life had become. Perhaps it always had been. I'd built him up as this great and powerful foe, but in reality, he'd never been more than a local gunrunner. He had some power, it was true, but his use of that power was petty and unimportant.

Never was that more apparent than when I watched him go about his day. Most of his actions were terribly mundane. He ate. He shopped. He talked with friends. But he was no criminal mastermind. In the grand scheme of things, he was just a petty criminal who managed just enough power to achieve some level of comfort. But with the city having fallen, much of that aura of invincibility he'd fostered had faded into the background. Now, he was just another guy.

Still, I followed him, convinced that it was all a facade. After all, he had once been an important man, at least within Nova City. Surely, he hadn't lost his taste for power. But everything I saw suggested otherwise. He had some influence, as evidenced by the number of people he spoke with, but it was a hollow thing. Perhaps my actions had broken him.

Eventually, I followed Gunther to what I suspected was his home. Carved into the rubble just like everything else, it was a tiny three-room domicile he shared with two other people.

Using Camouflage and Stealth, I watched as he greeted the other two people. Neither moved when he arrived. Nor did they even flinch at the sound of his voice. It wasn't surprising, either. One was a tiny, withered slip of a girl who was confined to a wheelchair, while the other just stared straight ahead, unseeing and inactive.

That's when something clicked in my mind.

I recognized the woman in the wheelchair. She looked far different from the person I'd met before—the one I'd thought I'd killed—but the moment I saw her eyes, I knew that I was looking at Dierdre, Gunther's cyborg bodyguard. However, without her cybernetic parts, she was about a quarter of her old size, and clearly, she wasn't capable of putting up much of a fight.

I watched as Gunther prepared a meal, then fed his two roommates. All the while, he spoke to them in what I supposed must have been meant as a soothing tone. I stayed like that for over an hour until I just couldn't take anymore.

I knew I shouldn't feel guilty. Those people had betrayed and tried to kill me. But seeing what had become of Dierdre—and the care with which Gunther treated her—tightened my chest and twisted my insides into knots. Justified or not, guilt enveloped my mind and threatened to overwhelm me.

In a lot of ways, their situation mimicked Nova City's fate. Greatness brought low. Power sundered. Potential dashed. And in its wake, only misery and weakness remained. Would that be my fate? I wasn't so different from Gunther, really. Certainly, I had some level of power, and so had he. But that hadn't saved him.

Of course, I didn't know the details of why he'd ended up with his current life. Perhaps he'd consciously chosen it after such a sound defeat. Or maybe I'd stolen his power, even if I hadn't managed to kill him. I didn't know, and I was past the point where I thought I could bear discovering more. So, without further ado, I pulled myself away from that scene and resumed my mission.

Still, the knot in my stomach remained, and as I traversed the tunnels that eventually led me to my destination, I couldn't shake the guilt threatening to strangle my mind. I thought I'd come to terms with what I had done to Nova City. And in a lot of ways, I had. I would never forgive myself for the single-minded dedication to vengeance that had led me down that path of inevitable destruction. But from a rational standpoint, I recognized that I didn't bear all the blame. The situation itself was partially responsible; without the Initialization, none of it would ever have happened. My uncle was guilty, too. He'd created the circumstances that ended with his death, which had in turn led me to seek revenge.

And Nora played her part, too. She'd set the bombs, after all. She had tried to manipulate me into letting her live. I didn't blame her. Not really. She was self-interested to the very end, and given everything I knew about her, the idea that she would take an "if I go down, everyone goes down with me" attitude was ultimately predictable.

But even so, it was my choice that had set everything into motion. If I'd gone a different direction or made one of a thousand different decisions, Nova City would still be standing. I accepted that, and I thought I had moved on.

I hadn't, though. Not really. Instead, I'd just pushed my feelings of remorse into the deepest, darkest corner of my mind where they could do nothing but fester. Now, though, Gunther's and Dierdre's fate had shone a light on my guilt, exposing it in all its toxic glory. I could barely stand it.

So, when I finally reached the facility housing the obelisk and the Confluence to which it was connected, I was not in a very healthy state of mind.

The chamber itself was perfectly spherical, with the concrete walls looking as if they'd been carved by a laser. The obelisk in the center was much as I remembered it—tall and red, with black trim—but that wasn't surprising. My uncle had once told me that it was nearly indestructible, and now, I couldn't help but believe it.

I had to progress through a checkpoint manned by shabby-looking guards before I was allowed to approach the obelisk. I also had to pay a fee—not surprising, given that the new city needed some sort of bureaucracy, which cost money to run. Then, when I laid a hand on the apparatus, I was prompted to pay another, much larger fee that probably went to maintaining the Bazaar itself.

Then, I was whisked up and away, eventually landing in the space station. Even though I'd made multiple trips to the Bazaar over the years, I was still astounded by the short journey through the atmosphere. It was one thing to fly around in *The Leviathan*, but it was something else altogether to do so without the obstruction of a ship. However, my flight ended after only a few seconds, and soon enough, I tumbled to the metallic floor of the Bazaar. As always, a sense of vertigo and nausea twisted through my stomach, but it passed after only a few moments. Then, I climbed to my feet and looked around.

The Bazaar looked much as I remembered it, with a crowd of people going to and fro as they went about their business. Some were dressed in what I would consider normal clothing. None looked destitute, but their outfits were well-worn and meant for work. There were plenty of others that were obviously aristocrats, though. Men and women who'd made deals with aliens, exchanging their loyalty for prosperity.

Once, I might have blamed them. But now? I had seen the other end of the spectrum, and I could certainly understand why someone would make that choice if it meant they could avoid poverty. Still, I couldn't help but look down on them. After all, their choice concerned more than their own fates. The entire world's future hinged on their inability to stand on their own two feet.

Pushing such thoughts aside, I quickly got my bearings and headed down the familiar halls in search of Gala. It took some time—maybe an hour—to reach her cube-shaped premises, but when I finally arrived, I found that she looked much the same as she always had. Which is to say that her appearance had a definite bovine cast to it, making her look like nothing so much as a minotaur from ancient myths.

"Mira!" she exclaimed when I walked through her door. She threw her arms around my illusory form—a quirk of her class that she was able to manage that feat, I'd been told—and hugged me tight. "What brings you here after so long? You're not in trouble again, are you?"

"Uh . . . Sort of?"

"What did you do?" Gala asked. The door slid shut behind me, ensuring our privacy. I didn't think anyone would be so bold as to eavesdrop—or if they were, that a closed door would stop them—but I trusted that Gala had plenty of defenses in place to prevent unwanted listeners.

So, secure in the knowledge that I wouldn't be overheard, I told Gala what had happened. First, I explained the ill-fated mission that had put me at odds with the Dengyts. She didn't react well to that knowledge, berating me for getting mixed up with "the core." I still wasn't certain what that meant—context told me that those planets were home to the elite of the universe, but beyond that, I was clueless.

Next, I told her about my investigation of the Pacificians, and she confirmed what Freddie had already told me—they were bad news no matter how I looked at it. After that, she cautioned me to steer clear of them.

"They have a habit of getting their hooks in people," Gala said. "Before you know it, you're lining up to join their collective, convinced that it was your idea all along. I've seen it happen."

"I'll be fine," I said. If there was one thing I knew about myself, it was that I wasn't likely to cede control, especially to a group of alien androids connected to a hive mind. "But here's the thing. I need to know about this group of aliens they're allied with." I told her what I knew of the elfin Rift-mining operation, then asked, "Am I missing anything? They're not some ancient clan of powerful warriors, are they? No big surprises, right?"

Gala shook her head. "No. They're probably not any stronger than a dozen other mining operations you've hit," she said. "Maybe a little smarter, but that's not saying much, given the sort of people who are willing to risk everything by mining on an Unintegrated planet."

"Anything I should know?"

"No. Not about them, at least. But I'll tell you again, Mira—stay away from those Dengyts. They're tricky little bastards," she said.

"I know," I muttered with a shake of my head. "The way they just snuck up on me—I didn't even know they were there, Gala. I still have no idea how they did it."

"Technology," she said. "You've got good equipment, Mira. Your uncle made sure you had a head start on everyone else on your planet. But your gear, it's basically trash to anyone from the core. Even on the outskirts, your weapons and armor are only a little better than average."

"Well, sell me something better."

"Can't. Even if I had the inventory, the system won't allow it."

"Why not?" I asked, frustrated. I prided myself on having the best equipment possible, and while that was true—at least on Earth—the knowledge that others had better gear was like a needle in my mind.

"Officially, it's because newly Initialized planets aren't responsible enough for the big guns," Gala said. "If you had access to some of the truly powerful weapons out there, you'd all end up killing one another. By the time the Initialization was finished, there'd be nothing but a dead husk of a planet left. And given that the system was created to deal with the repercussions of the Mist, that runs counter to the whole point."

"Who made the system, though?" I asked.

She shrugged her huge furry shoulders. "I've no idea. It's always been there," she said. "People from the outskirts like me aren't privy to that kind of information."

I looked away in frustration. Every time I thought I was on the verge of figuring things out, someone told me I wasn't allowed certain information. Given that, my ignorance wasn't really all that surprising. The only time I learned anything about the wider universe was when I stumbled across something I couldn't handle. I needed to change that, and fast, or else I was going to end up dead.

"What can you do for me, then?" I asked.

For a moment, I didn't think Gala was going to answer. But then, she glanced around before using some sort of ability. In my illusory form, I couldn't feel the swirl of Mist, but I'd seen enough skill activations to know one when I saw it. A moment later, she said, "Accept this information packet I'm about to send you."

"What is it?" I asked as the indicated packet arrived on the edge of my interface. I let it in, sequestering it in the same partition I reserved for information I stole from hostile terminals. I trusted Gala, but not so far as to give her unfettered access to my system.

"A contact," she said. "Information brokers are common in the wider universe. There's only one on this station, though. She's normally not available to people like you, but . . . Well, she owes me a favor. She can give you all the information you need if you insist on going up against the Dengyts, the Pacificians, or anyone else on that little planet of yours."

"And what's this going to cost me?" I asked.

"No cost. Just consider it me making good on a debt I owed your uncle," she said. "Speaking of—there's something else in that packet. Something Jeremiah wanted you to have. Just . . . Just don't access that part until you're back on the surface, okay?"

"He's been dead for years, Gala. Why are you giving this to me now?" I asked.

"I wasn't supposed to hand it over until after the Integration, but . . . Well, I figure you deserve to see what he left for you," she said.

"Do you know what it is?" I asked, trying my best not to dive right into the packet. I resisted the urge, though. I'd get the contact information for the broker, and then I'd worry about whatever my uncle had left me when I got back to my body on Earth.

She shook her head. "A message for sure," she said. "But more than that, I don't know. Jeremiah was a complicated man, and he wasn't exactly open, even with me. And I like to think we were friends. As far as a man like that has friends, at least."

I nodded. I wasn't sure if that was true, but Gala had always been a friend to me. That had to count for something.

In any case, I changed the subject, asking, "Any new arrivals? Did I tell you about the Dragon?"

That perked her right up, and she listened eagerly as I told her about the recent train heist—or more importantly, how I'd used my various weapons. When I'd finished, she said, "You get close too often. If it was me, I'd set up a mile or two away and just bombard my enemies with artillery."

"That's not always an option," I said. Though even if it was, I knew I'd never go down that route. I liked to get up close and personal, which was why I loved using my nano-bladed sword so much. "That reminds me—do you have anything better than my sword?"

"Guns are always better, and I have plenty of those."

"You know what I mean, Gala. C'mon. There's got to be something more advanced available."

"Guns. Even a bow and arrow is more advanced than a sword. There's a reason warfare moved past blades."

I fixed her with an annoyed glare. Finally, she rolled her bovine eyes and said, "Fine. There are options, I suppose. Energy blades are popular. So are elemental versions. You know, metal that's been imbued with some sort of elemental effect. Like lightning or ice or some other nonsense. But if you ask me, I'll always go with a nano-blade. They're sharp, no-nonsense, and you don't have to worry about recharging them."

"So, there's nothing better?" I asked.

"I didn't say that. That blade of yours is high-quality. Don't you doubt it one bit," she said. "But there's plenty of room for improvement. For instance, that metal is indicite. Good hardness. Solid durability. A great starter blade. But there are much better ones out there. You just don't have the Constitution to use them yet."

"What? I have plenty of Constitution," I argued.

"You really don't," Gala countered with a snort. "Come back to me when it's over a five hundred and we'll do some business. Until then, that little blade is as good as you're going to get."

I sighed, then said, "Fine. I'm a weakling. I get it."

"You're not even twenty-five years old, girl. You think you can compete with people who've lived ten times as long? Of course not. You still have a long way to go."

I knew she was right—especially after my recent losses—but that didn't take the sting out of it. However, there was one good thing about having my own place in the universe confirmed. Sure, I wasn't the strongest, but that just meant I had a lot of room to grow. And I knew precisely how to do that.

"What're you smiling about?"

"Just thinking," I said.

"About what?"

"That I've got a lot of training to do," I said. Then, I added, "Thanks, Gala. I think I need to talk to that information broker, then get back to Earth as soon as possible. It occurs to me that I'm in no way ready for what's coming."

CHAPTER THIRTY-THREE

INFORMATION

To Mira, Jeremiah was a godlike figure. Rationally, I think she understands that he was a flawed man and the product of a seriously messed-up situation, but from an emotional—and much more powerful—standpoint, he was everything she wants to become. If I do nothing else in my life, I hope I can prevent that from happening.

—Patrick Ward

I followed Gala's directions through the Bazaar, eventually finding myself in an area I'd never visited. That wasn't so surprising, really; it wasn't as if I visited the place all that often, after all. Couple that with the fact that it was enormous, and my unfamiliarity should have been expected. Still, it was a little unnerving to look around and see a wholly unfamiliar environment.

The setting wasn't so dissimilar from what I'd seen before. Each hall was lined with plasti-steel panels, curiously shaped lights, and subtle blue lighting, and the intermittent chambers were populated by the same cube-shaped shops manned by a wide variety of aliens that looked at me with unabashed suspicion.

Because I didn't belong.

It had been quite some time since I'd even seen another human being, which was my first hint that I'd gone off the beaten path. On top of that, the aliens didn't wear the welcoming expressions of shopkeepers like Gala. Instead, they looked angry at the intrusion, as if I'd interrupted something far more important than commerce.

But more than anything, I recognized something familiar in those alien faces. Or perhaps it was the environment itself. There was something about the dingy film covering every surface, the sometimes-flickering lights, or the overall demeanor of the population that made it clear that I'd come to the slums. Or whatever passed as such on a space station.

In a lot of ways, it felt like I'd come home. Back in Nova—and in the years since it fell—I'd spent quite a lot of time in the poorest parts of various cities. So, I could easily recognize the signs of poverty. Of desperation.

"Lost, little human?" grunted an alien who was leaning against one of the cubicles. He was a hulking creature with reptilian scales, a prominently ridged brow, and an upturned snout that made me think of the wild boars I'd seen in the wilderness. But as massive as he was, I didn't feel any real danger. After all, I was a mere projection. He couldn't hurt me.

Probably.

I wondered if that was truly the case, though. Through the use of some sort of skill, Gala could make physical contact. It would have been ridiculous to think that others couldn't do the same. And while the giant minotaur woman had only used that ability to hug me, these strangers would likely have other, more dangerous things in mind.

"No," I said. "Just passing through."

"Well, keep on movin'," he said. "You ain't welcome 'round here."

His accent was curious, and though I knew it had been manufactured by my Universal Language ability, I felt like it fit his appearance.

"Good to know," I said, pushing on.

Over the next few minutes, I endured many such comments, though I was quick to notice that no one tried to bar my way. Still, I garnered quite a lot of attention, which made me nervous. Once, I'd heard that aliens often thought humans all looked the same. Many had difficulty telling us apart. I could only hope that was true; otherwise, my passing would be noted, and there was a chance that some of my enemies would be able to trace my route.

That would bring trouble down on Gala's head. And while I thought her capable of dealing with whatever came her way, I didn't want to be the cause of any issues that might befall her.

So, I hunched my shoulders and continued on my way as I tried to remain as unobtrusive as possible. It really wasn't effective, but it was the best I could do under the circumstances. If I'd had my active skills available to me, things would have been different. I could have disguised myself with Mimic or used Stealth to remain unseen. But with my body back on Earth, that just wasn't in the cards.

Which left me feeling extremely vulnerable.

On Earth, I could depend on my skills, abilities, and attributes to see me through. But in the Bazaar? I was completely exposed.

I pushed forward until I finally arrived at my destination. It was a cube just like any other, though the glyph on the door indicated that it was the premises of the information broker.

I knocked on the door, and a few seconds later, it slid open to reveal what could only be described as a humanoid rat. It was only about four feet tall—big for a rat, but small for a person, I supposed—and it had all the hallmarks of a rodent. Small beady eyes. A long hairless tail. A narrow snout. You know—a rat.

"What'choo want?" it hissed.

"Uh . . . Gala sent me," I said. "She told me you could help me with an information problem."

"So cryptic," it spat. Literally, spit went flying with each word. "Come on in. Ain't got all day."

I reluctantly took the invitation and followed the ratlike alien into the cubicle. The interior was, in a word, disgusting. What looked like trash was piled in one corner, while boxes that still contained bits of food were strewn across the floor. There were even insects skittering here and there. As I stepped inside, however, I couldn't shake the feeling that something was wrong. I couldn't pinpoint exactly what was bugging me, though.

"What'choo wanna know?" it asked. Pointedly, the little creature hadn't bothered to introduce itself. Nor had Gala given me a name. Instead, she'd only provided a location and told me what kind of cost I should expect.

"Uh . . . There are some aliens—invaders, I guess—called Pacificians," I said.

"Nine thousand credits for basic information," it interrupted. "Forty for a more in-depth dossier. Two hundred thousand if you want everything I got."

"No. I mean . . . I'm not . . . Wait, two hundred?!" I exclaimed.

"Dangerous entities. Big money."

"But that's just extortion . . ."

Indeed, two hundred thousand credits was an extreme amount for a little information. Of course, the value of said information might very well exceed that sum, especially if you were at odds with a civilization like the Pacificians. Still, I wasn't there for information on them; indeed, I felt confident that I could discover what I needed on my own.

Besides, I didn't have two hundred thousand credits to spend. Perhaps I could come up with it, but running *The Leviathan* was extremely expensive, and so, I rarely had any accumulated wealth to speak of.

"It costs what it costs," said the rodent.

"Fine. Whatever. I'm not here about them, anyway," I said. "I'm looking into some of their allies." I explained what I knew about the elves in question. They were known as Ithids, and thankfully, information on their operations was far cheaper than the files on the Pacificians. Still, when I transferred the required ten thousand credits, it was with a degree of regret.

After all, I had the ability to gather information on my own, didn't I? That I'd had to pay for something I could get myself just seemed sloppy, and it left me feeling a little lazy.

I was just about to accept the credit transfer when I realized what had been bothering me ever since entering the cubicle. I watched as the same insect skittered across the floor in precisely the same way it had gone before.

It wasn't just similar, either. It was identical.

Which meant that none of it was real.

I was very familiar with holographic displays, and while mine weren't nearly as advanced as whatever the ratlike information broker was using, they still had many of the same issues. Like repeated patterns.

"You noticed, huh?" asked the information broker in an entirely different voice. "That's unfortunate."

Then, the entire scene shimmered. The trash disappeared, the stains on the walls vanished, and most importantly, the ratlike broker's illusory appearance faded away, revealing her actual form. She wasn't any bigger, but her rodent-like features were gone. Her fur had been replaced by purple skin, and her face had taken on something approaching human proportions.

However, I couldn't tear my attention away from her eyes, which were huge, oblong orbs speckled with pinpoints of light that made them look like miniature galaxies.

"What gave it away? It was too much trash, wasn't it?" she said. "I based the hologram on a slum I visited a few decades ago, so I'm sure it was accurate. Or was it too much? I'm told that humans associate rodent features with dishonesty and filth. Is that not the case? Was there some discrepancy?"

"I . . . It was the bugs," I said. "The hologram looped."

"Damn the ancestors, really?" she said. I don't know why I thought of her as female—her figure was androgynous enough that it threw her gender into question—but I felt certain about it all the same. "The bugs. I never thought of that. Now—would you suggest I remove the insects altogether? No. The more I think about it, the worse that sounds. The bugs tie everything together, don't you think? You can't have a disgusting trash pile without a few roaches, am I right?"

"I . . . Um . . . I guess?" I said, completely unsure of how else I was supposed to respond. The air of danger that had surrounded her had faded completely, but I got the feeling that, if I were to make even one wrong move, that could change. I had no basis for that, but I felt it in my bones.

"Oh, right—you're probably a little unsure of what's going on, aren't you?" she said. "Understandable. I'm trying something different on 2341-M. Earth, I suppose you locals call it. Seriously unimaginative name. May as well have called it dirt. But then again, that might just be the autotranslation at work. Perhaps your word for dirt was influenced by the chosen name for your planet, hmm? In any case, as I said—I'm trying something new with this Integration. Or upcoming Integration, as it were. Soon enough, you and your people will be flooding the Bazaar—also a silly name, by the way—looking for information. So, I decided to invest in a few new tricks just to keep you all on your toes. Still working out the kinks, as it were. So—what do you say? Bugs or no bugs? Now, be honest. At Infotech, your input is valued."

"Infotech?" I mumbled, still a little taken aback, as much due to the situation as it was because of her rapid-fire speech pattern.

"Oh. You don't like it, do you? I knew it was a silly name, but the one I really wanted was already taken," she said. "Well, I can't change it now, so you're just going to have to get over your issues. It's just a name."

"I . . . Um . . . I didn't say I didn't like it . . ."

She cocked her head to the side, and some of the little pinpricks of light within her eyes flashed. "So you didn't," she said after a second. "Do you, though? I don't. But I'm a bit biased, I suppose. I had my heart set on Goblsonger's Information Emporium. But my sister beat me to it, the bitch. Did I use that word correctly? My information says it refers to a female canine—curious creatures, those—but it also says it's meant as a derogatory term associated with . . . well . . . lots of unsavory things. Because my sister is quite unsavory, though she is not comparable to a female canine."

"I . . . I think it's probably a good idea just not to use the word."

"Well, that is just unacceptable!" she said, throwing one finger into the air. "I must fit in. Otherwise, no one will trust me!"

I wanted to point out that nobody was going to trust her if she kept trying to deceive them, but I thought better of it. Instead, I asked what seemed like an obvious question. "What's your name?"

"Kith," she said. "Kith Goblsonger. I know exactly what you're thinking. Another Goblsonger?"

"Uh . . ."

"Very common name. Like Sith on Earth."

"I think you mean Smith."

"Oh, no—Sith is definitely the right name. It's all over your history. Really—it's your planet. Perhaps you should get to know it a bit better instead of cavorting with a bunch of aliens."

"I'm not cavorting," I sighed. "I just . . . You know what, never mind. That's my bad, I guess. Is there anything else you can tell me about the Ithids?"

"No, no—it's all in the packet I sent you," she said. "But between you and me—and not to sound speciesist or anything—they are vicious little creatures who deserve to be wiped from the galaxy. With extreme prejudice."

"Right . . ."

With that, I accepted the transfer, exchanging the credits for the packet of information she'd promised. I only gave it a cursory glance to make certain that it contained the proper information, but in doing so, I saw that the Ithids were not elves in the same way that Askar had been. Instead, they were small, winged creatures that more closely resembled the fairies from Earth's mythology.

Except for the sharp teeth, faces that looked like someone had smashed them in with a hammer, and the fact that the photos included in the packet had them wielding weapons that were at least two or three sizes too big for their small bodies.

"Brutes," Kith said. "They always think bigger is better. And don't get me started on how they respond when you accuse them of having an inferiority complex."

"You say that like you have firsthand experience."

"I may have dated one a few cycles ago," she stated. "But in my defense, I was at a low point. My sister had just stolen my business's name right out from under me, and on top of that, this was the only Integration where I could manage a slot. I don't need to tell you how unlucky that is, what with the Dengyts running around as they are. Ugh. My luck just keeps getting worse and worse."

"S-sure . . ."

I barely managed to get the word out. I hadn't even mentioned the gnomes, but it seemed that their presence was common knowledge. And even other aliens were wary of them.

"And that's not even considering the Templar presence," she said. "Biggest mobilization in the past hundred cycles. There's something special about that little blue planet of yours, and everyone seems to know it. Except me, of course. You wouldn't happen to know what's going on, would you? Why are three major factions interested in Earth?"

"Three?" I asked. The Dengyts and the Templars were two of them, but I wasn't sure about the third. Perhaps she meant the Pacificians.

"Ah, but that'll cost you! No information for free. That's my motto. Not like my sister, whose motto is 'It's mostly accurate.' No professionalism there. But she got the good name, so of course she'd be the successful one. Right—which reminds me. I'll be sending you a questionnaire about your experience here. Now, be honest. My goal is to get better, and I can't do that without your input!"

Just then, another packet arrived. This one was labeled "Infotech (ugh, I hate that name) Customer Survey." I was tempted to refuse it, but then I thought better of it. Kith seemed a bit quirky, but if I could cultivate some sort of relationship with her, her information could prove invaluable. So, I accepted the transfer, sequestering it into a partition of its own before extricating myself from the situation. For her part, Kith seemed reluctant to let me go; she kept going on about her sister, and I kept nodding along as I backed away. I think she was a little lonely.

Finally, I managed to get away, and a few hours later—after visiting Ana, of course—I transferred back to my body on Earth.

If I was completely honest, I half expected that I'd arrive to find myself surrounded by Gunther and a bunch of hired mooks. It certainly would have fit with my recent string of bad luck. However, when I felt myself return to my body, I opened my eyes to see the same unassuming chamber I had left behind. No armed mooks. No vindictive gunrunners. Just a bunch of bored guards waiting out their shifts.

It was a little anticlimactic. However, as Patrick often said, "Boring can sometimes be a good thing."

I tried to remember that as I made my way out of the ruins of Nova City. Appropriately, the trip was uneventful, and before long I was back in the driver's seat of the ATAV and ripping across the terrain. I passed a couple of stray wildlings on the way back to *The Leviathan*, but nothing was really interested in barring my way.

Finally, I arrived back at the ship to find that no one had ventured within a few hundred feet. So, I quickly loaded the ATAV into the cargo bay, closed everything up, and headed to the cockpit.

That's when I got the surprise I'd been waiting for the whole time.

There he was, just sitting in the pilot's seat like he belonged.

"You visit the most wondrous places, Mirabelle," Alistaris Kargat said. "Tell me—did your visit assuage your guilt?"

I stared down at the Dengyt, unsure how to respond. Then, I yanked Ferdinand II from his holster, pointed it at the little alien, and pulled the trigger.

CHAPTER THIRTY-FOUR

THE BAD GUYS

I think it's important to see the good in the world. Sure, evil's out there. Bad things happen all the time. But to me, happiness is a choice we have to make every single day. Focusing on the negative will do nothing but make that choice harder and harder until it's just not an option anymore.

—Patrick Ward

The round hit Alistaris directly in the forehead, the momentum behind the shot sending him flipping backward into the ship's control console. Still, I wasn't surprised when, a moment later, he pushed himself to his feet, brushed imaginary dust from his jacket, and said, "Now, that was just rude."

"You're the one who broke into my home and snuck up on me," I said, still aiming Ferdinand II in his direction. I'd never intended the first round as anything but a warning shot; after all, the moment he had appeared, I'd sensed the powerful Mist shield enveloping his body. It wasn't quite up to the level of what Nora had used back in Nova City, but it was plenty powerful to absorb the impact from my least powerful weapon.

Things might've turned out differently if I'd brought the Dragon to bear.

But my shot hadn't been the result of simple pique. Instead, I'd had a good reason—or reasons, as it were—to pull my weapon and fire. First, I was annoyed. It was one thing to corner me in the middle of an unfamiliar city, but it was something else altogether to infiltrate my home and surprise me. I didn't know how he'd bypassed the ship's innate defenses or my Bastion ability, either, which had sent my level of frustration through the roof.

However, that wasn't even the biggest reason I'd shot him. Instead, ever since our first meeting, I'd longed to test his defenses. So, as I'd fired, I had paid close attention to the energy level of the Mist shield. The ripples were subtle, and the dip in power was barely noticeable, but the fact that it had been affected at all was a good sign. If that hadn't been the case—meaning that if the shield hadn't even wavered—I would've been at a loss as to how to solve my gnome problem. But that little ripple gave me hope. I couldn't overcome them yet—not with my current skill set or arsenal of weapons—but that wouldn't always be the case.

He continued to brush imaginary dust from his jacket, then ran a hand through his thick mane of white hair before saying, "Suppose you have a point. You'll forgive me a little drama, though, right?"

"Remains to be seen. What do you want?" I asked. Pointedly, I still hadn't lowered my weapon. It couldn't get through that shield, but it could still be effective in throwing him off-balance.

"Oh, put that little toy away. We both know you have no intention of trying to kill me," he said.

"I'm still on the fence about that," I stated.

"And what if I brought my friends along?" he asked. "You could be surrounded right now, and you might not even know it."

That was true. Or at least, on the surface, it seemed to be. However, I wasn't convinced. For one, our previous meeting had been much more dangerous for everyone involved, so it wasn't surprising that he'd have brought extra manpower—or gnomepower, as it happened—along. But this meeting was different, and so, I thought it was a reasonable expectation that he'd come alone. Or maybe with an extra soldier or two.

Second, I didn't feel anything amiss. If I'd been looking for it, I felt certain I would've felt Alistaris standing in the middle of my Bastion ability. My mistake was that I'd let my guard down because no one had ever bypassed *The Leviathan*'s security. Now, though, I was aware and alert, and I felt nothing. There wasn't the slightest ripple in the Mist, which suggested that Alistaris and I were all alone.

But most of all, I knew that if he'd brought a bunch of gnomes along as security, they would have reacted to me shooting him. The fact that no one had, told me that Alistaris had come alone.

Taken by themselves, none of those factors would have been enough to make me certain, but when they all came together, they painted a pretty good picture of the situation. Besides, even if I was wrong, he'd obviously come for a reason, and I trusted that to keep him from reacting too harshly.

Or maybe I was just trying to justify my own impulsive stupidity by assigning reasons after the fact. Either way, it was already done, and I needed to act accordingly.

"You didn't," I said with confidence that suddenly seemed like it had been built on shaky ground. "And anyway, you're fine. Didn't even muss your hair.

So, tell me what you want so I can refuse and we can both move on with our lives. You can go back to being a creepy stalker—or whatever it is you do for fun—and I can get back to—"

"You won't refuse," he stated with all the confidence I wish I felt.

"Didn't even refute the stalker comment, huh?" I said. "Says a lot about you, really. Do you just pick random women to creepily follow around? Or do you have, like, a list or something? Also, do you just get off on watching, or is there more to it? You know, the popping-up-out-of-nowhere thing? Or are there a bunch of little gnome bodies buried in your little gnome basement back home? I mean, I'd apologize for jumping to conclusions here, but really, you're not doing yourself any favors."

"That's not—"

"Seriously—how did you think sneaking into a woman's home was going to go? You didn't go through my stuff, did you?"

"Enough!" he yelled, slapping his hand on the arm of the pilot's chair. "I was not . . . It was just to prove to you that we can get to you at any time. And we can. That's it. There was nothing . . . creepy about it."

"Maybe you didn't mean it like that, but that's definitely how it came off. Just saying."

I considered shooting him again. Maybe multiple times until I made it through that Mist shield of his. It had limits—I'd already seen them—and I felt positive that I could find them. Still, the potential consequences of following through with that line of thinking brought me up short. If I pushed him too far, he would get serious. And if nothing else, I knew I didn't want to see that.

So, I switched gears and said, "Just tell me what you want, okay? We'll put this embarrassing little incident behind us."

He started to respond but then thought better of it. After that, he smiled. "Not bad. Putting me on the back foot, controlling the conversation—you're not terrible at this kind of thing."

"Wish I could say the same," I said. "But the whole creeping around other people's—"

"Don't act like you haven't done the same thing," he said. "But I'm not here to debate the morality of infiltration. I'm here to give you a job."

"And if I refuse?"

"You won't."

"Humor me."

"Fine—if you refuse, we'll part ways, and I'll come back with something else when I encounter a situation where your talents can be best applied," he stated. He held up one small finger. "But—if you continue to refuse our offers, I'll take that as you reneging on our deal. Then, we'll have to take things in another direction."

"You'll kill me."

"I will. Personally. Then, I'll kill everyone else that had a hand in that little fiasco of a heist," he stated. "You. Your pilot. The man with that ridiculous hat. The half elf. Those two you went to for help. Perhaps I'll destroy that whole city, just to be certain I got everyone."

"If you know who I am, then you know that kind of threat isn't going to sway me. I was presented with that kind of choice once before. You can go visit Nova—or what's left of it—to see how that turned out."

"Perhaps. But the promise remains. Do with it what you will," he said. "In any case, I believe I know you well enough to—"

"You don't know me at all."

"Don't I? You're not so difficult to figure out. A little girl who was thrust into a situation she couldn't control, then had the rug yanked out from under her—you responded by focusing on the one thing you think you can accomplish. But once you had your revenge in hand, you were confronted with the cost of your actions. You couldn't handle that. Not alone. So, you went off the rails, engaging in a host of self-destructive behaviors until, at last, your partner returned. Since then, you've tried to pretend you're not the same broken little girl you've always been. Usually, you resort to posturing—like shooting someone—or flippant comments to distract yourself from how doomed you really are. And right now, you're considering shooting me again just because you don't like what I have to say."

He wasn't wrong. Not about the being tempted to shoot him part, at least. The rest of it was just armchair psychology based on incomplete—and ultimately surface-level—information. Still, it hit close enough to home that I just about decided to shut him down, then and there, consequences be damned. But I managed to wrangle my annoyance into submission and say, "Tell me what you want me to do."

"Good choice," he said. "And not just because it's smart. I think you'll also like what I have to say."

"Just tell me what you want me to do and leave," I said. Indeed, I was already tired of the interaction, and I wanted to hear him out, shut him down, and then go back to my previous plans. After all, I still needed to peruse the information packets I'd gotten from Gala and Kith before beginning my surveillance of the elves.

"Very well," he said. "There are some Rifters I want you to eliminate. They're called the E'rok Tan, and they're some of the most detestable people you'll ever meet. I want you to kill them and destroy their mining operation."

"That's it?" I asked.

"That's it."

"What's the catch?"

I thought it was a valid question. It wasn't so different from what I normally did; I'd made quite a lot of money off of raiding alien mining operations. So, I didn't immediately reject the mission like I'd expected to.

"No catch."

"Oh, come on. There has to be a catch. You have plenty of people to do this yourself," I said. "Anything I can do, you can probably do better."

That hurt to admit, but it was true. Alistaris and the Dengyts had already proven that they had superior technology, and I suspected that many of their warriors were higher leveled and much more powerful. Sure, I probably had higher potential, but that didn't count for anything in the present.

"You must have figured it out," he said, looking slightly disappointed.

I shrugged. "I sometimes need things spelled out," I said. "So, start spelling."

His shoulders drooped, then he said, "I expected more from you. Oh well. Disappointment is a part of life, I suppose. It comes down to culpability. If we attack the E'rok Tan, we'll be in violation of the system's laws. It will ignore a few small mining expeditions—especially if they at least pretend to be in hiding—but when we start fighting among ourselves, it starts paying closer attention."

"But it'll let you hire someone to do your dirty work?"

"Indeed. Call it a loophole. It's no different from the other humans who have been working for various factions since the very beginning," he explained.

That made sense—at least on the surface. After all, people who'd thrown their lot in with the aliens were one of the first things my uncle had warned me about. So, what Alistaris was saying tracked with everything I already knew. Still, I was suspicious, so I asked, "And these Rifters—what makes them so bad?"

"Well, they have a taste for humans," Alistaris said. "Apparently, their planet was originally home to two dominant species. The E'rok Tan and a race of humans. Inevitably, there was conflict, and the E'rok Tan won. By the time the Mist enveloped their planet, the humans had been domesticated. I've never seen it, but they're kept as livestock. Horrible and barbaric practice, but it's part of their culture. In any case, the ones who came to Earth are far removed from their home planet—most of them have probably never even been there—but they still see eating humans as natural. So, if they're allowed to remain until the Integration, they will likely attempt to expand their human ranches."

"Expand? You mean they've already started domesticating people?" I asked.

"They have. It's a small operation. Perhaps a few thousand humans, most of which were born in captivity and have never known anything else, but . . . Well, it's still a disgusting practice, I'm sure you'll agree."

I ground my teeth. The very notion was indeed disgusting, but I wasn't certain I was the right person to solve the problem. What was I going to do with a few thousand people who'd been kept as livestock, anyway? They'd need to be taken care of, and I was ill-equipped to make that sort of commitment. Even so, now that I knew what was going on, I certainly couldn't just ignore it, either.

"Why?"

"I just told you why. With their history, the E'rok Tan see humans as cattle, and—"

"No—why do you want them gone? And don't tell me it's altruism, either. I might be ignorant of the wider universe, but I'm willing to bet that you don't care about a few humans. So, what's your real beef with them?"

"Beef?" he asked, cocking his head to the side. Then, recognition dawned on his face as he said, "Ah. The translation was a little slow there. Curious expression. In any case, the answer to your question is simple: we have a long-standing conflict with the E'rok Tan, and we have no desire to share a planet with them. If you refuse to do this, then we will attack their operation as soon as the Integration dawns."

"Sounds good to me," I said.

"They will be prepared for it, then. At this very moment, they are building defenses. If we let them dig in, removing them from Earth's surface will be very difficult. Likely, it will spark a war that will sweep across the entire planet," he explained.

I could see his strategy unfolding. First, he appealed to my emotions, casting the E'rok Tan as enemies of humanity. Then, he doubled down on that by explaining the stakes. If these aliens were allowed free rein, what was to stop them from enslaving the entirety of humanity? They had done it on their own planet, so it was a distinct possibility.

And I believed that Alistaris was telling the truth, too. He didn't need to lie.

After the emotional appeal, he'd thrown the consequences of inaction at me. If I didn't act, war would come. And that war would ravage the planet I called home, killing countless people in the process. I could stop that by simply taking the mission and doing Alistaris's bidding.

But just because I could recognize his manipulative tactics didn't mean they weren't effective.

"If I agree to do this, I'm going to need something from you," I said.

"I already said we would pay you for your trouble."

"No. Not that. I'm not talking about the money or the metals," I stated. "I'm referring to the people. Those . . . livestock you were talking about. If I kill the aliens, they'll need help. I want your agreement that you'll do what you can to rehabilitate them."

"That may not be possible."

"Then take care of them somehow. I don't know what is and isn't possible, okay? But I know we can't just leave them . . ."

"It may be more humane to simply euthanize them," Alistaris suggested.

"More humane? Or cheaper?" I asked.

"Both. You have to understand that—"

"No. You need to understand that this is the cost of my acceptance of this mission," I said, cutting him off. "I kill the bad guys, you save the victims. That's it. If that means euthanasia, then fine. But that's a last resort. I expect you to try everything else before you get to that point."

Indeed, I had no interest in helping those people myself. I wasn't equipped for the job. But that didn't mean I was okay with abandoning them. After all, I hadn't forgotten the scene of my first Rift, where the aliens had enslaved the local humans. Back then, I had been forced to kill those victims when they attacked me. I didn't want to revisit that same situation.

"You're asking quite a lot from me," said Alistaris.

"Same," I pointed out, banking on the fact that he needed me. Or rather, he needed the E'rok Tan gone. Perhaps he'd told me the truth about his reasons. Or maybe he hadn't. But the fact was that he wanted them dead, and I intended to use that leverage as much as I could.

He ran a hand through his wild white hair, then said, "Very well. We have protocols for situations like these. We can remove the implants and overcome the conditioning. The people will never fully recover. They have been fundamentally altered at a genetic level. Mostly, they're meant to be docile and dull, but they are a bit bulkier than normal humans. In any case, we can transfer them to our main facility where they will be given jobs, homes, and food. They will be as comfortable as we can make them. Assuming you hold up your end of the bargain. Do we have a deal?"

"I believe we do," I said, already mentally preparing for the job ahead of me.

CHAPTER THIRTY-FIVE

FAILURE

Morality is the privilege of the powerful.

—Patrick Ward

After Alistaris gave me a little more information on my target, I escorted him out of *The Leviathan*. To my surprise, a ship landed a moment later. It was small—maybe twenty or thirty feet long—sleek, and shaped like a bullet with wings. Looking at it, it was easy to imagine that it was a craft specialized for stealth and speed.

As Alistaris climbed aboard, I called out, "Remember your part of the bargain, Al. If those people end up dead, our next meeting won't be so pleasant."

He looked back and said, "You think that was pleasant? You did shoot me."

"I stand by what I said," I stated. He and his people might be incredibly powerful—far more so than I was—but I'd already proven that I could infiltrate their facilities and cause all sorts of havoc. If he didn't hold up his end of the deal and save those people, I intended to find out just how much chaos I could cause. Perhaps I couldn't kill them all—debatable, given that I had never really gotten serious with Alistaris or his team of invisible warriors—but I could certainly throw a wrench into their operations.

He just shook his head. "I keep my promises, Miss Braddock," he stated. Then, without another word, he climbed the rest of the way into the cockpit. Even as the door slid shut and the ramp retracted, the ship rose into the air and faded away. I could still sense it—barely—but I had to flare Observation at its maximum power to do so. Soon enough, it was gone.

But I didn't relax.

Instead, I quickly retreated into *The Leviathan*, sealed it shut, and began the arduous process of combing the systems for hostile Ghosts. And I found plenty. Alistaris hadn't spent his time idling about; instead, he'd planted thirteen Ghosts, each intended to track whatever happened within *The Leviathan*. Most were only surface level, which meant that he knew I'd find them. However, there were two buried so deep that I almost missed them. I crushed them all with ruthless efficiency before starting again from the top.

Like that, I spent the next six hours. Repeatedly scanning the systems probably wasn't necessary. I felt reasonably certain that I'd gotten all the trackers. However, reasonably certain just wasn't good enough. By the seventh hour, my repeated scans—each one going deeper than the last—bore fruit when I found the last tracker.

I unraveled it, then continued on for another few hours. I didn't find anything else, though. Finally, once I was absolutely sure that the systems were clean, I let myself relax for a few minutes. Then, I started searching for physical trackers. And I found plenty of those, too. In a lot of ways, it was a far more tedious process than combing the ship's systems for hostile Ghosts, but I was used to tedium, and the stakes were high enough to garner the entirety of my focus.

All in all, cleaning the ship took close to an entire day, but by the time I was finished, I'd found seventeen physical trackers. Each one was a tiny, matte-black plasti-steel disc that was perfect for remaining unseen. But thankfully, my Observation ability was more than up to the task.

Finally, when I was certain that I'd gotten all Alistaris's trackers, I slumped into the pilot's chair, mentally exhausted. I wanted to be angry, but I also knew that he was just doing what anyone would have done in his position. Besides, I was too tired to be annoyed.

So, after piloting the ship to a new location and instituting all my defenses, I took a shower and went to bed. After waking the next morning, I gave the ship another thorough sweep—finding nothing—before establishing my agenda. I had three things I needed to accomplish. First, I had enough information to infiltrate the Ithids' compound and hopefully use that to gain entry into Olympus, where I could commence my search for Cirilla's brother.

Second, I needed to open the packet my uncle had left for me. I knew that doing so wouldn't take long; it was just a file, after all. But I expected it to be emotionally draining in a way nothing else would be. Barely a day went by that I didn't think about Jeremiah, but most of those thoughts were muddled by time and distance. Suddenly confronting his final message to me was inevitably going to be emotionally draining. So, when looking at that packet, I felt a combination of anxiety, fear, dread, and anticipation that left my emotions tangled into something almost unrecognizable.

The last item on my list was to assault the E'rok Tan base of operations. I thought I was mentally prepared for what I would see there, but I also knew it would be a truly horrible experience. So, I had an overwhelming urge to put it off. I wouldn't listen to it, of course, but that urge to procrastinate was still there.

Sighing, I established my list of priorities, then dove into my interface and, after scanning the packet Gala had given me, opened it. When I did, a video of uncle appeared.

"Hey, Mira," the recording of Jeremiah said. "If you're looking at this, I'm probably dead." He ran his hand over his bald head, then sighed. "God. That's such a cliché line. Accurate but cliché. Anyway, I hope this finds you well after you finished your training. Maybe after you left Earth altogether. But if not . . . I'm sorry."

He sighed again. I could see from the background that he'd recorded the message in his room in the Dew Drop Inn back in Mobile. Maybe he'd done so right before he'd been killed. Whatever the case, it felt like I was looking back in time.

"I know I put a lot of pressure on you. You probably hate me for it. But I hope you appreciate that it was necessary," Jeremiah said. "This world . . . It's a terrible place. Sometimes, I wonder why I'm so driven to survive. It would be so much easier to just give in. To let death ferry me off into a better world. Your mother believed in heaven. Maybe that's where she is now. But even if nothing happens when we die, which is far more likely than some perfect world filled with angels, it has to be better than this hell, right? But I keep fighting. I keep scratching and clawing, even though I know we're all doomed. What does that make me? A glutton for punishment, maybe? I don't know."

I had never heard my uncle talk like that. The man I remembered had always been so sure of himself, so certain of his place in the world and how he intended to attack it. But this version of Jeremiah clearly had doubts. I'd always known my uncle had issues. He had been through so much, it would have been remarkable if he had come out of it psychologically unscathed.

But he'd never let that show. Not with me. As a result, the person in the video seemed almost like a different person.

"I wish I had something more to give," he went on. "Some great secret to pass on. A final gift, maybe. But I already put everything into giving you the tools to survive. I have to trust that you'll use those tools for their intended purpose. Survive, Mira. That's all I care about. Survive and escape this hell. Maybe the rest of the universe is better."

Briefly, he glanced away, and when he looked back at the camera, I saw wetness gathering at the corners of his eyes. "I love you, Mira. I don't think I ever said that enough," he said, wiping tears from his eyes. "You're so much like . . . You just remind me of your mother. And her father before her. I wish I could've been better. I wish I could have done more."

He sniffed, then ran his hand over his head again before continuing, "I just want you to know that I did the best I could. That was always the case. I screwed up so many times, Mira. Going back to the very beginning. Before that, even. I tried to save them. I really did. But I just kept failing. Over and over. I had to . . . I had to watch so many people die. At times, I tried to join them. I wanted to. I just didn't have the strength to do it myself. So . . . So I just kept throwing myself into danger. At the time, I was just so angry. So hopeless. I told myself I didn't care if I lived or died. I just wanted the invaders to suffer. But looking back, I was just trying to end it. That I somehow made it through is . . . is . . . It was one of my greatest regrets.

"And the best thing that could have happened to me," he went on. "I survived, and eventually, I found my sister. Your great-great-grandmother. She was a good woman who'd given everything she had to help her family survive. Only one did. Your grandfather. I tried to help him, too. But back then, I was too weak. And he was, too . . . He just didn't want the life I tried to give him. He lived a mostly ordinary life that was cut short when . . ."

He trailed off. Then, he said, "He didn't survive long after your mother was born. I raised her. I tried to give her every advantage. But she just wasn't . . . She didn't want it. I think I pushed her too hard. I think I tried to turn her into something she wasn't. And because of that, she rebelled. I wanted to respect her wishes, but . . . I just . . . I wish I'd have just let her live her life on her own terms. But I couldn't watch her throw her life away. So, I cut ties. I just . . . Well, when she was killed, I was . . . I was distraught. That's where that nickname comes from. Did you know that? I went on a rampage. I killed . . . hundreds of petty criminals. I didn't know who killed your mother, but I knew the type of person they were. So, knowing I couldn't only kill the one responsible, I just . . . I killed them all. They gave me the nickname after that. The Wraith. All because I . . . Everyone else thought it was terrifying. But me? It was just a reminder that I was a failure."

Jeremiah let out a long, drawn-out breath before continuing, "You know the rest. Or most of it. I . . . I didn't intend for this to be a history lesson. I didn't mean to burden you with my issues. But I guess it kind of fits. Don't follow in my footsteps, Mira. I know I turned you into a killer. You're probably good at it, too, judging by how well your training is going. But don't let that be all you are.

"Save someone. Help people. Do what I couldn't," he said. "But most of all, just survive. That's all I care about now. Everything else . . . It was just . . . It's all meaningless. The only thing that really matters is you surviving what's coming."

There was a knock at the door of his inn room, so after once again wiping his tears away, he said, "I think that's it, Mira. That's all I have to say. I'm sorry I wasn't better. I'm sorry I couldn't . . . I'm sorry I can't be there for you anymore. But I was never meant to survive. But you are. Remember that everything I put you through, I did it because I love you."

And then the video went black before cutting off entirely. It took a few seconds after that for me to realize that tears were running down my cheeks. I had always known that my uncle was a flawed man. But I'd only gotten a few rare peeks into his vulnerabilities. He had always been my anchor. My mentor. The example of what I could one day become.

To find that he was a miserable, broken man shouldn't have been surprising. I think I always knew. But to see it addressed so blatantly—it threw my entire world off-kilter.

And on top of that, it just highlighted how much I missed him.

It also made me think about my own path. I had no doubts that, if he had somehow known what I would do in Nova, he would be disappointed, largely because I was following in his footsteps. But was that any surprise? After all, I had him as a role model. Of course I was going to take my cues from him.

I leaned back in the pilot's chair and just stared at the ceiling. What was I supposed to do with that video message? How was I supposed to take it? It hadn't contained any new information. Not really. Even if I didn't think about it often, I knew my family history well enough. But those people were strangers to me. They'd had no impact on the person I had become.

It took me a few long minutes to realize that I was looking at it all wrong. That message hadn't been for me. It was for him. How lonely must Jeremiah have been if that was the only way he felt comfortable sharing his feelings?

After a while, I shifted the video to the back of my system, where it joined the Leviathan playlist my uncle had given me. I rarely listened to it anymore. Not because I didn't still like the music—I did. Rather, every time I heard those songs, I felt guilty. And I was reminded of my uncle's death.

But in that moment, it felt appropriate, so I queued up the playlist and just listened. I don't know how long I sat there, but by the time I pulled myself out of the funk, my tears had run dry, and I'd cycled through the songs multiple times.

"Okay. That's enough of that," I said aloud. "Time to get to work."

To that end, I headed to the bathroom, where I washed my face before sitting on the bed and perusing the second file I'd received. This one concerned the Ithids that had allied themselves with the Pacificians. I was pleased to see that they were not nearly as advanced as some of the other aliens I'd encountered, so I didn't anticipate any issues with infiltrating their base. Still, I spent quite some time combing through the file and memorizing their defenses before moving on to the final item on my list.

The E'rok Tan.

The compound itself wasn't anything special—just prefabricated plasti-steel buildings surrounding a familiar Rift aperture—but the setting was anything but what I'd expected. It actually took me quite some time to figure out what I was looking at, and when I did, I just shook my head and muttered, "Creepy."

On the surface, the area wasn't much different from a hundred ruined towns I'd passed through over the years. But looking closer, I saw what looked like rusted and overgrown rail lines suspended high in the air and surrounded by various oddly shaped buildings. It wasn't until I saw the remnants of a carousel—I had seen one back in the French Quarter of Nova City—that I pieced everything together.

It had been some sort of amusement park, abandoned since the Mist had changed the world. And the Rift—as well as the E'rok Tan base—was directly in the center.

I continued to study the map, soon finding the covered warehouse where they kept their livestock. I didn't see any humans, but the labels on the map were quite clear. The thought of human beings being kept like livestock was enough to make me gag in revulsion, so I pushed it away. Hopefully, those poor people wouldn't have to endure much longer.

After familiarizing myself with the setting, I turned to the section on the E'rok Tan themselves. They were tall, broad-shouldered creatures equipped with four arms, two legs, and jutting tusks. To me, they looked like someone had taken a boar and crossed it with a human before injecting the result with copious amounts of performance-enhancing drugs. Their bulging muscles and brutish appearance gave me the impression that I didn't want to challenge them in a contest of physical strength.

Which was good because I had no intention of going at them head-on. Instead, I planned to do things as quietly as possible—at least until it was time to go loud. By the time they knew I was there, they'd already be as good as dead.

Of course, that was barring any complications, which was unlikely. Plans were great and necessary, and sometimes, things went according to some predetermined strategy. As my uncle had once told me, "Everyone has a plan until they get punched in the mouth."

He attributed the quote to some long-dead prizefighter, and I'd taken the lesson to heart. The success of any mission didn't usually hinge on the quality of the initial plan. Instead, it was about adjusting to changing circumstances and thinking on your feet. And for better or worse, I'd had plenty of experience in adaptation. Hopefully, I wouldn't have to use that particular skill, but I'd learned that hope, for all its power, was usually the prerogative of the naive. In the real world, blind hope got people killed.

Preparation, planning, and adaptation were far more reliable.

CHAPTER THIRTY-SIX

THE BONES OF THE PAST

I never expected my life to end up like this. After my mom died and I started riding along with Remy, I thought I'd follow in his footsteps. We both did. But then he died, and I had to scramble for some way to stay relevant. I was so terrified Mira would leave me behind that I just went along with her plans. I still don't know if it was the right choice.

—Patrick Ward

A day later, I set *The Leviathan* down about a hundred miles from the E'rok Tan base. I might've been able to get closer—Patrick certainly could have, with his abilities—but I didn't want to chance being seen. So, after making sure that the ship's defenses were up, I used Bastion to ensure that it would be protected. After Alistaris's intrusion, it would have been easy to mistrust my ability, but I chose to focus on the fact that, over the past couple of years, it had done its job flawlessly. There was little reason to suspect that it wouldn't continue to do so.

Besides, I didn't have much of a choice in the matter. Not if I wanted to do what I'd come to do, at least.

Once the ship's defenses were up, I started toward the remnants of an old highway I'd seen from the air. When I reached it, I summoned the Cutter and was on my way. The going was a little rough, mostly owing to the poor condition of the wide road. About an hour after leaving the ship, I pulled to a stop before a giant skeleton draped across the road.

The bones were black, with some sort of silvery metal twisting through them. Whatever animal it had once been was huge—at least a hundred feet long and probably twice that in height—which made it one of the largest creatures

I'd ever encountered. Thankfully, it was long dead, without an ounce of meat left on the bones. Still, I could tell from the state of the skeleton that it had not died a peaceful death. So, I wasted no time before backtracking and going around. Even so, I didn't relax even a little bit until I'd left it far behind.

The next obstacle I found was a canyon that cut straight through the road. It was at least fifty feet deep and half again that wide, so I had to dismount and climb down and then back up before I could continue on my way. It was a curious thing—the E'rok Tan base was situated on a sizable plain, which meant that the ravine probably wasn't natural. I wasn't sure if some great creature had torn the earth asunder or if humans—or aliens—were responsible, but I wasn't eager to find out.

Over the next fifty miles or so, I encountered a few more obstructions, and I saw the remnants of the civilization that had once sprawled over the area. A few times, I saw small clusters of low-slung buildings that had likely once housed restaurants or fueling stations, but they had been rendered unrecognizable by the passage of time. It made for a forlorn sight, those buildings. Had they once flourished? Had people once taken them for granted? What had happened to the proprietors? I knew from my uncle's stories that most of the population had died when the Initialization had begun, so I knew there were unlikely to be any happy stories associated with the abandoned buildings. But still, I wanted to believe that the people had escaped. That they had survived. Perhaps their descendants lived in cities like Fortune or what was left of Nova City.

But probably not.

In any case, I maintained focus as well as I could until I finally reached a position about five miles away from E'rok Tan base. There, I dismounted the Cutter, embraced Stealth, and left the road behind. Traveling cross country was slow going, but I felt it was necessary in case the aliens had posted sentries at the obvious points of ingress. Along the way, I passed a few beasts—like a pack of wolves—but due to my abilities, they never knew I was there. A couple of hours later, just as the sun had begun to set, I finally reached my destination.

The abandoned amusement park was even creepier than it looked on the maps and in the photos I'd been provided. Some of that was due to the failing light, but even if it had been in the light of day, I think it would have still been just as eerie, albeit in a different way. I quickly found a stand of thick vegetation and settled down for some surveillance.

For hours, I remained motionless as I watched the derelict park, my eyes tracing the tubular lines of what I thought must have been roller coasters. If I would have encountered such a sight even two years before, I would've had no idea what I was looking at. However, Patrick had a habit of dragging me to new places, and only six months before, he'd taken me to a more modern version of an amusement park.

That had been a good day filled with laughter and fun.

Looking out at the abandoned ruins, I had a hard time believing that anyone had ever said the same thing about it.

Then, I heard one of the most disturbing sounds I'd ever heard in my life. There are a multitude of kinds of laughter. Giggles. Chuckles. Cackles. When Patrick laughed—like really let loose with it—he had a habit of letting out a cute little snort. The laughter that echoed through that ruined amusement park was different, though. The moment the sound hit my ears, a chill went up my spine, and my pulse quickened. A second later, I heard the staccato rhythm of gunfire, and the volume of the laughter increased. Then, suddenly, the gunfire ceased.

The laughter remained.

I swallowed hard, but I continued to watch. Throughout the rest of that night, I didn't hear another peep, but the memory was enough to engender caution. My packet hadn't said anything about whatever had made that sound, and I had no interest in confronting it unless I knew precisely what I was dealing with.

After dawn, I started feeling a little silly. I was a powerful warrior. A Tier 7 who'd spent countless hours training. I had superhuman attributes and a high-tech arsenal to back it up. I had nothing to fear. But every time those thoughts crept into my mind, the memory of that laugh returned.

So, I remained in place throughout the day, only taking breaks for food and biological necessities. I could go without sleep for quite some time, and I had no interest in resting until I figured out what I was dealing with.

Thankfully—or regretfully, depending on how I wanted to look at it—I got my first glimpse of the creature that next night when it ambled into my line of sight. At first, I only saw colorful fabric and a tall, lanky form before it once again disappeared into the derelict amusement park. But even that short glimpse was enough to make me want to abandon the mission altogether.

And when I got my second look, I almost turned tail and ran right then and there.

Then, a patrol of hulking E'rok Tan warriors strode into view. Each one clutched a rifle in one pair of arms while their second pair of arms remained free. There were seven of them, each muscular enough to make Nora look like a slacker.

Whatever power they had in those muscles was not nearly enough.

The creature swept in like a parti-color nightmare, all long, skeletal limbs and flashing claws. The first E'rok Tan warrior fell before any of them even knew what was happening. Even as the warrior collapsed to the ground, its thick neck nearly severed by the force behind those claws, the creature faded into the shadows, leaving only that horrifying laughter behind. When the remaining warriors started to panic, I didn't blame them.

Because I had finally gotten a good, long look at the thing.

I knew it was a wildling, but one unlike any I'd ever seen before. For one, it wasn't naked. Instead, it wore loose-fitting colorful clothing that would've been more at home on a children's entertainer than draped over the elongated and emaciated body of a monstrous humanoid.

The concept of a clown wasn't new to me. Though I'd never seen one in real life, they were a ubiquitous presence on the entertainment feeds I'd favored growing up. Sometimes, they were portrayed as fun-loving comic relief, but in the sorts of shows I never told Jeremiah I was watching, they were something decidedly different. It hadn't been a surprise to discover that many people had a phobia concerning the seemingly innocent performers.

Still, I'd never expected to encounter anything that lived up to those people's fears.

But as always, expectations often ran counter to reality. The evidence of that was the scene playing out right in front of me.

One of the warriors whipped around, firing into the shadows. Predictably, it hit nothing but the dilapidated ruins of an old carousel. But the distraction gave the wildling clown the opening it needed to eviscerate one of the other warriors. Of course, that brought more panicked fire from the remaining E'rok Tan.

Like that, the clown slowly picked them apart. One by one, they fell until only two remained. They looked at each other for a long moment before one seemed to reach a conclusion. It raised its rifle and fired, obliterating the knee of its fellow warrior before sprinting away.

It only got about twenty feet before the clown struck again, hamstringing the traitorous E'rok Tan. It mewled like a wounded animal, but its cries were only met with more cackling laughter before the clown finished it off. Finally, it turned its sights on the final remaining warrior, who was clutching its leg to try to stem the bleeding.

To its credit, the E'rok Tan managed to raise its weapon and fire, taking the wildling clown in the chest. But it had no noticeable effect.

The clown approached, swaying back and forth as if dancing to some music only it could hear. The E'rok Tan warrior fired again, but it did just as little good as the first shot. Still, the clown swayed forward until, at last, it reached its prey.

I watched in horror as the creature ripped the warrior apart, limb by limb.

And then, finally, everything went quiet.

That's when the feasting began.

More wildlings—tiny things that must've only been three or four feet tall— poured out of the brush and fell upon the still-warm corpses. Each of them was dressed similarly to the clown, almost as if it had been miniaturized.

Their appetites certainly hadn't shrunk, though.

Once, when Patrick and I had been camping on a tropical beach, I had seen a swarm of tiny fish—minnows, really—attack a whale. Thousands of them, tearing into the whale with vicious enthusiasm until there was nothing left but diluted blood.

That's what the tiny clowns reminded me of, and it was just as disturbing as it sounded.

It only took them a few minutes to completely devour the E'rok Tan warriors. They didn't leave anything behind. Not their bones. Not their clothing. Even their weapons were food for the clowns. And then, just like that, they scattered. Only the spindly wildling that was their leader remained.

And it was looking right at me.

A wide grin slowly crept across its face. Then, it raised one hand, palm up, crooked a finger, and beckoned for me to come.

My heart stopped. I didn't dare breathe. I could only stand there, staring.

I wasn't afraid because the wildling had seen me. Over the years, I'd learned to never underestimate anything that could survive life in the wilderness. And wildlings were usually at the top of the food chain. More, they often displayed strange abilities. Once, I'd seen one that could glide through the air like it had wings. Another time, I'd encountered one that could, for a short time, wreathe itself in flames. They were wild, vicious creatures with unpredictable abilities.

But none of them were intelligent.

Or so I'd thought.

That the clown appeared otherwise was a horrifying prospect, and not just because it had clearly enjoyed picking those E'rok Tan warriors apart. It had tormented them, maliciously and with obvious intent. And it had savored every second of their torture.

Given what the E'rok Tan had done, there was a part of me that considered it justice. However, it didn't take me long to recognize the dangers posed by an intelligent wildling. They were already powerful. But there was also a viciousness to them that I can scarcely articulate. As I knelt there, watching the ruins, I was reminded of what had happened to Heather. Before Edgar Russo had gotten ahold of her, she had been a completely nonviolent person. But after? She had changed, so much so that the rage had completely overwhelmed everything else. When I'd had to put her down, I had looked into her eyes, and I saw nothing left of the woman she had been.

If wildlings evolved into thinking creatures, they would sweep across the world, killing everything in their paths. Humans. Aliens. Animals. It wouldn't matter. They would only stop if someone killed them all.

There were plenty of philosophical questions there. What right did I have to condemn a creature to death? Doing so made me no different than the aliens I routinely killed. But the bottom line was that, while the threat seemed minor right now, there was every chance that, if left unchecked, it would grow into something far more serious. When that happened, it would be a them-or-us sort of war.

And as always, I chose the path that would see me living another day.

So, kneeling there behind those bushes, I decided to make a little addition to my plan. I still intended to kill the E'rok Tan, but I needed to take out the clown—or clowns—too. So, I started putting together some ideas on how to accomplish that.

It took me another two days—and a few sightings of the wildling clowns—before I felt prepared for my hunt. Just as I was mentally readying myself to stalk the creature and kill it, I heard a cackling peal of laughter echoing through the forest.

It seemed that, while I was watching it, it had been watching me, too. And it had completed its preparations before me.

Fear stalked up my spine as I shot to my feet. I was just about to take off at a dead sprint when I realized what was going on. That laughter—it wasn't just there for creepy ambiance. And it certainly wasn't a display of mirth. Rather, it was an ability, albeit a strange one.

Suddenly, everything clicked together. The E'rok Tan weren't as disorganized and panic prone as I'd first thought. Instead, they'd been subjected to the wildling clown's ability, which had flooded their bodies with terror, prompting a panicked response.

And I had very nearly fallen prey to the very same thing.

Only a second later, the rangy clown—it was at least nine feet tall, thin to the point of emaciation, and equipped with a set of elongated claws that capped each finger—burst through the brush in a whirlwind of motion. But then, it suddenly stopped and sniffed the air. My heart was pounding out of my chest, but I refused to move. Instead, I studied the creature. White paint—or perhaps that was its natural coloring—streaked its bestial, blood-smeared face, and it moved with jerky, sudden movements.

It stood there, head tilted back and sniffing the air, for a long few moments before it let out another peal of laughter. The cackling sound echoed through my brain, demanding that I run from the predator, but I clamped down on that urge with as much willpower as I could manage. Even as my every muscle screamed for release, I remained still and shrouded in my pair of concealment abilities.

The clown let out another, much louder cackle.

My knuckles whitened, and my muscles trembled with need as I forced myself to remain still. I had never felt such terror in all my life. Not when I saw that world-eating serpent in the spider Rift. Not when Nova City was falling apart beneath my very feet. It was all-encompassing and powerful enough to send tears running down my cheeks.

But I didn't move.

The clown was clearly confused and just as obviously incapable of detecting me beneath my layers of concealment. Still, it let out a few more cackles before moving on.

I still didn't move.

Not until the sun rose did I feel even a modicum of security.

As soon as I did, I retreated. For miles, I slipped through the woods, barely noticing my surroundings, until I finally reached one of those clusters of buildings I'd passed on the way in. I found the most intact one, swept it for life, and then found the most secure area I could. That's when I erected all my defenses.

First came the holographic display. Then, a pair of autoturrets that were just small enough to fit in my arsenal implant. And finally, I canceled the Bastion I had on *The Leviathan* before reapplying it to my current location.

Only then did I relax.

That's when the tears of frustration came. It was as if the stress that had built up throughout that seemingly endless night all came bubbling up at one time. And I couldn't stop myself from weeping. Nor did I try.

Sometimes, a few tears are what's necessary for a person to move on.

Soon enough, though, the residual fear turned to anger. At myself, for being weak. At the clown for putting me in such a vulnerable position. And at the E'rok Tan for not being strong enough to secure their own location.

By the time I recovered, I was furious. And determined to turn the tables on that damnable clown. To that end, I adjusted my plans, and once I was satisfied, I allowed myself to rest.

That afternoon, I dreamed of a horde of wildling clowns descending on me and eating me alive. It was not a pleasant rest, but by the time I awoke, I was ready to face them. If not because I thought it needed to be done, then so that I could face my own demons.

CHAPTER THIRTY-SEVEN

LIVESTOCK

There's so much we don't know about the world. We have no idea what's out there. Not really. And the rest of the universe is even more mysterious. Anyone who claims they know what's coming is lying.

—Patrick Ward

I approached the abandoned amusement park as quietly as I could manage. Usually, I could rely solely on Stealth and Camouflage to see me through, but the memory of how easily that clown wildling had taken apart the E'rok Tan patrol was the only motivator I needed to take extra care. I could only hope that it would be enough.

Over the past few hours, I'd made some plans in case my skills failed. However, if it ended up coming to that, my chances of survival would take a precipitous drop. Perhaps I would live through it, but it would likely take everything I had. On top of that, it would make accomplishing my mission that much more difficult, if not entirely impossible.

So, the stakes couldn't have been higher as I crept across what I suspected had once been a parking lot. Weeds, trees, and other foliage had managed to break through the great slab of concrete, but the space was mostly open. Being so exposed, the temptation was to hurry, to push through as quickly as possible. But I knew how wrong that could go, so I kept my steps careful and my breathing under control.

It was a good thing, too, because about halfway through, I caught sight of one of the smaller wildling clowns hiding behind a rusted-out hulk of a vehicle. It gave no indication that it knew I was there—my abilities had done their job, it seemed—but I was certain that it would quickly respond if it detected my presence.

As I continued to stalk across the disused parking lot, an echo of the panic I'd felt the night before lingered in my mind. It threatened to hasten my steps, which in turn, would cause a flicker in my abilities. If that happened, I knew I'd have to switch to my backup plan, which would in turn create all sorts of problems for me.

Chief among those issues was the question of whether or not I could even survive an encounter with that wildling clown.

Maybe.

But even if I managed to keep my wits—a big if, given its ability to terrorize anyone who heard its cackling laughter—I was experienced enough to recognize that it wasn't just any wildling. In fact, it reminded me of one I'd encountered years before when I was on my way back to Nova City after visiting Biloxi. Back then, that creature had nearly killed me. It had taken every weapon in my arsenal to put it down, and even then, it had been a close thing.

And this clown, it was stronger. I'd felt it the night before.

But what really worried me was the fact that it displayed signs of intelligence. It had toyed with those E'rok Tan warriors, baiting them into a trap before killing them. Was it true intelligence? Or animal cunning? I wasn't sure, and I really didn't want to find out the hard way.

So, my trip across the crumbling parking lot took nearly half an hour. Without my inflated attributes, I never could have managed it. I would have lost my balance. Or I would have become unfocused and made a mistake. Either would have cost me my life, as evidenced by the fact that I saw more than one small misshapen wildling clown along the way.

But they didn't see me, which I counted as a victory.

After completing my trek across the parking lot, I slipped beneath a turnstile and entered the park proper. Every subsequent step was an exercise in mental torture. The threat looming over me was unnatural. I knew myself well enough to recognize that, at least. Part of it came from my unsettling surroundings, but I'd traveled through plenty of ruins to know that the abandoned amusement park was only responsible for a small part of my anxiety. Instead, I focused on the subtle undercurrent of Mist hanging in the air.

The wildling clown had used an ability. Perhaps more than one.

I didn't know how that was even possible.

But then again, who was I to say what was and wasn't possible? I had only seen a fraction of what my own world, much less the rest of the universe, had to offer. For all I knew, all wildlings would eventually learn to use abilities. Maybe they were like the Templars or other mystics. Or perhaps some sick scientist like Edgar Russo had experimented on this particular batch of wildlings, giving them unnatural abilities.

I had no way of knowing.

And it didn't really matter. Not to me, at least. And not at that moment.

In an effort to keep my mind from wandering, I refocused on the task at hand. I only moved a few inches at a time, so my pace was absolutely glacial. But I'd spent countless hours training my ability to maintain focus, so my mind never wavered as I slowly made my way through the abandoned amusement park.

I passed dozens of old booths. Their paint was chipped, and much of the wood that had been used in their construction was rotten, giving me the impression that if I were to bump into one of the walls, they'd all come crumbling down. Inside were once-colorful stuffed animals, stained and decaying—but even so, it wasn't difficult to imagine what the park once had been.

Hours passed as, inch by inch, I continued along. In addition to more of the small wildlings—most of which were asleep—I passed beneath the rusted bones of an old roller coaster. Once, it must have been an impressive feat of engineering. But now, it looked like it would fall before a strong gust of wind.

There were other rides. One that looked like an overturned top, with chains dangling from its underside, the carousel I'd seen from afar, and a few other, less identifiable structures surrounded me as I kept going.

Every now and then, I stopped and placed an explosive on the ground. Otherwise, though, I continued on without stopping to investigate my surroundings.

Thankfully, I didn't see any sign of the wildling alpha. If I had, I might have lost my nerve. Not because I feared what it would do but, rather, because of the effects of that cackling laughter. During the previous night's encounter, I'd been more frightened than I'd ever been before, and I wasn't eager to revisit that terror.

Eventually, night turned to morning, and I finally reached my destination.

In the center of the amusement park, a huge plasti-steel wall loomed over everything. It was at least fifty feet tall, and I could feel the surging Mist of a shield encompassing its entire length. Atop the wall were the autoturrets and cameras that had been described in the file I'd been given.

Curiously, I didn't see any of the E'rok Tan warriors I expected to see.

Ultimately, it didn't matter, though. If my plan worked, I'd see plenty.

For the next couple of hours, I continued to creep around the amusement park, planting explosives and searching for the perfect place to hole up. I needed somewhere close to the E'rok Tan compound but still concealed. I found what I was looking for in an overturned replica of a pirate ship that some sort of creature had burrowed into. Whatever it had been, it was long gone, so I quickly set up shop within. I took a few moments to deploy my holographic display, which would hopefully work with my abilities to keep me concealed.

Once that was done, I took out a detonator and pressed the button that would ignite the charges I'd left scattered throughout the amusement park.

The results were . . . well, explosive.

In the space of a second, two dozen charges went off, one after the other. Then, a minute or so later, I detonated the second set. Then, a minute or two after that, a third set. Finally, I settled down to wait.

The idea behind my plan was simple. The explosions were meant to draw the E'rok Tan out of their base. I knew they wouldn't all go to check out what sounded like a battle on their doorstep, but I hoped that they would send enough that it would create gaps in their defenses. Because I could deal with Mist shields, drones, and autoturrets without drawing attention, but people were much more difficult.

Even if my plan didn't work out exactly as I wanted it to, I had no doubts that it would function as both a distraction as well as a means to thin the proverbial herd by means of creepy clown wildlings.

Still, as I waited, I couldn't help but feel a little anxious.

Soon, though, I heard the sound I'd both been waiting on as well as dreading. The wildling's cackle seemed to drift across the entire amusement park. And a few seconds later, the sound of gunfire joined in.

I couldn't be certain, but it sounded like at least a dozen weapons. Maybe more.

I detonated the final set of bombs, adding the sound of explosions to the mix. Hopefully, that would result in additional confusion.

Finally, after a few more minutes—during which the E'rok Tan waged war against the wildlings—I crept out of my hiding place and approached the wall. The Mist shield and the other defenses remained in place, but it only took a quick use of Misthack to temporarily power them down. Once they went idle, I climbed the wall and slipped over to the other side. As I hit the ground, I rolled to absorb some of the impact before coming to my feet, my assault rifle in hand.

But there was no one to fight.

Instead, I was confronted with a series of prefabricated plasti-steel buildings of a sort I'd seen many times before. For all that they came from a wide variety of civilizations, the alien invaders seemed to use much of the same infrastructure to construct their various bases. Each of the settlements I'd encountered also seemed to follow similar layouts, so it didn't take me long to get my bearings.

Now that I was inside, I had three goals. First was to find whatever passed for a storage area and steal everything that wasn't nailed down. My arsenal implant wasn't huge—not like Patrick's—but it would still hold a sizable amount of loot. And I intended to fill it to the brim.

Second, I needed to do the job I'd come to do and kill the E'rok Tan. To do so, I intended to set a series of bombs throughout the facility. After I detonated them, I would clean things up with my various firearms.

Normally, I would have used something like *Time Bomb*, but I was afraid that it would chain to the people I hoped to save. Strangely enough, explosives were the far safer option in that respect.

Which led me to my final goal: saving the people who'd been kept as livestock. I had a vague idea of where they were kept, but I needed to lay eyes on them before I could finalize my plans.

So, with those objectives in mind, I stalked through the compound, steadily placing bombs throughout. They looked similar to the charges I'd left outside, but they packed quite a bit more punch. I knew from experience that just one could bring down an unenhanced building.

And I used way more than that.

As I planted my charges, the battle outside the walls reached a crescendo. The wildling's cackle hung over everything, drowning out even the sound of gunfire.

Ideally, the E'rok Tan would finish it off while taking a bunch of casualties along the way. But I wasn't sure if that was feasible. The thing was obviously powerful, and I suspected that it wouldn't go down easily.

As I set the charges, I saw more than a few of the tusked, four-armed aliens. Each one carried at least one weapon, and they looked like they knew how to use them, too. Luckily, they weren't the most perceptive bunch, and I managed to remain undetected as I set about accomplishing my goals.

Eventually, I found the storage facility, which was a small, single-story building that was piled high with crates of low-quality Rift Shards. I took as many as my arsenal implant could carry. They really weren't that valuable, but they would suffice as fuel for *The Leviathan*, at least for a while.

I was just finishing up when the door to the storage building slid open to reveal a couple of the four-armed E'rok Tan. Both were carrying large metallic crates that contained Rift Shards.

"Glad I wasn't on duty," remarked one. "That thing out there . . ."

"It doesn't scare me," said the other in a remarkably feminine voice. There were no physiological differences between the two—aside from minor features like tusk length or eye shape—but I got the impression she was female.

"Then you're stupid," said the first as he set the crate down. "That thing . . . Wait, does this place look a little empty to you?"

The female shrugged. "Probably had a pickup," she said. "I don't—"

That's when I struck, slicing through her neck with my nano-bladed sword. She never even had an opportunity to react before her head tumbled to the ground. Without letting my momentum dissipate, I wheeled on the other tusked warrior and shoved my sword through his chin.

He was dead before I retracted my blade.

"Shit," I muttered to myself.

I hadn't intended to kill anyone before I set off the bombs, but I also wasn't going to take any chances. The moment the male had started asking questions, their fate had been sealed. Perhaps they would never have known I was there, but I wasn't willing to gamble on their lack of attentiveness.

After dismissing my blade, I dragged the pair of bodies into the corner and piled a few half-empty crates in front of them before throwing my holographic display down. It wasn't ideal—after all, I didn't want to leave my equipment behind—but I also had no interest in letting someone stumble across the bodies and raise the alarm.

Finally, I did what I could with the blood staining the floor.

None of it was perfect, but I could only hope that my subterfuge would last long enough for me to finish my mission.

By the time I left the storage area behind, the sounds of battle had died down.

Which meant the clock was ticking before I was discovered.

So, without any further hesitation, I continued on with what could arguably be considered my most important task.

When I extended my search belowground, I found the pens where the human livestock were confined. And I wish I'd never bothered to look. Sure, I would have felt guilty, but at least I wouldn't have nightmares.

For a few long moments, I just stared at them, unsure of what I was looking at. The figures were naked and so pale that I knew none of them had ever even seen the light of day. More, each one was so bulky and misshapen that they almost didn't even look human. Somewhere in the back of my mind, I recognized what was going on. The aliens had used genetic modification, hormones, and a very particular diet to ensure that each human had grown to outsize proportions.

But there were side effects, chiefly that they were almost entirely sedentary—probably due to the fact that their joints couldn't support their massive weight.

None of them wore clothes, and judging by their blank stares, they didn't seem to care. Perhaps they didn't even realize the value of modesty. Or maybe they couldn't comprehend it. In that moment, I understood why they'd been categorized as cattle. There wasn't even a trace of humanity or intelligence in their eyes.

The scene made me want to vomit.

But it also highlighted a problem. Even if I were to free these people, what was I going to do with them? I didn't even think they could make it up the stairs to the surface, much less know what to do once they got there.

No—for now, I had to simply leave them where they were while I dealt with everything else. And if they didn't make it long enough for me to call in Alistaris, perhaps it would be a mercy.

I left the cages behind, fully intending to come back. But in the back of my mind, I think I knew I would never lay eyes on them again. I didn't want them dead, but I also didn't want to be reminded of the horrors that threatened humanity.

But for a twist of fate, I could have been one of them. Just sitting in a cage, staring ahead with dead, lifeless eyes as I waited to be slaughtered and eaten by aliens.

I had always known that the universe was an unjust place, but the fact that such cruelty was allowed only served to cement that knowledge in place. And as I climbed the stairs back to the surface, I was beset by familiar anger, frustration, and most of all, cynicism.

I pushed it all down.

Suddenly, I wasn't so horrified by what the clown wildling had done to the E'rok Tan. In fact, it almost felt like justice.

Whatever the case, I pushed those feelings down as I set my mind to finishing my mission. To that end, the moment I found my way to a secluded corner of the compound, I settled in to wait. And once I was certain that any survivors of the battle with the wildling clown had returned, I retrieved my detonator from my arsenal implant and pressed the button.

As each explosion went off, filling the air with plasti-steel debris, E'rok Tan body parts, and clouds of dust, I tried to feel satisfied. But it was just too impersonal. If I'd had my way, I would have cut each and every one of them to pieces.

But that just wasn't possible.

In the end, I destroyed the whole compound without ever firing a shot. There were survivors, but they were so injured that, when I finally lopped their heads off, it could have almost been seen as mercy.

Finally, I opened a line of communication with Alistaris and said, "It's done. Come pick up the surviving . . . humans."

"Affirmative" was his only answer.

"And Alistaris—I don't want to know what you do with them," I said. "Just . . . Just do whatever you think is most humane."

With a sigh, I turned and trekked across the rubble-strewn compound, intent on finishing things off.

The wildling clown might have been fighting a fight I could get behind, but it was still a dangerous monster I couldn't let live. If something like that made it into a populated area, the results would be disastrous.

So, I once again embraced my various concealment abilities and set about hunting it down.

CHAPTER THIRTY-EIGHT

KILLER CLOWN

The world—probably the universe—is filled with horrible things. I know that, and I accept it. But I think there's just as much good out there. You just have to be open to it. To look for it. To embrace it. I want Mira to see what I see, but I just don't know if she's got that in her.

—Patrick Ward

I couldn't leave the E'rok Tan compound—and those horrible cages—behind quickly enough for my taste. But even so, I wrangled my emotions into some semblance of control as I stalked back into the surrounding amusement park. After all, the danger posed by the killer clown and its miniature followers had not abated, so precautions against detection were necessary.

Even so, my mind roiled with what I had seen. Or rather, the implications behind it. I had seen into those people's eyes, and I had recognized the lack of anything approaching intelligence or self-awareness. For all intents and purposes, they were no different from any other livestock.

Perhaps Alistaris could help them. I suspected that these people were not only the product of generations of genetic modification and pumped full of various chemicals to enhance their yield, but they were almost certainly under the effect of some pretty sinister implants. I could only hope that those implants could be safely removed and that doing so would allow the people to recover. But I had my doubts about the viability of such a hope.

I felt guilty about it, but I really didn't want to see the results. In fact, I wanted to forget about the entire thing altogether, mostly because I knew that it would only take a slight push in the wrong direction for the entirety of Earth's population to end up like that. Maybe they wouldn't become livestock bred for food, but mass enslavement was a distinct possibility. And given the proliferation of invaders already mining the Earth's various resources, there was every reason for the invaders to resort to slavery to meet their labor needs.

In the time Patrick and I were separated, I'd descended into a malaise of hopelessness. And rightly so. The Earth's population faced long odds, and to date, I had seen nothing to suggest we were capable of overcoming the forces arrayed against us. However, of late, I'd actively forced myself to see the other side of things. The people who'd managed to carve out productive lives, the families who'd remained intact, the cities that had thrived during the Initialization.

But with the sight of all those enslaved and dehumanized people, the hopelessness returned in force. My uncle had never intended for me to fight against the aliens. Instead, he had recognized the hopelessness of Earth's circumstances. Because of that, he'd utilized every asset he possessed in an effort to help me survive.

Not fight back.

Certainly, he didn't want me to be some sort of savior.

No—I was simply intended to survive and escape. From my uncle's perspective, nothing else was possible. And though I tried to resist that pessimistic mindset, I could feel it enveloping my mind. I knew that if I didn't actively try to combat it, it would overwhelm any sense of optimism I might have nurtured.

And maybe that was the point.

Perhaps that was my uncle's intention all along. Hope was a dangerous thing that often got people killed. If I didn't let it take root, then I could turn the whole of my attention to the simple goal of survival at all costs. If I already thought everyone was doomed, I wouldn't risk everything to save them.

But was that how I wanted to live?

And even if I did manage to survive, could I stand the guilt of standing by while the world—my world—was enslaved, killed, or worse? I didn't know myself well enough to answer that seemingly simple question. Selfish survival? Or potentially sacrificing everything in the hope that I might save a few people. What's more, I didn't even know if I could make a difference. I was just one person, after all.

Or was that just an excuse not to try?

Questions of that sort followed me as I stalked through the overgrown amusement park. Along the way, I saw evidence of my explosive distractions as well as the battle that had subsequently ensued. Part of the roller-coaster track had collapsed, more than one building had fallen, and there were still a few flames burning their way through anything dry enough to catch fire.

Part of me was saddened by the loss of so much history. Any other time, and I might have enjoyed exploring the area. But now, it was a war zone, and I was still a combatant. So, I pushed the intrusive thoughts out of my mind as I focused on what really mattered.

Eventually, I found the clown wildling huddled on the ground, surrounded by a pile of bodies. Some were the corpses of the smaller wildlings I'd seen before, but there were plenty of E'rok Tan bodies, as well. Most had been torn to shreds, which rendered them nearly unrecognizable. But there were enough that I could figure out what had happened.

Like the scene I'd witnessed when first arriving at the location, it was clear that the aliens had been ambushed and ripped apart by the lanky clown. But unlike what had happened in that instance, the invaders had given just as much as they got, and as a result, the wildling had been gravely wounded.

It was still alive, though one of its arms had been severed at the elbow. The other hung limp, and its legs were splayed across the overgrown ground as it propped itself against the splintered ruins of a booth. Among the bodies were decayed and discolored stuffed animals, most of which had been torn to pieces by the battle.

I watched as a dozen smaller clown creatures fell upon the alien bodies, ripping limbs from joints before bringing the results to the larger creature. It looked down on them with something like pride before taking their offerings.

The little clowns danced with satisfaction before returning to their grisly work. Like that, they fed the lanky clown wildling, and before my eyes, it began to heal. I had no concept of how it did so; no skill I'd ever encountered could do such a thing. But there it was, plain as day.

In fact, it reminded me of the Templars. I hadn't seen Isla heal me after my near-fatal encounter with the irradiated wildlings three years before, but I knew my own condition well enough to suspect that Templars—and other mystics— were capable of far more fantastic abilities than people like me.

According to Freddie, that gap would close as I continued to progress, but a wide gulf remained between my own skills and abilities and whatever the mystics could bring to bear.

So, following that logic, I had to assume that some wildlings were capable of similar feats. In fact, the evidence of just that was right in front of me. Perhaps the wildling was less powerful. Maybe its abilities were less pronounced. But even so, I felt confident in asserting that they followed along a similar path.

I just didn't know how it all fit together, though I vowed to ask Freddie if I ever saw him again. Or perhaps some of my contacts in the Bazaar would have an answer for me. Whatever the case, it was neither the time nor the place to ponder the nature of the Mist and how it affected people.

Because if I was going to kill this wildling, I needed to do so before it finished healing. Which, given the speed of its regeneration, was probably going to happen sooner rather than later.

So, I backed away for a couple hundred yards until I reached a huge wheel-like structure which was held upright by a series of pylons that extended from the ground to the center of the circle. The wheel itself was at least a hundred feet tall, and along the outer edge, there were carriages, many of which were barely hanging on.

In an effort to gain some altitude, I shimmied up one of the pylons until I reached the center of the wheel. Then, I climbed hand over hand until I reached the apex. Finally, I planted myself in the most intact carriage I could find and summoned my Pulsar. My perch swayed in the gentle breeze, but it presented an otherwise stable firing position as I brought the weapon to my shoulder and took aim.

Finally, as I sighted in on my target, I activated Empowered Shot, waited for it to charge, and then fired. The moment I squeezed the trigger, the unbearably thin clown's head jerked up, and it locked its eyes on me. However, by that point the ball of superheated plasma was already in the air.

The moment I sent the shot downrange, I repeated my actions, hoping to get another shot off before the creature could react.

Even though it couldn't avoid the shot altogether, the clown didn't remain idle. It flinched to the side with such quickness that I could barely even track the movement, and instead of the bundle of plasma burning its way through its forehead, the shot hit the clown in the shoulder.

The impact spun the wildling around, and by the time it landed, I had another shot in the air. This one was more successful, hitting the creature in the chest. However, I was unsurprised to see that, as lethal as my shots usually were—especially when empowered by my abilities—the thing was still up for a fight. It demonstrated this by leaping to its feet and avoiding my third, unempowered shot.

That's when it let out that evil cackle.

I was far enough away from the creature that I only felt a slight tremor of fear, so I was able to keep my wits about me as I continued to fire. Despite my flawless technique, I only hit with every third shot. The creature was just too fast, its movements too unpredictable. Still, I did what I could as it raced toward my position.

That's when I detonated a set of stun bombs I'd left behind during my initial positioning.

They weren't intended as more than a distraction. I didn't think that even my most powerful homemade bombs would do much damage, so I'd opted for shock charges instead. Upon detonation, each one sent out a bolt of lightning, which was accompanied by an incredibly loud sound and a flashing light. The results were predictable.

The lightning set the wildling's muscles to spasming as the auditory and visual stimuli overwhelmed its senses. It dropped to the ground in a brief seizure that I was more than willing to use to my advantage, and I continued to fire upon the wildling, peppering its body with a series of increasingly serious wounds.

However, as it quickly recovered from the stun bombs, I was shocked at its continual regeneration. Whatever the case, I had no choice but to keep going. I'd picked the fight, and I knew it wouldn't let me escape now that it knew I was there.

I kept up the barrage until, at last, it reached the base of the wheel. That was close enough that I could just barely reach it with Misthack, but when I tried to do so, I got nothing. Not surprising, really. I'd only ever encountered one nonsapient type of creature that I could affect, and that was in a Rift. For all I knew, those spiders were based on some other alien civilization. Regardless, the clown wildling was completely immune to my {Mistrunner} abilities. So, after I fired one last shot, I leaped to the next carriage before replacing the Pulsar with my assault rifle.

As I relocated, I used Explosive Shot and continued my bombardment. The wildling wasn't going to sit there and take it, though, and it wasn't long before it was skittering up the wheel's infrastructure like a mutated monkey.

My enhanced shots tore huge holes in the creature, slowing—but pointedly not stopping—its progress. Still, I continued to fire until the magazine ran empty. I used Instant Reload, following it up with another use of Explosive Shot before resuming my assault. Like that, I tore the creature to shreds, one exploding shot at a time.

Still, it kept coming until, at last, it caught up to me.

Just as it lunged toward me, I dismissed my assault rifle, summoned my blade, and sliced through the support cables holding the carriage aloft. Then, just as it reached me, I used Teleport to jump to another carriage almost twenty feet away. I gasped as the last of my Mist drained into the skill, but I quickly jammed a booster into my hip, giving me some level of relief.

I turned back to see the wildling falling more than a hundred feet before it hit the ground with an incredible impact. Immediately, the miniature versions of the clown wildlings raced forward, each one carrying an alien limb or hunk of muscle. I had seen that trick before, so I quickly exchanged my blade for my BMAP and opened fire.

Over the years, I had discovered that, while the mobile artillery platform was entirely capable of significant destruction, it was best suited for either of two very specific situations. The first was if I wanted to bring a building or slow-moving armored vehicle down. With the right ammunition, it was perfect for that sort of thing, and given its name, I felt certain that such circumstances were why the weapon had been built in the first place. But it was also well suited to one more situation: dealing with a large number of weaker enemies.

I had no illusions that my barrage of explosive rounds would kill the wildling clown, but I expected it would stave off—or at least slow—any regeneration abilities it might bring to bear. On top of that, I expected that the BMAP would make quick work of the little creatures that seemed to serve the larger one.

I emptied the BMAP's cannister, careful to avoid destroying the wheel structure's support pillars, and by the time I was finished, only charred corpses remained where the little monsters had once been.

But as I'd suspected, my efforts did little to finish the larger creature off, and by that point, it had begun to pick itself up. As it did, I noted that it wasn't doing so great. Even before I'd begun my assault, it had been wounded, but now, it looked like the walking dead, with huge chunks of its body missing. What remained was bloody, burned, or both.

Still, it was dangerous, and I needed to finish it off.

To that end, I climbed down the wheel, stopping every so often to shoot the creature a few more times. Doing so wouldn't kill it off. I knew that. But it would keep it off-balance and make it expend even more Mist—assuming that was what fueled regeneration—to heal.

Once I reached the bottom, I stowed my assault rifle away and summoned the Dragon. By that point, my Mist levels had recovered enough that I could use Explosive Shot. I did so, enhancing the weapon's ammunition before I brought the ungainly weapon around and aimed it at the wounded creature.

Then, I let loose.

The Dragon roared, spitting a ten-foot flame from the end of its corrugated barrel before sending more than thirty rounds a second to tear into the thing's battered body. The results were predictable, and over the next dozen seconds or so, I ripped it to shreds with my most powerful weapon.

But even then, it wasn't enough.

The Dragon's moving parts spun down, and when the smoke cleared, I saw a monster barely clinging to life. Missing an entire arm, and with a body that resembled mincemeat more than anything else, the creature still tried to drag itself toward me. It let out a gurgling cackle that carried with it only a fraction of its formerly terrifying power.

I ignored it.

Stowing the Dragon away, I summoned my nano-bladed sword and strode forward. I could have kept shooting. I probably should have. But I needed to dispatch it in a more personal manner. I needed the visceral satisfaction of feeling it hacked to pieces beneath me.

Otherwise, the fear might return.

Sure, I told myself that I just wanted to save on the exceedingly expensive ammunition the Dragon required, but the reality was that the wildling had terrified me. It had made me feel weak and powerless. And now, I was going to exorcise that demon the only way I knew how—by hacking it to pieces until it surrendered its grip on life.

And that's what I did.

Over and over, my blade descended. At first, it barely found purchase, but I persisted, bringing every ounce of my hard-won strength to bear. And slowly, I accomplished my goal. By the time I finished, I knew I'd picked up an audience, and when the thing finally died, I took a deep breath, turned to where Alistaris stood, and asked, "Enjoy the show?"

"I did not," he said.

"Good. Me, neither," I replied. Then, without another word, I whipped my sword out, sending a curtain of thick blood slicing through the air before I dismissed it. After that, I just shook my head and said, "Let me know when you finish relocating those people."

CHAPTER THIRTY-NINE

A UNIVERSAL SCALE

Sometimes, I have trouble remembering their faces. Remy. My mom. A dozen others I don't even want to think about. I can only imagine what it was like for Jeremiah. How lonely must he have been? How many loved ones must he have watched die? I don't want to end up like that. And I'm terrified that Mira is already on her way.

—Patrick Ward

I remained in the area for a little while longer, and in that time, I let my mind go blank. I didn't want to think about the things I had just seen. I didn't want to contemplate the future for those poor people who'd been sentenced to a life as livestock. Sitting on an overturned log and staring out at nothing, I felt a presence on the edge of my senses. Once it came closer, I asked, "Is it done?"

Alistaris—and I was certain it was him, identifiable by the light sound of his footsteps, the way he breathed, and the way the Mist swirled around him— didn't immediately answer. Instead, he approached and climbed up to sit next to me on the log. For a long moment, he remained silent before, at last, saying, "I'm sorry you had to see that."

"Sure you are," I spat, with far more venom than I really intended. "You've probably got a stable of humans stashed away somewhere, too."

"I would . . . I would never . . ."

I sighed, then hung my head. "I'm sorry," I said. "You probably don't deserve that. It's just . . . That was horrifying. I've seen some terrible things, Al. Like, really bad. But this . . . This was worse."

I really didn't have the words to describe how I felt. The idea that human beings could be reduced to unthinking livestock had shaken my foundations in a way nothing else could have. The only thing that came close was when I'd tried to rescue Heather from the clutches of Edgar Russo's experiments only to find that she had been converted into a wildling. But even that fell short on the horror scale, largely because, while Heather and the others involved in that experiment had been transformed, they'd still had some sort of agency. By comparison, the livestock people just remained in their cages with the completely blank expressions I'd seen in cattle.

They weren't human anymore.

They weren't even sapient.

They were simply human-shaped animals who had never known anything else.

"What the E'rok Tan do is a terrible thing," Alistaris said. "I told you in the very beginning that most people across the universe see them as . . . well, villains. There are exceptions. Always, there are exceptions. But the race as a whole is barely tolerated."

"But why? If everyone hates what they do, then why hasn't anyone dealt with them already?"

"There are wider concerns."

"Like cowardice?"

Alistaris sighed. "In a way, yes," he answered. "I have spent most of my life fighting against civilizations like the E'rok Tan, but when I go home, do you know the reception I get? People look down on me. We are a peaceful people—at least on the surface. We can afford to be because of our technology as well as our allies. But a few of us, we choose to fight against injustice. We have dedicated our lives to it. And yet, at home, we are seen as barely tolerated barbarians."

I looked away, trying to process that information. Then, I asked, "So, you're the good guys?"

"No. Not with the things I've been forced to do. But our mission is."

"And your mission is?"

"To fight against people like the E'rok Tan. To protect people who can't protect themselves. To make the hard choices so people back home can continue to live their lives in peace, never having to see things like what you just saw."

"So you say," I muttered. Lots of people claimed to fight for the greater good. I'd run across plenty of that in the past few years. But every single time, I'd discovered that their so-called heroism was a front for something horrible. Sure, they sometimes managed to do some good, but it was always a side effect rather than a purpose.

"I don't expect you to trust me," Alistaris said. "In fact, I'd be very disappointed if you did."

"Then why are we having this conversation if you know I'm not going to believe a word you say?" I asked. He was an alien, which was enough to garner my distrust. However, he had also threatened me, forcing me to do his bidding.

But he'd never really hurt me, had he? Was that simply a manipulation tactic intended to force me to do what he wanted me to do? Or was it evidence that he wasn't as bad as my first impressions might lead me to believe?

"Ask your friends about the Ark Alliance," he suggested. "Those people up in the Bazaar should be able to tell you all you need to know about who I am and what I represent."

I sighed, then stood up before turning to face him. With his legs dangling a foot or so above the forest ground, he looked so small. Almost like a child. Of course, that aura of Mist hovering around him ruined that perception almost as much as the thick beard and bushy white eyebrows.

"Why are you telling me this?" I asked. "You want something else from me, right?"

"I just want to help you," he said. "I want to help this world."

"Why?"

"Because it's my job. At this very moment, the worst people in the universe are poised to fall upon this world and turn the upcoming Integration into an invasion. And eventually, into extermination," he stated.

"Tell me something I don't know," I said. My uncle had always predicted that, when the Initialization ended and the Integration began, Earth would begin its descent into oblivion. That was his guiding star, and he'd spent years trying to prepare me for survival. So, having that confirmed by Alistaris was disappointing, but it wasn't surprising.

"They're called the Gomari Confederation," he responded. "Hundreds of systems, all working toward a singular goal."

"What goal?" I asked, already knowing the answer.

"Power. Influence. Survival," he said. "They target newly Integrated planets. They'll probably let some of the population survive. Some might even thrive. But most will be killed or enslaved. They'll strip this planet of every available resource, then abandon it. That's what I'm here to stop."

I shook my head. "I was told that you were mining something," I said. "That your people are—"

"I do not represent my people," he stated. "In any case, what the other Dengyts are doing is not what you think. It is harmless."

"According to you," I said.

"Do your research, Miss Braddock," he said. "Ask your friends about us. We are not your enemies."

"But you want to be friends, huh?" I asked.

"I want to come to an understanding," he answered. "I want to help this planet."

"You're the big, bad alien with all your technology, right? If you want to help, then you'll help. You don't need me."

"That's where you're wrong. Until the Integration is complete, the system restricts us. The same is true of the Confederates, though they have a preponderance of people who can and will flout those restrictions. We do not."

I didn't believe that one bit. If the so-called Alliance was constrained by the system, it was because they didn't want to pay the price of shedding those restrictions. Alistaris's characterization of the issue was simply an attempt to paint his people as the sympathetic underdogs.

"We are fighting on thousands of fronts throughout the universe," he said. "We are stretched thin, and your world is . . ."

"Unimportant."

"I was going to say ordinary, except as a proxy for a larger conflict."

"There it is. I bet if we had some nice, juicy resources that weren't available anywhere else, your little club would be all over it, huh?"

"If that was the case, your planet would already be destroyed. That's what happens to special worlds. The Confederates invade. We fight them. And eventually, one side or the other realizes that they can't win. And when they do, they come to the inevitable conclusion that they would rather destroy the planet altogether than let the other side reap the benefits of control."

"So you and yours do the same thing, huh? You want whatever we have."

"We will work with your people to bring this backwater up to universal standards," he answered. "That costs credits. Lots and lots of credits. We'll take part of what we need from your resources."

"There it is."

"You find that unreasonable?"

"It's a raw deal. It doesn't matter if it's you or the Confederates. No matter what, we get screwed."

"That isn't how it would work," Alistaris stated. "We only want to help. We'll show you how to build your infrastructure. We'll help you with defenses. We will—"

"You'll build a bright and shiny utopia," I said. "A pretty little cage for your pet humans. All the while, you'll strip us of whatever resources we have. Just like the Confederates."

"We're nothing like them," he growled, showing anger for the first time since the conversation began. "The E'rok Tan were part of the Gomari Confederation. What you just saw is what you can expect from them."

"Slavery is slavery."

"We don't take slaves. We have partners."

"When one side has all the power, and the other has none, there's not really a difference."

"You know that's not true. We are—"

"You're the good guys. Right. You covered that. Look, you can stop with your little pitch, okay? Right now, everything is just words. I'll need to see actions before I'll even begin to trust you. Starting with what you do with those people," I said, gesturing back toward the abandoned amusement park.

"We already have an agreement on that," Alistaris said. "Even if we didn't, we'd help them. One way or another."

I shook my head. I knew what he meant. In fact, over the past couple of hours, I'd wondered if death wasn't a better option than living a life like that. Not only were there logistical questions about how to take care of them, but there were ethical ones, as well. It was a complicated subject, but I knew that I'd rather die than live like those people.

Did that make me a bad person?

Or was I simply realistic?

I knew there were plenty of people who'd be horrified to hear my thoughts on the matter. To them, all life—even damaged beyond all recognition—was sacred. Patrick was like that, and it was one of the reasons I loved him. But I knew myself well enough that, if something like that happened to me, I'd hope that someone would show me the mercy of putting a bullet in my head.

Pushing those ethical concerns out of my mind, I asked, "Why do you want me, anyway? There are plenty of people out there who are stronger than me."

"I think you underestimate your own strength. And your potential."

My heart started beating a little faster. Did he know about the Tier 7 Nexus Implant? Maybe. After Disguise was replaced by the more active Mimic, I couldn't conceal my tier unless I changed my entire appearance. However, pinpointing someone's tier was no exact science, and the best anyone could do was to get a vague idea of someone's power. For instance, I knew that Alistaris was somewhere around Tier 4 or 5.

"In any case, we have contacted others like you," he said. "Negotiations are ongoing."

That was as expected. Powerful people were, by nature, suspicious; the quest for survival dictated as much.

"I'm guessing they're not going that well," I said.

"They are not, but we are hopeful. The fact remains that if humanity is going to survive and remain independent, you will have to fight for it," he said. "You don't trust me. I understand that. But I hope that you will come around. In the meantime, I implore you to investigate my organization. Ask your friends in the Bazaar about us. And when the time comes, you will see that we are on the same side."

"What about our agreement?" I asked, referring to the other two missions I'd agreed to undertake. "Are they going to be like this one?"

"They will be," he said.

"Good."

I didn't have much choice in whether or not I continued to work for him. So, I was relieved to hear that, maybe, I could do a little good along the way. Perhaps I couldn't really help the people who'd been enslaved by the E'rok Tan—they were probably a lost cause—but by killing the aliens, I'd prevented them from hurting anyone else. That had to count for something, didn't it?

Finally, he slipped down from the fallen log and said, "Until next time, Miss Braddock. Please, consider what I said today."

Then, without another word, he disappeared from my senses entirely. Even with Observation running, I could neither see, feel, hear, nor smell him.

I really needed to get my hands on whatever he was using to conceal his presence. Was it a skill? Or was it some sort of tech? Either way, it was impressive, and I wanted it.

I remained where I was for another few moments before taking a deep breath, then heading back to the highway. After mounting the Cutter, I took off through the untamed wilderness. I was a little distracted as my thoughts centered on my conversation with Alistaris, but I still kept Observation active. I knew precisely how dangerous the world could be, and I had no intention of enduring an ambush. Thankfully, nothing attacked me, and I arrived back at *The Leviathan* unmolested.

Even so, I didn't relax until I was on board *The Leviathan*, and even then, my thoughts continued to race through the events of the last couple of days. First, I'd had the initial encounter with that terrifying wildling. Its cackling laugh had been some sort of ability, I was sure, but the memory of the resulting terror—artificial though it was—remained in the back of my mind. Then, there were the humans who'd become livestock for the E'rok Tan. The only solace was that they were probably incapable of understanding the injustice they'd experienced.

But still, I would never forget their docile eyes and unthinking expressions. Or the way they were crammed into their cages, naked and with barely enough room to move.

I shuddered as I pushed those memories to the back of my mind.

It was beginning to get crowded back there. Eventually, I was going to have to deal with all my trauma. I knew that. Even with Combat Focus taking away most of its bite, it was still there, lurking at the edge of my perception and waiting to pounce on the slightest indication of weakness.

And finally, adding to my issues was my conversation with Alistaris. I'd always known there were aliens waiting to plunder the Earth, but until then, I had labored under the impression that it was an every-man-for-himself sort of situation. But if what Alistaris said was true, then my planet had a very difficult time ahead.

Wait—who was I kidding? Even if he was lying through his teeth, that was probably the case.

Regardless, I'd had a rough few days, and I was eager to take a few hours to simply relax. But first, I needed to get somewhere safe. *The Leviathan* was equipped with a superior defense system, but I had no doubts that plenty of the wildlife could overcome it. So, I took a deep breath and headed to the cockpit.

Only a few minutes later, I was zipping through the sky on my way back to Fortune. The trip took almost an entire day, so by the time I set *The Leviathan* down, I was exhausted. Physically, I could have probably kept going for a while longer. But from a mental perspective, I was absolutely beat. So, after letting Patrick know what was going on—keeping the details light—I retreated to the ship's living quarters where I showered, changed, and then went to bed.

What followed was nearly twenty hours of blessedly dreamless sleep. Even so, when I woke up, I was still groggy. So, I took a long, cold shower before heading to the kitchen and making breakfast. While I was eating some bacon and eggs—the real stuff, too—Patrick showed up.

He looked even groggier than I felt, with dark circles under his eyes and slumping shoulders.

"You okay?"

"Just trying to work through some unexpected issues," he said, plopping down. He reached over and grabbed a piece of my bacon.

"Hey!"

"I'll make some more," he said. "So, I got the sense that you didn't tell me everything over the Secure Connection. What's up?"

I leaned back and said, "It's been a tough couple of days."

Then, I told him everything. When I got to my description of the human livestock—I really didn't know how else to refer to them—I skated over the worst of it. But he knew me well enough to read between the lines, and he was suitably horrified by my story. Finally, I ended with a summary of my conversation with Alistaris.

"Do you believe him?" he asked.

I shrugged. "I don't know. I need to talk to some of my contacts in the Bazaar," I said. I intended to visit Kith when I had the time. If anyone knew the truth about the Ark Alliance and the Gomari Confederation, it was her. "I'll talk to Gala, too."

The way I figured it, I would get information from multiple sources, then cross-reference everything. If they all matched up, then I would start to believe Alistaris's story. Until then, I would treat it as the unverified information it was.

After I'd finished, Patrick said, "You know what? I think we both need a break."

"I can't afford a break, Patrick."

"I don't think we can afford not to take one," he said. "You're burning the candle at both ends. So am I. If we keep going like this, we're going to burn out. Besides, it's not like there's a time limit on any of this. If Caden has survived this long, he'll keep going for a few more days."

Caden. I'd almost forgotten about Cirilla's brother. And if I was honest, I didn't so much care about his fate as satisfying my own curiosity about the Pacificians. It was just more evidence that I was a much worse person than I wanted to believe, I think.

But Patrick was right. Despite being a bit blind to my own nature, I knew myself well enough to recognize that burning out was a very real risk. I'd toed that line back in Nova City, and because of that, I'd made a ton of mistakes. Moreover, I'd blinded myself to the implications of my actions, which was something I couldn't afford to do again.

So, I said, "Fine. What kind of break did you have in mind?"

"You'll see," he said with a smile.

DOWNTIME

Mira is like a bomb waiting to explode. It happened once before, and I've spent the intervening years trying to keep it from happening again. Not because I care about all the people she'll probably hurt. I do, but not as much as I care about what another Nova City incident will do to her.

—Patrick Ward

The next morning, I woke up feeling hopeful, satisfied, and well rested. For a long time, I just lay there next to Patrick, basking in the simple comfort of his presence. From experience, I knew how easily I could become untethered. He was my anchor. The one part of my life keeping me from backsliding into old habits.

It wasn't healthy, being so dependent on someone else. I knew that. In our world, a single instant could end a person's life, and I knew that if something like that happened to Patrick, the current version of me would not survive. I'd become something else. Something more like my uncle. Once, I might've considered that a goal. After all, he'd been powerful enough that his name was known across the world. People feared him, and rightly so.

But now? I had begun to see him for what he really was.

A broken man who was just trying to hold on long enough that he could leave something worthwhile behind. That's what I was to him. A chance at redemption. A brief ray of hope. In me, he had seen all the things he could have been.

And I was on the verge of going down the exact same road he'd chosen. Without Patrick, I would've already repeated many of his mistakes and gone past the point of no return.

In a way, that would have been easier. I could just give in to my demons and let them steer me into all the horrible things I was trying to avoid. I could simply destroy everything and everyone in my way. My climb to power would be quick and merciless.

But it would also turn me into something I couldn't stomach.

I opened my eyes to see that Patrick was already awake and looking at me. From anyone else, it would've been a little unnerving. But I could see the concern in his expression. I could practically feel it.

"What are you thinking?" he asked.

"How do you know I'm thinking anything? I just woke up."

"You've been awake for almost twenty minutes," he said. "Come on, Mira. You can talk to me. Tell me what you were thinking."

I sighed and closed my eyes, trying to steady myself. Then, a few moments later, I shifted away from him, instead turning my gaze toward the ceiling. Finally, I said, "I'm so close to the edge, Pick. Like, more than anything else, I just want to run from one alien camp to another, killing everything I find."

"We can do that."

I let out a long breath. "No. I mean . . . I don't know, Pick. If I do that, I'm going to get myself killed. Or worse," I said.

"Worse?"

"My uncle left me a message. I picked it up in the Bazaar," I said.

"What did it say?" he asked.

I shook my head. "Nothing new. Not really. He just wanted me to get out. To survive. Same as always," I said. "But the way he said it . . . I mean, he was broken, Pick. Like, really broken. When he was alive, I thought he was so strong. Like this great, immovable statue or something. He always knew all the answers. And nobody messed with him. He was everything I wanted to be."

I looked back at him and, after a second, continued, "But seeing that video, I noticed all the things I used to ignore. He was exhausted. Not physically, but emotionally. He'd already lost everything except for me. All he cared about was keeping me alive. I think . . . I think that's why he died. He was so single-minded that he just ignored everything else. Part of me thinks that, subconsciously, he let it happen just so it could end.

"And I'm terrified of going down that road, Pick. I don't want to be like him. Not anymore. I want more than that. But as much as I try to make different choices, I keep making the same mistakes he made."

"Then don't."

"It's not that easy," I said.

"Sure it is. Mira, you're in control of your own actions," he said. "I know you think you're just following in his footsteps, but the simple fact that you want to be better than him means you will be."

"I don't think it works that way," I said.

He shifted. "Think about it," he said. "What was his main goal?"

"Helping me survive."

"Then do the opposite."

"You want me to get myself killed? How does that—"

"You know that's not what I meant. No—I want you to find a better goal. Something less about simple survival and more about fulfilling a purpose," he said. "Because survival at all costs isn't enough, Mira. I think you know that. So did he, but what he went through changed him. It put him into a mindset he could never escape. So, he survived, but along the way, he lost everyone and everything that made him human. So, the question you should be asking yourself is what you really want. What's your purpose, Mira? Because without that, I just . . . I don't think survival is enough."

Purpose. It seemed like such an easy concept. But for so long, the only thing driving me forward was survival. That's what my uncle had given everything for. He'd sacrificed so much so that I could get strong enough to live through what was coming. But I'd only recently begun to recognize that he was just as flawed as anyone else. Maybe more so. And he'd passed some of those flaws on to me.

"How do I figure that out?" I asked.

"You're asking me like I know the answers," he said. "I don't, Mira. But no matter what, I'll support you. If you want to go on a rampage, I'm right there behind you. If you want to take off into the universe and become a pacifist farmer, I'll be there, too."

"Is that your purpose, then? Supporting me?"

"One of them, sure," he said, shaking his head. "But I'm not some side character in your story. I have goals, Mira. I have things I want to accomplish. But I love you, and that means I'm here to support you, even if it means putting my own stuff on hold for a little while. And I know you'd do the same for me."

I wasn't so sure that was the case. I wanted it to be. Desperately. But I wasn't sure if I was built like that. I was a little too selfish. But I guess that was just my uncle's influence shining through. Maybe recognizing that was the first step to changing my attitude.

"You're too good for me," I said.

"I know. But I'm here all the same."

After that, he leaned in and planted his lips on mine. The kiss didn't last long, but the following embrace was comforting in a way nothing else could have been. We lay there for a long time, just enjoying each other's presence.

Finally, after some indefinite amount of time, he said, "Come on. If we don't get up, we're going to be late."

"For what? You never said."

"You'll see."

"You said that last night . . ."

"Just trust me," he said with an impish grin.

I just shook my head and said, "That's not worrying at all. But okay."

With that, we both got out of bed, went through our morning routines, and then we were on our way. The flight only took a few hours, during which Patrick refused to let me know what was going on, but just after noon, we began our descent. When I looked out the window, I saw a city I didn't recognize.

It was old. Maybe the oldest city I'd ever seen, with weathered stone buildings and crisscrossing canals. It was also completely abandoned, with none of the trappings necessary for survival in the wilderness.

"What . . . Where are we?" I asked.

"Just a place I found a couple of years ago," he said as he landed *The Leviathan* in a small field near the city. "I don't know its name. But it's strange. Nobody comes here. Animals avoid it. But when I came here before, I just . . . I don't know—it just struck me as beautiful. And ever since then, I've wanted to show it to you."

"It's abandoned? No animals or anything?"

"That's what the local guide told me," he said. "And when I was here before, we didn't see any reason not to believe him. C'mon. I want to get settled in before dark."

"What happens then?"

"You'll see."

After that, he refused to tell me more. My stomach twisted into knots of anticipation as we disembarked and headed into the city. Up close, the age of the buildings was evident. They must have predated the Initialization by hundreds of years, and as we walked down the cobblestone streets, I found myself wondering about its history. How many people had lived there over the years? How many families had been raised? How many people had fallen in love? It was a humbling setting, and a little sad in its abandonment, too. But it also gave me a strange sense of hope, knowing that such a place had survived intact. It felt like people could simply move back in at any moment and resume their old lives.

A silly notion, of course. It had obviously been abandoned for a reason. But that idea clung to my mind all the same.

"You really do love this kind of thing, don't you?"

"What?" I asked, startled out of my reverie.

"History. You love it."

I shrugged. "I like thinking of what the world must have been like before all of this happened," I said. "My uncle told me a few stories, and I've heard a couple of other ones over the years. But it all feels so mysterious. It's fascinating.

They built all of this without Mist or alien technology or anything else. Just human ingenuity and hard work."

I had seen other evidence of the world that had been left behind. Monuments to my ancestors' abilities. A huge stadium where some unknowable sport had been played. Giant buildings where people had lived or worked. Huge craters where they'd used terrible weapons. It was evidence that humanity was more capable than our current situation might suggest.

There were some anachronistic features of the city, as well. An old car here, a bicycle there—there were even a few more modern looking buildings. But it was clear that the people in charge of the city had gone to great lengths to preserve their history.

We walked through that city, stopping every so often to admire particular buildings until, at last, we reached our destination—an ancient church with a bell tower that was taller than any other structure in the city. Patrick led me inside, and as we climbed the stone steps, I asked, "What brought you here before?"

"Resources. You'll see what I'm talking about when the sun sets."

"You keep saying that."

Clutching my hand, he looked down at me and said, "Because you keep asking the same questions. Just go with it, Mira."

That really wasn't my strong suit, but I resolved to do my best. The stairs were steep, and the climb took us quite some time, but eventually, we reached the top. When we did, I let out a gasp.

During our trek through the city and the subsequent climb up the steps, the sun had begun to set. So, when we reached the top of the bell tower, the lights floating throughout the city were clearly visible.

"What . . ."

"Mistflies," he said.

"You remembered."

I'd only mentioned it once, but Patrick had clearly been paying attention when I'd told him the story of Jorge pointing out the stag and the Mistflies outside of Mobile.

"Of course. This is what I wanted you to see, Mira. I know the world can seem like a terrible place. And it is. I know that," he said, turning to face me. He took both of my hands as he continued, "But there's beauty, too. You sometimes have to look for it, sure. And maybe you won't always find it. But it's there. Just waiting to be appreciated."

Jorge had said much the same thing back in Mobile, but when Patrick said it, it just hit differently. He led me to the edge of the bell tower, and I watched as the city's canals lit up with pink phosphorescent light.

"It's an algae. I don't know the name, but it's useful for some internal cybernetics. When I came here to gather some of it for experimentation, I couldn't help but think of you and that story you told me," he said. "And I thought maybe you needed a reminder of what your instructor taught you a few years ago. Plus . . . You know . . . It's kind of romantic, isn't it?"

At that, he released my hands, and a second later, a basket appeared in his hands. It had obviously been in his storage space, but it still came off as impressive—especially when he opened the basket, and all the smells of some of my favorite foods wafted out.

"Would you like to have a picnic with me?"

I smiled at him. "You really are too good for me."

As a response, he only pulled me close and kissed me.

What followed was one of the best nights of my life. Not because it was extraordinary—it was, but that wasn't why it meant so much to me. Instead, I cherished that night because of what it represented. The world was full of terrible things. I had seen plenty of them to recognize that much. But it was also beautiful.

Most of all, though, I knew that, no matter what else might happen, I would always have Patrick.

Of course, all good things must come to an end, and the next morning, Patrick and I returned to *The Leviathan* and headed back to Fortune. It had been a good break—one I had very much needed—but with the return to the city, my responsibilities came crashing back down. However, when I looked at the things I needed to do, I did so with a new perspective.

"Purpose," I said, watching Patrick cross the dock and head back to Cirilla's workshop. I'd been thinking a lot about what he'd said, and I had come to realize that he was right. I needed something to strive for that wasn't simply survival or more power. I needed to find my purpose.

Was it saving people? Maybe.

Could it be fighting against the aliens? Certainly, that felt like the direction I was going, especially with Alistaris's offer. There were plenty of other potential answers to the question of my purpose, but none seemed quite as right as fighting for humanity's independence, for Earth's future. But something was holding me back from committing.

I needed to confirm some of the things Alistaris had told me. Only then could I approach the problem with all the information I needed to make valid decisions. So, I headed back into the ship, and after telling Patrick where I was going, I returned to the remnants of Nova City so I could head back up to the Bazaar.

My trek through the city—and the Bazaar itself—was uneventful, and I soon found my way to Gala's shop. There, I asked her about Alistaris's claims.

To my surprise, she confirmed everything he'd said. There really was a universal conflict between the Gomari Confederation, whom even Gala considered the bad guys, and the Ark Alliance to which Alistaris belonged.

"They aren't saints," she said. "But they try, which is more than most can say."

After spending a little more time with Gala, I headed to Kith's premises and asked her the same thing. She ended up selling me a packet of information that more or less confirmed everything Alistaris had told me. There were some details he'd left out—like the fact that most of the universal powers thought the Ark Alliance cared more about beating the Gomari Confederation than about saving recently Integrated populations, but from a practical standpoint, his story checked out.

So, after thanking Kith, I left the Bazaar and the new version of Nova City and, once I boarded *The Leviathan*, headed back to Fortune where I started to make plans. They weren't terribly complex, but once I was finished, I felt a little better about my future.

I knew there was a chance that everyone was lying to me. I hadn't forgotten how adamant Alistaris had been that I ask my friends in the Bazaar about his organization. However, I knew I couldn't go through life without trusting anyone. So far, Alistaris had treated me well enough. He'd had every opportunity to kill or, if he wished, enslave me. But he hadn't, which told me that he was either playing the long game, or he was exactly what he claimed to be.

Either way, I intended to use him to fulfill my purpose. Perhaps it was naive. Maybe I was making a mistake. But if I could help humanity maintain its freedom, then that was what I would do. Anything else, and I wasn't sure I could live with myself.

CHAPTER FORTY-ONE

AN UNCOMFORTABLE JOURNEY

Sometimes, I wonder how it all started. Someone had to have created the Mist. Were they responsible for the Nexus Implants and the system? Or was it someone else? Did it all just spontaneously manifest, created by the Mist itself? There's so much we don't know, and I don't know if we'll ever learn the truth.

—Patrick Ward

Whoever categorized the Ithids as elves or fairies had clearly never encountered either. To me, they looked more like humanoid mosquitoes than anything else. At a foot or so tall, they were almost human in form, save for long, rigid proboscises jutting from their faces. Aside from that, each one was also equipped with a set of transparent wings that further solidified their insectoid appearance.

And there were thousands of them in the settlement spread out below me.

As I watched, I wanted nothing more than to send a few insecticide bombs— I'd seen them used in various cities when they were infested with mutated roaches, mosquitoes, or other pests—down there and kill them all. However, there were two major problems with that. First, I had no idea if that would even work, but given that they had access to Nexus Implants and the system, I had to expect that they had some way to mitigate such poisons. Second, I hadn't come to kill them. Instead, I was there to watch and wait until I saw a means to my end, which was to infiltrate the Pacifician city called Olympus.

Still, even knowing that I had multiple reasons not to kill them, I struggled to keep my weapons in my arsenal implant. If I had seen any human exploitation in the settlement, I don't think I could've kept to that resolution. Thankfully, all I saw were Ithids.

Most were just living their lives, not unlike what I'd seen in countless human cities. Others cycled through the nearby Rift aperture where they were mining shards. There were no humans present, and on approach, I hadn't even seen any ruins of the Earth's fallen civilization. No—the Ithid settlement was in the middle of nowhere; I reasoned that its isolation was probably the point. After all, they didn't look particularly powerful, and as such, they clearly wanted nothing to do with conflict—either with humanity or with the other alien invaders.

Even so, as I watched them from afar, I found myself growing increasingly hostile. I wanted to kill them. Not for anything they had done, but rather for what I suspected they would do in the future. Given the chance, would they be any kinder to humanity than the E'rok Tan? Would they take over the Earth and enslave the native population? My experience with aliens told me that they would.

But was that really the case?

Alistaris's claims, which I'd verified with Gala and Kith, suggested that there were plenty of aliens who had no interest in exploitation, oppression, or enslavement. Instead, the Ark Alliance fought against it. So, perhaps the universe wasn't quite as hostile as I'd been taught by my uncle.

Or maybe it was just a different form of exploitation.

I really didn't have enough information to make a determination. However, I was beginning to come around to the idea that my view of the universe was, at best, incomplete. At worst, it was needlessly pessimistic.

In any case, the Ithids were not my ultimate target, and waging a war against them—no matter how satisfying—would accomplish nothing. So, I continued to watch, noting the patterns of movement within the settlement.

Over the next two days, I gathered as much information as I could, but there was a limit to the effectiveness of my surveillance. In the end, there was only so much I could see from afar, and once I'd exhausted those limits, I decided to go ahead with my plan. So it happened that, two days after my observation began, I found myself creeping forward under the dim light of a half moon.

Cloaked in Stealth and Camouflage, I approached the wall surrounding the settlement. Unlike what I had seen in previous alien compounds, it wasn't made of plasti-steel. Instead, it was composed of some natural compound that the insectoid Ithids secreted from their proboscises. During my surveillance, I'd watched them squirt the yellow liquid into molds, where it hardened into similarly colored bricks they used as building material.

Even as I drew closer, I could feel the Mist incorporated into the wall. But it didn't feel like a Mist shield. Instead, it was more akin to what I associated with an ability. Perhaps that was what it was, given the source of the material.

In any case, it presented a problem—largely because, due to its natural origin, it was immune to my Misthack ability. However, during my surveillance, I'd seen enough to come up with a plan to get around the ocher wall.

To that end, I took a deep breath, backed away to get a good amount of momentum, and then set off at a dead sprint. Just before I reached the wall, I jumped high into the air. My leap took me about halfway up the wall, and at the peak of my jump, I used Double Jump, then Teleport to take me even higher.

My range wasn't impressive. Just a couple dozen feet, really. And using the ability drained every last drop of my Mist. However, it was enough to help me crest the wall; the only problem was that all my momentum was going upward, so unless I only wanted to get a peek over the top of the wall, it was useless.

Thankfully, I had a way to get around that.

The moment my Teleport completed, I jabbed a Mist booster into my thigh and discharged its contents. It took an instant for the Mist to flow into me, and when it did, I sighted in on the roof of a building on the other side of the wall and used Teleport. Once again, the Mist drained out of me, sending a spike of pain through my mind as I appeared at my destination.

There, I knelt, waiting to see if I'd raised any alarms.

Ten seconds passed. Then thirty. By the time a minute had gone by, I felt confident that I was undetected. That gave me leave to deal with the consequences of my strategy.

When I'd first discovered Mist boosters, I'd had very little use for the incredibly expensive pneumatic devices. As my abilities grew more sophisticated, though, I'd come to realize just how valuable they really were. However, soon after unlocking my Teleport ability, I had discovered that, like everything else in the world, Mist boosters came with a significant limitation. Chiefly, that my body was not equipped to deal with the aftermath of rapidly draining, artificially replenishing, and then draining my reserves of Mist again. In short, while I could use a strategy like I'd just employed to bypass the Ithid wall, doing so would leave me weakened and in pain that wouldn't fade until my Mist had naturally recovered.

It was a painful process that wasn't even remotely mitigated by my Pain Tolerance, but I'd spent plenty of time training myself to endure it. Still, it wasn't pleasant, and it took almost two hours for the pain to subside. By that point, I was certain that my presence was entirely undetected, which meant that I could move forward with my plan without further interruption.

The buildings within the walls were mostly constructed of plasti-steel, suggesting that the bricks were unsuitable for the purpose. I could see how that would be the case; nobody wanted to go through what amounted to a natural Mist shield just to return to their quarters. And even if the Ithids would tolerate that inconvenience, the resultant noise—or Mist resonance—would likely drown out any warning the wall might give.

Or maybe it was some other reason. I wasn't sure, and I was in no mood to investigate further. After all, I was behind enemy lines, and while I trusted my abilities to keep me hidden, I had no interest in testing their limits. So, as soon as I recovered, I slipped from the roof and headed toward my intended destination.

As I moved through the settlement, I got a better look at the Ithids, and while I was a little put off by their appearance—I couldn't get the notion of a humanoid mosquito out of my head—I saw no evidence that they were the enemies I expected them to be. Most weren't even armed, and they all seemed intent on completing their tasks and living their lives.

But they were allies of the Pacificians, weren't they? Even if the Ithids weren't evil, they had partnered with a race of aliens that wanted to subjugate and enslave humanity. As my uncle had once told me, you are who you associate with. And if the Ithids associated with the Pacificians, it just made them that much easier to paint with the same brush.

Then again, perhaps I was just trying to rationalize my own internalized hatred of all aliens.

In any case, I slowly made my way through the settlement, dodging Ithids along the way until, at last, I reached the supply warehouse that was my destination. It was a large, three-story building that contained all the materials the Ithids had mined from the Rift. There were shards, of course, but there were also other natural resources that were difficult to find elsewhere.

That was something else I'd learned in the previous three years. While Rift Shards were the big moneymaker for most Rift-mining operations, there were plenty of other avenues of profitability. Some Rifts contained rare ore. Others were populated by beasts whose hides, bones, and even organs were extremely useful. I'd even encountered one that offered a perfect environment for farming. And the list went on and on.

With the Ithids' Rift, the major export seemed to be a liquified metal that, according to the file I'd gotten from Kith, was useful for coating the hulls of spacefaring ships. I had no idea how it was supposed to work or what it was supposed to do, but I did know that it was the backbone of their relationship with the Pacificians—at least on Earth. And so, I quickly found my way to the section of the warehouse where they kept drums of the stuff.

When I got there, I was taken aback by the sheer volume on display. Hundreds of drums, all neatly stacked and waiting for transport to Olympus, stared back at me. What could Earth have done with those resources? What could humanity buy? I'd long since learned that money was the one true source of power in the universe. With it, even the weakest people could dig in and protect themselves. Money alone wasn't enough to make anyone a true powerhouse, but with enough of it, it could elevate an entire planet.

But with Earth's resources being plundered by invaders, we would never get the chance to establish ourselves. Nor would we have sufficient credits to protect ourselves. It was a vicious cycle that, once it started, was almost impossible to escape.

That was a problem for another day, though, and I forced myself to focus on the task at hand. With that in mind, I made my way to one of the barrels. Once I reached it, I used Misthack to open the lock and opened it up to reveal a shiny green liquid. I could feel the Mist radiating from within. However, the moment the air hit the substance, it began to solidify. I watched as, in seconds, it became a solid brick of gray metal that emitted no more Mist than mundane iron.

Such a finicky substance. Useful, I'd been told, but it seemed to be more trouble than it was worth. In any case, I gently tipped the barrel on its side and set about removing the now-solid cylinder of metal. It was much lighter than I'd anticipated—far less dense than most metals—so, with my Constitution, I had little trouble with the task. Soon enough, the barrel was empty, leaving me with a large cylinder of metal to dispose of. Fortunately, I was prepared for the problem, and over the next few minutes, I used my nano-bladed sword to slowly cut it into manageable pieces that I then stored away in my arsenal implant. It took most of my free space, but it really was my only option.

Once the metal had been disposed of, I pushed the barrel back into position and climbed inside, dragging the lid into place behind me. Once I was completely inside, I twisted the lid, then used Misthack to once again seal the barrel.

After that, I dragged another item from my arsenal implant. Even as the air inside the barrel dissipated, I placed a rubber mask over my mouth and nose and took a deep breath. I'd bought the respirator almost two years before when I'd targeted an underwater Rift-mining operation populated by amphibious aliens. However, I'd never gotten the chance to use it because, before I'd attacked, they'd packed up and disappeared completely. I'd never discovered where they went, but I'd kept the respirator in my arsenal implant in case I came upon a similar problem sometime in the future.

The item worked by using a combination of ambient and personal Mist to create oxygen. I was a little fuzzy on the actual mechanics of the process, but I'd verified that it would work almost indefinitely, so long as I kept my Mist reserves topped off. And given that I wasn't even using any abilities, that seemed like a given.

So, like that, I settled down to wait, occupying my mind by working on various Ghosts I'd neglected over the last few months. It was one thing to recognize that literally anything was possible with Ghosts, but it was something else entirely to expand my mind to the point where it was true. The fact was that everyone was limited by their own culture, personality, and creativity, and I was no different. My mind worked along fairly straight lines, and I had to stretch myself if I was ever going to create something truly different.

And as I'd discovered, that process was incredibly difficult.

The reality was that I just wasn't terribly creative. But that wasn't so bad, really. My Ghosts were still effective, and they worked well enough for me. That was all that really mattered, even if I knew I wasn't stretching the limits of what was possible. Even so, I found that trying to force myself to think differently was a viable exercise, so I persisted even if I knew it would never really give me any useful alternatives to my normal strategies.

Like that, hours passed into days, and I fell into a sort of hibernation. My mind was nominally active—I continued to work on my Ghosts and train via my old puzzle program—but my body fell into a lethargic meditation that was only sustainable due to my inflated attributes. Without them, I never could have remained contorted in that small space for more than a few hours, especially considering that I neither ate nor drank during that time.

But I'd trained myself to go without. And even if it wasn't pleasant, I was more than capable of eschewing bodily necessities for weeks at a time.

Still, when, almost a week later, I felt the barrel move, I had to suppress a sigh of relief. So long as the Ithids followed their normal protocol, my self-imposed ordeal would soon be over.

Another few hours passed, and during that time, I felt the barrel being jostled about. Eventually, though, I felt Mist gathering only a dozen yards away. That was my cue, and I immediately embraced Misthack and sent my senses out searching for the source of the swirling Mist. I quickly found it in the form of some sort of machine meant to scan the contents of the barrels. So, as I drew ever closer, I hacked into it, and when my barrel reached the scanner, I forced it to ignore my presence. Even though I trusted my abilities, I held my breath as it completed its scan, but I needn't have worried because, soon enough, I passed through.

Over the next forty-five minutes, I remained in place as the barrel was transported from what I hoped was the town at the base of the mountain and into Olympus proper. Eventually, it came to a stop, but I still waited another few hours before the moment of truth loomed before me.

I'd planned as well as I could, given the information I had. However, I had no idea what security measures Olympus had enacted. For all I knew, when I opened the barrel, I'd find myself surrounded by cyborgs. But during my research, I'd discovered that the city was locked up tight, with no real weaknesses in its outward-facing defenses.

As such, my only chance of entering the city undetected was my current means of ingress. Sure, I could have blasted my way inside. Or maybe, I could have snuck in using Stealth and Camouflage. However, my previous experiences with the Pacificians suggested otherwise, so I'd taken what I considered a safer route. As I prepared to climb out of the barrel, I could only hope that I was right.

After taking a deep breath, I used Misthack to unlock the barrel, then twisted it. With a discharge of air, the barrel's seal was broken, and I pushed the top off. I pulled the rubber mask from my face and took a deep breath before climbing unsteadily to my feet. Looking around, I saw that I was within a similar warehouse to the one where I'd started my uncomfortable journey.

And thankfully, I was alone.

With that, I climbed from the barrel and took my first step in Olympus.

CHAPTER FORTY-TWO

TO THE MOON

Sometimes, I wonder what it would be like if Mira and I just settled down somewhere. No more fighting. No more crazy missions. Just us living normal lives. I know it'll never happen, though. She would never be happy with anything ordinary.

—Patrick Ward

glanced around the warehouse, but I didn't see anything out of place. Nor did anything trigger my {Mistrunner} senses. As far as I could tell, it was just a normal warehouse, completely devoid of security—Mist based or more mundane. That lined up with my expectations. After all, when their city was so difficult to infiltrate, why would the Pacificians bother with elaborate defenses within Olympus?

After replacing the metal in the barrel, I resealed the lid and made sure that it looked undisturbed. Then, I used Stealth and set about exploring my location, eventually confirming my suspicions that it was a normal warehouse filled with identical barrels to the one I'd used to get into the city. Deciding that further inspection was pointless, I then started looking for a way out.

Soon enough, I found a door that I quickly Misthacked into. When I forced it open, I was confronted with an enclosed hallway—which surprised me because I had expected to end up outdoors. Even so, I didn't let it throw me off too much, and I quickly started down the wide corridor as I searched for another exit.

Curiously, the place was entirely deserted, and I didn't even detect any defenses. There weren't even any cameras, which I found more than a little odd. Seeing that, I resolved to be even more cautious than normal, and my pace slowed down considerably. It was a good thing, too, because only a few hundred yards down that inordinately long corridor, I was nearly trampled by a vehicle. I narrowly managed to dodge to the side as the thing raced past. As it sped away, the curve of the hallway took it out of sight. However, it remained visible for long enough for me to get a good look.

And I found it very odd.

For one, the thing actually had wheels which were clad in great knobby tires that would've been appropriate for trekking through the wilderness. That was odd enough, considering that the ambient Mist was easily thick enough to support hover vehicles. What was even stranger was that the vehicle was entirely sealed. I hadn't even caught a glimpse of the occupants because there were no visible windows. In fact, it looked like nothing so much as a sharply angled box on wheels.

Shaking my head, I wondered why the Pacificians had used such a vehicle, but there were no answers forthcoming, so I quickly moved on. I'd already gone a few hundred yards, but I kept going for hundreds more before I saw anything but the same repeating pattern of a modular hallway.

When I finally did, I couldn't help but let out a gasp.

Because I was obviously no longer on Earth.

In fact, I could see my planet in the distance—a blue-white-and-green orb that looked simultaneously far too small and more majestic than anything else I'd ever seen. The only thing that came close was when I saw the distant planet in the spider-infested Rift so long ago. But even that paled in comparison.

I was so startled that it took me a moment to notice the featureless gray landscape visible through the window.

Immediately, I tried to contact Patrick, but he was out of range. The same went for everyone else on my contact list. Even Gala and Dex back in the Bazaar were too far away to make a Secure Connection.

For a long moment, I stared out that window as I tried to make sense of what I saw. But only one thing seemed to fit. I wasn't on a space station. Nor was I on a ship. The rocky, gray landscape told me that much. So, I could only reason that, somehow, I'd ended up on the moon.

Which created a significant problem, largely that I had no notion of how to get home.

Since taking possession of *The Leviathan*, I'd taken the freedom it gave me for granted. And even without it, I knew how to get around the world. There were plenty of people who had ships, and there were public transportation options, as well. They all came with significant downsides—expense and a lack of safety being chief among them—but it was comforting to know that, if I needed to be on the other side of a continent, there was enough infrastructure to allow for it.

But now?

How was I supposed to get home from the surface of the moon?

I'm not proud of it, but at that moment, I started to panic a little. It's difficult to overstate just how shocking it is to suddenly look out a window and see the entire Earth thousands upon thousands of miles away. Perhaps I would have taken it much better if I'd expected it, but a thousand worries—ranging from how I was going to get home to what would happen if there was a leak in the window—crashed into me with overwhelming force.

I backed away from that window until my back hit the wall on the other side of the corridor. There I stood, my breath coming fast and shallow, until, a few minutes later, I managed to wrangle my anxious mind into some semblance of calm. Then, I forced myself to divide my problems into small, solvable chunks before organizing them in order of importance.

The first thing I needed to do was to figure out why the Pacificians had a base on the moon. I had some ideas about what its purpose might be, but I refused to even think about them until I had more information.

Second, I would have to find out how I'd gotten there. Because that was probably my only ticket home. If that wasn't possible, then I'd have to reevaluate based on whatever information I could uncover.

In truth, I couldn't make any real plans until I had more intelligence. So, in reality, nothing had really changed. Certainly, I was on the moon instead of in a Pacifician city called Olympus, but aside from the setting, my ultimate mission remained the same. With that in mind, I took a few deep breaths and then set off down the hallway.

Even so, I kept glancing to the other side of the hallway, half expecting it to burst before I was swallowed by the vacuum of space. Of course, I knew the moon had some sort of atmosphere, but to me, it would amount to the same thing. I could fight powerful enemies. I could survive in the dangerous wilds. But in space? I was just as vulnerable as anyone else.

It wasn't just the lack of oxygen, either. There was radiation out there. Extreme temperatures. And who knew what else had come with the Mist? For all I knew, the moon was crawling with just as many native monsters as Earth, only they were suited to that inhospitable environment while I was . . . Well, I was still human, with all the deficiencies that entailed.

But I couldn't allow myself to dwell on it. Not when I knew I was in enemy territory, and in more ways than one. So, I pushed those concerns out of my mind and focused on putting one metaphorical foot in front of the other. I needed to take one step at a time, or I'd be overwhelmed by the situation.

Like that, I continued down the hall, and eventually, I reached a three-way intersection. The corridor through which I'd been walking went off in either direction, but another path led to my right. I also noticed that it featured a slight decline, which suggested that it would descend underground.

I suspected that that direction would lead me to the Pacificians—if any even lived in the facility—but I wanted to keep going the way I'd been going. Because I'd learned over the years that, when mapping a new environment, it was important to keep to a pattern. Otherwise, it was easy to get lost.

So, I ignored the offshoot and kept going down what I was rapidly beginning to think of as the main hall. For two more hours, I walked, and during that time, three more vehicles passed me by. None saw through Stealth, but each instance left me breathless. I knew how thin my margins were, and I was not prepared for a fight.

By the end of the second hour, just when I was beginning to consider heading back to the offshoot I'd passed, the hall finally ended in a hangar.

In addition to a couple of ships, both of which looked like boxy cargo containers with wings, I finally got my first glimpse of the Pacificians. I slipped into the hangar and planted myself in an isolated corner while I watched. The men and women all looked disturbingly similar, with blond or brown hair and blue eyes, marking them as the same sort of androids I had seen back in Fortune. However, instead of blue, black, or brown robes, they were all dressed in green. I knew from my research—and the interrogation I'd staged back in Fortune—that the different-color robes marked these people as more important than most I had seen before.

Not that it mattered. They were all enemies. I didn't need to know precisely how they stratified their odd society.

In any case, I continued to watch as the Pacificians off-loaded crates from the ships and into the same sorts of vehicles I had seen racing along the hall. Once they were full, the vehicles took off the way I'd come.

I watched for almost an hour until, at last, the ships were completely emptied. That's when I realized that I might've overstayed my welcome. The androids all boarded their ships, and once everyone had done so, a door slid shut, sealing the hall away while a much larger set of doors swung out, exposing the hangar to the lunar atmosphere.

Or the lack thereof.

Immediately, the air rushed out of the hanger. I grabbed ahold of a nearby rail on the wall, then dragged my respirator from my arsenal implant. I barely got it in place before the air completely drained from the enormous hangar.

Instantly, I felt my body lock up as it was assailed by a biting cold I can't really describe. It was like I'd suddenly been encased in ice, though that wasn't entirely accurate, either. I knew from school that the surface of the moon could reach temperatures as low as two hundred degrees below zero, but knowing that and feeling it are two very different things. Fortunately, my Constitution gave me at least some resistance to the extreme temperatures, but even that wasn't enough to completely shield me.

In short, I froze.

Literally.

I only survived due to two reasons. First, I had air to breathe, and I forced myself to continue to do so. That kept my body running, albeit poorly. Second, my inflated attributes gave me superhuman endurance.

But even then, I knew it wouldn't be enough.

Thankfully, the two ships quickly lifted off and left the hangar behind. The doors swung shut, and with a hiss, the atmosphere within the hangar reverted to normal. I collapsed to the ground, and the impact made it feel like every cell in my body had shattered. Somehow, I managed to keep Stealth active—I think I hung on out of habit—and for a few long hours, I just lay there as my body struggled to combat the damage even that short exposure to the lunar atmosphere had done.

How long had those doors been open? A few minutes, at most. And it took me hours before I could even move, much less fully recover. However far I'd managed to come, my humanity was still intact enough that I couldn't endure the rigors of space. If I hadn't been in so much pain, I might've found that comforting, in a way. After all, I'd often wondered what my progression meant in terms of my continued humanity. Now, I knew that I was a long way off from pushing past my origin.

Gradually, I recovered, and eventually, I managed to grab a med-hypo from my arsenal implant and jab it into my hip. As the medication took hold, I felt a wave of relief; the hypo wouldn't heal me, but it did ease my symptoms enough that I could get out of the hangar and find somewhere more appropriate for recovery.

With that, I dragged myself to my feet, then stumbled out of the hangar and into the corridor. For the next few hours, I staggered down the hall until, at last, I reached the warehouse in which I'd woken. It still seemed deserted, and even if it wasn't, the chamber was big enough that I could lose myself in it without much chance of discovery.

So, that's what I did, eventually settling in between two rows of barrels. There, I continued my convalescence. I'd fought hundreds of battles over the past few years, but none had left me so thoroughly defeated as my brief brush with the lunar atmosphere.

As I recovered, I began to analyze my choices, and I came away extremely disappointed. The hangar doors hadn't looked any different than the other walls, but in retrospect, I should have expected them to open. After all, that was what a hangar was for, wasn't it? But I'd been so rattled by the setting that I hadn't been thinking clearly. And it had nearly cost me my life.

A few more minutes, and I would have died right there on that floor.

No fighting back. No heroic last stands. Just an ignominious death. Patrick would've never even known what happened to me. I would just disappear from his life.

For long hours, I berated myself for my carelessness. But then, I pushed that aside. I knew what I had done wrong, and more importantly, I knew how to fix the problem. So, I resolved to pay better attention, then set my mind to recovery mode.

As I sat there for days, I saw more Pacificians dropping off or taking barrels away. None of them were looking for someone like me, though, so I remained undetected. Meanwhile, I occupied myself the same way I always did—by working on my Ghosts. This time, though, I chose to tweak some of the ones I thought might see some use if it came down to a fight within the lunar station.

After almost a week, I finally recovered. It was a good thing, too, because my supplies had begun to run low. Much longer, and I would have run out of water. But now that I'd had a chance to think about my situation, I was eager to see what else the station had to offer. So, once I made certain that I hadn't left any evidence behind, I headed out of the warehouse and down the corridor until I reached the offshoot.

Then, I set off down that comparatively smaller tunnel, hoping that I could find some information I could use.

About a mile—as far as I could tell—down that tunnel, I started to see more androids. They all wore the same green robes, and unless I looked very closely, they were as close to identical as people could be. There were subtle variations, especially between genders, but they were so small as to be mostly unimportant.

The facility changed, as well, with the tunnel eventually giving way to a webwork of dormitories and living areas. I explored them all, though I found nothing of note until I stumbled upon a security terminal. With all the traffic, I could only connect to the terminal for a few seconds without risking detection, but in that time, I managed to download some basic information about the compound.

The moment I found an out-of-the-way corner of the facility, I settled in to give it a read. When I did, I discovered that the facility was meant to manufacture weaponized satellites that would, in turn, be deployed around the Earth. The files I'd downloaded didn't specify their purpose, but it didn't take me long to put two and two together.

The Pacificians intended to take over the world. And it seemed that I was the only person in a position to stop them. Because of course that would be the way it was.

I continued to read the file, internalizing the partial map that had been included. It didn't feature any helpful labels, but I could infer the importance of a few distinctive areas. The first was a huge set of rooms in the opposite direction from the hangar that I suspected would be where the satellites were assembled. I knew I'd have to check to make sure, but I felt confident in that assumption.

If I kept going through the living quarters, I would find another set of rooms, the purpose of which wasn't clear. I intended to check that first. So, after making certain I knew the way, I continued to creep through the facility. No one even suspected my presence, which was good because, even though I knew I'd have to eventually kill them all, I didn't want things to happen before I was ready.

However, when I finally reached the mysterious rooms that were my destination, I found my resolve not to immediately destroy the entire facility wavering.

I shook my head and muttered to myself, "It's always the same, isn't it? We're not people to them. We're just things to be used."

I was tempted to look away. I didn't want to see what was in front of me. But this wasn't like the situation with the people the E'rok Tan had turned into livestock. I couldn't call Alistaris in to handle the situation while I moped around and pondered the meaning of humanity. Instead, I was the only person around. So, I forced myself to look. I made myself see precisely what the Pacificians had done.

As I did, my fists tightened, and my heartbeat quickened. Never had my resolve to kill the aliens been so palpable. But before I could get to that, I needed to right some wrongs. So, I strode forward to see if I could save the people in front of me.

CHAPTER FORTY-THREE

A QUESTION OF MIST

There's something so satisfying about creation. I can take a bunch of seemingly unrelated pieces and put them together to create something far greater than the sum of its parts. It doesn't matter if I'm cooking, brewing beer, or building cybernetics—if I could just spend the rest of my life creating useful things, I'd be happy.

—Patrick Ward

For the longest time, I just stood there and stared at the scene laid out before me. There were hundreds of pillars, each at least twenty or thirty yards wide and descending thousands of feet into a huge circular hole that went on farther than I could see. Mist danced in the air, almost visible to the naked eye as it coagulated around the pods along the surface of those cylinders. Because the pods were transparent, I could see that each one held a naked person.

After a few moments, I remembered where I was, and I shifted away from the hall's exit, but my stare never really broke away from those people. I didn't know what was going on. I didn't know why they'd been imprisoned in such a way. But the sight triggered me in a way nothing else really had. Suddenly, I remembered why I hated the aliens—not just the Pacificians—so much. I'd let that hatred dissipate a little, but it came back in full force. They were the enemy—not because of some inherent evil. Rather, they were because they were invaders, and more importantly, they were far more powerful than humanity. As such, they had no restrictions on their actions. If they chose to enslave us— or to treat us as livestock, as I'd seen in the E'rok Tan settlement—then there was no one who could oppose them.

If the situations were reversed, humanity would be no better. I knew that. Our history proved as much. However, the people of Earth had something no alien ever could. Chiefly, they were my people. I was one of them. As such, it was easy to separate everyone into two sides: them and us.

And I wanted my side to win, not because of some moral imperative, but because if we didn't, I would fall the same as everyone else. In that way, I was just as self-interested as anyone else.

Of course, that wasn't the only reason for my mounting anger. My mind—and everyone else's, I think—was far more complex than that. I hardly ever did anything for only one reason, and this instance was no different. That's where morality came in. That's where pity reared its ugly head. There were a hundred other emotions racing through my mind, but they all coalesced into a simple objective: I needed to save those people and destroy the infrastructure of their prison.

So, after taking a few deep breaths, I got close enough to the first pillar that I could use Misthack. Predictably, the security of the structure was incredibly dense, but my training had prepared me well. So, even though it took almost twenty minutes, I managed to infiltrate the system and learn a little about what was going on.

And it shocked me at how uncomplicated it was.

The basic premise was that people functioned as natural Mist accumulators—at least to a point. When I'd first Awakened, I could only hold a tiny amount of Mist, but as I'd grown more powerful—partly due to my climbing Mist attribute, but also because of my higher levels—that amount had significantly increased. When I reached the cap on what I could hold, the regeneration of my Mist stopped. However, so long as I was missing some part of my capacity, it continued until my reserves were full.

The purpose of the pods was to constantly drain the prisoners' Mist, which was then collected and redirected by the pillars. I had no idea where it was going—that much information wasn't contained in the prison's system—but I resolved to find out. To that end, I disconnected my mind from that system and went searching for a security terminal, which I found only a few minutes later.

To my disappointment, though, it contained very little additional information, which meant that my investigation needed to continue. However, before it did, I located the controls for the pods and, after a little trial and error, figured out how to free one of the prisoners. I watched as a robotic arm extended from the edge of the cylinder, then plucked one of the pods from the closest pillar. Then, it set the globe on a cradle along the edge of the pillar, and a few seconds later, a hundred small tubes snaked out to connect with the cell. Finally, the tubes drained the pod, which deflated like a leaky balloon before disappearing altogether.

I'd kept my distance throughout the process, but once it was completed, I cautiously approached, only to find that the man in question was entirely unresponsive. I tried using a med-hypo on him, but he didn't even flinch, and only a few seconds later, the life drained out of him.

I stared in shock as a claw descended from above, latched on to the body, and dragged it up and away. And just like that, there was no evidence that the man had ever even existed.

That's when I heard footsteps coming from the hall. Without Observation, I never would've known anyone was headed my way, but with the ability running, I could hear them coming from hundreds of yards away. So, I retreated to the wall just to the left of the hall and, cloaked in Stealth and Camouflage, waited.

My vigil didn't last long, and soon enough, two blond androids strode into view. It took a moment for me to recognize that one was male while the other was female. Both wore green robes and carried rifles that looked almost as advanced as my own.

"It is probably a glitch," said the woman, passing me by.

"Indeed. The system still has a plethora of bugs," the man replied from beside her. "Soon, we will finish our mission and perfect the system."

"I hope so."

"Hope is for the weak," the man said. "Together, we make our own hope."

"Together," the woman agreed.

I followed them as they went toward the cradle where I'd just watched a man die, but after investigating it for a few minutes, the woman said, "Premature harvest. The third this month."

"Down from seven last month. Improvement."

"Indeed," she agreed. "Perfection is imminent. Together, we shall overcome."

"Together," he echoed.

A few moments later, the pair enacted some process by which the remnants left behind by the pod were drained into the floor, then, once everything was gone, they headed back the way they'd come. That left me with a choice to make. Either I could follow them, or I could continue to explore the facility until I learned more about what was going on.

I chose the latter, largely because I had proven that I could traverse the base undetected. However, people tended to complicate things, and while the two I'd just encountered were incapable of detecting me, there was nothing to say that others within the facility would be similarly restricted. So, simple exploration seemed to be the better option.

With that in mind, I continued to search the prison, trying all the while to ignore the people within those pods. None were conscious, so at least they probably weren't in pain, but that was a small mercy next to the reality of their imprisonment. The Mist continued to swirl around me as I spent the next few hours searching the cavernous room. However, I found nothing of note, save for another hall that led deeper into the facility. I knew from the maps I'd managed to download that it would loop around and connect to the yet-unexplored part of the base.

The connecting corridor was identical to the one I'd left behind, and it soon led me past a series of storage rooms. However, instead of drums filled with liquid metal, they contained complex components. If they'd been any smaller, I would have pocketed a few. However, my arsenal implant was too limited for that, so I noted the area before moving on.

Eventually, my exploration led me to an unmarked lift that descended farther underground. I didn't dare activate it on my own—I felt certain that doing so would trigger some warning within the facility's security system—so I settled down to wait for someone else to activate it. I got what I was looking for a couple of hours later when a group of green-robed Pacificians took the lift down below.

I rode along with them, undetected.

As the lift descended, I crouched in one of the corners. There were no rails, so the Pacificians were all clustered in the center, which gave me plenty of room to wait without the danger of running into one of them.

After a few seconds, the lift sped up until it descended into an enormous cavern. If it was less than a mile long, I would have been very surprised, and it was at least twice as wide and three times as deep. In short, it was an absolutely awe-inspiring space. But what was even more shocking was the contents.

Ships.

Each one at least twice the size of *The Leviathan*. However, where *The Leviathan* was clearly meant for transport and exploration, these were obviously machines of war. Sleek and bristling with weapons, the ships were far more advanced than anything I had ever seen before. That wasn't saying much, really, but the sight took me aback nonetheless.

As the lift continued to descend, I saw more details of what I suspected was a shipyard. There were black- and brown-robed Pacificians scurrying all around, but I couldn't really make much sense of what they were doing. I just assumed that they were building the ships, which, for all their size, were clearly incomplete.

When the lift finally reached the shipyard floor, I discreetly left it behind and found a secluded corner of the enormous chamber so I could continue my reconnaissance. However, even after a couple of hours, I hadn't managed to gather any more pertinent information. So, I continued on, looking for a terminal I could use to gather intelligence.

It took a while, but eventually, I found my way to what I suspected was the shipyard's command center. It was populated by more green-robed Pacificians, which spoke to its importance. More importantly, it housed precisely the terminals I'd been searching for. So, over the next hour, I slowly made my way inside, slipping through doors behind unsuspecting androids so as not to leave any record of my passage behind.

I didn't know if they paid attention to how many times the doors opened, but I wasn't going to take any chances. Not when I was so deep behind enemy lines and I had an opportunity to undermine their entire operation.

Eventually, I found my way to the command structure's operational center, where I waited for an opportunity to jack into the system. I didn't dare use Misthack, largely because it was very limited, both in scope and in the amount of access it could give. Instead, I intended to use my personal link to infiltrate the system directly.

The only problem with that was that the Pacificians, being androids, didn't really take many breaks. And when they did, others took their places. The whole thing operated with robotic efficiency, which made my task that much more difficult.

Still, no system is without flaws, and I merely had to wait until an opportunity presented itself. As it happened, I had to wait most of a day, which I spent crouched in a corner, my presence masked behind my abilities, before I finally got an opening.

The green-robed technician at the terminal told her colleague that she needed to refuel—which I took to mean that she was going to eat her dinner—which gave me the opportunity to creep closer, extend my personal link, and access her terminal. There were a half dozen other technicians in the room, but because of my abilities, none of them even knew I was there. However, I knew that if I didn't push through the terminal's defenses with alacrity, my intrusion into the system would quickly be detected.

Thankfully, I had plenty of practice doing just that, so I bent my will to the task, and one node at a time, the Mistwall fell before me. The puzzles—or locks, I suppose—weren't that difficult to overcome, but that tracked with everything I had seen so far. The Pacificians hadn't invested much time or effort in their security, and I could understand why. Their base was on the moon, and as such, it was almost entirely inaccessible to their enemies. Moreover, it took a very specific confluence of skills to infiltrate such a facility. It just so happened that I was equipped with precisely the right abilities to do just that.

And I wasn't going to squander the opportunity.

Over the next few minutes, I toppled one lock after another until, at last, their system was laid bare before me. I didn't take the time to read any of the files. I knew I was on the clock, so I simply downloaded as much information as I could, sequestering it in a specially made partition of my own system, before retracting my personal link and returning to my corner.

The entire operation had only taken five or six minutes, but in that time, I had mined enough data to fuel months of research. Soon enough, the female Pacifician returned, and when she opened the door, I used that opportunity to leave the command center behind. Retracing my steps, I quickly found an unused storeroom where I could settle in and rest while studying the information I had just acquired.

As I ate a ration bar and sipped from a bottle of water I'd had stored in my arsenal implant, I found my mind wandering back to thoughts of Earth. I'd been gone for a while, but that wasn't terribly abnormal. Sometimes, my various missions took weeks to complete. However, I usually kept in touch with Patrick, which was impossible given my current location. Was he worried? Or did he trust that I could handle whatever life threw my way?

Probably the latter.

He'd never shown anything but confidence in my abilities, and I didn't think he was going to choose now to start doubting me. That was comforting, after a fashion. Sure, he was wrong. There were plenty of situations I wasn't equipped to overcome. But his unwavering confidence in me made me want to live up to what he saw when he looked at me.

Once I'd finished eating, I took a few hours to sleep. I knew it was a risk, but I'd been going almost constantly for far too long without rest, and I knew that if I kept going like that, I'd start making serious mistakes. To ensure my safety, I used Bastion on the storage closet, trusting in *The Leviathan*'s built-in security systems to protect it back on Earth. And if someone managed to breach those systems, then . . . Well, it was just a trade-off I had to make. The ship was important, but I wasn't going to compromise my personal safety just to keep someone from stealing it.

Over the next couple of days, I rested and recovered. I hadn't been in any real fights since coming to the moon base, but I still hadn't fully healed from my brief brush with the lunar atmosphere. For all my abilities and inflated attributes, I was still human, after all. And nobody could have stood before that wave of cold, radiation, and lack of air without consequences.

Maybe my uncle could have, I amended. He'd survived for some time after being beheaded, after all. Surely, he could withstand extreme temperatures and a lack of oxygen.

I still had a long way to go before I reached that level.

As I recovered, I delved into the files I had stolen. At first, I had to wade through miles of irrelevant data, but eventually, I found my way to the important information. And as I read, my anger began to mount.

On the surface, the system wasn't complicated. The prisoners I had encountered were being used as Mist accumulators so that the Pacificians had the means to empower their fleet of ships and satellites. Without them, they'd have needed literal tons of Rift Shards—and not low-grade ones, either.

All those people imprisoned and eventually killed, and for what? So the Pacificians could save a bit of money? It was unconscionable.

But it was nothing compared to what I learned as I read further.

Those people weren't just random prisoners. They'd all volunteered, after a fashion. Of course, they'd thought their minds would be transferred to android bodies. The reality, though, was that the low-level Pacificians I'd seen back on Earth were just copies. Mind and body. The real people were sedated and sent to the moon to become batteries for the Pacificians' impending invasion of Earth.

What really tipped me over the edge was that the Pacificians actually were capable of following through with the promises they'd made. They could insert a human mind—or any other race's, really—into an android body. That was what they'd done with the higher-level Pacificians like the green-robed aliens I'd seen within the facility. But they'd chosen not to, taking the easier route of making simple copies.

The reality of it made my blood boil, and if I hadn't been determined to undermine the Pacificians before, I certainly was by the time I finished reading those files.

And now that I had all the information I needed, I started making a plan. It wouldn't be easy, but I intended to destroy the entire facility. Then, I would take the fight to Earth. They wanted a war? Well, now they had one, even if they didn't know it yet.

CHAPTER FORTY-FOUR

REEMERGENCE

In the old world, people had the luxury of solving their problems peacefully. But now? It feels like war is inevitable, and I don't think humanity is ready for those kinds of stakes.

—Patrick Ward

I searched through the compound, which was at least the size of a small city, looking for supplies. I only had so much room in my arsenal implant, and most of that had been reserved for necessities like ration bars, water, and ammunition, which didn't leave a lot of space for bombs. I had a few—enough to bring down a couple of buildings, certainly—but they weren't nearly enough for what I had in mind. Fortunately, there was a lot of overlap between ship- and satellite-making materials and the building blocks for explosives. I just had to gather them, then put them together, and finally, deploy the fruits of my labor.

Of course, there were other complications, like the fact that I had no way back to Earth. I had some ideas about how to go about that task, but they would all require me to add a few steps to my plans. For now, though, I would focus on the first step, which was to gather enough supplies that I could bring the lunar base down, with all the aliens inside.

To that end, I stalked through the halls, searching the various storage areas for appropriate materials. The first thing I needed was a catalyst, which I found after only a few hours when I stumbled upon a giant warehouse filled with barrels of liquified Mist. From the files I had stolen, I knew it was extremely volatile in that state—in fact, it was meant to power the satellites' main weapons, which in turn would be powerful enough to destroy whole cities—so I only had to take a couple of barrels to satisfy the needs of my purpose.

Thankfully, my Basic Explosives Handling ability that came with [Field-craft] was all I needed to safely handle the unstable substance. Once I had those two barrels stored snugly in my arsenal implant, I headed to a seldom-used corner of the facility and found an even more isolated storage room, where I removed the barrels and headed back out to find the other materials I needed.

My next goal was something that would ignite the liquified Mist. For that, I had to plunder the parts meant for the ships' engines. It would require some adjustment on my part to make it work properly, but that was what Improvisation and the oft-ignored Tinkering were for. I wasn't capable of building things as well as Patrick, but my abilities, especially in conjunction with Basic Explosives Handling, meant that making bombs was well within my wheelhouse.

Next, I needed to create remote detonators. What I had in mind was sophisticated enough that I didn't want to try to cobble something together. So, I chose to use the much smaller explosives I had in my arsenal implant. I'd have to dismantle them to get what I needed, but that wasn't such a big deal, considering I'd made them in the first place.

Finally, to give the new bombs a bit more punch, I intended to use some of the BMAP's incredibly destructive ordinance. This was the most difficult task because those shells were far more advanced than anything I could ever hope to create. Taking them apart and repurposing their pieces was easier, but only marginally so. Regardless, I'd done it before—albeit in much more appropriate circumstances, and with all the safety gear I could handle—so I didn't shy away from the task.

Still, as I set about dismantling those shells, my heart pounded out of my chest, and sweat poured down my face. But my hands remained steady as, over the next few hours, I did precisely what I intended to do.

And just like that, I had everything I needed to make a half dozen demolition charges whose yield was high enough that I couldn't even calculate how much damage I was going to do. I could only hope that it would prove to be enough to destroy the lunar base. Before I could figure all that out, though, I needed to actually assemble the bombs.

Once again, it took every ounce of focus I could muster, and even then, I had no idea if it would be enough, but over the next eight hours, I managed to put everything together. By the time I'd finished, I had six of the most powerful demolition charges I'd ever seen. I also had one barrel of liquified Mist left over, but I had plans for that, too.

So, with the first part of my plan done, I took a few hours to rest before embarking on the second task: planting the bombs. This proved significantly easier, but because I had to remain in Stealth the entire time, it took almost an entire day to place the half dozen charges throughout the compound. I tried to conceal them as best I could, but I knew that they would eventually be discovered. So, planting the bombs put me on the clock.

Without waiting to rest, I stopped by the warehouse where I'd first entered the compound, picked up the barrel I'd left behind, and unloaded the solid pieces of metal I'd packed back into it, before shoving it into my arsenal implant. Thankfully, I had just enough room.

Then, I started in on the third task: securing my exit. I knew good and well that this part of the plan would prove the trickiest. I was well suited to sneaking around the facility, especially given the passive state of the Pacificians' defenses. They had no reason to suspect that anyone could—or would—infiltrate their facility, and so, they were anything but alert.

That was soon going to change, and back in Fortune, I had discovered that they were more than capable of defeating me.

So, I had to be careful about fulfilling the parameters of my next task, which would involve me hunting down the compound's communications array, taking out any technicians inside, and calling for help. Once that was done, I would need to quickly escape the compound before detonating the charges.

And somehow, I would need to survive the ensuing explosion.

Initially, I'd considered trying to hijack one of the ships I'd found in the second hangar. However, I'd decided against it for two major reasons. For one, I had no idea how to fly those ships. Perhaps I could figure it out, but doing so would take time I probably didn't have. And there was always the possibility that I wouldn't be able to fly them at all. Again, I could probably get around any locks via my {Mistrunner} abilities, but there was no guarantee.

No—hijacking a ship was a bad idea that had way too many variables, which was why it was my backup plan. I would go down that route if I had to but only if my first option failed.

So, after planting the bombs in out-of-the-way locations throughout the facility, I headed back to the central command post where I'd stolen the files. The communications hub was located in a completely different room, but it was in the same area. So, I used the same route that I'd used before to infiltrate the area.

When I reached my destination, I noted that there were six technicians and two guards assigned to the communications hub. More than I would've liked but less than I'd expected. The Pacificians' security really was lax, and rightly so. I'd only infiltrated their facility by mistake, and there were probably only a handful of people in the world who had the skills to do what I intended to do. At best. There was also the very real possibility that I was entirely unique, at least on Earth.

Still, I was getting ahead of myself. I had a long way to go before I could start patting myself on the back.

To that end, I stalked forward and planted myself in the corner of the communications hub. It was still much closer than I would have liked, but I only had so many options. There were no convenient air vents or alleys this time, so I had to work with what I had available.

Once I was in place, I crouched down and used Misthack to initiate my infiltration. Overcoming the Pacificians' defenses was laughably easy, and I managed to bypass them in only a few seconds, which brought up the first Misthack menu:

Misthack successful. Options:
Reboot system
Overcharge
Disable cybernetics
Upload Ghost

I chose the fourth option, which brought up the Ghost menu:

Please select deck:
Assassination
Infiltration
Robot Disposal
Mass Murder
Annoyances
Wild Cards

I selected the third option, Robot Disposal, which brought up the final menu:

Select Ghost:
Scramble (Mk. XVII)
Explode (Mk. CXII)
Mass Disable (Mk. II)
Cascade (Mk. XXIV)
Drain (Mk. VII)

I chose the third option, which I'd created specifically for dealing with the Pacificians. *Mass Disable* wasn't a terribly potent Ghost. Nor was it complicated. The idea was a blend of *Time Bomb* and Disable Cybernetics, though with a few tweaks to make them work better against the robotic Pacificians. Its effect was just as the name suggested. Once I used it on a single enemy, it would gestate for a few moments before jumping to another. Then another after that.

It had a short range, and the ensuing disability would only last for about forty-five seconds, but for my purposes, it was more than enough to get the job done.

Once I'd uploaded the *Mass Disable*, I rocked back on my heels to wait for it to take effect. I could feel the Mist swirling—only slightly—as it leaped from one Pacifician to the next, and within a minute, every android in the room had been affected. Then, forty-five seconds later, they started to drop. At first, none of them noticed, but by the time the second one fell dormant, they started to react.

Before they could, I pounced.

My goal wasn't to kill them. Not yet. Instead, I only wanted to stall for time while the Ghost took effect. However, even that wasn't the easy task I would've liked it to be. My first mistake was dismissing the technicians and focusing all my attention on the guards, and it nearly got my killed when one of them leaped upon my back. I reacted in just enough time to use her momentum to flip her over my shoulder, but it was a close enough call that I knew I couldn't afford to discount any of them.

The battle that ensued was short and frustrating, and it was all I could do to keep them from calling for reinforcements. Thankfully, with every passing second, my Ghost had time to complete its gestation, and one by one, they fell dormant. Once the last one deactivated, the slaughter began.

With my nano-bladed sword, I hacked at the back of the first android's neck. It took me three swings to destroy the Nexus Implant and dislodge its head, but when it fell away, I saw a mixture of flesh, blood, and robotics that I hadn't expected. Vaguely, I recalled the Pacificians being described as organic robots, but even though I'd fought some of them before, this was the first time I'd encountered the reality of their composition.

The ones back on Earth had been different. They were entirely mechanical, which suggested that they weren't real Pacificians. Or perhaps it was because they were lower ranked. Whatever the case, I didn't have time to establish any theories. The moment I'd commenced my attack, the clock had started ticking. If I wanted to survive, I needed to get a move on.

To that end, I crossed to the communications apparatus, jacked into the terminal via my personal link, and used Mistwalk to infiltrate the system. In less than a minute, I had complete access, which I used in conjunction with Secure Connection to contact Patrick.

"Mira? I've been trying to contact you for the past—"

"No time to explain," I said, interrupting him before he could even ask the obvious question. "Long story short, I'm on the moon, and I need a pickup. Can you do it?"

"You took *The Leviathan*. I don't have a ship to—"

"Shit," I muttered. I had completely forgotten that I'd left the ship hidden outside of the Ithid settlement. It was only a few hundred miles from Fortune, but without a ship, Patrick would have to use more mundane transportation. The result was that, even if he could immediately find a viable ride, it would be hours before he managed to complete the trip. My heart sank. "I didn't think of that."

"I can make it work, Mira. Just give me—"

"No time," I repeated. "I'm about to blow this base up, and I don't think I can wait around for a few more hours."

It was true. If I'd thought of the issue beforehand . . . Well, even then, I'd have had to disable the Pacificians in the communications hub. As such, there was no way I could have made it work.

"Okay," I said. "I think I might have another plan. But if I don't get in touch with you in the next few hours, I need you to come get me, okay? I don't know if I can survive that long, but . . . Well, just come get me, okay?"

"The moon is a pretty big place, Mira . . ."

"Just start at the newest crater and expand your search from there."

"Crater? Mira, how big of an explosion are you going to make?"

"Honestly, I'm not sure. Big, though. Really big."

It would have to be, considering the size of the compound. But given how much liquified Mist I'd used, there was every chance that I might've overdone it a little.

"Look . . . In case I don't make it . . ."

"Mira . . ."

"I love you, Pick," I said. There was so much more that I wanted to say, but I just didn't have the time to do so. And even if I had hours, I probably wouldn't have known what to say. For better or worse, talking about my feelings had never been one of my talents. "I just love you, and I'm going to do everything I can to make it through this."

"I . . . I love you, too," he said. "Just . . . Just survive, Mira. Just survive."

I could tell that he wanted to say more, as well. Unlike me, he was eloquent enough to do so. But the time constraints hadn't faded.

"I will. I'll see you soon."

"Yeah. See you later."

Then, I cut the feed. For a long moment, I just stood there staring ahead, hoping against hope that I hadn't just spoken my last words to Patrick. Dying was one thing. I was prepared for that. But I wasn't sure if he could handle losing me, and even if he could, he'd end up miserable. That was gratifying, after a fashion, but it also shoved the weight of responsibility onto my shoulders.

I needed to survive. Not for my own good, but for his mental well-being.

With that resolution in mind, I made another call, this time to someone I really didn't want to speak to.

When it went through, I said, "Before you say anything, I just want you to know that I really didn't want to do this. But if you can come through for me here, I'm in. I'll kill all the aliens you want me to kill."

"Such a turnaround, Miss Braddock," said Alistaris. "And unless I'm reading this incorrectly, you're contacting me from the moon? I'm sure there's a story behind that."

"There is," I said. "But I don't have time. What I need from you is for you to come pick me up and get me back to Earth. I know you have the means to smuggle me past the quarantine. In return, I'll join your little party. Deal?"

He must have sensed my urgency because he didn't ask any other questions before saying, "Deal."

Then, I told him my plan. His tone told me that he was skeptical it could work, but he went along with it, anyway. Perhaps because I was expendable, and even if I didn't survive, I would still take out a group whose philosophy clearly ran counter to his.

Which was a bit suspicious, given the chain of events, but I didn't have time to put the pieces together. Instead, I pushed those thoughts to the back of my mind and focused on finishing my self-imposed mission.

Oh, and trying to survive, of course. That was a priority, as well.

Once I had an understanding with Alistaris, I cut the communication and reentered Stealth. It was just in time, too, because a moment later, a pair of guards rushed into the room. I used the distraction of them finding the bodies to exit the hub before quickly retracing my steps to the hangar containing the half-assembled ships. By that point, the place was swarming with armed Pacificians.

More importantly, I saw more than a few drones that were equipped with incredibly potent sensors. I knew from past experience that, if they came within range, even my Stealth ability wouldn't allow me to avoid detection.

Fortunately, I had ways around that.

So, for the next hour, I slowly made my way through the hanger. Along the way, I dodged drones and avoided the warriors. The drones I couldn't avoid soon fell victim to my *Scramble* Ghost, which, as the name implied, briefly blocked their sensory capabilities. Usually, I used it on cameras, but it was just as useful against surveillance drones.

Eventually, I reached the hall, which only made avoiding detection that much more difficult. With the narrow confines of the corridor combined with the swarming Pacificians, I had more than a few close calls before I finally reached the secondary hangar. There, I saw my way out.

The ships were blocky and looked anything but aerodynamic, which suggested they were intended only for space travel. But for my purposes, they would do just fine. The only issue was that they were surrounded by warriors.

My first instinct was to simply upload *Time Bomb* and wait for them all to die. But they were a little too spread out for that to work very well. Besides, with the base on high alert, it was only a matter of time before the Pacificians found my bombs. If that happened, my entire plan would be for naught. No—I needed to get out, and in a hurry. Otherwise, all my effort would have been for nothing.

So, after marking a route through the hangar, I took a deep breath, then set off. Even if everything went according to my plans—which I knew was extremely unlikely—I was in for a difficult road.

What was new, right?

By that point, being in mortal danger was almost normal for me.

CHAPTER FORTY-FIVE

OVERDOING IT

When Mira told me she was on the moon, I half expected her to tell me that she was going to use that as an opportunity to escape the situation on Earth. But in retrospect, I know that doing so never even crossed her mind.

—Patrick Ward

Still cloaked in Stealth, I stalked forward until the Pacificians came into range of Misthack. However, when I tried to infiltrate one of their systems, I got quite a surprise. The moment my awareness touched the Mistwall, it surged forward and enveloped my consciousness. It was only through a quick use of Rewind that I managed to avoid being completely overwhelmed.

It seemed that my enemies were prepared for a fight with someone like me. Perhaps they'd discovered my handiwork back in the communications hub. Or maybe their new defenses were raised the moment the alarm had been sounded. Whatever the case, using my {Mistrunner} abilities was not an option.

Which meant that I had no choice but to do things the old-fashioned way.

I stared across the hangar at my destination. It was a blocky ship that looked completely incapable of flight, which suggested that it was never intended to enter Earth's—or any other planet's—atmosphere. Instead, it was a spacefaring ship whose designers never had to worry about drag or aerodynamics.

But they could've at least made some concessions to cosmetics. Instead, they'd been content with designing a ship that looked like nothing so much as a trash can with a giant jet engine strapped to one end. Shaking my head, I reasoned that there was no accounting for taste.

Or maybe Pacificians, with their android bodies and pseudo-collective consciousness, didn't put much stock in appearances. Whatever the case, the way the thing looked didn't matter much for my plan, which consisted of tearing through a few hundred Pacificians, boarding the ship, and breaking free of the base. After that, I intended to put as much distance as possible between me and the facility before blowing it to smithereens. Once that was done, I'd contact Alistaris so he could come pick me up.

Simple, right?

But also difficult, considering that the Pacificians were obviously ready for me. Originally, I'd hoped to take them out with a Ghost like *Time Bomb*, but with whatever was blocking my access to their interfaces, that was just impossible.

As I'd thought before, there was no real choice but to do things the old-fashioned way. And I couldn't take my sweet time while doing it, either. Every passing second meant that they were that much closer to discovering my bombs. Those explosives weren't sophisticated enough to resist attempts at disarmament, either. So, if they were found, all my efforts would have been for naught.

No—I needed to get through that crowd of Pacifician warriors, and I had to do it with some urgency.

Fortunately, I had plenty of experience with that kind of thing. So, without any further hesitation, I retrieved a few spherical objects from my arsenal implant and, with an underhanded throw, sent them bouncing across the polished hangar floor.

The sound of those metallic devices hitting the floor was loud in the comparatively silent hangar, and in an instant, a hundred Pacifician weapons were aimed in their direction. However, they clearly hadn't expected a few silver balls, and as such, they hesitated before opening fire.

It was precisely the delay I'd hoped for, and soon enough, the balls rolled into position and exploded.

However, they had never been intended to hurt the Pacificians. Instead, because I was worried about damaging the ship that was my way out of the facility—and because I'd used most of my explosives to cobble together the bombs I'd left throughout the base—I'd chosen to use a trio of smoke bombs I'd had in my arsenal implant for months.

Usually, I didn't use them because they didn't really offer much utility that I couldn't get more easily with my abilities. But this was an opportunity for the little bombs to shine.

They exploded into dense white smoke that quickly spread throughout the hangar. A few Pacificians panicked and fired their weapons, but by that point, I was already among them, slashing out with my nano-bladed sword when I got close enough for them to detect my presence.

For the first dozen feet, it worked incredibly well, and for a moment, I thought I'd make it to the ship without issue. However, that hope was dashed when, suddenly, the drones came alive with a buzzing sound that echoed throughout the hangar. A moment later, the smoke—or fog, really—began to dissipate as the Mist that powered it was drained away.

I was still cloaked in Stealth, but that, too, dropped away only a second later when the drones emitted a piercing screech that forcibly cancelled the ability. I stumbled at the shock of it all, but I turned that into a roll as I stored my blade away, exchanging it for the Dragon.

Wheeling around, I let the weapon roar.

A dozen Pacificians fell to that initial burst, but these aliens were a cut above my typical enemies. So, even though the weapon was devastating, they quickly adjusted by deploying a series of directional Mist shields that looked like panes of blue glass. The Dragon's issue still tore into them, and I saw the shields waver before its might, but I knew I'd never get through them before reinforcements arrived.

So, I tossed a handful of flash-bangs out before stowing the Dragon and sprinting forward. As I did, a few of the Pacificians took aim, and I felt a series of shots thud into my hip. A quick glance at my health silhouette told me that those rounds hadn't made it through my infiltration suit or my subdermal armor, but they'd significantly undermined the integrity of my defenses. Only a few more hits, and they'd start doing some serious damage.

As I closed on the line of Mist-shielded Pacificians, I summoned my oft-ignored scattergun. Without aiming, I let it loose, sending a web of lightning crashing into those shields. It wasn't enough to bring them down, but it had the distinct benefit of sending hundreds of ripples across the shields' blue surfaces, obscuring my enemies' vision.

I leaped, then, when I reached the apex of the maneuver, used Double Jump. Rare was the opportunity to use the ability, mostly because it was far inferior to using Teleport. However, it had the distinct advantage of costing almost no Mist, which was a feature Teleport certainly couldn't claim. Even so, there weren't that many situations where it would be useful, so like my scatter-gun, it was usually ignored.

I sprang off a cushion of Mist, doubling the height of my jump, which allowed me to sail over the first line of Pacifician defenders. As I did, I pulsed Balance and twisted in midair before summoning my assault rifle and aiming at my enemies' suddenly exposed heads. The weapon barked, tearing through them without difficulty.

I knew it wouldn't kill them. They were far too durable for that. But I also suspected that they would have trouble seeing if their heads were half-destroyed. And if they couldn't see, they'd have a hard time shooting me.

After all, I didn't care about taking them out. The bombs would take care of that. Instead, all I wanted was to get through them. To that end, when I landed, rolling with my momentum before coming to my feet at a dead sprint, I didn't even bother looking back. Instead, I juked left, then right, zigzagging my way across the hangar as I sprayed bullets at anyone in front of me.

At the same time, I continued to toss out various grenades. None were meant to do damage. In fact, most of them were just prototypes I had stored in my arsenal implant in hopes of working on them in my downtime. Quite a few of them didn't even work properly. However, they all added to the chaos as I steadily sprinted toward the ship.

When I drew within range, I was very nearly decapitated by a blade that I only saw a second before it took my head off. I dropped to a slide that quickly became a roll. I found my feet just in time to see my attacker.

On the surface, he looked just like every other Pacifician I'd encountered. Blond hair. Blue eyes. A perfect facade for the robotic monster beneath. However, unlike his fellow androids, he wore a smirk on his handsome face.

He also held the largest sword I'd ever seen.

"Compensating for something?" I managed to say before he launched himself at me with an overhand attack that was so fast that it bordered on teleportation. I dodged to the side, narrowly avoiding the attack. The blade crashed into the floor, cutting a long groove in the metallic surface.

He yanked the blade away, but before he could recover and attack me again, I raised my rifle and sent a burst of gunfire his way.

That got a flinch.

Just a simple shudder as the bullets hit him. Nothing more.

"Shit," I mumbled.

He didn't respond. He didn't even acknowledge my gunfire. Instead, he rushed me, swinging that giant sword like it weighed no more than a feather. And it took everything I had to avoid being cut in half. Over the next few moments, I used every point of my enhanced Constitution to keep from being hacked apart. I used every ability I had at my disposal, as well, but he countered everything without difficulty.

I used Disengage, putting some distance between us, but that first clash had made something abundantly clear: I was completely outmatched.

And even those few seconds of delay had given the other Pacificians time to recover. Already, they'd started to close. In a moment, they would bury me under a barrage of gunfire. I needed to change the dynamic of the encounter. Otherwise, I wouldn't have a chance.

So, after glancing back toward the swordsman—who'd begun to advance—I came up with a plan.

That's when I turned and ran.

That seemed to surprise him, but that only lasted a second before he poured on the speed. In barely an instant, he caught up to me. But I was ready for it. When he reached me, I summoned my nano-blade and activated Riposte.

When my blade met his, I felt the force of it drive me into the ground. However, my ability endured, and I used that momentum to my advantage by letting it spin me around. My sword lashed out, neatly slicing through the tendon at the back of his ankle.

He stumbled.

And once again, I ran.

This time, though, I didn't use my feet, and I certainly didn't intend to keep going in the same direction I'd gone before. Instead, I used Teleport.

Instantly, I was standing at the ship's entry hatch. I yanked it open and dove inside, dragging it shut behind me, locking it the moment it was closed. Only an instant later, something hit the ship with enough force to nearly tip it over. Clearly, the swordsman had recovered, and he was very unhappy with the turn of events. Another impact sent a tremor through the ship, but I ignored it as I raced toward the controls.

As I'd expected, they were alien, and I had no idea what I was looking at. I didn't even know how to turn the thing on. Thankfully, I had a way around that. Even as a third impact hit the ship, I yanked my personal link from the Hand of God and jammed it into the ship's terminal.

Its defenses were laughable, and a moment later, my abilities translated the ship's controls, and I ignited the Mist engines. Thankfully, they spun to life within a couple of seconds, and I took off.

My next hurdle was the hangar doors, which remained shut. I solved that issue by taking control of the ship's weapon systems and creating my own exit. Even as I flew free—with a good deal less grace than if I was flying the familiar *Leviathan*—I heard another impact.

Clearly, the swordsman wasn't going to give up just because I'd escaped the facility. He was also obviously resistant to the extreme temperatures and lack of oxygen. Did androids have to breathe? Apparently not, as evidenced by his continued attempts to break into the ship.

I gained altitude, racing across the surface of the moon as I put as much distance between me and the base. Still, he continued his assault, banging against the door with enough force to send tremors through the ship.

I knew it could only take so much, but I also knew that I didn't have time to deal with him. So, I continued to pour on speed until, at last, I reached what I deemed to be a safe distance. I pulled the detonator from my arsenal implant, then pressed the appropriate series of buttons.

When my bombs exploded, the first thought that crossed my mind was that my idea of safe did not really correlate to reality.

A massive shock wave swept across the surface of the moon, catching the ship in its momentum. If I'd had a skill like Patrick, or if I'd been using the actual flight controls, I might have managed to keep it steady. But I didn't. And so, the ship went spinning through the thin atmosphere before colliding with a barren mountain.

It didn't stop there, either.

For miles, the ship tumbled across the lunar landscape. I tried to hold on, but at some point, my grip failed, and I was sent banging across the interior of the ship until, at last, I was knocked unconscious.

When I awoke a few minutes later, I was assailed by the sound of an alarm Klaxon. Red lights flashed, and I saw cracks spreading across the front window. Clearly, the integrity of the ship's hull had been breached, and it was only a matter of time before it failed entirely.

I picked myself up, noting that I was riddled with contusions, and I had more than a few broken bones. Most distressing was that my shin felt like it had been snapped in two. I didn't take the time to consult my interface, but I suspected that I'd have to take some drastic measures if I was going to avoid a lengthy recovery time.

Pushing those thoughts out of mind, I limped toward the ship's controls and, once again, tapped into the terminal. Once there, I found the communications array and used it to establish a Secure Connection with Alistaris.

"What did you do?!" he screamed, the first time I'd heard him lose his composure.

"I did what I said I was going to do," I stated as calmly as I could manage. It wasn't easy, given the amount of pain I was in. I also suspected I had a concussion, which made things even more difficult.

"You blew up half the moon!"

"That means I got all of them," I said, though I was more than a little distressed by his characterization of my efforts. I hoped he was being hyperbolic. "Look—I don't have much time. Can you track this signal?"

"Yes, but—"

"Okay. When you get here, I'm going to be in a barrel," I said. As I spoke, I dragged the stolen barrel out of my arsenal implant. "I don't have that much oxygen left, and when my ship's hull fails, I won't have much protection from the atmosphere. So, you'd better hurry up if you intend to save me."

"I should just let you die," Alistaris said. "The ramifications of what you just did . . ."

"Your choice. But think about what I just did. Think about pointing me at your enemies," I said, popping the top off the barrel. "Like I said before, I'm in. You want me to fight a war for you? Well, this is just my first step."

I heard him sigh before he said, "Fine. But let me know if you want to blow up any other celestial bodies."

"No promises," I said as I climbed into the barrel. Just as I did, the hull finally failed, and the oxygen within the ship raced out into the atmosphere. I pulled the barrel closed, dragged my respirator out of my arsenal implant, and settled in to wait. It was a few more minutes before the cold started to seep in, but it wasn't long after that before I felt my muscles start to lock up.

After about ten minutes, I felt the barrel jostling around, indicating that Alistaris had found me. However, only a few moments later, I heard muffled gunfire before everything went silent.

Soon, the motion of the barrel once again started, and only a little time later, the cold began to dissipate. Finally, the barrel popped open, and I pushed myself to my feet. I knew I made for a gruesome sight. I'd been through quite a battle, and the effects of the cold couldn't have been pretty. Still, I managed a smile when I saw Alistaris.

"Thanks for the pickup," I said.

Then, I collapsed. I didn't lose consciousness—I wasn't going to let that happen when I still wasn't entirely sure of the Dengyt's intentions—but I definitely wasn't completely aware as someone dragged me onto a stretcher.

"I have no idea how you're still alive," the gnome said as he loomed over my prone form.

"Just lucky, I guess," I mumbled before coughing up blood. Where that had come from, I had no idea. Clearly, I had some internal injuries.

But I had survived, and I had struck the first real blow against the aliens. That was a comfort. I coughed again, splattering blood all over my chin.

A small comfort, but a comfort nonetheless.

CHAPTER FORTY-SIX

THE NEXT STEP

When Mira blew up the moon, it was like a starting gun had gone off. Suddenly, the aliens were very aware that humanity had no intention of going down without a fight.

—Patrick Ward

The trip back to the surface was uneventful, though I did learn something extremely disturbing along the way. I sat in Alistaris's ship, which was a purpose-built smuggling vessel intended to get through quarantines and blockades. According to him, at least. I had no reason to distrust that, considering he'd just saved my life. Granted, he had his reasons for doing so—he wanted me to fight a war for him—but in my mind, that didn't really matter all that much. All I really cared about was that, without his intervention, I'd have died a lonely, cold death on the lunar surface.

In any case, that subject had been relegated to a position in the back of my mind as I watched the battle play out on a floating screen. In the video, I saw the battered form of the swordsman ripping his way through a mostly destroyed ship. I recognized the vessel as the one I'd worked so hard to board so I could ensure my escape.

Just as the swordsman ripped his way through the ship's fuselage, someone off-screen fired an energy weapon that tore a hole in his torso. That didn't immediately put him down, so he was quickly buried under a barrage of similar ordnance. He succumbed a few moments later.

"That guy was a real tank," I said.

Alistaris, who was sitting across from me, turned off the video, and a second later, the screen disappeared. I had no idea where it had gone, but it was just further evidence that I really didn't know anything about the wider universe.

"Indeed," the gnome said, running a hand through his white hair. The ship had been built for the much shorter Dengyts, so I was more than a little cramped in the small space. "That was Edrax Kel Tanimvan."

"Is that supposed to mean anything to me?"

"I suppose not," Alistaris allowed. "Suffice it to say that he is to his people as you are to yours. There is a great deal of mystery surrounding him, not least because he's been seen in multiple places at once. I had no idea he was even in this sector, much less in a hidden base on that little moon of yours."

"You didn't know about the moon base?"

"We did not," Alistaris admitted. "A shortcoming that will be the subject of some discipline, I assure you."

I sighed. If the well-informed Dengyts were ignorant of the base, then it was probably safe to assume that no one else had known about it, either. I'd only stumbled upon it by accident, after all.

"You've done the universe a great service," Alistaris went on. "That base . . . Do you know what it was?"

"They were building satellites and ships," I answered. "I'm guessing they intended it as a staging area for an invasion once the quarantine drops."

"Indeed. If that were to happen . . . We don't have the resources to fight such a force," he said.

"Why?"

"I'm sorry?"

"Why don't you have the resources?" I asked, leaning forward. Never before had I ever felt grateful for my relatively short stature. If I'd have been as tall as my uncle, I'd have been truly cramped in the tight space of the ship's cabin. "Seriously. If those android assholes could build a fleet of satellites up there, then why couldn't you? Why do you even need me?"

"We don't," he said.

"That's not what you said before."

"We want you. We don't need you. Your planet does, though. The fact of the matter is that this little world isn't that important to us. There are resources here, but nothing we can't get elsewhere and far more easily. The only reason I'm here at all is to oppose the Gomari Confederation."

"The Pacificians. Are they part of this group?"

"Allies. Not members. The Pacificians are one of the independent factions, and they span across multiple galaxies."

"Well, I'm killing them," I announced.

"You can't kill all of them."

"Sure I can. It just might take me a while," I stated. "I'll start with that city they planted on top of a mountain. Then I'll hunt down any other bases they might have. And once I get off Earth, I'll go to wherever they're holed up and kill them there, too."

"You say that like it'll be easy."

"Easy to say. Hard to do. But I'm pretty persistent."

"And what makes you think that will matter?" he asked.

I shrugged. "I did just blow up the moon."

He sighed. "You blew up part of the moon," he said. "By accident."

"Right. If I can do that without even trying, think about what I can do if I put my mind to it," I said. "Look—I don't expect you to understand, okay? Those robot bastards were using people as Mist batteries. Did you know? They copy their consciousnesses so it looks like they're giving people perfect lives. But in reality, they're just killing everyone, then using their bodies' regeneration to produce Mist."

"Some would argue that those aren't just copies."

"The Pacificians wouldn't be among the people who made that claim. I saw it in their files. They know what they're doing."

"And they believe they're creating new life every time they copy someone," Alistaris said. "I don't know if I can dispute that, either. They have free will. The ability to reason. Emotions. They—"

"They're just robots. End of story."

He sighed. "You are so naive," the Dengyt said. "There are dozens of sentient races of artificial intelligence. Most are entirely peaceful. The Pacificians are not, but—"

"Clearly."

I didn't dispute my naivete. I knew that I had no idea what the wider universe had to offer. But for my purposes, thinking of the Pacificians as advanced robots made things much easier. After all, if they weren't really people, killing them didn't pose any moral quandaries.

And that was as much as I wanted to think about that.

"We are getting too far afield," Alistaris said. "Before you can . . . do what you said you want to do, you need to help the Alliance."

"I remember what I promised," I stated. "But I want something else from you."

"Saving your life wasn't enough?"

"No. Not really."

He sighed. "What do you want?"

"I want you to help me get into Olympus," I said. "That's how I ended up on the moon. I tried to sneak in by barrel, but—"

"By barrel?"

"Long story. The point is that I could only find one way in, and that failed. I need you to help me enter that city so I can save someone," I said. I'd found some records that indicated that Cirilla's brother was being held within Olympus, and he wasn't alone. I didn't know much more than that, but I still intended to follow through with my promise and rescue him. But I also hoped to save the others, as well.

"That . . . That is more difficult than you know," he said.

I shrugged. "Get me in there and I'll take care of the problem they represent," I said. "Or am I wrong in thinking that you don't want them around? You said they're allies of the Confederation, right? Well, think of this as the first step in getting rid of the bad guys."

"That is a gross oversimplification of the situation," Alistaris said. "There are no good guys and bad guys, as you so simplistically put it. In fact, I was just telling the chancellor that—"

"Don't care. They've invaded my world. They've killed thousands. Maybe millions, by this point. And—"

"So have you."

"And they want to take over the world, oppressing humanity and strip-mining Earth," I said, speaking over him. "That makes them the bad guys, at least in my book. I don't care how you label them. You can call them glitter princesses, for all it matters to me. What does matter to me is that you give me the tools I need to do what I want to do."

"Which, to be clear, is to commit mass murder," he said.

"They're robots. I don't consider it murder."

"Most governments would disagree."

"Oh, stop pretending you care," I said, already guessing why he really needed me. I'd given it a lot of thought, and there was really only one reason for someone with his level of power to recruit me. "We both know you couldn't care less about any of that. You recruited me precisely because I'm not subject to whatever rules govern your behavior, right?"

"Is that a question? Or do you know more than you let on?"

"I have a brain, Al," I said. He winced at the fact that I'd shortened his name. "I can read the situation as well as anyone else. I know when I'm being used to fight a proxy war. I don't know what rules you think you need to follow. I don't know about repercussions or who's going to enforce any of it. But I think you want me to do exactly what I'm talking about doing so you can stand back and claim your hands are clean, all while your enemies die horrible deaths."

Alistaris leaned forward. "Just so we are clear—I don't care if their deaths are horrible, peaceful, or something in between those two extremes. I just want them dead," he said. "You are correct, though. The Ark Alliance has to follow rules of engagement as set forth by—"

"Again—I don't care. None of that affects me," I said. Still, I intended to contact Kith to get the real story. Just because I was okay with working for Alistaris, it didn't necessarily mean that I trusted him. He had no qualms about lying to me, so I had long since resolved to take whatever he had to tell me with a grain of salt. "Just tell me that you can get me into that city."

"I can probably get you into that city."

"Good," I said, slapping my knees for emphasis. "That's all I need for now. Besides, I think we're getting close."

Indeed, I'd felt that the ship's descent had slowed, and it didn't take a leap of logic to come to the conclusion that we'd reached our destination.

"You can feel that even with the inertial dampeners engaged?"

"Yup. I'm just that talented," I said. I'd been flaring Observation the entire time, but he didn't need to know that. The more in the dark he was about my abilities, the better. I'd already revealed far too much about my combat capabilities as it was, so I needed to keep some cards close to my vest.

He sighed and muttered something under his breath that sounded a lot like "arrogant child," but I knew that there was no way he was talking about me. Instead, I focused on the ship's descent, and only a few minutes later, I felt it settle into place.

When it did, I rose and said, "Well, thanks for the ride, Al." I gave him a little salute. "I'm guessing you'll give me a call when you're ready to get me into Olympus."

"Indeed," he said.

After that, I crossed the ship's cabin to the door, which opened when I drew near. Immediately, I was assaulted by hot, humid air. After spending so long in various climate-controlled areas, it was a welcome change. Sure, it wasn't comfortable, but it was familiar, which was all that mattered.

I left the ship behind, giving Alistaris a little wave as it lifted into the air and sped off. That left me alone in the wilderness. *The Leviathan* was only a few hundred yards away, and I covered the distance at a limp. When I finally reached my ship, I boarded and commenced with my customary sweep.

As I had already noted, I didn't trust Alistaris, and given that he'd already displayed a capability to infiltrate my ship and plant trackers, I wasn't going to take any chances. As it turned out, I found seven hidden tracking devices within the ship and three more planted on the exterior. I destroyed them all before activating Bastion and retreating to the bathroom, where I stepped into the shower.

That's when I broke down.

After everything I had been through, it had been all I could handle to keep my emotions under control. But now that I was alone, I didn't have any reason to keep up the facade. And as I sank to the shower's floor, letting the hot water fall all around me, I let my emotions fully take root.

There, I wept.

I didn't really think about any individual thing. Instead, my thoughts flowed from one horrible event to the next. I thought about the human cattle

I'd encountered in the E'rok Tan facility. I thought about the terrifying and curiously intelligent wildling clown. I thought about the human Mist batteries, about all those people who'd only wanted a better life but instead were killed and copied.

And I thought about the fact that I'd blown up the moon.

Not the whole thing, but enough that it was almost assuredly visible from Earth's surface. Which, in its own way, was the most disturbing thing I'd done. Not because I'd killed a few thousand robots. I was fine with that. And I wasn't even that concerned with the fact that I'd ended the lives of the brain-dead people the Pacificians had been using as Mist batteries. They were already dead, even if their bodies were being kept alive.

No—the biggest issue I had was with the sheer amount of destructive power I'd brought to bear. What was my limit? Did I even have one, aside from the size of the explosives I used? This time, I had simply torn a hole in the moon, but next time, I might do the same to the Earth. Or in a few more years, maybe I could even destroy an entire planet.

It was a disturbing thought, and I knew it would keep me up at night.

I don't know how long I sat there in the shower, crying as the water washed over me, but by the time I managed to push myself to my feet, I felt slightly better. Once, my uncle had told me that tears were a natural and necessary part of life. The act of crying could provide a much-needed outlet to relieve stress. At the time, I hadn't really believed him, instead thinking that it was a sign of weakness. However, in the years since, I'd discovered just how right he was.

Once I finished in the shower—and with my tears—I stepped out and used Secure Connection to contact Patrick. When he answered, he was understandably distraught, but I assured him I was okay. Soon after that, I told him that we'd talk when I returned to Fortune, but for the time being, I needed a few hours of rest before I headed that way.

He wasn't happy about the obvious dismissal, but he accepted it, nonetheless. And a few minutes later, I retreated into my bedroom, where I flopped onto the bed and almost immediately fell asleep.

Thankfully, I didn't dream.

A handful of hours later, I awoke, still groggy but well enough to pilot *The Leviathan* back to Fortune. The flight wasn't long, and before I knew it, I was setting the ship down in the familiar dock. I'd barely had a chance to shut down the engines when the forward hatch opened and Patrick came barreling inside.

A second later, he had his arms wrapped around me.

"I thought you were . . . I saw what happened up there . . . and . . . and . . . I'm just so glad you're okay," he said.

"Me, too," I said, suddenly feeling guilty that I hadn't contacted him the moment I was safe. I'd had my reasons not to—chiefly that I didn't want to use the Dengyt ship's communications equipment. I had no idea what they could do with that kind of information, so I'd waited until I was on board *The Leviathan*.

A mistake because Patrick had clearly been worried out of his mind.

"Tell me everything that happened," he said, finally releasing me and sitting in the copilot's chair.

And I did, sparing no details. He deserved to know everything I'd done, after all. It took a little while to recount the whole tale, and when I was done, he remained silent for some time before saying, "This just got a lot more complicated, didn't it?"

I nodded. "I think it was always going in this direction," I said.

Originally, I'd been committed to lying low until the Initialization completed. When the quarantine was lifted, I had intended to leave Earth behind. However, that had never really been an option. I wasn't so naive as to think that, if the Pacificians had been free to enact their plan, complete with a multitude of ships and satellites, they would have ever let us escape the planet.

It was always going to end in a fight.

We'd just been fooling ourselves by thinking otherwise.

"Have you seen it?" Patrick asked.

"Seen what?"

"The moon."

"I got a nice, close look, yeah," I said. I gave him a small smile, asking, "You were listening to my story, right?"

"I'm talking about from here," he said. "I think the whole world probably saw it."

I shook my head. When I'd arrived on the surface, I'd pointedly avoided looking up at the sky. And by the time I had set off toward Fortune, the sun had already risen.

"You should look."

I sighed, then nodded. After that, I followed Patrick out of the ship. By that point, night had fallen, and I looked up into the sky. There, amid a blanket of stars, was a silvery full moon.

In most ways, it looked the same as it always did. However, it only took a single glance to recognize the effect of my explosion. Alistaris had characterized it as blowing up the moon, and seeing the size of the crater, I couldn't really argue with that assessment. A full third of the moon had been affected by the explosion, tearing a huge crater in the lunar surface. It wasn't just visible with the naked eye; it was impossible to ignore.

"Would it make any difference if I told you that I didn't mean to do that?"

"I think that makes it worse, Mira."

I sighed. "Yeah. Yeah, it does."

CHAPTER FORTY-SEVEN

AN IMPORTANT MISSION

War is inevitable now. Maybe it always was. I don't know. It just feels like, somewhere along the line, we failed, and now we're just waiting to be buried by the consequences of our failures.

—Patrick Ward

Upon returning to Fortune, I had a few days to myself while Alistaris gathered the means to get me inside Olympus. I had already established that I wasn't capable of bypassing the Pacificians' defenses, so my ingress was wholly in his hands. I just hoped it wouldn't take him long to make good on his promises.

In the meantime, I would get some much-needed rest. I'd spent weeks running from one crisis to another, without much downtime in between. And even when I wasn't fighting for my life, I was occupied with surveillance. The only break I'd had was the night I'd spent in the fairy-tale city with Patrick, but even then, I was more than a little preoccupied with what had been going on.

So, the morning after I'd returned to Fortune, I found myself lying abed and wishing I never had to leave. Yet, circumstances conspired to rob me of my contentment when Patrick stirred and sat up. I complained, begging him to stay, but he said, "Can't. As much as I want to spend the morning with you—and I really, really do—I'm going to have to take a rain check."

"You make it sound like you missed a reservation at a fancy restaurant or something," I mumbled.

"I'm sorry. It's just that I'm on the verge of a breakthrough with the Mist circuits," he said. "The key to getting them to play nice with the more mundane circuits was this really rare element that only comes from Dead Zones. And even then, the conditions have to be just right for the specific mutation to—"

"Metals don't mutate. That's a biology term. With rocks and minerals, it's metamorphism."

"That doesn't sound right."

"It is. I read it somewhere," I persisted.

"Ah, somewhere. The most reliable and verifiable source known to mankind," he said loftily as he leaned in and kissed me. When he pulled away, he said, "I'll be free tomorrow, okay? The next day at the latest. Then we can do something special."

I grinned. "Like what?" I asked eagerly.

He shrugged. "I'll think of something," he said, and I believed him. Patrick had plenty of flaws, but commitment to keeping the spark in our relationship wasn't one of them. He always went above and beyond. By comparison, my own attempts at romantic overtures usually fell flat. For whatever reason, I just didn't think like that, even if I sometimes wished I could.

"What if I think of something first?" I asked.

"All the better," he said. "But honestly, I'd be happy just relaxing on a beach somewhere with you. You know, I have a new brew I've been researching on the local intranet. They use—"

"Uh . . ."

"If you really loved me, you'd try it," he said.

"Is that the gauge we're using?" I asked. "Because that doesn't seem fair."

"Ouch. My beers are not that bad, are they? There was that one you said you liked. You know, back in Australia."

"I said it was tolerable, not that I liked it."

"Same thing."

"It really isn't, Pick."

"Well, you'll like this one. I have a good feeling. I just need to let the yeast ferment. The key is to add a few grams of powdered Rift Shards. You know, for a little extra kick. And . . . Wait, where are you going?"

I'd already slipped out of bed and was walking toward the shower. I looked back over my shoulder and said, "No, no. Keep going. I'm totally listening."

Then, I stepped into the bathroom and closed the door. Using Observation, I heard him say, "It's not that bad . . ."

But it really was. Patrick was a great partner, but as much as he enjoyed brewing various beers and ales, he'd never had the knack needed to create something that wasn't overtly terrible. Every now and then, he'd come up with a tolerable brew, but I attributed that to the law of averages more than talent.

Once I'd showered—all the while lamenting the fact that he hadn't joined me—I stepped out of the bathroom and started getting dressed. By that point, Patrick had already dressed and had headed into the galley, where he was cooking something that admittedly smelled delicious. I followed my nose and found a pile of bacon waiting on me. I tried to sneak a slice, but he slapped my hand with a spatula, saying, "Wait for me to finish."

I rolled my eyes and considered simply going ahead. My attributes were high enough that I could steal a few slices without him even knowing. Probably. And even if he saw, he'd only be a little cross. It wouldn't be a big deal.

But I refrained, waiting until he finished scrambling a few eggs and toasting some bread. He'd somehow acquired fresh butter, too, which made all the difference in the world.

As he set the plate in front of me, I said, "This reminds me of the Dew Drop Inn back in Mobile."

"It reminds me of my mom," he said. "She always said that breakfast was the most important meal of the day."

"Sounds like a wise woman," I said, gesturing with a half-eaten slice of bacon. "But I'm a bit biased. All my favorite foods are breakfast. Except for gumbo. The real stuff, too. And jambalaya. Do you know how hard it is to find anyone who can cook that properly around here?"

"Impossible, probably."

"I've been all over the world, and I haven't found anyone who could make it like they did back home. I'd even take that synthetic stuff they had back in Nova."

In truth, I missed it more than I wanted to admit. But that might've been more about the nostalgia than the taste. I went on, "There was this diner back in the Garden. Terrible place that looked like it hadn't been cleaned in a hundred years. You know, the sort of place the Enforcers would shut down if they'd really cared about protecting the populace. Anyway, my uncle used to take me there every weekend. They made this cheap burger. The kind where it's all synthetic meat and faux bread. But there was this stuff they called Tiger Sauce that made it the best burger I've ever had."

"I doubt that."

"No, no—it's true. I'd give anything to get another one of those burgers. And the milkshakes? Oh my God, Pick. I would spend all week looking forward to those milkshakes," I said.

"My mom used to make this tofu lasagna. Objectively terrible stuff. Like, if you've tasted cardboard, you might get an idea what it was like," Patrick said wistfully. "But she tried so hard. Like, she'd spend hours on it, hand cutting the pasta, making the sauce—you know, the works. I wish I could go back and have one more lasagna dinner. I wish . . . I wish you could've met her. She would have liked you."

I had no idea how to respond to that, so I just reached across the table and gripped his free hand. We stayed like that for a few moments before letting go. After that, our meal progressed in silence without any nostalgic trips down memory lane.

Sometimes, I forgot that my story, while a bit bombastic, wasn't really all that unique. I wasn't the only one who'd lost people. Everyone had. Even Cirilla, who'd spent most of her life trying to play it safe, had lost her brother. How many others out there had experienced similar losses?

Was that the real reason I'd agreed to fight Alistaris's war?

Maybe.

Once we'd finished our meals, I bid Patrick goodbye, and he set off to work on his project. That left me once again alone. I was used to it. In fact, I often preferred solitude. But for the moment, I wished Patrick would have stuck around, at least for a little while. I wasn't typically clingy, but I just didn't want to be left alone with my thoughts.

Of course, we don't always get what we want, and soon, my mind went to the impending fight. Once Alistaris came through with his promise, I'd have to head into Olympus and rescue Caden, Cirilla's brother. And I knew I'd have to help anyone else I found, too. Otherwise, they'd end up as collateral damage.

Or worse.

I had seen what that looked like, and I had no interest in being responsible—even if it was only through inaction—for that happening to anyone else.

But that meant that I had a battle ahead of me. So, given that I'd used almost all my explosives in the lunar base—along with a lot of my other supplies—I decided that I needed to restock. Some of it, I could only get via the Bazaar. Fortunately, using *The Leviathan*'s communications system, I could put in an order for more ammunition. I did so, leaving a message for Gala that I was okay, but I didn't dare say anything else because I knew just how easily those messages could be hijacked.

It was why I usually preferred to do my business face-to-face. An ammunition restock wasn't enough to get anyone's attention, but if I started sending long messages, the wrong sorts of people might start to notice. After that, it wouldn't be long before my actions started having consequences for my acquaintances and friends in the Bazaar.

Once that was done, I finished dressing, using my self-styler to put my hair in a tight braid, and set off into Fortune. I caught one of the automated rickshaws, which took me to one of the local markets. Once there, I quickly found my way to a vendor who dealt in various chemicals.

I probably could have found an arms dealer, but I preferred making my own explosives. For one, they always seemed to work better like that, and for another, I didn't want to raise any alarms. Most of the materials I needed were fairly innocuous, so as long as I was careful—and cycled through a couple of identities as I went from one vendor to the next—I could avoid any undue attention.

Throughout the day, I found myself loitering near other shoppers and listening in on their conversations.

"You seen it, right? What could even do that?" asked a tall, slender man who looked as if he'd missed more than a few meals.

"It's the government, man," his friend, who was a short, corpulent man, said. "It's always the government."

"You think the council blew up the moon?"

"Not that government, Ricky. I'm talkin' about the real government. The ones really in charge. They been doin' it for years. They control everything."

Ricky shook his head and said, "That's dumb."

"Yeah, keep your head in the sand. I heard . . ."

That wasn't the only time I'd heard a conversation concerning my exploits on the moon. Most people were terrified, but there were probably just as many who were simply confused. But no one seemed to have guessed that the entire situation had begun in their city. Even now, the Pacificians were still operating out of their local headquarters. I was tempted to go in, guns blazing, but I held back, largely because I knew it wouldn't do much good.

No—I would keep going the way I was going while I waited on Alistaris to come through.

As the day went on, I continued gathering supplies. I bought a crate full of rations from one vendor, a few drums of necessary chemicals from various shops, and some little metal balls that would make for perfect grenade housings from a metalworking operation in the center of the city. In the end, I barely spent a few thousand credits, but I bought enough materials to build hundreds of grenades and quite a few larger demolition charges. I had all of it sent to Cirilla's workshop, where Patrick would store it away and bring it to *The Leviathan*. My own arsenal implant was far too small for that job, and I had no interest in making multiple trips across the city.

So, with my shopping done, I stopped by a nearby bar, mostly just to get the lay of the land. There, I listened to gossip while drinking a surprisingly decent beer. When the serving girl brought my second mug to me, I asked, "You brew this locally?"

"Yeah. Old Kev does. He calls it his masterpiece," she said.

"Well, it's definitely good."

Once she was gone, I finished my beer, paid, and set off toward the door. Along the way, I had an idea, though, so as soon as I hit the sidewalk outside, I took a right turn and headed toward a nearby alley. When I reached it, I ducked inside and, after making certain that no one was looking, activated Stealth.

Secure in my concealment, I strode down the alley, turning when I reached the corner of the bar. Then, I sprang to a half-open window, which I pushed ajar and slipped inside the apartment above the tavern. It didn't take me long to search the place, and I soon found a sizable notebook filled with various ale recipes. Flipping through it, I only understood half of what I read, but that didn't matter.

It wasn't for me, after all.

I didn't have the heart to simply steal the book. Instead, I spent a few minutes taking careful still shots of the pages, which I sequestered in a corner of my interface usually reserved for sensitive and dangerous material. Odd, that it had most recently held files detailing the Pacificians' horrific practices, and now it was home to a bunch of brewing recipes.

With that done, I replaced the book and retreated, not dropping Stealth until I'd reached the alley. Then, I let it fall away and headed back out to the street. It was a trivial use of my abilities, but I still felt it was worth it.

In any case, I wasn't finished.

Over the next few hours, I hunted down some more materials. This time, I wasn't concerned with various chemicals that, when combined, made for powerful explosives. Instead, I was gathering the makings of something that was arguably more important. Once I was finished, I headed back to *The Leviathan* where I got to work.

I'd only just finished when Patrick returned.

He looked exhausted, but I hoped that my efforts would brighten his day. So, without preamble, I announced, "I got something for you."

As I stepped close, holding the gift I'd spent so much time on behind my back, he said, "Huh? What? Mira, I—"

Grinning, I thrust the present into his chest, saying, "Here. Open it. Now."

"Um . . . Alright?" he said, obviously surprised. I usually wasn't much of a gift giver, so his surprise was probably warranted.

In any case, he opened the box—I hadn't had the chance to wrap it—and looked inside. He reached in and retrieved a book. Its cover was wooden, without embellishment; that had been the most difficult component to source, but I'd found a local craftsman who whipped it together in only half an hour. Then, I'd gone to a bookbinder—the only one in the city—and paid a small fortune to get the woman to put it together.

"What is this?" he asked, flipping open the book. The paper had been more expensive even than the bookbinder's services, but at least it hadn't been difficult to find. "Is this your handwriting?"

"It is," I confirmed. That had been the most tedious part of the project, but I'd managed it all the same.

"Are these . . . These are beer recipes," he said, flipping through the pages. "Where did you get this?"

"I made it," I said.

"No, but where did the . . . I mean . . ."

"Do you like it?" I asked. "I just thought . . . You know, you do so much for me. I almost never get you gifts or take you anywhere special. So, when the opportunity to . . . uh . . . acquire these recipes presented itself, I thought of you."

"I . . . I don't know what to say . . ."

"Say you'll follow these recipes instead of the ones you usually use," I said. "Oof. Low blow."

"Just callin' it like I see it," was my smiling reply.

"Seriously, Mira . . . This is . . . I can't imagine a better gift. Thank you," he said, shaking his head. "Really. Thank you. I wish . . . I wish I could stick around, but I'm just here to grab a quick nap before heading back to work."

"I figured."

Indeed, Patrick barely took any time to himself, and when he did, it didn't last long. He was just as dedicated to his project as I was to my own. That was probably why we worked so well together.

The rest of the night went by without much fanfare, and the next morning, I awoke to an empty bed. That was fine. Patrick had his project, and I had work to do, as well. So, after eating a breakfast of oat porridge, I spent the next few hours training. After that, I started building bombs.

Or grenades.

Same difference, really.

Whatever the case, I was an old hand at the process, but I still used my well-trained focus to good effect as I built one grenade after another. Some were simple fragmentation grenades, but I also built flash-bangs, smoke bombs, and a half dozen other varieties meant to solve very specific problems.

It was almost meditative, building bombs, and like that, time flew by until I realized that day had passed well into night. Once again, I went to bed alone.

CHAPTER FORTY-EIGHT

PREPARATIONS

My beer really isn't that bad. I don't know why Mira hates it so much. It's not good. I'll grant that. But it's not that bad.

—Patrick Ward

The dawn of a new day brought with it a palpable sense of anticipation that I couldn't really place. I spent most of that day training, and when I finished, I took a look at my long-ignored status:

NAME	Mirabelle Lisa Braddock		
CLASS	MISTRUNNER		
LEVEL	45 (98%)		
CONSTITUTION	244/325		
MIND	271/325		
MIST	219/325		
SKILLS	7/7		
SKILL NAME	Skill Tier	Modifiers	Abilities
CYBERNETIC MASTERY	Tier 5 (92%)	300% Efficiency	10 Cybernetic Slots
COMBAT	Tier 5 (97%)	+75% Damage (All) +100% Speed (Melee)	Empowered Shot (D) Double Shot (D) Combination Punch (D)

| | | +60% Accuracy (All) +50% Range (Firearms) +75% Reload Speed (Firearms) +25% Damage (Small Arms) +25% Range (Small Arms) +25% Accuracy (Small Arms) +50% Damage (Heavy Weaponry) +15% Range (Heavy Weaponry) +50% Rate of Fire (Heavy Weaponry) +25% Damage (Melee) +25% Accuracy (Melee) +25% Movement Speed +25% Jump Height | Pummel (D) Engage (D) Disengage (D) Mark Target (E) Barrage (E) Explosive Shot (E) Multishot (E) Shatter Shot (E) Instant Reload (E) Riposte (E) Execute (E) Double Jump (D) Teleport (D) |
| INFILTRATION | Tier 5 (15%) | +95% Effectiveness (Stealth) +25% Effectiveness (Deception) +15% Effectiveness (Charisma) | Stealth (D) Camouflage (D) Deception (D) Mimic (D) Observation (D) Charisma (E) Interrogate (E) Distraction (E) Vanish (E) |

		+15% Effectiveness (Mimic) +25% Effectiveness (Bluff)	Bluff (F) Chameleon (D) Sense Deception (E) True Sight (E) Vanish (F)
MISTRUNNER	Tier 5 (91%)	+75% Speed (Misthack) +75% Processing Speed (Mistwalk) +75% Durability (Mistwall) +15% Ghost Strength +25% Ghost Stability +25% Infiltration Stability +50% Processing Speed +50% System Defense +20% Damage (All)	Mistwalk (C) Misthack (C) Mistwall (C) System Redirect (D) Disable Cybernetics (D) Overcharge (D) Surge (E) Plague (E) Rewind (E) Skeleton Key (E) Backlash (D) Mental Fortress (E) Assassinate (F)
FIELDCRAFT	Tier 5 (99%)	+50% Combat Effectiveness +50% Effectiveness (Triage) +50% Recovery Speed +25% Medication Effectiveness +25% Less Food/Water Required	Triage (D) Basic Explosives Handling (C) Combat Focus (C) Pain Tolerance (D) Resistance (D) Foraging (D) Improvisation (D) Regeneration (D) Universal Language (E) Stabilize (E) Mend (E)

		+25% Less Sleep Required +50% Endurance +25% Effectiveness (Combat Focus) +25% Effectiveness (Regeneration) +25% Explosives Yield	Bastion (D) Tinkering (F) Share Map (D) Waypoint (E) Combat Map (D) Secure Connection (C) Ignore Injury (E) Focused Will (D)
DEMOLITION	Tier 5 (99%)	+50% Explosive Radius +50% Explosive Strength	Blast Shield (C)
ACROBATICS	Tier 5 (99%)	+100% Proprioception	Balance (C)

Destroying the Pacifician lunar base—as well as all the killing I had done leading up to that event—had provided quite a boost to my levels. With that came a significant increase in the potential of my individual attributes. I hadn't taken huge strides in the actual values associated with my Constitution, Mind, and Mist, but that was due to the fact that I hadn't had much time for focused training. However, I had made some gains, so I was reasonably happy with my progress in that arena.

Regarding my individual skills, I'd continued my climb toward the peak, reaching Tier 5 in each of them. All but one of them—[Infiltration]—had reached ninety percent progress, too. Soon, I would maximize all my skills, which filled me with a mixture of satisfaction and anxiety. Satisfaction because there was nothing quite like achieving a goal, especially when there was a verifiable benefit to doing so. But I was also anxious about what would come next. The skills didn't go past ninety-nine percent progress in Tier 5, so I couldn't help but wonder how I would motivate myself going forward.

Of course, there was the possibility of combining skills, but I'd yet to stumble across any information about how that was done. And I'd tried, too. All I'd been able to learn was that it was possible, with no details forthcoming.

I'd done it before, though. When I'd gained my {Mistrunner} class, a few of my skills had merged. So, I could only hope something like that would happen again, though I wasn't sure how reasonable an expectation that was.

In any case, I chose to focus on my excitement and the sense of pride, rather than the anxiety, that came with my progression.

Next, I moved on to my individual skill trees, starting with [Combat]:

Tree	**Combat: Tier 5 (97%)** <Focus for Modifiers>			
Branch	Small Arms: Tier 5 (97%)	Heavy Weaponry: Tier 5 (99%)	Melee: Tier 5 (94%)	Movement: Tier 5 (99%)
Tier 1	+25% Damage	+50% Damage	+15% Speed	+5% Movement
Tier 2	+25% Range	+15% Range	+25% Damage	+25% Jump Height
Tier 3	Ability: Explosive Shot	Ability: Shatter Shot	Ability: Riposte	Ability: Double Jump
Tier 4	+25% Accuracy	+50% Rate of Fire	+25% Accuracy	+15% Movement
Tier 5	Ability: Multishot	Ability: Instant Reload	Ability: Execute	Ability: Teleport

Not much had changed with the [Combat] tree. The skill itself was on the verge of reaching the pinnacle, and the individual branches weren't far behind. Two—Heavy Weaponry and Movement—had already done so. The skill also came with a host of modifiers that I sometimes took for granted. I'd even hidden them because the list had gotten a bit out of hand.

In any case, I moved on to [Infiltration]:

Tree	**Infiltration: Tier 5 (15%)** <Focus for Modifiers>			
Branch	Spycraft: Tier 5 (82%)	Stealth: Tier 5 (1%)	Deception: Tier 5 (12%)	Sensory Input: Tier 5 (1%)
Tier 1	+15% Effectiveness (Deception)	+15% Effectiveness (Stealth Abilities)	+15% Effectiveness (Deception)	+25% Effectiveness (Observation)

Tier 2	+15% Effectiveness (Deception)	+25% Effectiveness (Stealth Abilities)	+15% Effectiveness (Mimic)	+25% Effectiveness (Observation)
Tier 3	Ability: Charisma	Ability: Distraction	Ability: Bluff	Ability: Sense Deception
Tier 4	+15% Effectiveness (Charisma)	+15% Effectiveness (Stealth Abilities)	+25% Effectiveness (Bluff)	+15% Effectiveness (Sense Deception)
Tier 5	Ability: Interrogate	Ability: Vanish	Ability: Chameleon	Ability: True Sight

As with [Combat], not much had really changed with [Infiltration], save that it had finally reached Tier 5, which gave me an additional fifteen percent Stealth effectiveness. The Stealth branch had also reached Tier 5, giving me an additional ability called Vanish. During my most recent training session, I had tried it out a few times, but without real enemies, it was difficult to tell just how valuable it was. It was also entirely untrained, which meant that the ability itself hadn't progressed from the lowest grade. I would have to change that going forward, but I suspected it would be next to useless in the coming conflict.

As for its effect, it was fairly simple. Using it would allow me to become invisible, if only for a few seconds. So far as I could tell, it was intended to get me out of combat for long enough that I could make it to a location better suited for Stealth. Not the most useful ability in its current incarnation, but I suspected that, once I'd had a chance to train it, it could prove to be a powerful tool in my arsenal of abilities.

Next, I looked at the skill tree associated with [Mistrunner]:

Tree	**Mistrunner: Tier 5 (91%)** <Focus for Modifiers>			
Branch	Misthack: Tier 5 (99%)	Mistwalk: Tier 5 (13%)	Mistwall: Tier 5 (99%)	Combat: Tier 5 (81%)
Tier 1	+15% Speed (Misthack)	+25% Infiltration Stability	+15% System Defense	+5% Damage (All)

Tier 2	+15% Ghost Strength	+25% Processing Speed (Mistwalk)	+25% System Defense	+5% Damage (All)
Tier 3	Ability: Surge	Ability: Rewind	Ability: Backlash	+5% Damage (All)
Tier 4	+25% Ghost Stability	+25% Processing Speed (Mistwalk)	C-Grade System Defense	+5% Damage (All)
Tier 5	Ability: Plague	Ability: Skeleton Key	Ability: Mental Fortress	Ability: Assassinate

[Mistrunner] had been Tier 5 for quite some time, with its associated branches reaching the maximum tier, as well. However, I couldn't help but feel a sense of satisfaction as I saw how close each of those branches—save for the one associated with Mistwalk—was to reaching the peak, too.

The same could be said for [Fieldcraft], which was easily my most advanced skill. Even though I knew what I'd see, I still took a moment to look at it:

Tree	**Fieldcraft: Tier 5 (99%)** <Focus for Modifiers>			
Branch	Medic: Tier 5 (99%)	Survival: Tier 5 (99%)	Communication: Tier 5 (99%)	Utility: Tier 5 (99%)
Tier 1	+50% Effectiveness (Triage)	+25% Less Food/Water Required	Ability: Universal Language	+25% Effectiveness (Combat Focus)
Tier 2	+50% Recovery Speed	+25% Less Sleep Required	Ability: Share Map	+25% Effectiveness (Regeneration)
Tier 3	Ability: Stabilize	Ability: Bastion	Ability: Waypoint	Ability: Ignore Injury

Tier 4	+25% Medication Effectiveness	+50% Endurance	Ability: Combat Map	+25% Explosives Yield
Tier 5	Ability: Mend	Ability: Tinkering	Ability: Secure Connection	Ability: Focused Will

The skill had long since reached the pinnacle of Tier 5, and the individual branches had done so not long after. Some of the resulting abilities were often ignored—like Mend, Stabilize, and Focused Will—but I knew they were still valuable. Going forward, I would need to incorporate them a little more.

The problem was that I had a glut of abilities, and even with my Mind attribute increasing my cognition speed, I could only handle so many at a time. So, I'd fallen into the trap of only using my favorites. It was something I needed to remedy because I was only using a portion of my skill set.

I resolved to do so, but it wasn't as if I could simply flip a switch and do it. It would take long practice and focused effort. I could only hope that I'd get the chance to fix the problems.

After inspecting my progress, I spent the next few hours working on my Ghosts. Some, I just tweaked, but others, I decided to entirely rewrite. Some people liked to meditate to relax. Others exercised. Me? I worked on my Ghosts. Not only was it necessary if I wanted to push the limits of my abilities, but it was also soothing, slotting the various components together until I had created something that was far more than the sum of its parts.

Like that, time passed. One day passed into another, and before I knew it, I'd been in place for almost a week. By that point, I'd entirely healed from my ordeal on the moon—largely due to my copious use of Mend. The ability was intended as a shortcut to effective triage, but I'd discovered that if I used it consistently over the course of a few days, it could accelerate my already prodigious healing by a significant margin.

I also continued to train, using the ship's Mistrunner training protocols. Not because I would see numbers go up on my status but, rather, because I strove for perfection. I knew I'd never reach that lofty goal, but I also knew that, in battle, completing a Misthack or a Mistwalk even a second more quickly could be the difference between life and death. And though I often took a pessimistic—or even cynical—view of life, I desperately wanted to survive.

It wasn't until the tenth day after my return to Fortune that I received a visitor. For once, Alistaris didn't simply appear in the ship. Instead, he actually knocked on the hatch. When I opened it, I was surprised to see a strange holographic display overlaying his tiny form.

"What's that?" I asked.

"Oh, you can see through my disguise. I suspected you could," he said. "May I come in?"

I shrugged and let him inside. "Let me know if you plan to leave any other trackers," I said. "I had to spend almost three hours searching the ship last time you were here, and I don't think either of us wants me wasting that kind of time on something trivial."

He raised his eyebrows and asked, "Are you sure you got all of them?"

"Not really," I admitted. I knew his technology was far more advanced than anything I could bring to bear, and he wasn't shy about using it to his advantage. It wouldn't have surprised me at all to find that there were multiple trackers and listening devices throughout *The Leviathan*.

But if there were, there was nothing I could do about it. I'd searched, using both my own abilities as well as the ship's built-in security to hunt down what I could. If there were any other bugs in the ship, I wasn't going to find them.

"I pledge to refrain from any further violations of your privacy," he said, following me to the ship's common area. I hadn't cleaned it over the past few days, so there were a few empty cartons that had once contained cheap processed food populating the table. Alistaris eyed them with barely disguised disgust. "The things you people eat . . ."

"Not much in the way of choice," I stated. It was a lie. I could have easily sourced plenty of fresh food, but that would have taken time and effort. And there was a part of me that was just used to eating junk, so it was somewhat comforting. I wasn't going to admit that to him, though. Instead, I sat down and asked, "What's up? You have a plan to get me inside."

"I do."

"Okay? Spit it out," I said, throwing my arm over the back of the bench seat. It wasn't the most comfortable position, but I wanted him to think I was relaxed.

The little Dengyt climbed into the chair across the table, and once he was situated, he said, "It's not simple."

"Oh? How so?"

"We can't be seen working against the Pacificians," he stated. "Not before the quarantine is lifted. And even then, our direct involvement will be minimal. This has to look like humans fighting back. Otherwise, it doesn't work."

"You're afraid of blowback."

I didn't know anything about galactic politics, but I'd already established that the Ark Alliance wanted to use humanity to fight a proxy war against their enemies. Technically, that didn't include the Pacificians, but because they were allied with the Gomari Confederation, the situation was firmly entrenched in a gray area.

I'd opted to use that to my advantage.

I told myself it was because I wanted to make good on my promise to rescue Cirilla's brother, Caden, but I knew my resolution to bring the Pacificians down was rooted in something far more personally impactful. I had seen what they did to people, and like the E'rok Tan, they deserved to die.

And I was the one who was going to facilitate that.

"I am. I'm also wary of breaking the quarantine too overtly."

"Why? You're already here."

"The system can be tricked. It's just a program meant to help people harness the Mist. But you're caught trying to circumvent its restrictions, it will punish you."

"Yeah, but how?"

"Death is the kindest punishment. Some people have been crippled, their Nexus Implants rendered inoperative. Its punishments are varied and extensive."

"What about people who don't have Nexus Implants?" I asked. "Mystics like the Templars."

Alistaris's expression darkened. "Templars," he spat. "They talk about justice and peace, but do they ever act? No. All they care about is their own power, their own influence. And killing rogue mystics. They care nothing for all the people who have fallen before groups like the Gomari Confederation. They are too concerned with preserving their so-called political neutrality to actually do any good."

"The ones I've met seemed okay," I said.

"That's because you've never had to depend on them. That's because you've never watched your friends die while a Templar stands idly by and does nothing," he said. "All while they claim moral superiority. They act above us, but they're no different. They pretend neutrality because they are too cowardly to fight against true injustice. They talk about justice and virtue, but when it comes time to translate those pretty words into action, they shy away."

"A group of them saved me once," I stated.

"Oh, they'll save people. When it suits them. But their aid is shrouded in self-interest. Never forget that," he said.

That wasn't my experience, but I hadn't had many interactions with Templars. And I certainly had no idea how they conducted themselves in the wider universe. So, I chose not to pursue that topic any further.

"So, what's the plan, then?"

"I have contracted a team of specialized combatants to bring the shield down," he said. "You will have to be in position when they commence their attacks. When it comes down, you will only have a few minutes to get inside."

"Who are these specialized combatants?" I asked.

"I will not reveal their identities. Neither did I tell them who you are," he said.

I didn't like it, but I saw the benefit of keeping everyone separated. That way, if any of us were captured, we couldn't reveal too much information. Still, I asked, "How are they bringing down the shield?"

He refused to answer that, as well, simply insisting that they would succeed in their assigned task. I asked a few more questions, but I couldn't get much more information out of him. In the end, he gave me a time and date before making it clear that I would have only one chance to infiltrate Olympus.

"What about the people inside?" I asked. "How am I going to get them out?"

He shook his head. "That is not my concern. I told you I would get you in, and this is how I'm doing it," Alistaris said. "Beyond that, you are on your own."

"I suppose that's fair."

"Once this is finished, we'll meet and discuss the future," he said, climbing down from the chair. It would have been comical if it wasn't for the fact that I suspected he was more than capable of killing me. I didn't know how strong Alistaris really was, but I knew enough that I didn't want to test him.

"Looking forward to it."

After that, I escorted him out of the ship. Once he was gone, I gave *The Leviathan* a good once-over to ensure that he hadn't somehow left behind more bugs. I didn't find any, which made me more nervous than if I had.

Once that was done, I set my mind to the problem at hand. I had a little more than a week until Olympus's shields would come down, and in that time, I needed to figure out a way to rescue Caden and the others the Pacificians had imprisoned in the city.

CHAPTER FORTY-NINE

INGRESS

Finally creating the working prototype of my armor was a huge moment for me. I knew it wouldn't really close the gap between Mira and me. But I felt it would make me a little less of a liability. I'm still not sure if I was right or wrong.

—Patrick Ward

I pored over the map of Olympus, memorizing my route. I knew it wouldn't be easy, but I thought that, so long as Alistaris came through, I had a real shot at rescuing the prisoners. I still had no idea what the Pacificians wanted with all those people—or why they hadn't simply been copied before sending their brain-dead bodies up to the moon—but I expected it would be something terrible.

Because it always was.

Just once, I wanted to find some aliens who were actually helping humanity rather than enslaving them. But I knew just how unlikely that was. Even Alistaris and his ilk only wanted to use us to further their own agendas—and that was likely due to the fact that people like me were expendable. It was a firm reminder that, in the wider universe, humanity was only as safe as we were useful.

Or dangerous.

I endeavored to become the latter. When everything was said and done, nobody would mess with me—or Earth—unless they were ready for a knock-down, drag-out fight. Only when that thought crossed my mind did I realize that I'd wholly committed to the war Alistaris had recruited me to fight. And it had nothing to do with him, either. The fact of the matter was that I was tired. Not physically, but I was so done with walking into alien installations and finding that they'd done something terrible to a group of humans.

The first time I had seen it was outside that very first Rift, when the Casto-rix had enslaved the local human population via slave implants and skills that had equated pleasure with obedience. Those humans had gone insane when I'd killed their masters, forcing me to kill them. And ever since then, I'd seen one instance of enslavement after another, each more disgusting than the last, culminating with the E'rok Tan keeping people who'd been genetically altered to the point of becoming unthinking cattle.

By comparison, what the Pacificians had done was nothing. It was still hor-rific, but it was difficult to compete with monsters who literally bred and ate sentient beings.

Perhaps there were good aliens out there. Alistaris and his Ark Alliance very well might fall into that category. However, I wasn't going to hold my breath expecting them to save humanity. They would oppose the Gomari Con-federation, but if it came down to a choice between humanity and achieving their goals, I knew precisely which decision they would make.

Was it fair? Was it just?

No. Not at all. But that was the nature of the world. And of the universe, it seemed. I'd tried to move away from my pessimistic attitude. Down that cynical road lay ruin. Yet it was difficult to look at the world with any sense of optimism when everything I saw continued to show me just how naive positivity was.

"You alright?" asked Patrick, who'd spent the night in *The Leviathan* for once. He slid into the chair across the table from me. "You've been staring at nothing for, like, an hour now."

I blinked, letting out a sigh. "Studying," I answered. "I'm tired of going into situations unprepared. The last few missions have been difficult."

Indeed, they had. For the past few years, I'd tried to be extremely careful, gathering as much information as I could before commencing any attack. But ever since that ill-fated heist with Askar, Isaac, and the others, I'd been forced into one desperate situation after another. And I intended to change that going forward because I knew just how lucky I was to have survived so far.

"You know what I think."

I did. Patrick had made it abundantly clear that he didn't really trust that Alistaris and his Alliance had our best interests at heart. I agreed with that assessment, but I wasn't going to let it dissuade me from doing what I felt I needed to do. Patrick, by contrast, was adamant that we should simply lie low until the end of the Initialization. The moment the Integration dawned and the quarantine dropped, he wanted to leave Earth behind.

Conveniently, he'd neglected the very simple fact that doing so wouldn't really solve anything. In fact, it would likely create more problems than it solved. After all, where would we go? And more importantly, what would we do once we got there? I was very good at what I'd been trained to do, but I didn't think I could just settle down and become a shopkeeper or something.

I was a warrior, and a warrior without a battle to fight is, by definition, useless.

Of course, Patrick insisted that we would figure it out. I knew it was all based on a desire to protect me. He'd seen how my various battles had affected me, and he didn't want me to backslide into the habits I'd developed after Nova's fall.

I respected that, but I couldn't let his worries deflect me from my budding purpose. For so long, I'd been passively surviving. I had no issues targeting aliens, but I'd had no interest in fighting a war. That had begun to change. I knew Alistaris had his own agenda, that he was using me, but I could accept that so long as he followed through with his promises of support as humanity fought against the incoming tide of invaders.

They were coming. My uncle had known that. But he'd given up on fighting against them because he didn't think there was any way to win. Alistaris and his Alliance gave us a chance, and I wasn't so jaded that I was willing to turn that down.

"I know," I said. "But this is our shot, Pick. With his help, we might be able to fight the other aliens off."

"Or we might just be exchanging one set of oppressors for another," he pointed out.

"I talked to Kith, and she said—"

He raised his hands and interrupted me, "I know what you found out. I read the files, same as you. The Ark Alliance is the real deal. But for all we know, that's just propaganda."

"Everything is propaganda, Patrick," I said. "There's no such thing as an impartial source of information. Every file we read has some inherent bias. But I've got it from multiple sources that the Ark Alliance isn't interested in colonization or conquest. They don't try to take a planet's resources. They don't enslave its people. Their whole thing is to let each population live on their own terms."

"From what I read, their whole thing is to oppose the Gomari Confederation," Patrick said.

"Because they're the bad guys," I pointed out.

"Does that make the Alliance the good guys?" he asked.

I shrugged. "The lesser of two evils," I stated. "I'm not blind, Pick. I know what they are. They might have started out with principles, but the Alliance is just using us. I get that. We're a means to an end. Earth is just another proxy war for them."

"So, why go along with it?"

"Because we don't have a choice!" I said, slapping my hand on the table. "We don't, Pick. I know you think we can just zoom off into space and leave everything behind. But I know you. I know you could never do that. It would eat you up inside, thinking about what you left on Earth. Because you know what'll happen if we don't fight back, don't you? Maybe they won't enslave everyone. Not officially. But they'll bring their technology and equipment and soldiers, and they'll turn this planet into—"

"I know, Mira."

"Then why are you fighting me on this? I have to do it."

"I know that, too."

"Then what's wrong?"

"You go down this road, I don't know if you're coming back," he said.

"I've survived so far," I pointed out.

"Oh, you'll probably live. That's what you do. But you'll leave a lot of death and destruction in your wake," he predicted. Before I could counter that, he went on, "And I couldn't care less about any of them. If you kill them, they probably deserved it. But I worry about you. I worry that it'll be worse than it was after Nova."

"It won't."

"You say that, but I'm not sure I believe it. You like to act like an unrepentant killer, Mira. And you can be, so long as you're dealing with the bad guys. But when it comes to . . . collateral damage . . ."

"I hate it when you call them that. People shouldn't be called collateral damage."

"I know. But you know innocent people are going to die. You'll probably have to kill some of them yourself. Are you going to be able to live with yourself if you have to make a decision between accomplishing your mission and killing a few innocents?"

"I've done it before."

"And it almost broke you, Mira."

"It won't this time."

He shook his head. "I hope you're right. I do. I just . . . I don't know, Mira. I don't know the right answer. I just hate that we're put in this situation," he said.

I locked my eyes on his. "War isn't pretty. Innocent people are going to die," I said. "It's not about weighing lives. Nobody can do that. It's about conviction. Commitment to the mission. The aliens need to be stopped, and I'm going to help stop them. Whatever it takes."

"That's what I'm afraid of."

After that, we both went silent. I didn't know how to respond, and he didn't have anything else to say. We could have repeated our arguments, but at that point, we would've just been talking in circles.

I certainly understood Patrick's point, and until recently, I had been of a similar mind. But the fact that I now thought there was an alternative, that humanity had an opportunity to fight a war and win, had altered my thinking. Then, once that was combined with the atrocities I'd seen in the past few months, I couldn't just run away. Not in good conscience, at least.

I hoped he could find it in him to understand.

Eventually, Patrick changed the subject to his project. His recent breakthrough had been just as impactful as he'd expected, and they were nearing the point where a viable prototype could be constructed.

"What combat capability are we talking about?" I asked.

"At first? Not much," he admitted. "We've got to build the weapons systems from scratch, and that means reverse engineering whatever we want to integrate into the armor. Then, we've got to make it play nice with existing systems. After that, we'll have to work out the kinks, troubleshoot any additional problems, and then—"

"You could just say you've got a long way to go," I chided with a grin.

"We do," he said, returning my smile with one of his own. "But it'll be durable right out of the gate. So, there's that."

"What are you calling it?" I asked.

He shrugged. "Not sure. I think—"

"The Turtle."

"What?"

"The Turtle," I repeated. "Think about it. It'll have strong defenses without many weapons, right? And you said it was slow."

"I didn't say that."

"It is, though, right?"

"I mean, it's not fast, but—"

"The Turtle," I repeated once again.

"I'm not calling it the Turtle."

"So you say. So you say," I said.

"You're going to call it that regardless of what I want, aren't you?"

"I am."

"I hate you."

"No you don't."

He sighed. "Whatever. Look—I'm going to head back to the shop," he said, pushing himself to his feet. "But . . . I mean . . . Just reconsider what I said, okay? Don't go making any big commitments without considering the repercussions."

"I always do," I said.

"You think about how it'll affect your mission. Or other people. You never think about what it'll do to you. Just once, I'm begging you to take the time to consider whether or not this war, if it comes to that, is worth your sanity," he said.

I knew it was useless to argue with him, so I just said, "I'll think about it."

"That's all I ask."

Then, after leaning in and giving me a kiss, he left *The Leviathan*.

Once he was gone, I retreated into my system, where I continued to study Olympus's layout. A few hours later, I got what I'd been waiting on when Alistaris initiated a connection. I accepted it, asking, "Is it time?"

"It's time," he answered. "Do you know where to go?"

"I do."

"Then good luck," he said. "In six hours, the shield is coming down. Stay alive. We can't get any use out of you if you're dead."

Even though he couldn't see me, I nodded and responded, "Pretty sure we're on the same page about me not being dead."

"Indeed."

And with that, he canceled the connection. I took a deep breath, then went over my last-minute checklist. After making sure that I had my supplies squared away, I initiated a Secure Connection with Patrick and let him know that I was going. We'd already discussed it, so he simply said, "Good luck. I love you."

"Love you, too."

Then, it was time.

So, I headed to *The Leviathan's* cockpit, and a few minutes later, the ship was in the air and flying across the landscape. I covered the distance between Fortune and my designated landing zone in only an hour. Then, I activated Bastion before leaving the ship behind. I opted for the Cutter, and soon enough, I was weaving my way through the wilderness as I headed toward Olympus.

It was a little more than two hours before I caught sight of the city on the mountain, and once I pulled to a stop, I gave it a quick once-over, establishing that it was almost entirely unchanged from my last stint of surveillance. So, after dismissing the hover bike, I set off on foot until I reached the outpost at the base of the mountain.

According to the files I'd read, it was sparsely populated with Pacifician soldiers, and it was only intended to serve as the gateway to the city proper. As such, it was well fortified and manned by cameras, guards, and enough drones to make any infiltration a pain. Thankfully, I had a plan to bypass everything.

It took me a few minutes to find the abandoned well that was a remnant of whatever settlement had existed before the Pacificians took over the area. Once I found it, I didn't hesitate to leap over the edge and plunge into the depths. I splashed down into ankle-deep murky water.

Then, I ran my hand over the wall, searching for the hole Alistaris's people had dug. He'd promised to get me into the city, and if I was going to do that, I had to go through the outpost first. So, he'd been obligated to ensure that I did so unseen. Thus, the tunnel that I found only a few seconds later.

I climbed inside and slithered forward. Inch by inch, I covered almost two hundred yards until I tumbled out into a storage cellar. Looking back, I saw that it had been concealed behind a holographic display. It wouldn't fool anyone for long, but it didn't need to, either. Once I reached my destination, it didn't matter if the Pacificians discovered the tunnel.

In any case, aside from bringing Olympus's Mist shield down, that was as far as Alistaris was going to go. From there on out, I was on my own. Which was fine by me. I appreciated his help, and it had kept me from having to waste a bunch of time disabling cameras and drones, but I'd always worked better when I didn't have to depend on anyone else.

Perhaps that said something about me.

In any case, I quickly searched the cellar, finding the stairs that would lead up to the ground floor. When I did, I engaged Stealth and, after using a combination of my {Mistrunner} senses and Observation to confirm that no one was on the other side, I opened the door and stepped through.

What I saw was the expected supply depot that had been marked on my map. I didn't bother inspecting the crates or boxes. Instead, I quickly crossed the distance to the side door, then headed into the neighboring alley. Cloaked in Stealth, I crept forward and took stock of the situation within the outpost.

As far as I could tell, it was business as usual. Upon learning that the Pacificians were androids connected to a central mind, I'd expected them to act like a bunch of robots. However, what I saw was no different from any other settlement. For the most part, the Pacificians were just trying to live their lives.

Most probably didn't even know that they were only copies of real people.

Using Stealth, I quickly made my way through the outpost, not stopping until I reached the lift that would take me up the mountain. I only had to wait for a few minutes before it descended from on high. When it did, I boarded alongside a half dozen Pacificians and a couple of heavy trucks laden with supplies.

Then, it ascended.

This was the tricky part, and I tensed as the lift quickly covered the thousand or so feet to the top. Ahead, the Mist shield loomed, glimmering, ominous, and blue. According to the schematics I'd been given, it was a unique shield that never came down. The only people who got through were Pacificians or the ones they'd marked via some unknown method to which I had no access. There were no nearby terminals. No targets to Misthack. And it extended in a dome around the whole city. To put it bluntly, it was impregnable without the benefit of an all-out assault.

Which was precisely the plan.

But first, I needed to get into position. Once the lift reached a certain point, I climbed atop the rail and, seeing a likely handhold, leaped to the nearby cliff face. For a moment that seemed to stretch into eternity, I sailed through the air. But then I hit the side of the cliff with an impact that, if anyone was paying attention, would've looked extremely peculiar, considering that I was, for all intents and purposes, invisible. Thankfully, by that point, the lift had risen another thirty feet, and the chances of anyone seeing me from the ground were nil.

I hung there, my fingers aching as I clung to the smallest of handholds.

Then, I started to climb.

Five minutes later, I reached my designated position. The shield was only eight inches away from my face—close enough that the Mist practically singed my eyebrows. Then, I checked my timer. I had arrived ahead of schedule.

Twenty minutes.

That's how long I needed to wait. So, that's what I did. Thankfully, my attributes were high enough that I could do it, but no matter how inflated my Constitution was, there was nothing comfortable about hanging a thousand feet above the ground with only the strength of my fingers to keep me from plummeting to my likely death.

Maybe I could survive such a fall.

Probably, actually.

But there was no way I could do so without significant injury. And considering I was surrounded by enemies, the fact that I could live through the fall was mostly inconsequential.

The minutes passed slowly, and I couldn't stop myself from frequently checking the clock imbedded within my interface. I tried to distract myself, but that was a tall, nearly impossible task. So, in the end, I just settled on watching for the signal.

I got it nineteen minutes after I'd reached my position. Just on time, then.

The final seconds passed, and I tensed, ready to spring into action. And finally, the time came.

And at first, nothing happened.

Five seconds passed. Then ten. Twenty. And still, nothing.

I was on the verge of contacting Alistaris when I felt something coming. I glanced to the north, and at first, I didn't see it. And when I did, my jaw dropped.

I had expected a lot of things. Perhaps they'd planted a bomb. Or maybe they'd convinced someone to turn coat and disable the shield. But what I hadn't expected was to see three miniature suns arcing through the air on a collision course with Olympus.

I closed my eyes, but as they drew closer, I could feel the roiling Mist speeding in my direction. I braced, tightening my grip to such a degree that the rock beneath my fingers started to crack. I didn't care.

Not with what I felt coming my way.

And then they hit, one after another. The first sent a ripple of Mist flowing through the shield. The second sent another. But the third . . . The third brought it down altogether. The shock wave of the impacts stripped me of my Stealth, but I couldn't worry myself with that. Instead, I scrambled forward, leaping from one handhold to another as quickly as I could. In seconds, I'd covered ten feet.

Then twenty. The Mist roiled, heralding the reactivation of the shield.

Thirty. I still wasn't safe. If it completed activation before I made it to the top, I would be obliterated. The sheer energy of the Mist would tear me apart, regardless of how much Constitution I could boast.

Just as I felt it activate, I dove over the lip and rolled to safety. Immediately, I reactivated Stealth and Camouflage, then looked around. I had reached the top of the mountain. Now, the real work could begin.

CHAPTER FIFTY

SETTING THE STAGE

People change. We grow. We regress. Our priorities shift, and we commit to courses of action that would've once seemed unthinkable. Never was that more apparent than when I realized that I didn't want to save the world. I didn't really care about a bunch of innocent strangers. When it came down to it, all that really mattered to me was that Mira and I survived. Everything else was secondary. But Mira—she's different. She talks the talk, but when it really comes down to it, she would give everything up if it meant beating the aliens.

—Patrick Ward

The top of the mountain had been flattened into a plateau, upon which rested a large disc reminiscent of the ones in Nova City. On top of that was a city sizable enough to house hundreds of thousands of people. Until I went through the shield, I hadn't realized just how widespread the Pacificians' efforts really were. But looking at the towering buildings that comprised Olympus, I couldn't escape the fact that, if even half those structures were occupied, their operations were far more ubiquitous than I'd expected.

It was a sobering thought, and one that reinforced my determination to make them pay for what they had done.

So, once I got my feet underneath me, I set off across the grassy expanse between the reactivated Mist shield and the outskirts of the city. As I did, I studied my surroundings, and once again, I was surprised by what I saw. The knowledge that everything had been built by hive-minded androids had prepared me to expect the city to be composed of a bunch of featureless boxes. In my mind, the architecture wouldn't be so different from what I'd seen back in Nova, but without any of that city's individualistic flourishes.

And in a way, I was right. It did look like Nova. But rather than the utilitarian designs so common in poor districts like the Garden, it took its cues from the more affluent platforms like Lakeview. Glittering glass, shining steel, and green topiary abounded, making Olympus look paradisial. Upon first glance, the place didn't even look occupied. It was more like a series of statues than a place meant for habitation.

But as I drew closer, that perception proved erroneous when I saw the robed inhabitants. Some were clad in brown. Others red. Still others wore yellow or green or a number of other hues. I knew that those colors were indicative of social status, but I had no idea how any of that worked—especially considering that, according to everything I'd read, they were a completely egalitarian society. Wealth had no place in their culture, save for when they dealt with other civilizations. And given that they were all connected to the same hive mind, the Pacificians were supposed to have an entirely collectivistic view of life.

Clearly, even in such a supposedly equal society, there was some degree of stratification. In truth, that felt like the most relatable thing I'd seen from the Pacificians. People—even hive-minded androids—needed some hill to climb. They needed goals. And in the absence of money, there was usually power to fill that void. Or social status. Or countless other means of differentiating between the high achievers and everyone else.

Because some people were simply more valuable to a society than others.

I couldn't help but wonder where I'd fit into such a system. Was I valuable enough to warrant a gold robe, which as far as I could tell, was the highest rank in Olympus? Or would I be clad in brown?

I liked to think that I was inherently special. Everyone did. But the difference was that I had results to back me up. I had accomplished great things in the past handful of years. Terrible. But great, too. Did that mean I was special? Or had I just started ahead of everyone else?

I only let myself dwell on that for a few seconds before I dismissed the subject. It didn't matter. I couldn't change my past. I couldn't go back and keep my uncle from passing on all the advantages I'd used to get ahead. I could only keep moving forward and hope I made the right choices to justify that investment.

With that in mind, I continued across the open area until something twinged my {Mistrunner} senses. I stopped midstride, and it was just in time, too. Because the moment I focused on what I'd felt, I discovered that I'd been walking across a killing field populated by hundreds of autoturrets. They were sequestered below the turf, but they were there, nonetheless.

And to my horror, my foot, which hovered a few inches off the ground, had been on the verge of crossing a barely detectible web of Mist that would no doubt activate the turrets. I stood, balanced on one foot and cloaked in Stealth, as I sent my awareness out. And when I did, I discovered just how lucky I'd been.

Running from one end of the lawn to the next, which was a couple hundred yards wide, was a latticework of Mist. How I'd managed to get even a few steps without setting off an alarm was a mystery. Was I just that lucky? Or had my senses subtly guided me to safety? I had no idea, and I was in no position to figure it out.

I glanced skyward. I'd begun my infiltration at night, so the place was still bathed in darkness. However, that wouldn't last much longer because dawn was only a couple of hours off. Once the sun rose, even Stealth wouldn't be enough to keep me hidden. Not unless I settled down and refused to move, which was not an option.

No—I needed to cross the killing field before the sun rose, or bad things were going to happen.

My first thought was to simply Misthack into the governing systems, shut off the autoturrets, and then continue on my stroll toward the city. However, that turned out to be a nonstarter because, despite my studious practice, the Mistwall around the systems in question were completely impenetrable. Try as I might, I couldn't bypass them. Perhaps it would've been possible if I'd had a hard connection and a few hours, but there was a distinct difference between what I could do with Misthack and Mistwalk, and I'd run headlong into the former's limitations.

So, with that out of the question, I focused on the web of Mist itself. The one good thing was that it was entirely static, which was lucky because, if it had been in motion, I'd have already tripped the alarms. As it was, I just had to keep my senses about me, and I felt confident that I could weave my way through them.

With that in mind, that's what I set out to do.

In theory, avoiding those thin strands of Mist was easy enough. But in practice, doing so was an exercise in tedium, body control, and focus. Fortunately, I was well trained in each category, and over the next ninety minutes, I crossed the lawn. Sometimes, it was as easy as stepping in the right place, but at other times, I had to contort my body around the Mist with only a fraction of an inch to spare. If I hadn't been cloaked in Stealth, I would've made for a curious sight, but in the end, I made it to the outskirts with plenty of time to spare.

In the shadow of one of the buildings, I took a few minutes to rest. From a physical perspective, the crossing hadn't been terribly tiring, but as an exercise in focus, it had been more than a little draining. But I could only afford a little time to reset my mind before I needed to move on.

As I did, I got a closer look at the Pacifician society. And I was sorely disappointed by the mundanity of it all. When I'd considered a city full of robot people, I'd expected to find a wholly different sort of society, but what I saw wasn't so different from what I'd encountered in a dozen other cities. People still had to eat and sleep and endure all life's other necessities. The only difference was that, in Olympus, there wasn't any crime or filth.

Seeing that, I couldn't help but wonder if they had the right of it.

Of course, such would never have been possible with humanity at the fore. Our very nature prevented it. We were dirty, self-interested, and destructive, and there didn't seem to be any way around that. All we could do was implement policies to counteract the worst of our nature.

For a while, I just wandered through the city. With Stealth concealing me, I wasn't worried about anyone noticing my presence, and before long, I found my way to the first stop on my list of targets.

In truth, it didn't really matter where I started. Eventually, I'd get plenty of coverage. But I'd developed a plan to maximize the spread of the Ghost I intended to utilize. So, with that in mind, I crept into what I'd dubbed the central command station. Fortunately, with the city locked down, they didn't have much use for surveillance of fancy defenses.

There were cameras and drones, but they were low quality and easily bypassed. I had half expected the attack that had very temporarily brought the shield down to change that, but the moment the Mist shield had gone back up, the Pacificians in Olympus had gone back to normal.

Likely, they had some sort of strike force hunting down the originators, but the city itself had been largely unaffected. As I'd expected, based on the files I'd read—but even knowing what to expect, I was grateful to see that the intelligence I'd gathered was correct.

In any case, there were no major obstacles between me and my first destination, and the few hurdles I had to clear were easily bypassed. Soon enough, I found myself as deep behind enemy lines as I could've ever hoped.

That's when I picked a target—a woman in a gold robe—and used Surge, which would enhance the next Ghost I used, then activated Misthack. After bypassing her strangely anemic defenses, I chose to upload a Ghost from a specialized deck I'd prepared specifically for the mission.

The Ghost in question, which I'd chosen to call *Extermination*, took most of its structure from *Time Bomb*. It still required a significant gestation period before it could activate. However, it would remain inert unless I triggered it. That meant that, over the course of the next few days, I could infect the entire population. Unbeknownst to them, every time one of the infected made contact, they would spread the Ghost to someone else. Eventually, it would blanket the entire population.

With *Time Bomb*, that never would've been possible. It would've gone active well before everyone was infected. But with *Extermination*, that just wasn't the case.

The second change I'd made was that it would only affect androids. While in the lunar base, I'd had plenty of time to study the Pacificians, and I'd used that information to create a few very specialized Ghosts. *Extermination* was one of those, but I had a couple of others in my deck just in case things went wrong.

The upside to all those limitations was that *Extermination* was extremely deadly. I didn't for one second think that it would kill off the entire population. But I felt confident that it could handle most. And besides, it was only the first stage of my plan.

Over the next day, I traveled all over the city, making certain that I got as much coverage as possible. Then, I found a secluded corner of a mostly empty building where I settled in to wait for the Surge-enhanced Ghost to complete its gestation period. Three days later, the notifications that the Ghost was ready started rolling in. At first, it was only a handful, but soon enough, hundreds, then thousands flew past. That lasted for another day until those notifications came to a trickle, then ceased altogether.

Like that, the saturation point had been reached, which freed me to enact the next part of my plan.

Of course, that included bombs. Lots and lots of bombs.

Each was tiny. Barely bigger than my thumb, but they were packed full of a high-grade explosive compound I'd created myself. By themselves, they weren't good for much. But when placed at just the right points? With my modifiers, I hoped they would be enough to bring the buildings down.

I didn't have enough to destroy every building in the city. However, I did have enough to target the most important ones. In the majority of cases, I had no idea what purpose those buildings served. Instead, I just aimed to bring down the ones frequented by the higher-ranked Pacificians. That they'd color coded themselves just made my job that much easier.

The infiltration of each building took all my combined skills working together. Stealth to keep from being seen. Misthack to bypass locked doors and disable cameras and drones. Mistwalk to access security terminals and download building schematics so I'd know precisely where to put my bombs. And on a couple of occasions, I had to utilize my combat skills when bad luck or coincidence forced me to fight.

Fortunately, I remained undetected, and I kept my body count to a minimum.

Over the next four days, I was like a ghost haunting Olympus, and eventually, I finished my task. One command, and I could bring down almost two dozen of the city's most important buildings.

By that point, the stress forced me to take a break, and I spent the next day resting.

Once I felt refreshed, I started in on the third part of my plan by targeting the building I'd marked as the hub. It was in the center of the city, but unlike many of the other important structures, barely anyone ever visited. The only reason I'd recognized it as important was because of the sheer amount of Mist it contained. So, seeing that, I had resolved to check it out, and when I did, I discovered that it was the apparatus by which the local Pacificians kept in contact with the central mind.

I had no idea how it worked. But all my sources of information—Kith and Alistaris, mostly—said that the Pacificians were not a true hive mind. Each individual had some degree of autonomy, but they were still all connected. And the structure at the center of the city, which was shaped like a giant dimpled ball with a huge spire at its crown, was the means by which they maintained contact.

At first, I considered simply destroying it along with the rest of the important buildings, but then I thought better of it. I knew I was taking a risk—after all, at any point, my bombs could be detected—but my idea demanded due diligence. So, I retreated to the mostly empty building that I had established as my temporary base of operations and settled in to start working on some new Ghosts.

It took me almost a week to get it mostly right.

The result wasn't perfect, and using it would do nothing on its own. However, when taken in tandem with *Extermination*, I hoped it would give the Pacificians every reason to avoid Earth in the future.

Or maybe I would start some kind of intergalactic war.

Which was fine by me, if I was honest. As far as I was concerned, we were already at war. I was just taking things to the next obvious step for someone with my skill set. So, armed with my new Ghost, I headed back to the hub and, over the next hour, gradually gained entry. It was slow going because the security was a good deal tighter than anywhere else in the city, but I was more than up to the task.

Soon enough, I found myself in the center of the building and looking across a catwalk that extended to the midpoint of the structure's spherical interior. The Mist in the area was thick enough that it had manifested as blue vapor, which filled the building with a dense fog that felt almost solid. I stepped out onto the catwalk and slowly made my way to the consoles at the center.

At each one sat a silver-robed Pacifician. I didn't know what that color meant, but I reasoned that it denoted some importance. It didn't matter. They needed to die if I was going to accomplish my goals. However, I knew that killing them would eventually set off the alarms, which in turn meant that the last part of my plan would be a race against time.

So, I understandably took a few minutes to compose myself and, for the thousandth time, confirm that I knew the remainder of my plan. Step by step, I went over everything I needed to do to finish my mission until, at last, I felt I was ready to kick things off. Once I did, I took a deep breath, letting the fog-like Mist soothe me before I took the final few steps that put me directly behind my first target.

She was a woman, and like so many other Pacificians I'd seen, blonde-haired, blue-eyed, and with the sort of artificially perfect features that instantly put my hackles up. I pulled a nano-bladed dagger from my arsenal implant, and then, without missing another beat, activated Execute before stabbing her in the base of the skull where I knew it would do the most damage. I caught her before she could fall, then leaned her forward so she wouldn't immediately alert the others.

Then, moving swiftly but with care, I dispatched the next. And the next after that. The fourth one gave me some trouble when she suddenly turned, wide-eyed, and started to say something, but I mercilessly buried my dagger in her forehead. That didn't kill her—not immediately—but it certainly stopped her from reacting before I snatched her blonde hair, yanked her head forward, and buried my other dagger in the vulnerable base of her skull, destroying her Nexus Implant.

And just like that, all four were dead.

Which put me on the clock, so I yanked my personal link out of the Hand of God, then plugged it into the massive terminal. The defenses activated immediately, but over the next few minutes, I bypassed them, one after another, until the system finally opened up to me. When it did, I felt something looming in the virtual distance. Something powerful. Something I could scarcely comprehend. It wasn't a physical being but, rather, another entity connected to the system, and I knew it was only a matter of time before it noticed me. So, without further hesitation, I uploaded the Ghost I'd prepared specifically for that moment, then disconnected.

That was when an expected but still unwelcome alarm sounded.

I'd hoped I would have a little more time, that I would get out of the building before they knew I was there. But that just wasn't in the cards.

So, I took off, abandoning stealth as I crossed the catwalk as quickly as my feet would carry me. It only took a second, but when I reached the door leading to the rest of the facility, a pair of androids loomed before me. I didn't hesitate, and neither did they.

In an instant, the sound of gunfire filled the building. I dashed to the side, peppering the pair of guards with explosive rounds from my assault rifle. By itself, the weapon was incapable of taking them down—not quickly at least—but with my skill enhancing the ammunition, it was more than up to the task of taking them out of the fight.

My barrage didn't kill them, but I didn't need it to. Instead, I only cared about getting them out of the way so I could secure my exit, which was precisely what I did. And as soon as I was in the clear, I used Vanish, then once again embraced Stealth and started the long and arduous process of creeping past the rest of the guards.

Fortunately, Olympus didn't have the security capabilities of the lunar base, so aside from a few close calls, I had no trouble making it out of the building and to the relatively safe haven that was my temporary base.

Once there, I triggered the explosives. Then, I activated my Ghost. And finally, as the city collapsed into chaos and ruin, I set off to complete the final part of my mission.

CHAPTER FIFTY-ONE

THE PRISONERS

We're playing with forces we don't understand. Every detail I uncover about the way Mist circuits interact with cybernetic parts shows me just how ignorant we are. We don't know what the system really is. Nor do we know where it came from. Not really. We're just scrambling to keep our heads above water. Meanwhile, the aliens have known how to swim for years.

—Patrick Ward

Buildings crumbled as my carefully placed demolition charges destroyed the supports necessary to keep them upright. With Mist, miracles were possible, but no structure could stand when its foundation had been sundered. The same was true when it came to the androids that had built Olympus.

Extermination was no simple Ghost, and I'd spent countless hours perfecting its construction. So, I was unsurprised to see Pacificians dropping left and right, dead before they even hit the ground.

While its structure was anything but simple, the purpose of the Ghost was as uncomplicated as any I'd ever created. It was there to kill. That was it. And in the case of the Pacificians that were my target, the easiest way to accomplish that goal was to sever their connection with the Nexus Implants at the base of each android's skull.

With a human—or any other biological entity—that strategy wouldn't result in instant death. Eventually, they would succumb, either dying or becoming wildlings, but in terms of immediate effects, they would only lose access to their skills. But with androids like the Pacificians, the effects were much more abrupt. They were creatures of Mist, and as such, they couldn't exist without it.

So, without their Nexus Implants, they were just bundles of cybernetics, without will or direction.

So, in effect, even as I destroyed the buildings' foundations, I did the same to the Pacificians.

I jogged through the city, maintaining Stealth along the way. It wasn't perfect, but amid all the chaos, no one was looking for a shimmer in the air. Instead, the stronger Pacificians who'd managed to resist the effects of my Ghost were far more concerned with the death and destruction all around them.

And it was glorious.

I was never one to revel in murder. Certainly, I'd felt a certain sense of justice upon killing people who I thought deserved it. But I'd never felt anything as satisfying as when I watched thousands of Pacificians drop dead. They were people. I knew that. It didn't matter that they were cybernetic. They were, each and every one of them, capable of independent thought and emotions. But even so, I had no qualms about killing every last one of them.

This was no Nova City. In Olympus, there were no innocents.

Except for the people I intended to save. So, I ran through the wide avenues, a smug sense of satisfaction enveloping my mind. I was so busy patting myself on the back that the resultant inattention very nearly got me killed.

Not by Olympus's defenders. But, rather, because of my own actions.

Above, one of the elevated trains the androids used for transportation jumped its tracks and crashed into the street in front of me. The impact jolted me out of my self-congratulatory malaise, and I leaped. However, as the train screeched across the pavement on a collision course with my position, I knew I wouldn't make it over. So, I activated Double Jump and sprang off a cushion of Mist, narrowly dodging the out-of-control train. It smashed into one of the remaining buildings—I had only destroyed the ones I'd deemed important, after all—and the individual cars began to buckle upward.

Which presented another problem, considering I'd barely managed to clear the train in the first place. I desperately tried to activate Double Jump again, but like many abilities, it came with a cooldown that prevented chain activation.

I fell.

The train rose to meet me.

But right before it smashed into me, I activated Balance, then, using the increased coordination that came with the ability, twisted in the air before planting one foot on the train's fuselage. I sprang away, using it to change directions, and flew through the air before colliding with one of the building's windows. It shattered on impact, the glass cutting my clothes to pieces. Thankfully, it was incapable of slicing through my infiltration suit, though, so I was almost entirely unharmed.

Still, I picked up quite a few scratches on my face and exposed hand.

I ignored them as I hit the ground at a roll, then leaped to my feet and sprinted through the building. Fortunately, the Pacificians only used a handful of floor plans for their buildings, so I had no trouble navigating my way through the maze of halls. As I did so, though, the building shook, telling me in no uncertain terms that the collision with the train had compromised the integrity of its foundation.

I dashed through the building as it crumbled around me, and when I saw another window, I didn't hesitate to lower my shoulder, cover my face, and dive through the glass.

Once again, I found myself falling through the air. Chaos reigned all around me as the air was filled with the sound of falling buildings, a citywide alarm, and crashing vehicles below. I hit the ground hard, and even though I absorbed some of the momentum by rolling, I felt the impact in my bones. I didn't break anything, but I knew I'd come very close.

But that pain was easily ignored, courtesy of my Pain Tolerance, and the moment I found my feet, I was once again running. A second later, the sound of gunfire sent me diving for cover. Bullets tore into the concrete and ripped holes in the hover car behind which I'd hidden.

Apparently, some of the survivors were paying more attention than others.

I peeked over the hood to see a half dozen Pacificians surrounding me in a half circle. Above them flew a trio of surveillance drones. With their powerful cameras and other sensors, they would render Stealth useless.

Not that I thought that was an option. It was one thing to sneak around and remain undetected when nobody knew you were there. But it was something else altogether to do so when the enemy was alert and looking for you. Possible? Sure. But only when ineptitude reared its helpful head. Looking at the enemy warriors, I didn't think that was likely.

The first thing I did was try to Misthack them, but predictably, I found their defenses impenetrable. Perhaps if I'd had a hard connection via my personal link, I could have done something with Mistwalk, but as the matter stood, I wasn't getting through. Not surprising, given that they'd managed to survive my first Ghost. I knew some would, but I estimated that only ten or fifteen percent of the Pacificians were strong enough to resist the effects. Some of those would have been killed by falling buildings or in the chaos I'd created, too.

In any case, only the strongest would have made it this far, so I knew I had my work cut out for me. It was a good thing, then, that I had some tricks up my sleeve.

I summoned my Pulsar, used Explosive Shot to enhance the entire magazine of ammunition, then activated my newest ability, Vanish. The moment I disappeared, I rose from cover, activated Multishot, marking all five targets, then used Execute before finally activating Empowered Shot. I knew the invisibility that came with Vanish wouldn't last long, so I immediately took aim, waited the requisite second for Empowered Shot to take effect, then fired.

On its own, the Pulsar was already an extremely powerful weapon, and it was made even more so by my significant modifiers. Then, that damage was further enhanced by Explosive Shot. And finally, using Execute multiplied that already augmented damage by five hundred percent.

The results were explosive, if predictable.

The primary shot hit with enough force that it looked like the most powerful Pacifician simply ceased to exist above the waist. The remaining four targets took less damage—the trade-off of being able to hit multiple enemies at once—but with all those enhancements running at once, it didn't really matter. One exploded, showering the immediate vicinity in gore. Another had a hole torn through her torso. The third reacted to the sound of the gunshot quickly enough that he almost dodged. But almost wasn't enough, and when the round took him in the shoulder, it destroyed that side of his chest. Another was cut in half at the waist, and though she didn't immediately die, I quickly took her out with another shot from the Pulsar.

That left one enemy and a handful of drones. Not bad for two shots, but it had the detriment of using almost my entire store of Mist. Fortunately, I had a couple of Mist boosters to solve that problem, and in the chaos, I jammed one in my hip and discharged its payload.

Even as the booster took hold, I was moving. By the time my first step hit the pavement, I'd already exchanged my Pulsar for the assault rifle, and as I strafed to the side, I peppered the lone remaining Pacifician with a barrage of unenhanced gunfire.

He took it without any real damage, but that wasn't the point. Instead, I only wanted to drive him back and keep him off-balance while I relocated to a position where I could take aim at the drones. A few moments later, I'd sent three concentrated bursts of gunfire downrange, and the comparatively defenseless drones were destroyed.

That left only one enemy.

And I knew precisely how to deal with him.

I continued to fire, and though my aim was true, he'd begun to recover from the shock of seeing his comrades so thoroughly destroyed. Which was bad for me because he was carrying a weapon that looked a lot like the Dragon.

As it spun up, I slid into cover behind another wrecked hover car. The weapon roared, and a barrage of bullets tore through the car. Bits of metal flew into the air before, finally, it exploded into a ball of blue, Mist-infused flames.

The weapon spun down as its ammunition was spent.

It was at that point that, having used my recovered Mist to fuel Teleport and get behind him, I stabbed him in the base of the skull. He didn't immediately die. He was too strong for that. Instead, he stumbled forward, then tried to whip around to attack, but even if his Nexus Implant hadn't been destroyed, it had been damaged enough to affect him. So, his movements were slow. Clumsy. And ultimately, useless.

I danced around him, hacking at his neck. The first blow cut deep, but he still didn't fall. The second hit the same spot, and the third finally destroyed that Nexus Implant. By the time he fell, my breathing was labored, and when he hit the ground, I couldn't keep my shoulders from sagging.

Using that much Mist in such a short amount of time was hard on the body, and even I wasn't immune to the consequences of that kind of tactic. But given how strong those Pacificians had to have been to survive my Ghost, I hadn't wanted to take any chances.

And I'd survived while they'd died. So, my strategy was probably the right one.

Either that or I'd gotten lucky. It was easy to misjudge success as the result of good decisions rather than the host of other factors, ranging from good fortune to overpowering the situation. In any case, I wasn't in any position to second-guess my actions. I'd made it through, and that was all that mattered for the moment. I would reassess and adjust accordingly once I finished the job at hand.

With that in mind, I left the scene of the brief battle, pausing only to make certain that my opponents hadn't carried anything useful. Once I confirmed that they hadn't, I set off toward my intended destination. By that point, the situation within the city had mostly stabilized, though the Klaxon of the alarm—which seemed to emanate from all the still-standing buildings—continued to sound. In addition, the entire city was cloaked in a cloud of dust, which made my job that much easier.

Still, along the way, I was nearly discovered on multiple occasions. Sometimes, it was just a drone, but there were a few more survivors than I'd anticipated. Each of them wore gold or silver robes, so I knew they were higher-ups. And I struggled to stop myself from killing every one of them I saw. The only reason I didn't was because I had a job to do. Once I completed it, I would be free to kill as many of them as I wanted.

So, I maintained my Stealth, dashing from one shadow to another as I used the cover of the dust cloud to mask the evidence of passing. Like that, I crossed the city, and by the time the sun set, I'd reached my destination.

It was a huge set of doors, at least thirty feet across, and it was guarded by a full squad of Pacifician warriors in shimmering orange robes.

That was the first I'd seen of that color, which I took to indicate that they were somehow special. Each one carried impressive-looking weaponry, and I knew that if they'd managed to survive my Ghost, they were strong opponents.

Any other time, and I might have left them alone, but I needed to get through those doors.

So, a fight was necessary.

Fortunately, they were standing out in the open and I had the entire city at my back, so I had multiple places to hide. It was a perfect battleground for me to show my skills.

So, I retreated into a nearby building before climbing to the roof. Once there, I familiarized myself with the location, then stepped close to the edge. Then, I once again drew my sniper rifle and took aim.

As I marked my targets—both mentally and with Mark Target, which would help me keep track if they scattered—I lamented the fact that using my heavier weapons was out of the question. There was a reason that the buildings in the general area had remained untouched; I didn't want to block those doors. So, for that same reason, the Dragon and the BMAP weren't really options.

Hopefully, it wouldn't matter.

This time, I didn't use all my abilities, largely because doing so would drain most of my Mist. I only had one booster available, so I needed to be a bit more circumspect about how I used my abilities. So, I chose a more traditional avenue of attack when I used Empowered Shot, took aim, and fired.

I didn't watch the results of that first shot. Instead, I quickly moved to the next. And the next after that. I shot two more times before I pulled back and took off across the roof. When I reached the edge, I leaped, and when I'd reached the halfway point between the first building and my destination, I activated Double Jump. Springing off of a plane of Mist, I easily covered the distance to the next roof.

By that point, the remaining orange-robed Pacificians had taken aim at my previous location and were currently trying to tear it down by way of copious gunfire. Fortunately, the cloud of dust still hid me.

So, I took aim once again. I'd only killed two of those orange robes, but the others I'd shot had been injured. An acceptable outcome.

More, if it worked once, I had no qualms about doing it again.

So that was precisely what I did, moving from one building to the next. I skipped one here and there, and I made certain not to follow any discernible pattern, but over time, I took them all out. By the time I'd finished, I found myself wondering why they hadn't called for help.

But then again, the entire city was in shambles, the vast majority of the population had been killed by my Ghost, and there were other, far more sensitive assets that needed to be guarded. In fact, after what I'd done to their lunar base, they probably expected me to go for the power core below the city. I'd considered it, but I'd opted for something a little less destructive, mostly because I was afraid of overdoing things like I had on the moon.

Whatever the case, I waited for a while to make sure that no one was going to take the orange robes' place. And once I judged that it was safe, I descended from my perch atop one of the buildings and approached the gates.

Finally, I'd reached my primary goal. Now, I just needed to head down, rescue the prisoners, and then finish the job.

Sighing, I realized that I still had a ways to go.

So, without further delay, I stepped close to the terminal governing the doors, then, after connecting via my personal link, Mistwalked into the system. A moment after I'd breached its defenses, the doors slid open to reveal a long, sloping tunnel.

With a shake of my head, I once again embraced Stealth and stepped inside. The tunnel itself followed a fairly steep decline, and only a hundred yards in, I reached a switchback. Then, a hundred yards later, another. And another after that. In that manner, I followed the tunnel as it led me deep underground.

Finally, after what felt like at least a few miles, I reached a large chamber. On one side was an elevator whose size reminded me of the lifts used at the Nova City gates. If it was less than thirty yards wide, I would have been surprised. At present, it was loaded with hundreds of carts full of raw ore.

I wasn't concerned with that.

From the files I'd read, the ore itself wasn't particularly valuable except in large quantities. The mine over which the city had been built was deep, though, and so long as they had the labor to tap into it, the Pacificians managed to subsidize the cost of the entire city. So, the mine itself was valuable, but not to someone like me.

In any case, I was far more concerned with the men and women huddled in the center of the room. There were about a thousand of them—at least according to the records I'd read—and each one of them had failed to join the Pacificians. Because of that, they'd been put to work as slaves.

Others, like the ones I'd seen during my first time surveilling the city, had been sent elsewhere, but most had ended up in the mines. One such prisoner was of particular concern to me.

So, I stepped forward and let my Stealth drop. They noticed me straightaway. One shouted something at me, but I ignored them as I approached. When I came within a dozen feet of the crowd, I raised my voice and said, "I'm looking for Caden Montague."

A young man that matched up to the photos I'd seen pushed his way through the crowd. He looked like he'd lost a little weight, but I felt certain it was the man I'd been sent to find. "What's going on? Are you—"

"I'm here to rescue you," I said. Then, I looked at the others. There were less than a thousand. A lot less. If I'd had to guess without taking the time to count, I would've put their numbers at less than thirty. I added, "You all should come, too."

"Rescue?" Caden asked, cocking his head to the side. "From what?"

I got a bad feeling from his tone. "Uh . . ."

"Where are Heaven's Chosen?" came a voice from the crowd.

"Have they come to raise us?"

"Is it time?"

"Oh, thank the Collective!"

I took a step back.

"She's not one of Heaven's Chosen!"

"Get her!"

It was at that moment that I realized that I'd made a huge mistake.

CHAPTER FIFTY-TWO

THE POWER OF MANIPULATION

Deep down, we all know that anyone who says they can solve all our problems is lying. But it's so easy to just surrender control, to let someone else take responsibility out of your hands. That's why the Pacificians were successful. It's just human nature.

—Patrick Ward

My assault rifle was up in less than a second, and before they could take one step, I'd put the first one down. As he fell, I swept the weapon back and forth, shouting, "Back the fuck up!"

Surprisingly, they did just that. But Caden demanded, "Why? Why would you do that?! He was so close!"

"To what? They're not here to solve your problems, idiot," I growled. "They're just killing everyone and copying them. You can't be this stupid."

But I knew better. If there was one thing of which I was absolutely certain, it was the breadth of human stupidity. It was especially pervasive with the sort of people who wanted a bunch of aliens to solve their problems. I understood, and there was a part of me that sympathized with their situations. I knew just how insidious addiction could be—I had seen it firsthand—and poverty and food insecurity were just as bad. The draw was easy to see.

There was something else buried beneath that pity, though. Something that shamed me. I hated them for their perceived weakness. I knew it wasn't all their fault. But I also couldn't help the revulsion coursing through my mind. I shoved it aside, focusing on the task at hand.

"You," I said, pointing my weapon at Caden. "You're coming with me." I glanced at the others. "The rest of you, you can come, too. I've arranged for transportation to somewhere safe. But I'm not going to force you."

"You'll force me, though?" Caden demanded.

"Most definitely."

"What? Why?"

"Because I made a deal," I said. "Now, if you all stay . . . You know what? I'm not sure what'll happen. But it probably won't be good. The Pacificians are done on this planet. Maybe not today. Maybe not tomorrow. But I'm going to kill every last one of those assholes. So, maybe don't pick the wrong side."

With that, I stepped forward and, too quickly for Caden to react, grabbed him by the arm. I yanked him off-balance, and he stumbled after me as I backed away. "So?" I asked the others. "What's it going to be?"

They didn't answer. Instead, as one, they surged toward me. I probably could have escaped, but I'd have had to leave Caden behind. Even with him in tow, I didn't have to kill them.

But I wanted to.

I'd come to rescue them, and they'd rewarded me with aggression? I knew they had been manipulated, but in that moment, I didn't care. So, I fired.

I didn't even have to use any abilities. Just the weapon, my modifiers, and a mind full of anger, regret, and revulsion. They couldn't stand before that, and in seconds, I'd cut the entire group down. It wasn't even difficult, which probably should have been a little concerning. It wasn't, though.

"You . . . You killed them . . ."

"And if I didn't promise your sister I'd get you out of here, I'd kill you, too. Or I just wouldn't have worried about trying to rescue a bunch of morons who joined a cult," I said. I gave him another tug, which unbalanced him once again. "Now, come on. I want to rescue you, but I'm not so invested that I won't tell your sister that you were dead when I got here."

I was keenly aware that my initial goal had been to rescue all of them. Or was that just an excuse for my anger? I wasn't sure. And I was in no position to think about it any further. Perhaps I'd tackle that issue once I escaped and was safe. To that end, I contacted Alistaris and said, "Got my package. I'll be—"

I never got the chance to finish my sentence. Instead, I pushed Caden to the side as I dove forward, narrowly dodging the blade aimed at my neck. I rolled, coming to my feet and firing at the man who'd just tried to kill me. I didn't bother with witty repartee. Nor did I hesitate. I just fired, sending a barrage of bullets downrange to hammer into his chest.

He flew from his feet and skidded across the floor. I kept firing, then used Instant Reload before continuing with a second magazine. The superheated plasma rounds ripped into him, tearing his red jumpsuit to pieces and sending bits of Realskin misting into the air.

But I knew it wouldn't be enough.

Because I recognized him. Or rather, I recognized the giant sword still clutched in one of his hands. It didn't make sense, though. I'd watched him die. Alistaris and his Dengyts had killed him back on the moon, hadn't they?

Clearly not, because there he was, struggling to rise even as I peppered him with a barrage of bullets. My magazine ran empty, and I didn't dare use Instant Reload again. It would drain most of the rest of my Mist, and I suspected I'd need everything I had left if I was going to escape alive.

It was just the opening he needed, though. Even as I smoothly transferred one magazine into my arsenal implant and replaced it with another, he sprang to his feet and rushed me. Moving so quickly that it looked like a teleport, he was on me in less than an instant.

I ducked under a horizontal swing of that massive sword, then used Combination Punch to aim a pair of strikes at his ruined midsection. The first barely did anything, but the second pushed him backward. I followed up with another jab, building the power of the fourth and final punch—an uppercut that took him right in the chin. The impact lifted him off his feet and shattered his jaw.

If I hadn't administered the blow with the Hand of God, I felt certain that it would have destroyed my fist, as well. As it was, the nigh-indestructible cybernetic was completely unharmed.

The android couldn't say as much, and as he sailed through the air, I dragged the Dragon from my arsenal implant, used Explosive Shot, and let loose.

The massive weapon roared, ripping through him with a couple thousand rounds a minute. And with Explosive Shot enhancing each shot, the damage was devastating. I tore him to pieces, one round at a time, and by the time the Dragon ran dry, he was in pieces. But I didn't dare assume he was dead.

So, I exchanged the Dragon for the BMAP, then reached down to grab a stunned Caden by the hair before dragging him to the exit. Once I reached the sloping tunnel, I took aim at the collection of parts—they were still twitching, and unless I was seeing things, the pieces had begun to drag themselves back together—and let loose with Shatter Shot.

The round sailed through the air, hitting the pile of parts dead center and filling the room with a massive conflagration. By that point, I was already sprinting up the ramp and dragging a struggling Caden along behind me.

As I outran the ball of fire, I screamed through my Secure Connection, "Change of plans. Only one passenger. You ready for my pickup?"

"No!" he screamed. "The Pacificians had another . . ."

There was a massive explosion over the connection before he continued,

"There's three other gunships in the air! We can't get to you, much less take that shield down!"

"Shit," I growled. "Great intel."

"I'm aware."

"Am I on my own?" I spat.

"For now. Good luck," he said.

It was all I could do not to roll my eyes. If I was honest with myself, I would've admitted that I should have expected as much. Alistaris had taken great pains to conceal his involvement, which meant that he couldn't bring the full weight of his organization to bear. On top of that, he was so preoccupied with secrecy that it was always going to negatively affect the operation. In this case, he'd missed something he should've—and would have if he'd been fully focused on the mission—seen.

But it was fine.

I had a plan B.

I just needed to cross the city in order to implement it. So, when I finally reached the end of the tunnel and burst free into daylight, I wasted no time before summoning the Cutter. I tossed Caden over the seat, telling him, "You move, you die. Got it?"

He nodded, clearly terrified. I didn't blame him. After the firepower I'd just shown, I would've been afraid, too. But I didn't have time to think about things like that because, just then, a pair of men in red jumpsuits and carrying giant swords burst onto the scene. They skidded to a stop, aiming their weapons at me.

"What the hell?" I muttered, my mind working overtime. With two more in my way, it seemed reasonable that I hadn't just fought the same man I'd battled in the lunar station. Instead, there were multiple copies of the same—or a similar—man.

Which was absolutely horrifying.

I took off, the Cutter accelerating faster than either of them could react. Or that's what I thought until I was forced to skid sideways across the pavement just to avoid a thrown sword that ended up embedded up to the hilt in a nearby wall.

I righted the hover bike, then sped off, thanking my luck that those powerful androids seemed to have a thing against guns.

The city blurred past as I left them behind, and soon, I was dodging between wrecked vehicles and circling fallen buildings. Behind me, Caden let out a gasp, clearly surprised by the level of destruction.

In truth, it hadn't been nearly as bad as I'd expected. Sure, there were dead androids scattered throughout the city, but there were plenty that had survived my carefully created Ghost. It was just evidence that, even in an ideal situation, it wasn't a perfect solution.

Not yet.

But I still had a long way to go before I tapped all my potential. On top of that, I knew that there were ways to get more power out of skills. Specially made cybernetics could boost all manner of skills. And finally, there was the issue of my skills themselves. I refused to believe that reaching Tier 5 in each category was the end of my road. If it was, then my uncle wouldn't have been nearly as powerful as he'd been.

No—I still had a ways to go. I just needed to keep going, and things would open up. I was certain of it.

I sped through the city until I saw something that brought me to a screeching halt. "Shit," I spat, looking at the blockade. There were seven red-jumpsuited androids, a dozen others in green robes, and a handful of hover cars stretched across the street. I turned and tried to go around, but I quickly found that every other road was blocked—some by the rubble of fallen buildings, but others with heavy defenses including Mist shields—as well.

It was clear that they were trying to hem me in and force me to fight the men in red.

There was a part of me that just wanted to ditch Caden and use Stealth to bypass them. But I'd made a promise, and even if I had failed to rescue any others, I wanted to at least get him to safety. With Observation, I could tell that there were hundreds of people converging on my position. I didn't have time to look for another way out. I had no choice but to break through the blockade.

"So be it," I said, pulling the BMAP back out. This time, I exchanged the normal ammunition for something even more destructive—at least to a bunch of robots. I slammed the cannister in place, then took aim with one hand while keeping my other on the hover bike's accelerator.

I sat there, staring at my enemies.

They stared back.

And then, I took off.

The Cutter was the highest-quality hover bike I'd seen on Earth, and it was capable of truly blistering speeds. I used every ounce of its power as I tore down the street, swerving left, then right to avoid piles of rubble. And then, when I came into range, I used Shatter Shot before firing the BMAP's payload.

The round traveled in a low, lazy arc before thudding into one of the cars. But it didn't explode. Neither did the following seven shots.

I didn't stop, though. A hundred yards away, the green-robed androids opened fire. I swerved, keeping to a zigzagging pattern as I closed to fifty yards. Then twenty. When I was only ten yards away, I detonated the rounds I'd fired from the BMAP.

With a deep, reverberating sound, they discharged a blanket of Mist designed to disrupt cybernetics. The androids—even the ones in red jumpsuits—collapsed into seizures as I piloted the hover bike through the blockade and to the relative safety of the open street.

The rounds were called MDGs—or Mist-disruptive grenades—and I'd gotten them special after getting back from the moon. They had cost me a relative fortune, and it was even more expensive to get them shipped down to Earth. But in hindsight, they were well worth it. The ordnance was largely useless in most situations, and against anything but androids, it would do nothing but briefly disrupt cybernetics. However, against robots and drones, it was reputed to be extremely effective.

Against androids, as well, it seemed.

The rest of the way was easy going, and soon enough, I arrived at my destination—the small hangar they maintained. Unfortunately, it too was guarded, though only by a single man. Predictably, it was an identical android to the ones I'd fought so far—right down to the overlarge sword clutched in one hand. He held it out to the side, with the wide blade stretching parallel to the ground.

"Get off," I said.

"What?"

"If you're on this bike when this goes down, you're going to die. So, get off. If you make me chase you after I kill this asshole, I'm going to break your legs."

"I thought you were here to save me . . ."

"You're still saved with broken legs."

He didn't comment any further, and soon enough, I was alone on the back of the Cutter. I knew good and well that the only reason I'd survived so far was because I hadn't fought fair. The one that had ambushed me was the closest, and that had required me to empty my entire arsenal. But now, the Dragon was empty, and I didn't have the Mist to use Instant Reload. I'd also used my entire stock of MDGs—probably unnecessarily, but I hadn't wanted to take any chances—so I didn't have my secret weapon.

No—if I was going to beat this latest challenger, it would be without any tricks or overwhelming firepower.

Which meant that I wasn't terribly confident in my chances. However, I didn't have much of a choice. I couldn't go back. Even now, I was certain that whoever was left in the city was closing in on me. I needed to get to that hangar and get out with some alacrity, or I'd be overwhelmed.

So, I summoned my Pulsar, took aim, and used Empowered Shot. I fired a second later, but by that point, he was already moving. My shot still hit him in the shoulder, spinning him around, but he quickly righted himself, and then he was on top of me. I fired without aiming, hitting him in the chest. It knocked him off-balance, and I took off.

The Cutter was fast.

He was faster.

And even as I tore off across the tarmac in front of the hangar, he recovered and closed in on me. I whipped around, drawing my sword at the same time, then accelerated in his direction. The move took him by surprise, but he still managed to block the swing that came only an instant later. It threw me off-balance.

And then, disaster struck in the form of a giant blade slashing through one of the Mist vents at the bottom of my hover bike. It exploded, flipping the Cutter into the air. I tumbled free, hitting the ground on my shoulder. Flaring Balance, I rolled, then dragged Ferdinand II from the holster at my hip. As I rolled to my feet, I fired blindly behind me.

I heard the rounds thud into my attacker before I twisted around, sword in one hand and pistol in the other. It was just in time to see him leaping in my direction and aiming a two-handed overhand attack at me.

I dove to the side, firing another shot in his direction. It went wide, and his blade bit deep into the concrete of the tarmac. I fired again, this time hitting him directly in the head. The round tore the Realskin from his metallic skull, but he was otherwise unaffected. So, I fired again. And again. Even as he turned and slowly walked toward me, I kept shooting until Ferdinand II went dry.

He smirked—a macabre sight, when half of his metal endoskeleton was on full display. I pushed it from my mind as I exchanged Ferdinand II for my assault rifle. I had just enough time to jam a new magazine into place before he reached me.

I tried to dodge his giant blade, but it was a feint meant to disguise his true attack. Even as I overbalanced to avoid the blade strike, he kicked out, taking me in the chest. I felt ribs break as I was launched through the air. I landed a moment later, then skidded across the pavement until I came to a stop.

Spitting blood on the ground, I looked at him only forty or fifty feet away. Then, I returned his smile with a smirk of my own before I said, "That all you got, big boy?"

Then, I raised my assault rifle and bathed him in a hail of gunfire. He darted forward, heedless of the barrage of bullets. They thudded into him, ripping his Realskin away as I charged.

And like that, our battle continued.

CHAPTER FIFTY-THREE

ROUND TWO

I don't want to spend the rest of my life fighting a war. I know the cause is just. I get that. But why does it have to be us? Why can't we just leave and let someone else shoulder the weight of resistance?

—Patrick Ward

As I dropped into a slide, the android's sword neatly severed a solid inch of my braid. I lashed out with my own blade, slashing the back of his knee before my momentum carried me out of his immediate range. I knew he wouldn't let me escape so easily, so I slammed my foot into the ground and leaped high into the air. As I flipped, I brought Ferdinand II around and fired. The round took him in the face, tearing through more of his Realskin but leaving only a scuff mark on his metallic skull. It did throw him off-balance, though, so his follow-up attack—a sweeping strike that might have bisected me—went wide enough that it only barely nicked my stomach.

I landed in a crouch and skidded across the tarmac.

The android sneered at me, but he didn't speak. Instead, he ripped the remaining flaps of faux skin from his skull before tossing it aside.

"That's better," I growled. "No more hiding behind your mask, huh? Must be freeing."

He snarled, then raced forward. His sword ignited with blue Mist as he swung, but by that point, I was already gone. I dove aside, rolled, and came up firing again. The bullets continued to thud against him, but even with all my modifiers, it just wasn't enough to get through his impressively sturdy Constitution.

I knew he wasn't indestructible. It had taken an entire magazine from my Dragon, but I'd killed the one that had attacked me in the mine. But reloading that particular weapon took time that I didn't have.

I dragged a grenade from my arsenal implant, then tossed it in his direction. It exploded into a dense cloud of white smoke. Then, I turned and ran. When I got a couple dozen feet away, I used Vanish, then embraced Stealth.

I knew it wouldn't last. An android as advanced as my enemy probably had all sorts of ways to see through my ability, and the smoke grenade wouldn't change that fact. But I didn't need long to drag my Pulsar from my arsenal implant. Then, I used every ability I had.

Mark Target, so I could see through the fog.

Then Explosive Shot, which drained a good portion of my remaining Mist. I hoped it would be worth it.

Next, I used Execute, increasing the damage of my next shot by five hundred percent. It was only usable so long as I was undetected, but with the smoke and my Stealth, I satisfied the requirements.

Finally, I activated Empowered Shot.

After waiting a second, I fired. The ball of molten plasma tore across the tarmac, parting the smoke on its way to hitting my target directly in the chest. The impact sent him flying backward, but I didn't dare wait to see the damage. Instead, I tossed out another grenade—this time, a flash-bang—then canceled my Observation right before it exploded.

Even with my eyes closed and my hands clapped over my ears, the effect was nearly overwhelming. And that was with Blast Shield blocking the worst of it. Surely, the android—whose momentum had sent him tumbling across the pavement—was much more affected.

Using that window of opportunity, I took off, tossing yet another smoke grenade out. I sprinted away as fast as my legs could carry me. Then, when I thought I'd made it far enough, I wheeled around and repeated the process. Even as I layered my abilities, the android was picking himself back up. I could only see an outline—the effect of my Mark Target ability—but that was enough.

I fired again.

This time, he reacted far more quickly than I could have anticipated, and the deadly shot only clipped him in the shoulder. Even that sent him spinning to the ground, giving me further opportunity to relocate.

For the next few minutes, that's how the fight went, and I used an entire magazine of sniper rounds to tear him to pieces.

But it wasn't enough.

I knew it even as I fired the last shot.

I needed more power. I needed the Dragon. As I exchanged the Pulsar for the huge weapon, I could only hope that I'd have enough time to reload. I should have known he'd never give me that chance.

The smoke cleared, and I looked on with horror as I saw the result of my bombardment. Most of his flesh was gone, exposing his metallic endoskeleton. His jumpsuit was nothing but tattered red cloth that did nothing to hide his ravaged body. But he was still alive, and though he was dragging one useless leg and one of his arms hung limp, he didn't look like he intended to stop.

The Dragon took a long time to reload, and it involved deft manipulation of my arsenal implant to do so. In perfect conditions, finishing the process would take at least thirty seconds. It was too bad, then, that he only gave me fifteen before he sprang at me.

I raised the Dragon to block, but to my horror, his Mist-wreathed sword sliced right through it—not a great thing when it had so much Mist coursing through it. Knowing what was coming, I dropped it, but before it had fallen more than a few inches, it exploded.

I was thrown backward, and the android went in the other direction.

I don't know how far I went, and for the briefest of seconds, I passed out. And when I finally managed to shake myself back to reality, I saw the aftermath of the explosion. A crater—maybe ten feet across—marred the tarmac. A couple hundred feet distant, the android was picking himself back up. His sword was gone, and all his faux flesh had gone with it. Instead, he'd been reduced to nothing but a heavily damaged endoskeleton.

I pushed myself to my feet, cataloging a hundred wounds along the way. The silhouette in my interface that was supposed to indicate my health was almost entirely red, which couldn't have been good. But it didn't matter.

I wasn't going to stop just because I was half-dead.

So, dragging my assault rifle from my arsenal implant, I used most of my remaining Mist to empower it with Explosive Shot, then took aim. I fired. The android, who'd so far been almost entirely unaffected by that weapon, didn't even bother to dodge. It was his mistake because the explosion had clearly taken its toll on him, at least as much as it had affected my health. I didn't know if it was the lack of skin—perhaps it functioned as some sort of armor—or that I'd finally injured him enough that he didn't have the Mist to maintain his defenses. Or perhaps it was something else entirely. I had no idea, but what I did know was that this time, my shots tore through his torso, sending metallic shards flying and puffs of Mist into the air.

He staggered under the barrage.

I advanced, heel to toe, just as my uncle had taught me so long ago, and continued firing. The first magazine did the most damage, empowered as it was by Explosive Shot, but the second was effective, as well.

But by the time I reached the android, I was running low on both Mist and ammunition. That was fine.

My blade needed neither.

As I drew the sword, the android tried to respond. But by that point, it had been reduced to a quivering pile of damaged parts. I kicked it over, exposing the Nexus Implant at the base of its skull. I raised my sword, then brought it down in a swift, vicious slash. It wasn't enough. So, I did it again.

And again.

And again after that.

Finally, the Nexus Implant shattered, and the android fell limp.

Breathing hard, I stood there, staring down at the monstrous thing. Then, I spat on it before dragging my last Mist booster from my arsenal implant and jabbing it into my hip. As it discharged, I used Stabilize, which sent a pulse of healing Mist through my body. It was expensive and only marginally effective, which was why I almost never used it. It was only meant as a last-resort sort of ability to keep someone from dying. And for that, it was great. In my current condition, it improved my health by only a little, but I hoped it would be enough to get me to safety. I watched my silhouette turn from red to orange, which was probably all I could've hoped for.

Then, I exchanged the booster for a med-hypo, which I jabbed into my hip, as well.

With that seen to, I limped toward where Caden had taken cover. At the same time, I dismissed the Cutter. When I reached the man, I asked, "Are you hurt?"

"H-how . . . How are you still standing?" he asked.

"Just lucky, I guess. Are you hurt?" I repeated.

"Uh . . . No . . ."

"Good," I said, reaching down. I grabbed him by the upper arm, then pulled him to his feet. "Let's go."

As I dragged him along, I heard the distant sound of Mist engines and footsteps as the remaining Pacificians descended upon my position. I estimated that they were about a minute out. Maybe less. Which meant that I needed to hurry.

Marshaling what strength my body had left, I limped into the hangar. There, I saw five ships. They were small, and normally, they were only used to transport resources from the surface to the lunar base. But for my purposes, they would do just fine. So, I selected the first one, then used Misthack to disable any locks before boarding the ungainly ship.

"Sit," I said, shoving him into the copilot's seat as I took the controls. "And strap in. This'll probably get bumpy."

Then, I dragged my personal link from the Hand of God and plugged it into the control terminal. I could've piloted it the old-fashioned way, but I'd found that, with unfamiliar craft, using Mistwalk was much easier for me.

"Probably should've opened the main doors for this," I muttered, firing up the engines. "Oh well. We've gone too far to worry about that now."

"Um . . ."

I ignored Caden as I directed the ship to lift off. It did, though I could tell that it wasn't built to hover. So, I used Mistwalk to accelerate through the thin doors. They came down with a crash, and as we broke through, I saw that every Pacifician in the city had descended upon the hangar.

"Guess it's time, then."

I finally activated the Ghost I'd uploaded into the main communications hub. For the barest moment, nothing happened. But then, suddenly, the Pacificians—each and every one of them—exploded.

So did the rest of the buildings.

And, unfortunately, the ship tried to, as well. Because I was connected directly to the system, I managed to cut it off, but the same couldn't be said for the ships that remained in the hangar. The force of the multiple explosions buffeted the ship I'd commandeered, nearly sending us into the ground. But I barely kept it aloft long enough for the dust to settle.

"What did you do?" gasped Caden, looking out the window at the devastation. Olympus had fallen, and it had taken every Pacifician in the area with it.

"Completed the mission," I said. The purpose of the Ghost was simple. It was intended to destroy their connection to the hive mind. Clearly, doing so had activated some sort of fail-safe. A good thing, as far as I was concerned, even if their self-destruction was unexpected.

I saw a few figures in red coveralls and amended that assessment. Most of the Pacificians had exploded. The elites—I still wasn't sure how that worked— clearly hadn't.

It didn't matter. The Mist shield had fallen, which meant I was free. Still, the ship was unsuited to the task before us, and it had been damaged in the series of explosions. So, I barely managed to keep it aloft long enough to escape the city's vicinity.

Still, it did its job, and when I set it down, we were more than a dozen miles from the destroyed Olympus.

That's when I got a communication request from Alistaris.

"What's up?" I asked, establishing a Secure Connection.

"What did you do?" he asked.

"People keep asking me that."

"Just answer the question," the Dengyt ordered, his squeaky voice hoarse.

I told him, omitting any details as to how I'd accomplished the feat before asking, "Why? Thought you'd be happy about this."

"You have no idea what you did, Mira."

"The job I set out to do."

"And so, so much more. Reports are still coming in, but it looks like whatever you did severed the connection between this sector's local governor and the rest of the Pacificians."

"I have no idea what that means," I said.

"The governor is the hive mind in charge of their population," he said. "You just . . . You just killed millions of Pacificians without even meaning to."

"Good."

"Good?"

"I don't think I stuttered there. This is a good thing, Al," I said. "I told you before—I intend to kill every last one of them. This just means I got a little bit of a head start."

"I don't think you understand . . ."

"Yeah? Well, explain it to me."

"You just started a war," he said. "A real one."

"War was always coming," I argued, though his assertion was a little worrying.

"Not like this," he said. "When the Initialization is over, you'll have real armies to contend with. Not private security forces, either. That's what was going to come, and you'd have had a chance against them. But now? Mira, even if you and the other earthlings manage to win somehow, your planet will be destroyed."

"Then help us," I said far more calmly than I felt. The implications of what he'd said were enough to send a chill of fear up my spine. "That's your thing, right? You and your little Alliance can—"

"It won't just be the Gomari Confederation now," he said. "The Pacificians have allies, and they'll descend upon this planet with the intention of carving it to pieces. And they'll do it under the guise of protecting their ally. They won't have to hold back, either. I can see it now. The Pacificians will call you a terrorist. They'll say you attacked them unprovoked. It won't get them support from anyone. Not really. But it will muddy the waters enough that, by the time anyone gets around to caring about all those poor, dead earthlings, it'll be too late. Then, the bottom-feeders will show up. Pirates. Mercenary groups. Private corporations. They'll all try to get what they can out of it. They won't be gentle, either. They'll kill anyone who gets in their way."

"What are you saying, Al?" I asked. "You aren't going to help?"

He sighed. "Of course I'll help," he said. "But it won't be the entire Alliance. Our presence here will be limited, just like before. The only difference is that we just had the deck stacked against us. We won't succeed."

"Yeah? Well, I disagree," I said. "But we'll figure that out later. For now, I'm going back to Fortune to return this idiot to his sister. Then, I'm going to take a few days to recover. After that . . . Well, we'll see."

"Good luck" was all he said before severing the connection.

Given what Alistaris had said, I could well understand his exasperation. I'd just made his job all the more difficult, and there was every chance that he'd end up dead in the coming conflict. I was sure he had plans to escape that fate, but in war, plans had a tendency to fail. But even knowing what was coming, I couldn't bring myself to regret my actions. For one, I'd had no idea that severing the connection between the Pacificians and their hive mind would have such explosive results. But even if I had known, I would have done it anyway. After all, I hadn't forgotten what they had done, and my resolution to kill them all still stood.

Besides, it wasn't as if anything had really changed. Earth was still going to be inundated by aliens that meant to bleed the planet dry.

I sat there for a long moment, then turned to Caden and said, "Come on. We need to get out of the area. There were still some of those assholes left, and you can bet they're going to be after us."

Indeed, at least some of the powerful elites in the red jumpsuits had survived, and I would have been surprised if they were the only ones. If I had to guess, severing that connection had only killed the weakest Pacificians. Although, if what Alistaris had said was true and the effect had gone farther than just Earth, perhaps I'd really made a dent in their population.

After all, they'd all exploded, hadn't they? Surely, there would be some collateral damage.

In any case, that was a question for another day because, as I'd told Caden, we needed to vacate the area, and fast. So, I led him out of the ship, summoned my Cutter—which was damaged but still operational—and sped away.

After an hour following an old, mostly crumbling road, I veered off and took shelter in an abandoned building. I took a few moments to set up Bastion, then set about treating my wounds. They weren't as severe as I'd expected—probably because of my use of Stabilize—but my infiltration suit had definitely seen better days.

"I don't know how you're even alive. Do you know who that was you were fighting?"

As I bandaged a wound in my stomach, I shrugged. "My buddy Al told me his name, but I can't remember it."

"Edrax Kel Tanimvan," Caden said.

"Yeah. That was it."

"He's . . . He's, like, the strongest person I've ever seen," Caden stated.

"First, not a person. He's a robot with a copy of someone's brain imprinted on him. Second, clearly he's not the strongest, considering I just killed him," I said.

"He's not dead. That was just one of him."

"And how many bodies does he have?" I asked.

He shrugged. "I don't know. Hundreds, I've heard. They didn't exactly tell us everything."

I sighed. "What the hell were you even doing there? I mean, I get it, I guess. Life's hard. But you don't look like an addict," I said. "And your sister clearly cares about you. That's more than most people get."

"I . . . It's . . . It's embarrassing," he said.

"I assure you, I can't really think any less of you. So, lay it on me. Why did you join a cult? I'm sure you didn't know they were going to copy your brain, then kill you. But you seem at least smart enough that you had to have seen the red flags," I said.

"It was a girl. She . . . She ended up getting converted right away. I was sent down to the mines where they said I could earn my own conversion," he said. "We had it all planned out. We were going to have a life together. But now . . ."

"Well, she's gone. Dead. Even the copy of her probably went down with all the rest. So, my condolences, I guess? Now, shut up," I said. "I've got to concentrate on something."

"What?"

"Shut up or I'll shut you up," I muttered.

And blessedly, he went quiet, which allowed me to focus on my status. With thousands of kills—maybe even millions—under my belt, my level had sky-rocketed. And it seemed I'd hit a threshold when I reached level seventy-five.

I read the message with a mixture of shame, anticipation, and excitement:

You have reached level 75. Please choose a class evolution from the following options:

I didn't immediately look at the choices. Instead, I took a deep breath, then sighed. I'd jumped thirty levels in a single afternoon. I knew from experience that such a leap forward wasn't the product of only a few thousand kills. I didn't want to think about it, but clearly, Alistaris hadn't been exaggerating. I'd killed millions with my little stunt.

EVOLUTION

I sometimes wonder how I can be with someone who can do the things Mira has done. Aside from the morality of killing literal millions of people, I often look at her and see someone that's so far above me—at least in terms of power—that we're barely even the same species.

—Patrick Ward

I stared at the notification, wondering how I was supposed to react. On the one hand, I was excited about the possibility of evolving my class. Becoming a real {Mistrunner} had changed everything, instantly giving me far more power than I'd ever thought possible. And since then, I'd only grown stronger. So, it stood to reason that I would experience a similar increase when I chose to evolve the class.

But on the other hand, the weight of my actions was overwhelming. I had killed millions. Alistaris had claimed as much, and the number of levels I'd gained supported that suspicion. Despite my lack of guilt—we were at war, and they were enemies—there was no way I could uncaringly kill so many people. Even if they were androids who depended on a central hive mind, they were still distinct enough that, under the strictest definition, they were at least close to being designated as people. Certainly, Alistaris seemed to think of them in that way.

And I had killed millions.

Sighing, I pushed those thoughts aside. I couldn't allow myself to get tangled in the resulting emotions. So, after sequestering them in the back of my mind, I moved on to the choices laid out before me.

The first was {Wraith}, which had the following description:

{Wraith}—You flit from one shadow to the next, bringing desolation in your wake. Requirements: [Combat] (Tier 5), [Fieldcraft] (Tier 5), [Infiltration] (Tier 5), Kill Count >1,000,000. Abilities Granted: Silence, Invisibility, Domineering Presence, Genocide

Upon reading the name, I got a little choked up. That was what they'd called my uncle. The Wraith. A legendary fighter, feared all across the world. And the class clearly lived up to that description. I wasn't certain as to the effects of the abilities granted, but from the names and the class's requirements, I felt sure that they would be powerful.

However, the kill count and the name of the final ability left me a little wary. I knew I was on the verge of fighting a war, and like any war, there would be plenty of death to go around. If I wanted to win—or at the very least, make the aliens pay a steep cost for victory—I would have to kill thousands. Maybe millions. So, Genocide seemed appropriate for my circumstances.

Still, I couldn't divorce the word from the negative connotations. Genocide implied the death of innocents. Combatants, too. In fact, it was characterized by the death of an entire population. And while I'd killed millions of Pacificians, I hadn't really meant to do so. My intention was to simply cut the androids off from their hive mind. That they'd died was an unintended consequence of my actions.

Besides, I still wasn't entirely certain where the Pacificians sat in regard to whether or not they were really people. They seemed like they were, but that didn't mean anything. At best, they were person-like.

Or maybe I was just clinging to that so I could excuse my actions.

In any case, I moved on to the next choice:

{Hacker}—You have spent countless hours perfecting your ability to Misthack, infiltrating thousands of systems and felling hundreds of enemies through the use of Ghosts. Requirements: [Mistrunner] (Tier 5), [Infiltration] (Tier 5). Abilities Granted: Hack (replaces Misthack), Overwhelm, Inflict Error

I frowned. The class, though seemingly powerful—I was especially interested in an evolution of Misthack and whatever benefits that would bring—was a bit of a disappointment. It said nothing about any of my other skills, which suggested that it was probably much more focused than my current class.

And given that I was on the verge of fighting a war, it felt a little shortsighted to disregard any potential weapon, even if the specialization might make Misthack much more powerful.

So, I pushed it aside and looked at the next class evolution:

{Devastator}—You are a peerless combatant, developing a wide array of skills devoted to battle. Requirements: [Combat] (Tier 5), [Fieldcraft] (Tier 4), [Demolition] (Tier 5). Abilities Granted: Conjure Weapon, Fortify Position, Entrench, Devastate

"That's more like it," I said. I certainly liked the sound of those abilities, and {Devastator} definitely looked like the sort of class I'd need to inflict maximum carnage on my enemies. However, it was held back by the lack of focus on my [Mistrunner] abilities. Sure—they wouldn't just disappear, but if possible, I wanted something that could take advantage of all my skills.

So, I moved on to the fourth option:

{Hidden Blade}—You are a killer. A blade in the dark. A weapon meant to destroy anything in your way. You will use any available method to accomplish your goals. Requirements: >[Combat] (Tier 5), [Demolition] (Tier 5), [Mistrunner] (Tier 5), [Infiltration] (Tier 5), [Fieldcraft] (Tier 5), Kill Count > 7,000,000. Abilities Granted: Attrition, Infusion of Mist, Overwhelm

Upon reading the requirements, I couldn't help but let out a gasp. For one, the fact that the system granted me credit for killing more than seven million people was quite a shock, and I certainly wasn't sure how to feel about it. Pushing past that, the skill requirements were intimidating. That I'd met them was both frightening and, if I was honest with myself, a little gratifying. I'd worked incredibly hard to progress my skills, and to see it rewarded gave me a sense of accomplishment.

Still, I moved on to the next choice:

{Mist Warden}—You are a defender. An avenger. A vengeful avatar who will protect your home using any means necessary. Requirements: [Combat] (Tier 5), [Fieldcraft] (Tier 5), [Infiltration] (Tier 5), [Mistrunner] (Tier 5), [Demolition] (Tier 5), [Cybernetic Mastery] (Tier 5), Kill Count > 5,000,000 in defense of your home, Tier 7 Nexus Implant. Abilities Granted: Orbital Strike, Planetary Defense, Mist Deprivation

My jaw dropped at those requirements, and an audible gasp escaped from between my lips when I read the abilities the class would grant. The only reason I didn't immediately select {Mist Warden} was because of the class's description. Avenger I understood. Vengeful avatar made sense, too. But I'd never really been a defender.

Except maybe I was.

Perhaps my commitment to the coming war was why I had been given the opportunity to select a class that looked incredibly powerful.

I sighed. Did I even need to go through the pros and cons of each option when the final choice seemed to be head and shoulders above the rest? Probably not. But I chose to do so anyway, going back and forth as I considered the potential strengths and weaknesses of each class. Most of it was conjecture, though, and at the end of the day, I made the only choice that made sense.

You have chosen the class {Mist Warden}.

Merging skills: [Combat], [Demolition], and [Fieldcraft], resulting in [Warfare]. Disengage, Double Jump, Stabilize, and Mend lost. All other abilities maintained or evolved.

Merging skills: [Infiltration] and [Mistrunner], resulting in [Espionage]. Skeleton Key, Rewind, Bluff, and True Sight lost. All other abilities maintained or evolved.

Evolving skill: [Acrobatics] into [Combat Maneuvers].

Evolving skill: [Cybernetic Mastery] into [Mist-Infused Body]

I didn't know how to react to the transformation. Sure, I'd expected something like what had happened, but in no way, shape, or form had I anticipated that my seven skills would merge into four. Suddenly, I had three open slots, which meant I needed to head to the Bazaar sooner rather than later.

Before that, though, I needed to catalog the changes. First, I'd lost a few useful abilities. Disengage was one I'd used sparingly, but I didn't like the loss of Double Jump. And the sudden disappearance of Mend and Stabilize would definitely hurt. I didn't use the abilities that often, largely because they were both very situational, but if the appropriate situations were to come, I would definitely feel the lack.

As for the ones I'd lost when [Infiltration] and [Mistrunner] merged into [Espionage], I was a little less disappointed. I could count on one hand the number of times I'd used any of the four, and Skeleton Key had never actually seen use. It wasn't that the ability wasn't useful but, rather, that I always preferred to use Misthack or Mistwalk to bypass any system's defenses. Anything else would be a wasted opportunity for training.

"What are you doing?" came Caden's voice.

"Nothing. Shut up," I said, opening my status.

NAME	Mirabelle Lisa Braddock		
CLASS	MIST WARDEN		
LEVEL	75 (0%)		
CONSTITUTION	247/535		
MIND	273/535		
MIST	222/535		
SKILLS	4/7		
SKILL NAME	Skill Tier	Modifiers	Abilities
MIST-INFUSED BODY	Tier 0 (0%)	500% Efficiency of Cybernetics	5 Cybernetic Slots
WARFARE	Tier 0 (0%)	+300% Damage (All) +75% Fewer Bodily Requirements +125% Recovery Speed +50% Medication Effectiveness +100% Endurance +150% Explosives Yield +100% Effectiveness (Combat Focus)	Empowered Shot (D) Double Shot (D) Combination Punch (D) Pummel (D) Engage (D) Mark Target (E) Barrage (E) Explosive Shot (E) Multishot (E) Shatter Shot (E) Instant Reload (E) Riposte (E) Execute (E) Teleport (D) Triage (D) Basic Explosives Handling (C) Combat Focus (C) Pain Tolerance (D) Resistance (D) Foraging (D)

			Improvisation (D) Regeneration (D) Universal Language (E) Bastion (D) Tinkering (F) Share Map (D) Waypoint (E) Combat Map (D) Secure Connection (C) Ignore Injury (E) Blast Shield (C) Focused Will (D)
ESPIONAGE	Tier 0 (0%)	+150% Infiltration Abilities +200% Mistrunning Abilities +100% Processing Speed +100% Damage (All)	Stealth (D) Camouflage (D) Deception (D) Mimic (D) Observation (D) Charisma (E) Interrogate (E) Distraction (E) Vanish (E) Chameleon (D) Sense Deception (E) Vanish (F) Mistwalk (C) Mishack (C) Mistwall (C) System Redirect (D) Disable Cybernetics (D) Overcharge (D) Surge (E)

			Plague (E) Backlash (D) Mental Fortress (E) Assassinate (F)
COMBAT MANEUVERS	Tier 0 (0%)	+150% Proprioception +50% Movement Speed	Balance (C)
OPEN			
OPEN			
OPEN			

It was much as I'd expected, though I was a little surprised to see that many of my modifiers had been combined. I fiddled with it a little, and I saw that I could expand those categories to see the individual effects. However, I didn't feel the need to micromanage things to that degree, so I left the cleaner display as the default.

As I'd expected, after I opened my status, a familiar warning flashed across my HUD:

Warning: You have recently lost three (3) skills. Replace them within sixty-two (62) days (Earth or Planet 2341-M) or you will forfeit the potential and any attributes exceeding your new, lower potential.

That wouldn't be the huge loss that it was the first time I had seen that message. Still, I wanted to avoid it if possible, which highlighted my need to visit the Bazaar as soon as I could. For now, though, I focused on my new skill trees, starting with the one associated with [Warfare]:

Tree	**Warfare: Tier 0 (0%)** <Focus for Modifiers>			
Branch	Arms: Tier 0 (0%)	Explosives: Tier 0 (0%)	Fieldcraft: Tier 0 (0%)	Command: Tier 0 (0%)
Tier 1	+25% Damage (All)	+50% Explosives Yield	+100% Endurance	Ability: Planetary Defense

Tier 2	+25% Damage (All)	+50% Explosives Yield	+50% Effectiveness (Combat Focus)	+100% Effectiveness (Planetary Defense)
Tier 3	+50% Reload Speed (Firearms)	Ability: Selective Explosion	+150% Effectiveness (Regeneration)	+100% Effectiveness (Planetary Defense)
Tier 4	+50% Rate of Fire (Firearms)	+100% Explosive Radius	Ability: Stasis	Ability: Aura of Command
Tier 5	Ability: Overclock	Ability: Replicate Charge	+200% Defense	Ability: Orbital Strike

Like the modifiers I saw on my status, the new tree looked a lot simpler than before. Instead of enhancing specific abilities or facets of my skills, the new modifiers granted broad increases. And they weren't weak, either. If I managed to progress all the way to Tier 5 in any of the branches, I would gain a significant amount of power.

Next, I moved to the tree for [Espionage]:

Tree	**Espionage: Tier 0 (0%)** <Focus for Modifiers>			
Branch	Infiltration: Tier 0 (0%)	Mist Manipulation: Tier 0 (0%)	Reconnaissance: Tier 0 (0%)	Assassination: Tier 0 (0%)
Tier 1	+25% Infiltration Effectiveness	+50% Mist Abilities	+25% Effectiveness (Observation)	+50% Damage (Stealth)
Tier 2	+25% Infiltration Effectiveness	+25% Mist Abilities	Ability: Sensory Mask	+50% Damage (Stealth)
Tier 3	+50% Infiltration Effectiveness	+100% Mist Abilities	+50% Effectiveness (Observation)	Ability: Sense Weakness

Tier 4	+100% Infiltration Effectiveness	Ability: Mist Spike	+25% Effectiveness (Observation)	+15% Damage (Stealth)
Tier 5	Ability: Mist Cloak	Ability: Mist Deprivation	Ability: Perfect Recall	Ability: Target Weakness

[Combat Maneuvers] didn't have a tree associated with it, but that didn't make it any less powerful. The movement-speed modifier alone was incredibly potent, and I could already imagine how I could use that to my advantage. However, I could also sense that it was going to take quite a bit of training before I could use the full effect of my new speed.

The same could be said for [Mist-Infused Body]. The modifier for my cybernetics was insane, but I was a little disappointed that the number of slots available had dropped. But that disappointment didn't last long. I didn't really depend on many cybernetics, anyway.

I sighed, leaning back against the wall.

It was at that moment that Caden chose to attack me. I saw it coming, of course. My new class had come with a significant improvement to every aspect of my body and abilities, so when he tried to stab me with a blue-glowing knife, it was like he was moving in slow motion. So, slapping the knife away was easier than breathing.

I heard his wristbone snap upon impact, and my other hand shot out. I rose to my feet, feeling every injury I'd sustained in the recent battle, and wrapped my fingers around his neck.

"Why would you do that?" I asked.

"Because you ruined everything!" he screamed. "All my friends . . . Everyone is dead because . . . because of you!"

I sighed. "You would have died, anyway," I said. "That's what they do. They copy your brain, then kill you."

"Better than—"

Before he had the chance to finish his sentence, I infiltrated his system via Misthack, then used a Ghost to knock him out. It happened in the space of a second, surprising me with how easily I'd torn through his innate defenses. His system's Mistwall was laughably flimsy—most people's were—but it still usually took me a few seconds to bypass them. Already, my new class and skills were showing their worth.

Sighing, I dropped him, then relaxed before dozing off. I awoke only a couple of hours later, but by that point, the injuries I'd sustained felt much better. They hadn't completely healed, but it wouldn't be long, either. The benefits of my increased recovery speed, I supposed.

Shaking my head, I contacted Patrick. Or I tried and failed.

Again, I attempted to establish a Secure Connection, but no matter how many times I tried, the results were the same. My heart jumped into my throat, and my stomach twisted into knots as I imagined all the reasons my Secure Connection might have failed. None of them were good.

So, it was with that in mind that I threw Caden over my shoulder and left the building behind. Once I reached the road, I summoned the Cutter, mounted, and sped off. It would take me a few hours to reach Fortune, but I was determined to cut that time in half, starting with my trip back to *The Leviathan*. Luckily, my new modifiers trivialized moving at such high speed, so I had no trouble keeping up as I sped across the landscape.

Still, I could only go so fast.

At some point, Caden woke up, but I ignored his terrified screams as the Cutter ate the ground before us, and soon enough, we arrived at the ship. I wasted no time before getting it into the sky.

When I saw the smoke twisting into the air, I knew the worst had happened. But I still held out hope that Patrick had somehow escaped the destruction I knew I'd find upon reaching Fortune. When the city came into view, I saw that half the city had been destroyed. Most of the buildings had fallen, and the ones that still stood were structurally unsound.

Still, I kept hope alive as I sped toward the dock, where I set *The Leviathan* down. Many of the other ships had experienced much the same fate as the city. When I spotted the dockmaster, I wasted no time before approaching him to demand, "What happened?"

"The city . . . People . . . They just blew up. All over town. I don't know . . . I just . . . My own wife . . ."

My stomach dropped.

It was my fault.

When I'd activated the Ghost that had severed the connection between the Pacificians and their hive mind, I'd seen the remaining citizens of Olympus explode. And given the number of kills with which I'd been credited, it was clear that it wasn't an isolated occurrence. Clearly, their infiltration into human society was far more ubiquitous than anyone suspected.

"Your wife," I said. "What did she look like?"

"Huh?" the stunned man muttered. I repeated the question, and something about my expression must have gotten through his grief. He explained, "She was . . . dark-skinned. Like you. But she . . . I don't know . . ."

Then, he reached into his pocket and retrieved a tablet, which he turned in my direction. There on the screen was a plump woman who could only ever be described as homely. I think that's when I realized how erroneous my assumption had been.

Until that moment, I'd thought that every Pacifician looked the same. Blond or brunette. Blue-eyed. Perfect bone structure. But clearly that wasn't the case.

In a daze, I re-summoned the Cutter and left the dockmaster behind. Caden said something to me, but I didn't hear him. Instead, I soon found myself racing between crumbling buildings. I ignored all the carnage. In the back of my mind, I recognized that the number of casualties had to be ridiculously high. I only saw a few bodies here and there, though. Most had been buried by the fallen buildings.

Soon enough, I reached my destination.

Cirilla's workshop, like so many others, had collapsed into a pile of rubble.

CHAPTER FIFTY-FIVE

A BACKHANDED VICTORY

World Killer. That is the title she would eventually earn. And seeing that first mass execution . . . What she did to the Pacificians opened a lot of eyes and got a lot of attention. It's terrifying, what she can do, and the fact that we're on the same side doesn't do much to mitigate that fear.

—Alistaris Kargat

I fell to my knees, staring at the pile of rubble that had once been Cirilla's workshop. The neighboring buildings had met a similar fate, and the rest of the city looked like a war zone. Once again, I'd inadvertently destroyed an entire city. After what happened in Nova, I'd vowed to never make that kind of decision again.

And I hadn't.

Still, millions had died. The casualties weren't just limited to the enemies. Instead, when the Pacificians had self-destructed, they'd taken thousands more with them. Maybe millions. I didn't think my kill count included that number, but whether the system gave me credit or not, I knew it was all my fault.

Beside me, Caden muttered, "This is . . . This is her . . . This is Cy's building . . ."

"This is what your friends did," I said. It wasn't strictly true, but I wasn't blind to the fact that the Pacificians held at least some of the blame. Just like Nora, they'd adopted a policy where, if they died, they intended to take everyone else with them. Later, I would learn that it was a deterrent. A shield against the sort of attack I'd just implemented. The rest of their enemies knew.

I hadn't.

But my guilt didn't care about my ignorance. In fact, it just made things worse. I should have known. My research should have been more thorough. I should have asked Alistaris. But I hadn't, and now, I was responsible for thousands more deaths.

It was one thing to know that I'd killed millions of enemies. I felt guilty about it, but it was a shallow emotion, easily overcome because I knew, at the end of the day, it had been necessary. If I didn't kill the Pacificians and other invaders, they would enslave or exterminate my people. I was fighting a war, and so, it was justifiable—at least in my mind.

Certainly, others would disagree. I was sure that plenty of people would look at me and see a monster. But my actions meant that they had the freedom to criticize me. They were alive to disagree. My conscience could bear that thin layer of guilt, so long as I had accomplished my goal.

With the collateral damage, though, things got messier. That blanket of guilt grew thicker and thicker until it felt suffocating.

Still, I could bear that. I could live with it.

The burden that I couldn't shoulder, though, was the knowledge that, because of my flippant actions, Patrick had died.

No last words. No tearful goodbyes. Just a dead body buried beneath a mountain of rubble.

Tears fell down my cheeks, but my sadness, my guilt, and my self-recrimination—it all felt hollow. The struggle felt meaningless next to my loss. Patrick was all I had. And now, he was gone. Dead. I would never again drink his terrible beer. No more nights on the beach. No thoughtful outings. No simple mornings where we just enjoyed each other's company.

I was well acquainted with the finality of death. I'd watched the recording of my uncle's death often enough that I could remember every single detail. And since then, I'd seen so many lives ended that I'd long since lost count.

I carried that with me wherever I went.

But Patrick's demise was different. I felt it far more keenly than even my uncle's death. It made me nauseous just thinking about it.

I was busy wallowing in that miasma of guilt, anger, and sadness when the pile of rubble shifted. At first, I didn't see it, and when more rocks came tumbling down the mountain of broken cement, I thought nothing of it. It wasn't until a huge rock rolled down the pile that I took notice.

"What . . ."

Then another followed, with a cascade of more rocks coming soon after. And then another. Soon enough, it was clear that something was moving under the pile. That's when I bounded forward and, using every bit of strength at my disposal, started digging. I tossed chunks of cement aside, one after another until, almost an hour later, I caught sight of a sliver of white metal.

"Patrick!" I shouted. "Is that you?"

At that moment, someone tried to initiate a Secure Connection. With my heart beating out of my chest, I accepted the prompt. And when I heard Patrick's voice echoing in my mind, tears once again traced lines through the dirt and grime on my cheeks.

"Mira? Is that you?" he asked, his voice clearly strained.

"It's me!" I shouted. "Are you okay? I'm trying to—"

"I'm . . . I'm alive," he said. "But . . . But I'm not okay, Mira. My legs . . ."

"It doesn't matter," I said. "Just hold still. I'm going to get you out. Just hang on, okay? Just hang on!"

With that, my efforts were renewed. At some point, a few other people—including Caden—joined me, but I paid them little attention. Slowly, the pile of rocks shrank until, at last, I caught sight of Patrick.

He was inside the cockpit of his armored suit, which was at least three times the size of a human being. However, the plasti-glass was shattered, exposing an interior that had been painted red with blood. For his part, Patrick was barely conscious, likely due to blood loss. But he was alive.

That was all I cared about.

I tore the cockpit open, then descended upon him. I went to activate Stabilize, but I was horrified to find that nothing happened. That's when I remembered that my class evolution had robbed me of the ability. At the time, I hadn't considered it a huge loss. I rarely used the ability, after all.

But now?

I needed it.

It wasn't there, though.

"Please . . . Don't," Patrick coughed. "The armor's the only thing keeping me alive."

"But . . . But we need to get you to . . . We need to get you a doctor . . ."

I turned and shouted for assistance, but none of the people responded. Clearly, they didn't have the skills to help. So, I did the only thing I could think of—I established a Secure Connection to Alistaris.

"What?" he asked.

"I need your help. Now," I said.

"I'm not your—"

"I need a doctor. A real one. I don't care how you do it, Al. Just get someone to Fortune."

"I don't respond well to demands."

"Do it or I'm out. No war. Nothing. In fact, I'll turn my attention on you and yours. Do you want that? Knowing what I can do, can you afford to make an enemy out of me? But if you help me right now, you'll have my loyalty. I'll kill whoever you tell me to kill. I'll murder whole worlds if that's what it takes."

"We can't—"

"Don't tell me what you can't do," I spat, anticipating his response. The aliens were supposed to keep a low profile while the quarantine was still in place. Otherwise, they risked the ire of the system. "All I want to hear is how you're going to help."

"I . . . Hold on," he said.

I could practically hear the wheels turning in his head. I wasn't just an asset. I'd proved that I had the power to turn the tide of any war. Certainly, I wasn't all-powerful, and I was sure that there were plenty of defenses my enemies could engage to keep me in check. But if they were worried about me, then they couldn't focus their whole attention on other threats.

And if I chose to go all out, things were going to get very messy for any-one who wanted to invade Earth. I still didn't think we could win. My uncle was strong, too, and he'd thought it was a hopeless cause. But I could make things incredibly unpleasant for my enemies. I didn't need to kill them all. I just needed to make Earth unprofitable.

I thought I might be able to kill enough for that goal.

Almost a minute passed, and in that time, I tried to comfort Patrick. It wasn't easy, seeing him in such a state. I couldn't see his injuries, but I suspected they were extensive. He kept muttering about his legs, but I didn't dare move him so I could diagnose the problem. Even if I was willing to do so, without Mend and Stabilize, there was nothing I could do.

Still, I did use a med-hypo in the hopes that it could ease his pain and pre-vent the onset of infection. It wasn't much, and if I was honest, I took the step more to feel like I was doing something rather than any hope that I was helping.

Finally, Alistaris said, "Okay. I have a surgeon on the way. He's human, so there shouldn't be any issues."

"Thank you!"

"Don't thank me yet," he said. "You owe me. Remember that when the war begins."

After that, he severed the Secure Connection.

I reached out to stroke Patrick's cheek, then said, "It's going to be okay, Pick. There's someone coming to help. You're going to be fine."

He mumbled something unintelligible. The painkillers from the med-hypo were already doing their job. For the next twenty minutes, I stayed by his side until, at last, someone spoke from behind me.

"Miss Braddock?" a soft voice said. I turned to see a heavyset man carrying a large bag. Behind him was a hover van. "I'm Dr. Hassan. Our mutual friend sent me to help."

After that, things got a little blurry. Dr. Hassan and a few others helped retrieve Patrick, but when I saw the ruin of his lower body, I couldn't help but despair. Still, I put my faith in the doctor, who directed his helpers to put Patrick in the back of the hover van. I tried to follow, but I was quickly brought up short. I didn't dare object as they closed the van's doors and started working on him.

For hours, I paced back and forth. At some point, I realized that Caden hadn't moved. He was still standing there, staring at the pile of rubble. I didn't know what to say, so I just ignored him. Eventually, the crowd dissipated, and the sun dipped below the horizon.

Finally, the doors opened, and Dr. Hassan stepped out.

"Is he . . ."

"He's alive," the doctor stated. "But there are issues. We had to amputate his legs, as well as one of his arms. In addition, he needs a few prosthetic organs if he wants to live for more than a few more days."

"I'll . . . I'll get them," I said.

"He also needs a competent cybernetic engineer," the man stated.

"I'll get that, too."

"The cost will be—"

"I don't care about the cost," I interrupted. "I've got money."

After that, I arranged for Dr. Hassan to take care of Patrick while I went up to the Bazaar. It wasn't ideal—I didn't want to let Patrick out of my sight—but he wouldn't live through a trip to the Bazaar. After I transferred a veritable fortune to him, Hassan agreed to take care of him.

A few minutes later, I was allowed into the back of the van, where I saw Patrick. Or what was left of him. Half of his face was bandaged, and both of his legs ended at midthigh. His left arm was missing, as well, having been amputated up to the shoulder.

His eye fluttered open when I knelt beside him.

"Fancy meeting you here," he said, his voice weak.

"I'm sorry . . ."

"Nothing to be sorry for."

"This . . . This is my fault," I said.

Over the next ten minutes, Patrick explained what had happened. I was surprised to learn that it was Tate, Cirilla's girlfriend, who'd been the Pacifician. When she'd self-destructed, she'd immediately taken the other woman with her. Patrick, who'd been working on the armor, lived through the initial explosion, but the collapsing building had nearly killed him. Somehow, he'd managed to drag himself into the armor, so when the building completely fell, he'd been protected.

It was only by sheer chance that he'd survived.

"It's not your fault, Mira," he said after I explained why Tate had self-destructed. "You couldn't have known."

"I should have, though," I stated. "I need to be better, Patrick."

"You will be."

I sighed. I appreciated the faith he had in me, but I wasn't sure if I agreed. To date, I'd shown myself to be nothing more than a blunt object. I had power. I could kill with the best of them. But I seemed incapable of mitigating the collateral damage. It had happened in Nova and again with the Pacificians. Because of me, thousands of innocents had died.

And the worst part was that that was a conservative estimate. The real number may well have been in the millions.

It was easy to simply tell myself to get over it, to focus on my evolution, Patrick's survival, and the fact that I had, ostensibly, won the battle. But that wasn't how my mind worked, and I couldn't help but wallow in the guilt of so much death. Patrick's situation had brought it all home in a way that simple statistics never could.

Eventually, Patrick could no longer remain conscious, and I left him in the doctor's care. With that done, I headed to *The Leviathan* and flew to the ruins of Nova. Cloaked in Mimic, I rushed through the city and found my way to the obelisk that would transfer my consciousness to the Bazaar.

Once I reached the space station, I headed straight to Dex's shop, where he sold me a series of cybernetics that would repair the damage Patrick had sustained. None of them were the highest quality, but I got what I could afford.

Then, I headed back.

Everything became a blur as I returned to Fortune. Along the way, I contacted Alistaris and asked—well, demanded, really—that he put me in touch with a talented cybernetic engineer. He did just that, and over the next two days, I set about finding, hiring, and transporting the cybernetic engineer back to Fortune.

Once we arrived, the woman—named Fiona Rhyne—went to work. The procedures took most of a day before she declared the operation completed. When I went inside the hover van—which was a mobile surgery center—I found Patrick arduously pushing himself upright. Half of his face had been replaced by a metal dome, and both of his legs as well as his left arm were robotic.

But he was alive.

When he saw me, he gave me a small half smile before saying, "You know, most of this stuff could be considered an upgrade. So, maybe I should thank you for—"

I didn't let him get another word out before I practically tackled him. I threw my arms around him and buried my face in the organic part of his chest. There, I sobbed. I'd held it in for the past few days. Ever since I'd left for Nova and the Bazaar, I'd forced myself to focus on the task at hand. But now that I knew he was going to make it, I couldn't contain my emotions any longer.

"I thought . . . I thought you were . . . I didn't think you were going to make it . . ."

He patted my back with his hand of flesh, saying, "I'm fine. It's going to be fine. Lots of people have cybernetics."

I knew that was true. I'd seen it for myself. Back in Nova, almost all the Operators had replaced limbs with cybernetic versions. Still, it was one thing for someone to choose that route and something else altogether for it to be thrust upon them. I knew Patrick had never intended to go down that path, and the fact that he'd been forced to do so was tragic.

Between sobs, I said as much.

Patrick responded with a hearty laugh. "Tragic? This is a miracle, Mira," he said. "Do you know how few people would've survived something like that? I'm lucky."

That certainly was an optimistic way of looking at it.

"And besides, I did it."

"Did what?"

"I finished the armor," he stated. "It's probably damaged, but before Tate . . . you know . . . blew up, I got it working."

"You think it survived?"

"I do. And I want to dig it out," he said, swinging his new legs off the cot. He quickly overbalanced and fell over, though I caught him before he tumbled to the floor. "Whoa. That's . . . going to take a little getting used to."

Of course, that brought more tears.

"It's fine, Mira. All that matters is that we're both still here and that we're together. Everything else is secondary."

And as I hugged him close, I couldn't really disagree.

ABOUT THE AUTHOR

Nicholas Searcy is the author of Death: Genesis, Mistrunner, and Path of Dragons, all of which were originally released on Royal Road. He enjoys writing, reading, spending time with family, sports, and, of course, a good cup of coffee.

Podium
DISCOVER
STORIES UNBOUND
PodiumAudio.com

9 781039 454378